"You're so lovely to look at, it makes a body ache," Meghan whispered shyly.

"Ah, Meghan," Revelin sighed and lowered his head until his lips rested lightly upon hers.

The shock of his mouth lasted only a moment. His breath was hot, his mouth a furnace upon her tender skin, and then her mouth blossomed under his, offering heat for heat, kiss for kiss, pleasure for pleasure.

The darkness wrapped them in its intimacy as he cupped her shoulders and drew her lightly against him. Meghan clasped her arms about his neck and closed her eyes, giving up the world beyond the breath of his tall strong body.

Whatever it was he wanted of her she wanted him to have it...

* * *

"Fans of Ireland will enjoy this tale of love and turmoil set against the pageantry of Elizabethan times." —**Rebecca Brandewyne, author of** *And Gold Was Ours*

"A wonderful adventure! A wonderful love story! I enjoyed it immensely." —**Roberta Gellis, author of** *A Tapestry of Dreams*

"Four stars—highest rating! Reads like a beautiful, romantic fairy tale... has an evocative atmosphere of the total beauty of Ireland." —*Romantic Times*

P9-CFR-873

ATTENTION: SCHOOLS AND CORPORATIONS

WARNER books are available at quantity discounts with bulk purchase for educational, business, or sales promotional use. For information, please write to: SPECIAL SALES DEPARTMENT, WARNER BOOKS, 75 ROCKEFELLER PLAZA, NEW YORK, N.Y. 10019.

**ARE THERE WARNER BOOKS
YOU WANT BUT CANNOT FIND IN YOUR LOCAL STORES?**

You can get any WARNER BOOKS title in print. Simply send title and retail price, plus 50¢ per order and 50¢ per copy to cover mailing and handling costs for each book desired. New York State and California residents add applicable sales tax. Enclose check or money order only, no cash please, to: WARNER BOOKS, P.O. BOX 690, NEW YORK, N.Y. 10019.

ROSE
OF THE MISTS

Laura
Parker

WARNER BOOKS

A Warner Communications Company

*This book is dedicated with love to my mother,
whose love of language inspired me.*

WARNER BOOKS EDITION

Copyright © 1985 by Laura Castoro
All rights reserved.
Cover art by Bob McGinnis

Warner Books, Inc.
75 Rockefeller Plaza
New York, N.Y. 10019

 A Warner Communications Company

Printed in the United States of America

First Printing: September, 1985

10 9 8 7 6 5 4 3 2 1

ACKNOWLEDGEMENTS

A novel with an historical setting requires many hours of research. My thanks to Barbara Perkins of the Dallas Public Library who spent hours tracking down the right books. Thanks to Sue Cooper and Kitty Wilson who shared their love and knowledge of Ireland with me. Thanks to Tony, my Irish guide, who knew the name of every flower and ruin between the Skellig Rocks and Dublin.

THE LORDSHIPS
AND THE PALE

N

ATLANTIC
OCEAN

LOUGH SWILLY

RATHLIN ISLAND

NORTH CHANNEL

Dunluce
MACDONNELLS

LA TYRCONNELL

DONEGAL

FINN

BANN

EARL OF TYRONE

O'DONNELL

O'NEILL

O'NEILL

U L S T E R

LOUGH NEAGH

BLACKWATER

Armagh

EARL OF CLANCONNELL
(TURLOUGH LUINEACH)

Newry

Sligo

O'CONNOR

CLARE
ISLAND

GLEN BAY

CONNAUGT

O'CONNOR

O'ROURKE

CAVAN

Dundalk

Drogheda

IRISH
SEA

O'MALLEY

EARL OF CLANRICARDE

Athlone

O'CONNOR

M E A T H

BOYNE

Dublin

EARL OF THOMOND

Galway

O'BRIEN

EARL OF KILDARE

BUTLER

Kildare

O'BYRNE

O'TOOLE

LD. BALTINGLAS

SHANNON

FITZGERALD

Limerick

EARL OF DESMOND

Cashel

L E I N S T E R

EARL OF ORMOND

FITZMAURICE

FITZGERALD

M U N S T E R

SUIR

Kilkenny

BUTLER

MACMURROUGH
KAVANAUGH

Trake

MC SHEEHY

LD. ROCHE

Waterford

DESMOND

Wexford

ST. GEORGES CHANNEL

FITZGIBBON

MACCARTHY
MORE

BLACKWATER

SOUTH

LD. BARRY

FITZGERALD
Cork

O'SULLIVAN

SULLIVAN BEARE

MACCARTHY
REAGH

Kinsale

Desmond

Tyrone & Clanconnell

Ormond & Kildare

Dublin Pale

Thomond & Clarincarde

0   MILES   50

0   KM   50

IRELAND, CIRCA 1579

THE IRISH LAND
ABOUT 1600

MILES
0 50
0 40 80

ATLANTIC
OCEAN

NORTH
CHANNEL

RATHLIN
ISLAND

LOUGH SWILLY

FOYLE

LOUGH FOYLE

ARTHUR HILL

BLANK

DERRYVEAGH MTS.

DONEGAL

SPERRIN MTS.

LOUGH NEAGH

FINN

ERNE

BLUE STACK MTS.

DONEGAL BAY

LOWER
LOUGH
ERNE

DARTRY
MTS.

Dungannon

U L S T E R

BELFAST LOUGH

BLACKWATER

PASS OF THE NORTH

Armagh

STRANGFORD
LOUGH

MOURNE
MTS.

Newry

Sligo

UPPER
LOUGH
ERNE

LOUGH
ALLEN

OX MTS.

LOUGH
CONN

MOY

CLARE
ISLAND

CLEW
BAY

C O N N A U G H T

PARTRY MTS.

LOUGH
MASK

SUCK

LOUGH
REE

INNY

C A V A N

Dundalk

LOUTH

DUNDALK BAY

Drogheda

BOYNE

M E A T H

TWELVE
PINS

LOUGH
CORRIB

Galway

GALWAY
BAY

SLIEVE
AUGHTY
MTS.

SHANNON

Athlone

BOG
OF
ALLEN

LIFFEY

Dublin

IRISH
SEA

LOUGH
DERG

L E I N S T E R

WICKLOW
MTS.

Limerick

SHANNON

Askeaton

LOUGH
GUR

MOORE FOREST

WEED

GOLDEN
VALE

Cashel

ANBROW
VALLEY

Clonmel

Kilkenny

BLACKSTAIRS
MTS.

SUIR

Enniscorthy

GALMOYE
(Slan)

MULLAGHAREIRK
MTS.

Tralee

Smerwick

SLIEVE MISH. MTS.

DINGLE BAY

LOUGH
LEANE

BLACKWATER

GALTEE
MTS.

BALLYHOURA
HILLS

KNOCKMEALDOWN MTS.

COMERAGH
MTS.

Lismore

Dungarvan

Waterford

Wexford

ST. GEORGE'S CHANNEL

MAC GILLYCUDDY'S
REEKS

BOGGERAGH
MTS.

LEE

Cork

M U N S T E R

Youghal

BANTRY BAY

Kinsale

ELEVATIONS

▲ 2000'-3000'

△ 3000' and over

Chapter One

Early-morning mist banked the forest, stretching wispy fingers back into the darkness. Under the silent canopy of ancient oaks the light of dawn had not yet found a path. Night creatures, dulled by the impending morning, had crawled to their places of rest while the day creatures had yet to stir with the warmth of sunrise. The only sounds were the creaking of dew-drenched limbs, the distant whispering of the topmost leaves, and the rumble of water unseen yet never far away in this land.

Into this twilight world fled Meghan O'Neill, the sound of her bare footsteps muffled by the spongy carpet of moss.

A frosty stinging filled her lungs, and she shivered beneath her *leine*. Until a year ago she could run for as long as she desired. Now her chest ached from the bouncing weight of her full breasts, but she did not dare stop to catch her breath. She had made a mistake in going near the settlement, a mistake which would cost her her life if she did not hide quickly.

Only when she spied a fresh print on the path did Meghan pause and dip a slender finger into the impression. It was the

1

hoof mark of a wild sow, weighing perhaps twenty stone. Foreboding coursed through her. Where there were tracks there was certain to be the danger of the animal. Instinctively, like one of the forest's wild creatures, she raised her head and tossed back her tangle of blue-black hair to breathe deeply of the cold, wet air. It was soft, perfumed with the rich, pungent smells of molding leaves and the acrid sting of green wood, but it held also the unmistakable rancid odor of a wild boar.

Then suddenly Meghan was overwhelmed by a familiar sensation. Her vision narrowed to a pinpoint of light, and her body began to tremble. She pressed her fingers over her eyes but it did not help. With a whimper of resigned fear, she gave up the struggle, closed her eyes, and waited.

Most often the visions came to her in dreams, the knowing yet unknowing, the sense of inevitability, which she could not alter or even understand. She could not remember when the first dream had come to her or when she had realized that she was not reliving memories but was enveloped by visions of things yet to be.

The vision came swiftly, as if it were aware that there was little time, and it was the same as that of the night before. Vivid images stirred behind her lids, then flared full-blown; she saw blood-soaked moss and torn flesh, and the stench of death invaded her nostrils, the smell of blood nearly suffocating her.

Gasping, Meghan opened her eyes wide and the vision vanished as the distant cries of angry men and boys came to her ear.

"Dinna ye see her, Rory?" cried a man.

"Aye! She ran this way. Nae doubt she's found cover!"

"Runnin' like the divil himself was on her," answered a third male voice as the heavy footfalls neared. "Do we nae give chase, man?"

"Aye, that we will! Ye lads circle to the right, the rest take the left. She'll nae go far in them black regions. Rory, fetch the hounds! They've the scent of her."

Meghan froze for an instant, her nostrils quivering with the scent of wild boar and the fetid musky odor of men. Which was the more deadly enemy? Dare she try to warn the men of the danger she foresaw when she knew they meant her harm? She touched the knife strapped to her left forearm. It was puny protection against armed men or a boar.

The question was answered as a fist-sized stone whizzed past her left shoulder with barely an inch to spare.

"There! There!" came a cry behind her. "I see her! Come on, then, or we'll lose her!"

Meghan had lived her entire sixteen years in the wild, and she reacted as an oft-hunted creature would. With the instinct of a fleeing doe, she showed her pursuers a quick flash of her back, then ducked behind a wall of trees and crouched among the ferns that grew thickly at the base of an oak. But as the clamorous cries of the men grew stronger and she realized that her hiding place would soon be discovered, she jumped up, grasped the tree trunk, and began to climb.

The tree was difficult to scale, not one she would have chosen to climb for pleasure, for its trunk was broader than the span of her arms. She gained the first inches upward by digging her hands and feet into niches in the bark, which shredded the skin of her bare toes and fingers as it yielded grudgingly the purchase she sought. Inch by inch she pulled herself higher, uncaring that as she stretched for a handhold her wool tunic tore at the armhole.

"I dinna see her!" cried a man crashing through the underbrush just feet from the tree. "Faith! We've lost her," he exclaimed in disgust, and fell to swearing roundly as he stopped under the limbs of the tree to which Meghan clung like a squirrel.

His voice frightened Meghan into stillness. With her heart pounding so hard in her throat that she feared it might leap out, she listened to his labored breathing.

"May the good Lord come 'twixt us and the evil we pursue," a second man said as he joined the first. "Ye seen her plain as me, Shaun," he continued. "A great clot of blood hanging from her face, the mark of the divil. Could be she's turned her monstrous self into some great beast."

"Nae!" Shaun replied. "'Tis a vast tricky place, a forest. She'll have found herself a hiding place. Wait till Rory brings the hounds. They'll flush her out quick enough."

"The stone I heaved at her found its mark, I'd swear," the second man boasted. "Still, I dinna see a single drop of blood anywhere about. Think she were a spirit, Shaun, aspyin' on God-fearing folk? Nae good will come of it, and there's a truth!"

"Were she a spirit, she'd nae have run away from the likes o' us," Shaun rejoined. "She were human. Still, the mark was on her, and we'll be doin' ourselves nae mischief to stone that one. 'Twill be bad luck else. Rory?" he bellowed suddenly. "Where's that lad when a body needs him? The hounds will have forgot the scent."

Cold and damp from the dew, lungs pained with every breath of chilled air, Meghan felt herself slipping from the branch. She had been chased more than a mile by the men. They were wrapped against the morning chill in heavy gray mantles, but her shawl had been lost as she fled across the meadow. Swept by a new surge of fright, she commanded her trembling muscles to lift her upward as she clutched the lowermost limb. They refused to move, leaving her hanging by her arms.

Then the sound of the hounds unhooked her fatigue-locked muscles. The distant baying of those great wolf hounds was more frightening than the sound of the men at her heels. If the dogs discovered her, their great jaws would tear her to shreds within seconds. Drawing on the last of her strength, she pulled herself up to chest level and threw a slender leg over the branch to straddle it. A moment later she was balanced on tiptoe, stretching for a higher, safer limb.

The herders came confidently into the dark forest, shouting and carrying torches and clubs. As their dogs drove all before them, the racket sent startled wild creatures scurrying in every direction.

Frightened by the din, a boar raced through the heart of the forest. A cowardly creature by nature, it was running away. When it found its path blocked, however innocently, by the two men beneath the ancient oak, its instinct for self-preservation took over. Black bristles rose on its hump as it tucked its head down, baring the sharp points of its yellow, curving tusks.

In her fright, Meghan had forgotten the smell of the boar, and her pursuers were too angry at the loss of their prey to heed it. Now the fresh scent came sweeping over her, and she turned to look toward the ground. To her horror, she saw the boar break from the brush nearby.

The sow paused a moment, its small eyes judging the two men. Quick-footed despite its size, it shot forth like an arrow from a crossbow when one of the men turned and fled. One saber-sharp tusk caught him in the ankle, and he screamed as he stumbled and fell.

Turning instantly, the sow charged again to gore the half-risen man in the chest and then toss him aside with a heave of its great head. It found an escape in the underbrush just as the hounds broke into the clearing under the oaks.

"Ah, God! The beast's killed Shaun!" his companion cried, rushing to the fallen man as the hounds began to close in, drawn by the scent of boar. He kicked away the first of the hounds to reach the battered body, then swung his club at another, threatening but not delivering blows as he shouted, "Keep away! Keep away from the poor lad!"

"'Twas the she-divil what done that!" one of the newcomers whispered in fear as he crossed himself. The rest of the men did likewise and fell silent at the sight that greeted them.

"God strike me dead if she dinna!" Shaun's companion replied. "Ye seen her, every one of ye. She's a divil, that 'un," he continued, caught up in the fever of his imagination. "She growed great tusks the like of a most monstrous boar, all black bristles and such, and killed Shaun, may God have mercy on his soul. She must be stopped!"

Though the others nodded, none of them moved in the direction in which the boar had disappeared.

"'Twill be time enough for killin' when Shaun's been proper laid out," one man suggested. "May the Lord God lay waste to the divil's hag what did this filthy deed!"

Confused by the irrational anger directed at her but stricken with guilt nonetheless, Meghan watched as they lifted the dead man and carried him away. Finally, when they were out of sight and the forest was silent once more, she turned away and buried her face in the crook of her arm.

She cried softly at first, but as the terror receded, a sense of guilt overwhelmed her and her tears became heaving sobs.

It had happened just as she had dreamed it. The boar had come and killed, and she had not been able to prevent it. The herders were right: it was her fault that a man was dead. If the men had not been looking for her they would not have been in the forest.

It no longer mattered to her that the dead man had been trying to catch and kill her. She could remember only the terror-filled nightmare that had predicted the herdsman's death. She had dreamed of death but had not known whose until it was too late to prevent it. Why could she never understand enough to stop what was about to occur? The knowing and yet not knowing was a torment, a curse.

Absently her fingers traced the outline of the pebbly-textured birthmark the size of an acorn that curved across her left cheek an inch below her eye. This was the reason why she had been told to keep to herself, out of sight of strangers. It was the reason why Una, her kinswoman and companion, made her pull her shawl over her face when they encountered people on the road. It was the reason why they had lived apart from people since the day Meghan was born. She bore the "mark" of the otherworld.

Tears cascaded down Meghan's cheeks. She hated the dull-red mark that turned the color of blood when she was frightened or blushed. Once, when she was eight, she had tried to scrape it off with a piece of bark, but Una had caught her at it and had given her a sound thrashing with a switch. Una said it was not her place to deny what she had been given at birth and that she must live with the burden of the mark.

Ever since Meghan had been old enough to remember, the clansmen of Ulster had viewed her with suspicion. They whispered among themselves and made the sign of the cross when they glimpsed her cheek, as though they might become tainted by her presence. Yet, the wariness of the clansmen was better than the utter fear she invoked among the peasant herdsmen of Louth. No one in the settlements surrounding the O'Neill clan fortress at Lough Neagh had ever raised a hand against her. She had been safe there in Ulster; it made no sense for her and Una to have left. Surely Una would change her mind and take her home again.

One night, a little more than a year ago, Una had suddenly packed their meager belongings and brought her south from their homeland. Una had not explained the need for the sudden journey, nor had she allowed Meghan to show her face at all once they set out. They had journeyed south for days until they reached the county of Louth. For the last year they had lived here in seclusion, hidden from the world and from the joy of being with other people.

Meghan sniffed back new tears. She was so lonely, more so in the last few months than ever before in her life. In all her life she had never had a friend. Even in Ulster, those few brave souls who came to call on Una were careful not to stare at Meghan or touch anything she touched. She liked people and envied the happiness of the families she sometimes glimpsed when they did not know she was about. That was why, when Una was away bargaining for goods in a neighboring settlement, Meghan would crouch in the reeds on the bank of the river to watch the herders who lived in the clearing near the forest.

She had been going there this morning, just to watch and wait, and to sound the cry of alarm if the boar of her nightmare appeared. Long ago she had learned to heed the warnings of the "sight," as Una called her troubled dreams. But she must have been observed on an earlier visit, because men had been waiting in ambush when she arrived at the water's edge. If not for her acute senses and her swift legs, she would have been caught.

The cold had seeped slowly into her body and now she began to shake like a leaf in the wind. Beneath her shift, the tips of her breasts puckered in a way that half-delighted, half-frightened her. Shyly she touched one breast, its tender fullness new and unfamiliar.

Within the past year her body had changed so quickly, creating new curves and hollows, that she could not become accustomed to one change before another surprised her. Only a few months earlier she had awakened to a gnawing ache in her lower belly and found herself bleeding below. Una had soothed her fright but warned her to expect such a thing to be a monthly occurrence thereafter.

"'Tis a sign that ye be a woman now, and sure 'tis cause enough for lament," Una had said, and then had refused to discuss it further.

Suddenly and inexplicably ashamed, she jerked her hand away from her breast and wrapped her arms tightly across her bosom. Una said that the changes of her body were manifestations of the devil, charms to tempt a mortal man's soul. Una had said it, with a twinkle in her eyes, Meghan remembered, but that did not allay the uncomfortable feeling that her kinswoman was speaking the truth.

But why should the devil do such a thing to her? She had seldom been in the company of men; the only one she had ever exchanged more than a word with was an Ulster monk who had regularly visited them to instruct her in reading and writing. Yet, the herders, too, called her a devil. Were they right? Did her mark make her so ugly that men could not bear to look upon her face?

With a shuddering sigh, Meghan leaned back against the tree trunk and stretched her legs out along the limb. Only then did she notice that her legs were criss-crossed with fine bloody scratches that had begun to sting and itch. Rubbing the chafed skin only smeared the blood. After a moment she gave up and stared at her hands. The fingertips were badly scraped, as were the soles of her feet. In consternation she examined the rend in her shift, which exposed her from armpit to waist. Sharp-eyed Una would be sure to ask how she had come to such mischief.

Remembering the dead man, she groaned in sorrow. If Una threatened her with a thrashing for spilling a crock of milk, Una would surely beat her mercilessly for having roused the herders against them. She must do something, and quickly.

Following an urge that had been with her since childhood, Meghan sought the sky. Moving steadily up the tree, she concentrated on the changing patterns and colors of the canopy of leaves. Finally, near the top, she pushed back a branch that blocked her view and smiled up into the warmth of the early-morning sun.

In the distance, the tops of the Mourne Mountains rose above the mists, their rugged forms littered with ancient gray boulders and clinging wet grasses. Here and there, a hillside pasture was visible, its lush greenness bringing unexpected tears to Meghan's eyes. Overhead, a lark called, its note sweet and clear as the blue sky on which sea clouds sailed. She was at the top of the world.

The thought quickened Meghan's pulse. The dazzling gold and green shimmer of beauty lifted her spirits out of a world of misery. She no longer feared the dark forest below with its deep shadows and uncertainties. Surely the peace and happiness that now was just beyond her reach would someday be hers.

The branch she stood upon was slim and supple, swaying and dipping playfully beneath her weight in the spring breeze. Perhaps by summer Una could be persuaded to give up this hiding and return to Ulster.

"Please, soon!" Meghan whispered fervently to the day.

The climb down to the ground took longer than the climb up. When she touched the damp earth once more, Meghan was again hushed and worried. She had yet to find a way to keep Una from being suspicious about her appearance. As she reached down to scratch a new itch, an idea came to her. She would bathe in the pond at the edge of the oak grove; that would remove the dirt and soothe her scratches.

She made her way toward the water confidently. The herdsmen believed her a demon capable of turning herself into a wild boar at will, and they would undoubtedly come again into the forest to search for her, but she knew they would not follow her to the pond: they thought it was enchanted.

When she reached the marshy waters of the small pond, she stood for a moment watching a water bug skimming across the glassy surface. The pond was little more than a sunken bog, its surface deceptively calm. In its amber and brown depths lay a swaying forest of reeds in which an unsuspecting swimmer might be caught.

Certain that she was alone, Meghan stripped off her tunic, flung it on the bank, and dived head-first into the silent water, her knife still strapped to her wrist.

Her slim body slipped unimpeded through the soft, smooth water. Like a thousand gentle fingers the cold water soothed and caressed her body. Savoring the freedom of weightlessness, she arched her back and swam in slow, graceful somersaults just beneath the surface. Finally, when her need for air forced her to the top, she struck out with deliberate strokes across the water, her yard of blue-black hair trailing like a banner of silk ribbons.

As she had in the treetop, she felt the intoxication of happiness winding up through her. In the water she was as insubstantial as a leaf. Neither fish nor ducks resented her intrusion into their realm, nor did they care whether she was blemish-free or marked. They swam away only from the hands of predators. Ugliness did not frighten them.

Aye, I am ugly, Meghan thought as she flipped over onto her back and opened her eyes to the hazy morning light. She had looked at her face often enough in the glassy surface of the pond to know.

She discounted the reflection of the large, velvety blue eyes that stared back at her from the green-brown water and the lustrous tangle of inky tresses that surrounded the delicate angles of her chin and brow. She saw none of her beauty, only the vivid birthmark that marred the creamy smooth texture of her left cheek. Sometimes she would squint until her image blurred and the red mark seemed only a shadow on her cheek. Then she could make believe that it was gone entirely. Or she would drape her hair forward over her left eye to cover the mark, and pretend that she looked like everyone else.

Yet, I am not like everyone else. Meghan sighed and closed her eyes. She would not think about it.

The snort of a horse on the opposite bank took her by surprise. Alarmed, she slipped noiselessly beneath the surface. Several swift kicks carried her into the reeds growing thickly in the shallow water, and wriggling free of their slick coils, she came up for air among them. Then she crouched and waited.

Before long she heard the voices of her unwelcome companions. First there was a great splash beyond the sea of reeds where she hid, followed by a large dog's joyful barking. In that instant the morning sky exploded with life as geese, ducks, and cranes took flight in fear for their lives. A moment later she heard a man's shout.

"Heel, Ualter! Heel, you great beast!"

Meghan tensed. The words were spoken in a tongue which, though she did not speak it, she recognized as English.

When the dog continued to thrash at the water's edge despite

11

its master's command, the voice roared again, "Go ahead and drown yourself, you ungainly cur! I'll not be sharing my cloak with you this night."

Her heart pounding in fright for the second time that morning, Meghan slipped the knife from the thong that held it securely to her wrist. Its narrow but deadly blade shone like silver in the misty light as she waited behind the blind of weeds.

Perhaps, she hoped wildly, they would simply pass on. But that hope bolted when she heard the creak of saddle leather and the man dismounted with what sounded like a groan of pain. An instant later, the reeds behind her rustled and a covey of quail, flushed by the dog, raced toward the woods for cover.

Meghan gripped her knife more tightly. If the dog's attention was drawn to the birds, he would surely spot her.

But the animal did not come her way. He was content, it seemed, to wade back and forth, barking incessantly. Finally, after another sharp command from his owner, he ceased barking and the splash of water died.

For a long, nervous minute Meghan remained perfectly still and listened. They were not going away. She could hear the man speaking softly in his unfamiliar tongue to his pet but she could not tell what they were doing. The voice came no closer, but it did not retreat.

Curious and needing the advantage of observation, Meghan reluctantly moved toward the voice, keeping only her head above the surface. The lazy ripples made by her passage were so slight that she knew no one would notice. At last she found a thinning in the pond weeds and looked for the first time at the intruder.

Ever after, whenever she saw something beautiful, she would remember that this man bathed in the morning light was more beautiful.

Angled sunlight, illuminating the pond mist like a sheer saffron flame, surrounded the man in a brilliant golden haze. Everything about him was golden, from the amber sheen of his skin to the rich color of his hair, from which dawn's light struck gilded sparks. He stood still, his face in three-quarters' profile, and Meghan caught her breath. His was a mysterious face, unlike any she had ever seen before, with its smooth cheeks, straight mouth, and long jutting nose. Cut short, his fair hair waved closely about his head. He was bare to the waist, his green velvet doublet lying in the grassy bank. Broad in the shoulders, his tall and well-muscled form was lithe, not bulky.

As he moved toward the water, she noticed the bandage on his right forearm, through which blood had seeped, and the smears of mud on his boots and leggings and on his brow. He walked stiffly, as if he had injured his hip or knee, but at the water's edge he dropped gracefully onto the grass and began muttering to himself. In quiet curiosity she watched him tug with difficulty at his thigh-high boots, speaking swear words that she did not need translated. He was injured and was impatient with his awkwardness.

Had he spoken her language she might have been tempted to aid him. But she was not certain that he was even real. The men who had chased her that morning were thick-bodied and hairy, their features half-hidden beneath unkempt beards and wild streaming hair that reached to the middle of their bare backs.

Once before, in Ulster, she had hidden and watched O'Neill warriors who stopped to camp near her home. They were muscular and tall and wore wolf skins and bright yellow mantles across their shoulders, which they shed to bathe in the Blackwater. Fascinated, she had stayed and watched until Una had come looking for her. And so she had learned that men were mostly the same. Save for the amount of hair on body and face, she had decided that the only difference among men was in their size.

But this man, if he was a man and not a fantasy, had scarcely any hair. What little there was was the color of wild honey.

Meghan still held her weapon. From the corner of her eye, she kept track of the overeager dog prancing back and forth behind his master. He was a huge beast, nearly as tall as she, with a reddish brown coat and dark markings on his ears and muzzle.

"There!" the stranger cried triumphantly as he tossed a boot aside. The second came off more quickly, and then he stood once more. Meghan did not see him unfasten his leggings. It seemed to her that they merely fell away from him and then he stood as God had made him.

Never having learned modesty, Meghan studied him with open interest. His legs were long and shaped by supple muscle, but that was not what most attracted her. Nestled at the base of his belly in a shadowing of golden curls was the proof of his manhood. Whatever else he might be, he was a man.

As she gazed at him, Meghan felt a curious stirring inside her, not unlike the quickening of her body near its monthly cycle. The feeling surprised her, for she had never experienced it at the sight of a man before. But he was unlike any man she had ever seen. Perhaps the herdsmen were right; the pond was enchanted and the man was the work of magic.

Unable to understand but willing to feed the strange languor stealing over her, she traced the slope of his spine with her gaze, lingering on the tight swell of a buttock, on the contoured muscle of his thigh, and then rising again to blink in wonder at the pure gold of his hair. It made her feel as warm and happy as she had when she climbed to the top of the oak and turned her face to the morning sun.

A golden haze stole softly over the opposite bank, wrapping the man in a mantle of amber light. When it had drifted on, only the dog remained, standing tall, straight, and perfectly still.

Gasping in surprise that the man had suddenly disappeared from her view, Meghan forgot her fears and stood up. Then the water heaved about her and she realized that he had dived into the pond. Not wanting to be found, she dropped down and began moving back into a denser region of the reeds, only to pause in fresh amazement as she heard the man's voice. He was singing . . . in Gaelic!

> *There is a distant isle,*
> *Around which sea horses glisten:*
> *A fair course against the white-swelling surge—*
> *Four pillars uphold it. . . .*
>
> *Unknown to us wailing or treachery*
> *In the familiar cultivated land,*
> *There is nothing rough or harsh,*
> *But sweet music striking on the ear.*
>
> *. . . A beautiful game, most delightful,*
> *They play sipping at the luxurious wine*
> *Men and gentle women under a bush,*
> *Without sin, without crime.**

Resisting the urge to continue to spy on him was futile. Drawn by his charming voice, she stretched out in the water and allowed herself to float back toward the break in the reeds. The water's chill would have driven her out long before now, but there was no safe way to leave while the huge dog sniffed the air expectantly. What harm, then, she asked herself, could come from watching the man until he left?

He was floating on his back and Meghan was not surprised to see a smile upon his face. The urge to swim to his side was powerful. He seemed friendly, a kindred spirit in this place that she thought of as hers alone. Without conscious thought she slipped her knife back into its place. But a lifetime of caution kept her from joining him. If he saw the mark on her

*The Voyage of Bran, eighth-century poem.

face it might frighten him away, or, worse, he might try to kill her as the herders had.

Even when he drifted across the pond, so close to her that she could see the pale light of his eyes, she did not move. Yet she drank in every bit of him. When two yards separated them he stood up in the shallows and began washing the blood from his injury, and she noticed that he was young. The blond stubble of beard on the strong angles of his jaw and chin pronounced him full grown, but he had only recently come of age, she guessed.

Fascinated, she watched as the breeze stirred rippling shivers across his broad back. She too shivered, and as her teeth began to chatter she wondered how long she would be trapped in the water. With relief she saw him dive back toward the center of the pond, heading for the opposite shore and his horse and dog.

Meghan clasped her hands tightly over her naked shoulders, but the cold pierced bone-deep and her shivering intensified. For a moment she entertained the impulse simply to leap from the water and run into the woods. The man could easily be evaded . . . but, alas, not the dog.

Her wary gaze moved to the bank, where the dog stood at the water's edge waiting eagerly for his master. Panting, his open mouth revealed large sharp teeth, and his black eyes kept watch on the lake surface. A shudder of revulsion quaked through Meghan. The baying of hounds after her own blood was too fresh in her mind for her to admire the handsome animal. She would miss the man when he left but she would be glad when the beast was gone.

The dog was the first to realize that something was wrong. He moved out and began pawing the water, whining like a puppy. Following his lead, Meghan turned her attention back to the pond. Its surface was smooth again, with no sign of the stranger. Then she saw the faint bubbling near the center.

Though she could not see through the murky water, an inner vision revealed a man suspended beneath the surface, his body bobbing and swaying like a puppet at the end of the reeds that gripped his wrists and ankles. Without hesitation she pulled her knife from her wrist, clamped it between her teeth, and dived toward that telltale sign.

The sun had climbed higher in the sky but its rays could not penetrate far into the marshy water. Still Meghan kept her eyes open as she propelled herself deeper into the muddy green underworld. She did not think of failure. It never entered her mind that she would not find him. She hoped only that she would be in time.

As she reached the tops of the long sinewy weeds she drew back instinctively. Their touch was like the licks of long wet tongues across her stomach and legs. This was what she had been taught to avoid.

Her hesitation lasted only a moment. The golden-haired stranger was down there; the writhing nest of snaky weeds had wrapped themselves about him and held him in a death grip. He had no weapon to free himself. She had to find him.

Although her skin shrank from the cold reedy fingers that reached out to her face and body, she plunged deeper into the forest of underwater growth, one hand stretched out in the darkness in search of her goal. When she felt a man's shoulder under her palm, the solid hard warmth of his skin triggered a leap of joy within her. Already her lungs were aching. With a hard kick she forced herself deeper, reached blindly lower to grasp him under the arm, and then tugged. Only then did he respond. His arm came up and, incredibly, shoved her up and away. Caught unprepared, Meghan floated helplessly to the surface.

She broke the surface gasping for air, confused and amazed. Was he a madman? Or had he thought her some monster of the deep come to claim him as its meal? It did not matter. A flip and a kick sent her straight back down. This time she didn't hesitate as the reeds grazed her. Without seeing, she knew where he was.

She found his head first, when the springy texture of his

hair moved through her searching fingers. Slipping behind him to stay out of his reach, she ran a hand down his back until she encountered his bonds. Both legs were caught in the leathery grip of the reeds. Small but sharp, her blade sliced through the wet tentacles that clung to him. He was no longer hostile, but he did not even try to free himself as she worked to release him. She hacked more frantically at the vines.

He must live! He must!

The thought became a chant in her mind. She could not bear another death on her conscience.

When finally he floated free, rising past her like a bubble, Meghan sheathed her knife, grasped him about the waist, and began to kick with all that was left of her strength. They rose slowly. It seemed an eternity to her until they reached the air. When his head broke the surface her gasps sank them again and again until she could control the heavings of her starved lungs; but not once did she release her burden.

"You're safe! You're safe!" she whispered against his cheek as she started for the shore, the stroke of her free arm carrying them.

In deep water she maneuvered him easily, but as they reached the shallows the man became an ungainly weight. Finally Meghan gave up swimming and began dragging him, one hand under each armpit, as she struggled for sure footing on the slick bottom.

Suddenly the water behind her erupted with splashing and barking. A moment later, Meghan was pushed flat as a great weight leaped onto her back. Hair streaming water cross her face, Meghan righted herself and came face to face with the stranger's pet. The dog was even bigger than she remembered, nearly chest-high and baring teeth that could grind her bones, but she was too angry to be terrified.

"Get away, ye great beastie!" she roared in a furious tone and heaved an armful of water at the dog.

Without waiting for the animal's reaction, she turned and

grabbed the man, whose head had slipped under the water. Pulling and tugging, she brought him to the bank, keeping her gaze averted from the animal who stood watching her. No doubt he waited to see if she meant his master harm.

When she reached the grassy bank, she lifted the man by his underarms and tried to drag him onto the land. He was heavier than she had thought and her efforts met with only partial success. Once his shoulders and chest cleared the water, she found she had no strength and lowered him onto his back. Squatting, she paused to draw several fresh breaths, knowing that he would not slip back in.

"No thanks to ye!" she muttered as the dog came hesitantly forth, his head lowered, and poked his nose beneath his master's. After a brief inspection, he began to whine.

"He's nae dead!" Meghan said sharply, and pushed away the dog's muzzle as she bent over the man. He could not be dead; she would not have it so.

But a look at his face was not reassuring. He lay absolutely still, his face as translucent and pale as mother-of-pearl. Annoyed and frightened, Meghan gently shook his shoulder.

"Awake, man! Ye must nae be dead!"

She laid a hand on his chest, but she could not be certain that she felt anything more than the throb of her own pulse in her fingertips. She knew nothing of dead people, had never touched one. The small animals she and Una snared were different: their rapid heartbeats and quick breathing were easily detected. She shook him again.

"Open yer eyes, man! Dinna be dead!"

Once more the dog poked his muzzle against the man's clammy cheek and licked it twice before lying down beside him. The man did not respond.

Terror awakened within Meghan. One man had died before her eyes this day. Now she had risked her life to save another. He could not be dead.

"Wake up! Wake up!" she cried in frustration as she fell on

him, pummeling his chest and stomach with her hard little fists. "Ye mustn't be dead! Ye foolish, foolish man! Ye should nae have gone so deep! Great brute! Ye mustn't be dead! Ye mustn't!"

The dog, confused by the girl's actions as she pounded his master and screamed abuse, barked and leaped excitedly upon her, knocking her flat.

Looking up into bared teeth, the dog's paws on her chest, Meghan lay perfectly still while tears obscured her vision. If the man was dead, she no longer cared what happened.

The man's cough startled both girl and dog.

Encouraged by the sound, the dog leaped away from her and to the man's side.

When Meghan pulled herself upright she saw that his lungs and stomach were beginning to expel the pond water that had nearly drowned him. Quickly she moved to his side and turned him onto his stomach as the heavings continued. This she understood. She had nearly drowned once and had never forgotten the feeling. She knew that he would live if the water came out of him.

After his spasms stopped, she cradled the stranger's head in her arms, holding him quietly as he lay insensible in her embrace.

The minutes passed slowly and soon her arms ached and her naked body quaked with the cold, but she was afraid to release him. By force of will she had pulled him back from death, and now, holding him, she believed she kept him safe. The dog lay a few feet away, his head on his paws but eyes ever watchful.

Slowly a little color came back into the man's face, and the blue ring around his lips faded, leaving a faint trace of pink. Meghan watched eagerly for those signs of life, willing him to stay in the world with her. His closed eyes were deep set beneath golden brown brows, the jaw hard and square, and the nose bold and blunt tipped.

He was so beautiful, she thought as she slowly rocked him, more beautiful than any other being she had ever seen. And she was responsible for saving his life. Surely, then, she could not be the devil people claimed.

Shyly she stroked the bright hair turned dark by the water, and one damp curl entwined itself about her finger. Yet he did not move. Fear reawakened within her as she felt the clammy texture of his cheek. His skin was as cool as that of a fish. Anxious for reassurance, she bent over and rested her cheek against his.

"Dinna die," she whispered against the corner of his mouth, and was rewarded with a feathery sigh of his breath against her lips. The touch sent a quiver of pleasure through her. Emboldened by his stillness, she cupped his cool cheek in her hand and turned his face until her lips lay lightly against his. "Dinna die," she whispered again into his mouth, as if her words held the gift of life.

His lids fluttered, the dark lashes stirring on his cheeks, and Meghan drew away, trembling in anticipation. Then his eyes opened and he looked straight up into her face.

For a long moment they stared at each other. She had not known what to expect, had only wished the life to stir within him once more; but the instant their gazes met, Meghan knew she would never forget a single line or curve of him, nor would she ever want anything of life but to be looked at by those wondrously deep green eyes.

She watched his expression change from confusion to wonder and then amazement. Until that moment she had not realized that he was staring . . . at her cheek.

Clamping a hand over the mark, she leaped to her feet. Only one thought filled her head as she fled back into the forest: perhaps he had lived because he had not looked upon her face until now.

Chapter Two

When Revelin Piers Butler opened his eyes, his first impression was one of utter peace. He seemed suspended, disconnected from the earth and even from his body, as though he floated in the soft light of morning. He felt himself part of the amber air, shimmering, floating, riding the gentlest of breezes. Above his head spread green and gold distances. The sunlit regions of ray and shadow swirled and changed before his eyes, now green, now gold, now the blackest of greens.

Finally it was too much. He shut his eyes against the vibrant beauty of the light. Yet, a feeling of melancholy gripped him, for he knew he would never see such light again.

Green water now swam before his mind's eye, sluggish dung green with purple depths that filled him with regret. He did not want to die, not yet, not when the day was so lovely, the year in its springtime, and he so full of unfulfilled promise.

Were those tears that dampened his cheeks, or was it the wet embrace of the marsh pond? He could not tell. But he was sinking, gliding deeper and more quickly with every moment until there was only the icy cold depths of brown water and the slick wet arms of death's embrace. . . .

When he awakened again it was to the security of the ground beneath him. He could feel the cushion of grass and the jut of a rock at his back, but he had no desire to open his eyes this time. Heaven or Hell, it could wait a little longer. . . .

There was the cool breath of morning in the air. It tickled his nose and roughened his exposed flesh with goose bumps. He felt his manhood shrivel and his belly tremble. Nothing in his religious education had predicted that Hell would be so mild and sweet. Perhaps, in spite of his father's dire predictions to the contrary, he had earned Mercy's Grace and Heaven. The thought pleased him, and a smile that did not quite form quivered on his lips.

He felt no longer capable of surprise. He did not open his eyes when arms enfolded him. When a gentle hand pushed the hair from his cool cheek, he felt only gratitude. He had heard that sailors, who feared drowning above all else, would sometimes throw themselves into the sea in hopes of sharing a mermaid's embrace. If this were the embrace they sought, he marveled that a ship ever returned to shore. She was warm and soft, her breath scented with wild strawberries. He turned his face into the warmth and found the pillow for his cheek to be a tender round breast. His eyes opened then and he realized that he was, after all, still capable of surprise. Surely the most beautiful girl in the world was bending over him. And she was naked.

Enormous sea-blue eyes looked down at him, and a sensation not unlike drowning, but much more pleasant, moved through him. A tendril of hair, as pure a blue-black as a raven's wing, brushed his cheek as she moved closer. Her soft red lips parted, capturing his cool mouth for an instant, and then he was again staring at her tempting breasts only inches from his face.

Was he her lover? He could not remember; could not remember anything beyond a painful tumble when his horse had stepped into a rabbit hole. But one thing was becoming increasingly clear. He had not died. This time when his manhood stirred there was no shrinkage but a sudden filling. The urge to reach for her, to bring those tender lips down upon his own once more rushed through him, but he found he could not so much as raise a finger. He was as weak as a babe.

What jest was this? Why could he not move? What held him? Bonds . . . chains . . . or the girl?

In near panic his gaze met hers again and she responded to his silent question with a look of fear. Her hand flew to her left cheek, then she leaped to her feet and was gone.

"Don't go!" He must have said the words aloud, for they echoed loudly in his ears, but she did not come back.

Then more than a hundred pounds of Irish wolfhound settled on his chest, and Revelin found himself without breath to repeat the request. A long, rough tongue salivated over one cheek and then the other before the owner of the odoriferous breath backed off Revelin's chest.

Cursing roundly and imaginatively, Revelin lay for a moment staring at the trees above him. And then it came back to him, slowly but completely what had occurred, memories of who he was and where he was . . . and why.

A mist too fine to be called rain blanketed the clearing where four hungry and saddle-weary men shared an evening meal beneath the shelter of a canvas tent.

When the last of the meat had been carved from the roasted joint, Sir Richard Atholl raised his tankard in a solemn toast. "God be praised He did not condemn me to life as an Irishman!"

Two of his three companions chuckled appreciatively and downed the contents of their cups. This ritual had been repeated each evening around their campfire for more than a fortnight as the four men traversed the uncharted areas of Ireland beyond the English Pale of Dublin. But the rain-drenched day had taken its toll on the one Irish-born gentleman among them; the toast was one barb he no longer intended to tolerate.

Revelin looked up from his untouched ale with an expression that was unusually grim for a man of twenty-three years. "I doubt the good Lord took particular care where your mother dropped you."

The words, though softly spoken, cut short the agreeable laughter. Sir Richard's narrow, almost lipless mouth lost its parsimonious smile. "Sir! You insult my mother's memory!"

Revelin shrugged, his muscles stretching the limits of his leather jerkin. He did not relish a fight, but neither did he fear one. "How else would you have me answer your attack upon my own?"

"He has you there, Atholl!" Sir Robin Neville broke in, adding his infectious laughter. Slight of size, and with a trace of freckling above his precisely cropped blond beard and mustache, Neville was the only man present dressed in courtly fashion with a Spanish ruff at his throat and ribbon cross garters. Not even the twin miseries of cold and rain had dampened his spirits. His blue eyes gleamed with high spirits. "You forget that the sod you scrape from your boots each evensong is sacred to Butler."

He reached out and placed a familiar hand on Revelin's shoulder, choosing to ignore the tensing of muscles beneath his touch. "Though Ireland's home to Rev, he's a man whom the queen has seen fit to commission as her emissary."

Sir Richard Atholl raised his chin a fraction to better the effect of looking down his long beak of a nose as he regarded his young companions. His somber brown Reformation clothing and his thinning cap of light brown hair made him appear much older than his thirty years. "For all her astute and superior nature, our beloved queen is not above her maidenly weaknesses," he said censoriously. "A strong form and an unlined face ever finds favor in court these days. Yet, I am reminded of the saying: 'The fairest skin may cover the sourest fruit.'"

Robin's fingers dug into Revelin's shoulder to hold him still. "You dare to suggest that our wild Irishman has caught the fancy of our sovereign?"

Robin turned a thoughtful gaze on Revelin, as though seeing him for the first time. "I admit that he exceeds my height by some inches and that he's not ill made, for all that he refuses to submit to the manly itch of a beard and shaves his cheeks. Still and all, 'twould be a shame to cover so square a chin with bristles. Aye, he makes a pretty specimen for the tenderhearted ladies."

He turned quickly to Atholl and winked. "But I reject his pretensions to our sovereign's heart. He's only a stripling. Whereas I am—"

"—A greater fool than that blackguard who attempted to sell us a diseased cow for meat this morn!" finished John Reade, the fourth member and the acknowledged leader of the party.

Reade's bulky, heavily muscled shoulders moved restlessly beneath his leather jerkin as he reached to wrap a broad hand about his tankard. Below a jut of heavy black brows, his dark eyes shone with contempt as they moved from one to the other of those seated with him. "If the three of you will persist in this battle of the witless, I'll seek the solitary company of my bed." So saying, he drained his cup.

"That would be a novelty," Robin exclaimed with a guileless smile. "Solitude in your bed," he continued. "I never knew you to prefer your own company when a compliant wench was at hand."

The four men glanced out the open tent flap to where their lone servant had retired for the night wrapped in a blanket beneath a canvas lean-to. John Reade said he had hired Flora, an Irishwoman, as their servant; but the others had quickly accepted the fact that she was John's whore.

"Slut!" Sir Richard declared, his lean face tight with disapproval. "Gaelic slut! Pocket of disease-ridden foulness! They all seek a man's mortal soul to serve it up to their master in Hell!"

The speech was answered by Robin's laughter. "Such passion, Atholl, and before the second keg's been broached. That bodes well for the potency of the ale. I could use such fervor to guard me against this deuced mist!" Turning up his tankard, he drained it.

Sir Richard rose, his face livid. "I was tempted to decline Her Majesty's generous request to be her eyes and ears in this popish wilderness when the names of the other members of this company were made known to me. However, my acceptance does not force me to sit and be ridiculed by my detractors! I bid you good night."

"Alas! I fear I've upset our Presbyterian friend," Robin remarked when Atholl had retired out into the fine mist.

"Your court-jester airs will yet land you in trouble, Sir Neville," John grumbled. "But, as to that, I've little stomach for the sermonizing of that self-righteous prig myself."

"He does wax tedious," Robin agreed as he twisted the huge ruby carbuncle ring on his left hand. "I wonder that he came at all."

"The conversion of sinners is his mission, I'm told," Revelin said sourly. "He might have done better to set his sights on the company of hangers-on at Whitehall."

"He might have at that," John said with a sneer as he eyed Robin over the rim of his tankard. "Purple taffeta and lace trunk hose. God's body! If not for the scraggly bearding upon your cheeks, I'd believe that a skinny-shanked wench in gentleman's clothing sat before me!"

Robin rubbed his ring, blew his breath against the dull ruby, then extended it toward the light of the campfire. "Really, John, you stoop too low to wound. I fancy a lesser barb might have served."

He raised his eyes slowly to the larger man's face, his lids lowered seductively in perfect mimicry of the best London courtesans. "To cast me in the role of a woman does little credit to your vision . . . or your taste."

"The devil take you!" John roared, rising menacingly to his feet. His hand went to the Spanish dagger he wore at the waist of his doublet. "Extend your gibbering tongue once more and I'll split it for you!"

Robin nodded agreeably. "At your leisure, Reade. I would consider first, however, that 'tis the strain of the day that wearies you rather than my mild jests.

"A pox on this weather!" he continued, wiping the misty damp from his brow with a scented handkerchief retrieved from his sleeve. "I fear I will rot clean through before ever I dry out. Rev, man, can you do nothing about the plaguey poor weather? 'Tis bad hospitality, if you ask me."

Revelin watched anger change to frustration on John's tight face. Each of them knew that John could ill afford to provoke a challenge. The queen did not appreciate quarreling among her men, and John had recently spent six months as a guest at the Tower for a similar infraction. His new post as leader of this expedition had been nothing more than a royal slap on the wrist for a soldier of his ilk.

"A plague upon the pair of you!" John spat at last and left them.

"One day you will provoke him beyond control," Revelin said quietly when they were alone.

Robin's fine blond brows rose in astonishment. "You fear John wants my head on a pike? I thought he merely chose argument as the fastest method of settling his supper."

For the first time that evening, Revelin smiled. It was well known that John suffered from a sensitive digestive system and often complained of dyspepsia. "In truth, none of us has the stomach for this journey. There's little for us to learn in this weather. Every hill, every glen looks the same wherever we ride. I must number my sketches to tell them apart. We might as well return to Dublin."

Robin smiled. "I do not mind the damp by half. 'Tis the

company, present companion excepted, that tries my patience. Even John's surly temperament is preferable to Atholl's. Without him I would have fallen happily into some debauchery or another before now. Why, just this morning on the road I spied as sweet a pair of eyes as ever enticed a man to damnation. Alas, Atholl saw the gaze and routed the wench with one of his bombastic oaths. God's life! I never met a sourer disposition where women are concerned. If this is what the Reformation does to a man's appetites, I'd sooner follow a man of your stripe, for all its dangers."

Revelin smiled but did not reply. His secret sympathy for Catholicism was both a source of consternation to his uncle, the earl of Ormond, and a potential danger to himself. Robin might infer much, but he had no concrete evidence and Revelin was not about to enlighten him. Instead, he changed the subject: "What is your opinion of the day's sketches?"

Robin looked at the bundled papers that lay on the table between them. "They're clever, Rev, you know that. As to their military merit," he shrugged, "you must ask John. A map is as much good to me as a plow: I can use neither. But our sovereign wants every inch of Ireland charted, and you do your share. After all, your future at court depends on the success of the mission."

Though Robin's words mirrored his own thoughts, the reminder from one he had regarded as indifferent to court politics made Revelin sharpen his gaze in interest. "Tell me, Sir Robin, why I'm in need of your words of encouragement."

Robin leaned closer and lowered his voice. "I know you do not take kindly to any remark made against your uncle, the earl of Ormond, but you would do well to ask yourself why he did not want you to accept the queen's commission when he had sponsored you at court himself. Could it be jealousy? After all, he did not endear himself to our queen when he went to war against the Fitzgeralds at Affane. Four years have passed since the conflict, and yet he remains in London as balm for her temper over the occasion." He smiled impishly. "Certain rumor has it that the queen may be looking for a more 'loyal' Butler to place at the earl's right hand."

Revelin stroked his chin thoughtfully, his mind shifting through Robin's tidbits of information. It was true that the queen was still known to swear roundly when reminded of the temerity of the earls of Ormond and Desmond in engaging in battle with private armies on soil nominally under British control. Yet, no one before had dared to whisper in Revelin's ear that the queen's anger with Thomas Butler, the earl of Ormond, had reached the point of disaffection. Why was Neville so loose-tongued concerning the queen's wants and desires this night?

Revelin sipped his ale, unwilling to be hurried by his curiosity. Either Sir Robin Neville was an idle intriguer whose conjectures had no foundation, or someone had confided something to him, in which case he was a man to be regarded with suspicion. Could his information have come from the earl of Leicester, his uncle's personal enemy at court?

After a few moments, Revelin said easily, "Come, Robin, who am I that the queen should think so highly of me? In any case, Her Majesty knows my loyalties are hers as much as the earl's are."

Robin smiled impishly. "You're not dull, Butler. You accurately surmised the queen's humor before we left Whitehall. While she's loath to engage in war, she is aware that the Irish question must be settled sooner or later. Isn't it wiser to test loyalties before the matter becomes a contest of armies? Our sovereign refused the earl's request to release you to his household. Instead, she sent you home on a mission of her own design. Does that not speak of intrigue?"

Revelin chuckled. "Do I look like a rebel?"

Robin reached for the pitcher and refilled their tankards with ale. "When men like Perrot and Sidney have the queen's ear, 'tis only a matter of time before this quaint little land is carved

31

up like the Christmas goose. Why, even that untutored West Country campaigner Carew has persuaded the Dublin Parliament to uphold his claims to the barony of Idrone in Carlow. 'Twas thought to be Butler land, was it not?" He shrugged. "Loyal men, Rev, are what the queen needs most, and she's willing to be generous for that loyalty."

Revelin knew a comment was expected of him but he remained silent. He had been in court circles too long to be led into voicing an indiscreet opinion that could be carried back to the queen. Ormond was his uncle and his foster father; nothing would induce him to speak against the man. Besides, Neville seemed already to know, or to suspect, a great deal too much.

Robin said pleasantly, "It may be that John Reade is not indifferent to the gleam of gold."

At Revelin's questioning glance, he continued, "Our mission is to map the Ulster countryside so that the army can plan strategy should war come. You are the artist; Atholl, blast him, is our conscience. But John Reade is yet another matter."

Revelin eyed the foppish courtier before him with new respect. Behind the lethargic demeanor was a strong and quick mind. "What of you, Robin? Where lies your path?"

Robin smiled his bland smile that hid so much. "Why, Rev, my friend, when I'm here I'm out of reach of my father. What more could a son of Lord Neville wish for? I do not fancy myself the landlord of an Irish estate. But you may believe the matter takes up more than a night's lodging in John's head." He leaned forward suddenly. "And so that you will not think me napping on other accounts, I know Lady Alison Burke will expect you to prove worthy of an Irish land grant for services rendered to the Crown."

Revelin started at the mention of the lady's name, spilling a bit of ale down his front. "Damn you for your presumption!" he muttered as he brushed the liquid from his leather jerkin.

"Sir Revelin Butler, the lovesick calf!" Robin chuckled. "'Tis a splendid title for a sonnet, do you not think?"

"I think I'm for bed," Revelin answered as he rose and pulled his woolen cloak about him.

"You may rest assured that your secret is safe with me, for I wish you luck with the fair Lady Alison. You've set your sights upon marriage to a Protestant Irish landholder's daughter, a rare enough commodity. Were I you, I would keep an eye open for other suitors. Nay! You'll have no more from me than that. I grow weary with the sound of my own voice. *Au revoir!*"

Revelin found his quarters no less and no more than they had been since riding north out of Dublin. His tent was poorly pitched, its poles finding uneasy purchase in the sodden ground. The cot that served as his bed was spotted with mildew and clammy to the touch. But the sight of Ualter curled up before his cot brought a smile to his face. Here was one companion of whose company he never tired.

With a curse of discomfort, he wrapped his cloak more tightly about himself and lay down in it. Every joint in his body ached with cold and his muscles with fatigue. Sleep was the only cure for those ills.

As always, as soon as he closed his eyes, visions of Lady Alison Burke came to keep him company in the solitude of his tent. At the journey's beginning he had delighted in recalling with great detail the inflections of her speech, the exact tilt of her head when she listened attentively, and even the number of turns in the golden curl that she wore in the middle of her brow. But tonight the image had faded. Even his favorite memory of her, dressed for hunting with her hawk perched upon her glove, refused to resolve within his mind's eye.

Suddenly a hand on his shoulder brought Revelin awake with a cry, and he reached automatically for the hilt of his dagger as he threw off his cloak.

"'Tis I, Butler."

Revelin stared up in the dark, finally making out the features of the face above him. "What brings you here, Sir Richard?" he grumbled in annoyance.

The sound of tinder being struck was followed shortly by

the dim glow of an oil lamp, and Atholl's lean form appeared before him. "Listen carefully," he said softly. "I do not wish the others to become curious, so I must be brief."

Revelin swung his legs over the side of his cot and ran his hands through his hair. He threw a dark look at his dog, whose head rose expectantly, but decided against turning him loose on Atholl. However, had the dog attacked his unwanted guest beforehand, Revelin might not have come quickly to Atholl's aid. "Well, Sir Richard?"

Atholl's eyes stayed a moment on Revelin, as if weighing some matter, then he nodded. "You have not adopted all the sins of our English courtiers, I see."

Revelin's gaze followed his and he realized then why the older man was staring at his bed: Atholl was pleased never to have found a woman sharing Revelin's bed, even in Dublin.

"I find nothing in these wilds to my liking," he answered, uncertain why he could not declare his lack of desire for other women now that he knew himself to be in love with Lady Alison.

Atholl nodded. "There's nothing to compare with the purity of body and soul, a thing rare and therefore more pleasing in youth."

Revelin bit his lip and frowned. The compliment was not a particularly flattering one. "I've sampled enough of the flesh's delights," he offered with a hint of challenge in his voice.

"The indiscretion of youth," Sir Richard answered agreeably. "It's a folly of most young men."

Revelin let a great yawn escape him. "You wanted something?"

"I notice that you approve of our leader no more than I," Atholl began. "Reade has no feeling for the momentous occasion that may yet arise from our trip through Hibernia. He is a man of the flesh, a soldier whose family rose to prominence through dastardly deeds perpetrated under the aegis of a grossly debauched sovereign."

Revelin rubbed his eyes, the grit of sleep stinging them. Atholl's sermonizing on the proclivities of Henry VIII could find no less-willing audience than he. "I beg you save this speech for a more brilliant hour, Sir Richard."

The older man smiled. "You've come so far, Revelin, I would not like to think you could be persuaded back to the popish mire from which you've risen."

Finally, with that declaration, Atholl received Revelin's full attention. "What?"

"The devil has many snares and lures, my boy, with which to deflect a man from his ultimate design. I have seen this country from which you came, and I have wondered at your escape. Its beauty is so lush, its smells and sights more sensuous than a harlot's. Why should this be?"

The old man's pale features took on a light of life, glowing like the wax of a candle just before the flame dies. "In the throes of tonight's prayers the answer came. This place cannot be the Eden it seems. Therefore it is a false paradise, a temptor's garden of beauty, an illusion, a crumb to tempt the unsuspecting and cheat him of a taste of the true paradise. And yet a man born to the very sin of this false paradise may yet escape it!"

Revelin had ceased listening, and his lids closed briefly over his eyes. This was no time for the confessions of a zealot. It was a rude surprise when he found himself suddenly crushed in an embrace that smelled loudly of camphor rubbed onto an unwashed body.

"You! You are my example!" Atholl boasted when he released Revelin. He laid a bracing hand on the younger man's shoulder. "You are the example of what good can be wrought in this land if only the virtues of Christian principle can be brought to the Irish. As for my harsh words at supper, they were not meant for you. I cannot hold your degenerate Gaelic background against you now that I have seen its true purpose. We will be fast friends after this, that I promise!"

With an agility that both surprised and relieved Revelin,

Atholl disappeared from his tent as silently as he had come.

"He's mad!" Revelin muttered and, dowsing the oil lamp, returned to his cot. If the discomforts of the daily travel in territory without roads but with a plentitude of bogs and marsh flies were not enough, he had somehow unwittingly won the friendship of a man he neither liked nor found easy to tolerate.

"A plague upon you, Revelin!" he grumbled to himself in a sleepy voice. "You cannot even keep a proper enemy!"

Revelin blinked as the gossamer wings of a pond fly touched his lashes and flitted past to light upon the bridge of his nose. With a flick of his finger he removed the intruder. The memories of the night before had returned intact. At dawn, all he had been able to think of was ridding himself of the promised company of Atholl. He had ridden ahead of his group to be free to mull over plans of his own, which included marriage to Lady Alison, if he could win the queen's approval for it. Then, too, Robin had given him food for thought. If Robin was the queen's or Leicester's spy and John an intended usurper of Irish land, Revelin would need to tread warily, indeed. His troubled thoughts had so occupied him that he had not seen the rabbit hole into which his mount was about to step. . . .

He raised his left arm and frowned as he looked at it. There was a deep gash in his forearm where it had struck the sharp edge of a stone. He had come to this pond to wash off the telltale signs of mud, realizing that the others would make merciless sport of him if they learned of his spill. While swimming he had become entangled in the reeds and nearly drowned. The girl! The girl had saved his life!

For an instant he recalled deep blue eyes looking down at him from a delicate face. So real was the memory that he reached for the vision, but it vanished and he caught only a handful of air for his effort.

Disappointed, he let his hand drop back onto his bare chest. She had been here, bending over him. He would swear to it. Or had it been a dream?

He sat up. This time his muscles responded. Looking about, he was satisfied to find his horse chewing the succulent grasses along the water's edge while his dog sat at his feet. But the girl was nowhere in sight.

"Ualter!" he greeted, and groaned a moment later as the huge animal leaped upon him. "Down, Ualter! Down," he ordered, pushing with partial success to free himself from the dog. With one last lick of joy the animal sat back on his haunches, his nuzzle pushed forward inquiringly.

"Did you see her?" Revelin questioned as he scratched the ruff of fur under the dog's chin. "Well? Where is she?"

As if the dog understood the question he stood up and ran a few feet away, then swung about and barked excitedly.

Revelin grinned. "You're teasing. I believe you know nothing about her."

Ualter's ears lay back and then sprang forward again as he shot past his master and raced around the edge of the pond. Revelin watched skeptically as the dog rooted about in the tall grasses, frightening a flock of ducks who had thought themselves well hidden. In the meantime, Revelin reached for the first of his clothing and began to dress.

Finally, with a yelp of pleasure, Ualter grabbed a length of fabric and bounded back to his master.

"What is this?" Revelin murmured, then whistled appreciatively as he unfolded the cloth and realized it was a linen shirt like the local peasants wore. She had been naked. *This must belong to her. So she was real after all*. The thought gave him a warm rush of pleasure.

He folded the garment and tucked it into the front of his doublet. But when he had pulled on his hose and boots, he found himself staring out across the marshy waters in thoughtful contemplation. He had a desire to see the girl again. No, it was more like an urgent flood in his blood, quite unlike anything he had ever experienced before. Yet he did not know where to begin. She could be a member of any family within miles. The memory of wide blue eyes, unbound silky black hair, and an astonishingly lovely face would be of little help.

Revelin closed his eyes, pushing impatiently against his lids with his thumb and forefinger. There must be something he could remember that would make his search easier. The memory came back so quickly and sharply that it made him laugh out loud.

"She wears a rose!" he said, bending over to lift Ualter's muzzle and bring the dog's eyes to meet his. "She has a blood-red rose upon her left cheek! With that mark we shall find her, Ualter. That we shall!"

Chapter Three

"Ah well, it's home ye've come at last," Una remarked at the sound of footsteps. "Come in, lass." She beckoned the shadow that paused in the doorway. "I've saved ye a wee morsel."

Reluctantly, Meghan moved into the range of the dull glow from the smoky peat fire in the center of the floor.

"What's—?" As Una's gaze swept her niece's nakedness, the handle of the butter churn slipped from her hands and she rose from her stool. *"May—geen!"*

Belatedly, Meghan raised her hands to shield the parts of her body not hidden beneath the cascade of her hair, but she could not hide the fresh scratches on her arms and legs or the leaves and thistles that had caught in her hair as she ran home through the forest. The excitement and terror riding high and hard within her had crowded out consideration of anything until now.

A look of innocence came into her eyes. "Ach, Una. 'Tis not so bad as ye be thinking."

"What am I thinking, lass?" Una pinned her with the full scrutiny of her canny gaze. "Ye run off before sunrise without a word, and now ye come back looking like the fairies pulled ye backwards through a bog. And where's yer *leine?* Have ye no shame? Take me mantle and cover yerself," she commanded as she swung the garment from her shoulders.

Guilt and misgiving chased across Meghan's features as Una placed the mantle across her shoulders. The rough woolen fabric chafed her outraged skin but there was also warmth within its scratchy folds and she accepted it gratefully.

"Now, let's have a look at ye." Una gripped Meghan's chin and tilted her face to the light to study her overly bright eyes. Where she was not splashed with mud, Meghan's fair skin was rosy with exertion—or perhaps something more. "Well, lass? What's become of yer tongue?"

Not for the first time in recent months Meghan tingled with resentment of Una's authority over her. For a moment she stared stubbornly at the ceiling of the tiny wicker-work hut. Was she never to have secrets to keep or share as she chose? She was exhausted and sore, and her feet ached with cuts and stone bruises. Despite that, a warmth encircled her, an emboldening warmth fed by the memory of a man with amber hair and green eyes. No, she would not tell Una of the meeting at the pond. It was too special, her emotions too fresh to expose them to the older woman's harsh judgment.

"I was attacked by a wild beast," she blurted, not knowing where the words came from. Lowering her gaze, she met Una's look of disbelief. "Truly!" Born with a fertile imagination and raised on Gaelic lore, Meghan's lie quickly matured into the full fabric of a story. "'Twas a horrid creature with huge fangs and claws so sharp they'd flay a man with a single stroke!"

Una's carroty brows rose for an instant before her eyes narrowed skeptically. "And so, how would ye have me believe ye escaped so fierce a brute?"

Meghan's imagination faltered until the stinging sensation

of her palms reminded her of her first adventure of the morning. Triumphantly she held them up for the older woman to see. "I climbed a tree!"

Una chuckled and shook her head, disturbing the thick plait resting on her shoulder. Once the plait had been carrot red; now it was grayed with age. "I'm nae so great a fool as to believe that tale. Beast, is it? I'd as lief believe ye'd been with some man."

Meghan's gaze slipped away as a guilty blush suffused her cheeks. Was there some difference in her, she wondered, that her aunt suspected what she hoped to keep secret?

Alive to every nuance of her niece's moods, Una did not miss the change as the girl's face warmed to scarlet. "Meghan, lass, what have ye done?" She caught her niece's shoulder and tried to catch her chin but Meghan kept her head lowered.

After a moment, Una released her with a sigh. "I'd nae have believed it possible but—" She paused to pass a hand over the sweat on her brow. When she glanced up there was a new look in her eyes, a kind of desperate knowledge. "There's a man somewhere who knows the answer to me questions. Would ye deny me that, Meghan?"

Meghan's gaze fastened on the long neat rills of dirt raised by the bristles of Una's broom as if the earthen floor held clues to what her answer should be. Her lie had been spontaneous, uncalculated; and now that Una had seen through it, she had no choice but to revert to the truth.

"I did not run from a beast," she admitted reluctantly. "There were herdsmen in the forest. I—"

"Herdsmen?" Una repeated in horror. "Ye wicked, wicked lass! Ye know better than to go near the settlements. A thousand times I've warned ye. After one glimpse of yer face, should a babe sicken or a cow abort her calf, they'll descend upon us like wolves upon a wounded stag!"

Fear washed through Meghan as she raised a protective hand to her left cheek. Una's anger was no easier to bear than the unfounded wrath of the herdsmen. "'Twas a dream that made me go there," she confided. "It came to me in sleep last night. I sought to learn if 'twas true."

"The dreams." Una sighed in defeat, her strong square shoulders sagging. It had been many months since the visions had visited Meghan. She had hoped, had dared to believe, that they were gone once and for all. Now that hope was dashed. Leaving Ulster had not broken the link with the otherworld. "'Tis always the same. What's a body to do against such temptation?"

"It foretold a man's death," Meghan whispered.

Una gasped and crossed herself. "Mercy's Grace be upon ye, child, for the burden of such evil knowledge."

Meghan blinked back the tears that roughened her voice. "Why do the dreams come to me? What am I that men must fear me so?"

The older woman shook her head. "'Tis not for ye or me to say what brings the sight. Ye must learn to keep the visions in yer heart, tell no one. I do what I can for ye. There's been no cause for any to wonder what more a mother could have done for ye."

It had been many years since Meghan had voiced the question, but now it held a new urgency in her mind. "Why will ye never tell me who my mother was and what happened to her?"

"Ye had no mother, to tell a plain truth!" Una snapped, turning a blind eye to the expression of hurt on the girl's face. "But enough of that." A new horror electrified her face. "Meghan, lass, ye didn't lead the herdsmen here?"

"They didn't see me," Meghan lied, fearing what Una would do if she knew the truth. "I did climb a tree. When they passed by, I went to the pond to swim, but a noise frightened me and I ran away. That's where I left my *leine*."

She lowered her gaze before speaking, but Una seemed not to notice. Her own expression had softened a trifle. "Well,

there'll be no more of that. Ye're to keep away from the settlements after this. 'Tis only a mercy they didn't set eyes on
ye, or I'd not offer a stone's worth for another safe night."

Chastened by the reminder of the danger in which she had
placed them, Meghan said nothing more.

Turning, Una lifted an oak piggin that was half-full with
milk. "There's been enough mischief afoot this morning to
spoil the butter." She glanced doubtfully at the churn and then
back at Meghan. "Ye know what's to be done."

Meghan nodded. It was churning day. Churning was a tick-
lish process subject to the whims of witches and fairies. Everyone knew that. Una had never said so, but they both understood
that Meghan's dreams were a gift of dubious origin. If the
butter failed to break, there was no doubt where the blame
would be laid. That was the reason why Una had banished her
from the house every churning day since she could remember.
The "whiteflesh" was their staple for the summer. A failed
churn meant a starving week.

"Ye'd best take this. 'Twill be nothing else till evening."
Una plucked two oatcakes from the basket on the hearth.

Without a word, Meghan reached for the cakes, which were
generously spread with the last of their butter, then stepped
out of the hut into the morning air. A nameless but very real
guilt gnawed at her, bringing back her desperate need to be
assured that she was not some malignant evil, capable of rousing hatred at a stranger's single glance.

If only she were brave enough to explain to Una about the
man at the pond whose life she had saved. Then perhaps Una
would not be so angry with her. Yet, telling the truth would
not change the fact that the herdsmen had seen and pursued
her and believed she had changed herself into a wild boar and
killed one of them. She had seen fear chalk Una's face at the
mention of a vision of death. If she learned that the vision had
come true, Una might turn away from her forever. No, she
must not speak.

She chose a tree not far from her doorway and sat down among the rosy spikes of foxglove and lacework ferns that grew at its base, resting her back against the trunk.

Meghan closed her eyes, squeezing them until dizzying colors cartwheeled behind her lids and then merged into a single image of beauty that was the golden stranger's face. This was not one of her visions, which came in a guise altogether different from this mingling of fascination and fear and . . . and something more. She had dared to touch him, to hold him tightly to her as if he were an unexpected gift of great value. So little time, so brief a moment had he been hers. Now there was only the remembered satiny coolness of his lips under hers. The memory touched her, astonished her senses with delight. Though she had wished it with all her heart, he had not been hers to keep. And she knew instinctively that sharing the bursting sweetness of her experience with Una would only dim its beauty.

"Be silent," Meghan admonished herself softly, as though the trees would hear and respond, "be silent and pray that the herdsmen will give up their search."

Reluctantly, she licked the last of the butter from her fingers and gathered the large folds of Una's cloak tightly about her. But when she started off toward the nearby oak grove where their sow and piglets hunted moldy acorns as fodder, there was a secret smile upon her lips.

Watching from the shadow of the doorway, Una had waited patiently for the girl to finish her meal and disappear into the woods. Sighing with relief, she returned to her stool and began churning with furious determination.

For sixteen years she had lived apart from people, caring for a child who was not her own. In the beginning it had been simple to raise a babe away from the world. But Meghan was no longer a babe. Each day she ventured farther, expanding the limits of her world until she knew the country better than did her aunt. Fear for their lives had made Una abandon Ulster for the wilds of the south. Now a new threat was upon them, one that loomed larger than the troubles that had made them flee their homeland. Meghan had become a nimble, fresh-budded woman.

"And more's the pity for the pair of us," Una muttered. "Any man with breath in him would yearn to lie upon her thighs . . . till he got a good look at her face. Then there'd be the devil to pay!"

The priest who had baptized Meghan had said it was no sin to be born with the mark of fairies. Only time would tell whether the mark was for good or ill. Except for the mark, she had been a wee fair babe with the creamiest of skin, velvety black hair, and eyes that seemed to see into a body's soul.

Una paused for a moment, resting her forehead against the dash handle. Though she had raised Meghan from birth, she could not say she had spent a comfortable hour in the girl's company. Meghan was a constant reminder of the guilt Una bore. But even that would have been endurable had the girl's "dreams" not begun. They had come first in the summer of Meghan's sixth year. After that, the fear of impending danger seemed ever with them, for Meghan possessed a gift of the "sight."

Guiltily Una crossed herself. Perhaps the priest's advice was the best solution. Perhaps Meghan's true calling did lie with the Church. Once safely behind convent walls, Meghan's dreams might stop, and her blemish would no longer pose a threat. Yet, how could Una give up the girl whose every look reminded her of her beloved sister Maura?

Una's gaze softened at the memory of Maura Fitzgerald— a lass no man in Munster could pass without commenting on her beauty. Her skin held the richness of fresh cream and her lips were as red as ripe wild strawberries. In the end, her beauty had entrapped her. It won for her, against her desire, the passion and jealousy of a man who later became known as the greatest chieftain in all of Ireland, Shane the Proud, "the O'Neill" of Ulster.

It had been expected that Maura would bear Shane a male

heir. But after two days of labor, Maura lay dead, and the babe . . .

Una clasped her hands together. "Lord in Heaven, I've lived not a day without the memory. And so Ye well know. But I'm a simple woman. May I not be held in account for what was done out of pity for a poor wee babe's life. 'Twas her birthright!"

Tears gathered and ran down Una's full cheeks, though she told her herself the deed was history and Shane O'Neill was dead. A year earlier his handsome head had been lifted from his shoulders through the cunning of the O'Donnells, his clan's ancient enemies. The head had been tarred and sent to English Dublin, thrust on a pike, and hung from the northwest gate for all to see. All of Ulster was aflame with the treachery perpetrated by the O'Donnells. Shane had been a hard man, more feared than liked, but he had won the admiration of Irish nobility by standing firm against English aggression in his homeland.

Yet, Shane's death had awakened new fears in Una. He had made many enemies, not all of them O'Donnells. His death would bring either an invasion of Ulster by the English or the massacre of Shane's heirs by other O'Neills as they fought for the title of "the O'Neill." Either way, there would no longer be protection for herself and Meghan. This was the beginning of their exile in fear.

After a quick glance at the entry, Una dropped to her knees by the corner of the turf fire and began gently to scrape away the dirt from behind the blaze. The dirt lifted easily, having been dug up frequently. Finally a corner of rough cloth appeared and Una grasped it and tugged, freeing a weighted bundle from its hiding place. When the thong tied around it was loosened, she carefully unwrapped the cloth to reveal the jeweled hilt of a sheathed blade.

Stones of amethyst, translucent rock crystal, and amber gleamed dully from the gold work. It was a weapon of great workmanship and value, a piece of artistry worthy of a nobleman. With trembling fingers she withdrew the dagger from its sheath. Light flashed off the blade, whose only blemish was a single rusty-brown streak along its fine edge.

Una bit her lip until it bled, but her eyes remained fixed upon the dagger. No, she would not give Meghan up to the Church just yet. Lives had been lost to preserve the secret of Meghan's birth. Now that Shane was dead, Una alone knew the truth. Even in her fear she believed that the visions that came to Meghan were proof of her special nature and that the gift should not be given even into God's service unless Meghan herself wished it.

"But 'twill be poor comfort for the like o' ye, Una Fitzgerald," she whispered as she furtively retied the bundle. "If a vision of the truth should come over Meghan one fine day, ye may still answer for yer part in the deed!"

Not until dawn, when rain hissed upon the heath sod that roofed the hut, did Meghan close her eyes and allow herself the pleasure of sleep. For the past four nights she had lain wide-eyed in the dark, listening. A snap of a twig or a rustle of leaves might mean there was a lurker in the woods.

But night after night the only sounds she heard were the faint scratching of her rush mattress when she moved and Una's low sonorous breathing as she slept. When a lightening of the sky signaled the approach of dawn, relief flooded her body, weariness dragged her lids shut, and Meghan tumbled down the rabbit hole of sleep.

Then, as it had each morning, came the dream of the stranger at the pond.

Water, cool and sweet, spangled her lashes and smoothed her hair into an inky flood upon the surface of the willow-green pool. Where sunlight touched the water it melted into liquid amber or merged into the trembling lavender shadows cast upon the surface by oak boughs. Between the amber and green Meghan swam in lazy strokes that sped her across the top of the water toward . . . toward . . .

He stood on the moss-covered bank. Only a golden mantle of daylight clothed his strong shoulders, which sloped into the beautiful arch of his firm young back. His angular hips balanced perfectly the tight curves of his buttocks and the long muscles of his legs.

A dark wing of cloud swept before the sun, its shadow a phantom rider on the land obliterating the amber from the lake, and then the man, too, was gone, eclipsed in the blink of an eye.

The first flutter of unease moved in Meghan's stomach like a swallowed sliver of ice. The strange fluttering intensified, filling her with a foreshadowing of fear. This was not right. This was not the scene as she remembered it.

She raised her hands before her eyes to blot out what might follow, but the dream that was not a dream would not be denied. The water leaped suddenly, drenching her in a frigid shower that tore an uncontrollable gasp from her. She opened her eyes. Mud-streaked currents swam before her eyes, and then she spied the horror.

Una floated below her, her sturdy, compact body undulating with the currents. Reeds held her, viciously wound in Gordian knots about her ankles and wrists. Una's mouth was distorted in fear, her eyes wide with despair. She was drowning, dying!

Desperately Meghan clawed at the water, trying to reach her aunt. She could not lose Una. She was only a hand's breadth away. And then their fingers brushed.

The water exploded with light. With no more substance than that of a falling star, the light dwindled. It wavered an instant, flared, and died, taking Una with it.

A scream rolled up from deep within Meghan and poured from her in an impotent wail of misery.

* * *

Suddenly a callused hand stopped Meghan's mouth. Surprised by the sting of tears on her cheek, she wondered if she was still caught in the grip of the nightmare.

"Meghan, lass," Una whispered near her ear as she eased the pressure of her hand over the girl's mouth. "We have visitors. Not a sound!"

Meghan sat up. She heard first the hissing of the dew-drenched grasses as many feet traversed the open field between the forest and the hut. Then came the voices of men who made no attempt to be quiet. Cold sweat replaced the tears on her face. Without seeing them she knew that what she most feared had happened: the herders had found them.

"Don't go out!" she whispered, grabbing her aunt's sleeve. "Maybe they'll go away."

Una gently freed her arm. "Keep hidden and there's naught to fear. We've braved strangers' comings and goings before." She touched Meghan's face, lightly tracing the mark on her cheek. "'Tis said the fairies protect their own. We could make use of a bit of luck."

"Please! Don't."

The raw edge of Meghan's voice puzzled Una. "Meghan, lass, have ye seen something? Was it a vision that frightened ye?"

"No! No!" Meghan whispered quickly.

"Well then," Una said with a smile. "There's naught to fear."

Naught to fear. The words were false, but Meghan clamped her lips shut. The dream had not been right. Always before when she had relived the encounter by the pond she had succeeded in saving the stranger's life. This time the ending had changed.

A shout from the yard startled Meghan, but Una did not pause a second time. She threw back the wool drape hung before the doorway and stepped out into the day. "Ach! If it isn't a grand welcome I see before me this fine soft morn," she greeted.

Pausing, she used the excuse of lowering the woolen flap over the entry to observe the dozen men who had come armed with sickles and staffs. *There's trouble, Una, lass,* she thought as she turned to face them.

"And what brings ye to my hut? Ye'll be lost, I'm thinking. Or is it food ye seek? Well? Have ye not a word to spare?"

One man moved forward out of the crowd, his grizzled beard framing his hard mouth as he answered her. "We be chasing the divil's own."

"The devil, ye say, on so fine a morning?" she replied mockingly. "Did he steal yer herd?" She gestured to where her two cows stood tethered. "Ah well, he didn't reive mine." In challenge she added, "Ye'll not be saying I took me two from the brawny likes of ye?"

"Tell her, Coilean!" voiced a younger man who stepped forward holding a garment in one hand. "This is what brings us. The dogs had the scent till the rain came." With that he threw the garment on the ground before Una.

Bending over, her eyes on the challenger, she picked up the garment and her heart skipped a beat. It was Meghan's cloak. Her tongue passed quickly over her lips. Meghan had lied to her, but there was no time now to seek out the truth.

"Ye great hairy beast!" she spat, hurling the cloak back at the young man. "'Tis a sad day for wooing when ye must come slavering after the flesh of one wee lass with clubs and dogs."

"'Tis no bride we seek," the young man replied. He stepped closer to the old woman. "'Tis a she-divil must answer our wrath. She killed one of our own, not a week past!"

Una stood her ground in the face of grumbled epithets. The men were tense but not overly eager for a fight. The stench of their fear was in the air. Like a warm decay it permeated the cool breath of the spring morning. She had lived many dangers in the forty years of her life, and, as always, danger cleared her senses. She could use that fear to her advantage.

"Killed a man? One wee lass against yer number and ye were bested?" Her sneering laughter echoed across the clearing. "If ye were me, I'd not be telling that tale."

"She were a divil, I'm tellin' ye," the young man maintained, shaking his staff in her face. "Ye saw!" he cried, turning to his companions. "We all saw the bloody mark on her face. She were spyin' on us. When we gave chase she turned herself into a wild boar and gored our Shaun."

"She killed him!" cried another man.

"Aye, she killed Shaun!" added another.

The hairs on Una's neck stirred. Despite their obvious distortion of the truth, she realized that they must have seen Meghan the day she went to spy on their settlement, but it did not follow that they knew Meghan lived with her.

"This talk of devils and such, what has it to do with me? I'm no lass, and ye can see for yerselves there's no mark on me. Be off with ye before I think up curses enough of me own to shrivel yer short hairs!"

The implied threat sent a shiver through the throng of men, their mutterings low and anxious in response.

"Maybe she's changed herself again, Rory," the old man said to the young herdsman. "She did such in the forest."

"Put her to the test," a voice cried, and was instantly answered by others:

"Aye, put her to the test!"

"A test!"

"Test her!"

The urge was hard upon Una to fall back before the threatening voices, but she did not dare do so. No real harm would come to her as long as none of them suspected that Meghan was in the hut.

The men hesitated; they had no desire to lay hands on the old woman while memories of Shaun's gored body still haunted them. The decision was made for them when a stone was thrown from the back of the crowd.

Una staggered, surprised by the unexpected blow to her head. Before she could recover, another and then another stone found their marks on her hip and thigh. Gasping in pain, she struggled to maintain her footing.

"Curse ye for a mean-hearted lot!" she cried as a rock struck her leg. With a sickening crunch she heard her kneecap give under the jolt and she tumbled forward onto her knees.

A roar of approval went up from the men as they reached for more stones from the rocky ground.

"Stone her! Stone her!" became a chant as rocks rained down on the old woman.

Ignoring the blood streaming from a cut at her brow and the ringing pain in her head, Una threw her arms heavenward and cried, *"Mallacht na mbaintreach agus na ngalrach ort!"*

The ancient curse checked the men, their voices breaking off in mid-sentence. Stones tumbled from their hands as they hurried to cross themselves in prayer against the power of the old woman's words.

"The curse of the widows and orphans on ye!" Una repeated, tearing at her braid until her long graying hair streamed over her shoulders and face. Solemnly she once more raised her face to the sky and cried, "Not another night of yer lives by a warm fire, not another day of yer lives under a clear sky!"

For a long moment no one spoke, and then the man called Coilean stepped forward, a dagger in his fist. Grabbing Una by the hair, he lifted her head and pressed the blade to the bare arch of her throat. "I've nae fear of dyin'. If my life be cursed for avengin' Shaun, so be it!"

Suddenly from within the crowd a girl's voice rang out. Swiftly, silently Meghan had slipped in among them, and now, eyes wide with horror, she cried, "Don't kill her! 'Tis me ye be wanting. Let her be!"

Una's worst fear had come to life. "A quick death and God's peace upon us," she whispered as she closed her eyes.

* * *

From the imposing height of horseback, Revelin looked down into the hideous face. It was moon round, moon pale, and hairless. An uneven gash, as though cut by an impatient hand, opened as a toothless, dribbling mouth. Flat nostrils where a nose should have been gave it a piggish look. Blank, lashless eyes of milky blue gazed unseeingly at him. Blind. Where arms and legs should have been there were only pathetic webbed stumps. Held in his mother's arms it was hard to tell whether the idiot child was two or twenty, but its sex, uncovered in squirming, was male.

Restraining himself to an inward shrinking, Revelin said calmly, "No. A girl." Inhaling deeply, he grappled with his impatience, then sounded out the Gaelic words distinctly: "I am searching for a girl. So high." He bent in the saddle to indicate a height five feet from the ground. "Her hair is black. Her only mark is a rose upon her left cheek."

The members of the settlement murmured and shook their heads. There was no one among them who fit that description.

"Ye be looking for a particular changeling?" questioned a bold man as Revelin resignedly turned his mount away. "Ye were as readily chasing the rainbow's end. One or another, 'tis all the same when said and done, 'tis folly to court the fairies!"

Folly. The word hummed through the air after Revelin like an angry bee as he urged his horse into a canter. For nearly a week he had been searching for the elusive slip of a girl he remembered no better than the remnant of a pleasant dream. Perhaps the man was right. At every settlement he passed he stopped to ask, yet none of them seemed to understand his quest. In the past three days he had been shown a wall-eyed old crone, a crippled girl of eight, a badly burned woman of twenty, and now the idiot boy. Changelings all, or so their kinsmen claimed. Perhaps the object of his quest was even less than that. It was said a drowning man dreams many dreams.

He touched the torn shirt tucked inside his cloak and smiled. She was no shadow or drifting gossamer of a regretful man's last thoughts. She was real, and he would find her. But not today.

"Ualter, heel," he called to the dark quiet form sitting patiently at the edge of the settlement. Instantly the dog sprang forward, his long legs bringing him easily to pace beside the horse. "She's not here," Revelin said, as though he felt the animal was owed some explanation. "It seems we must give up the chase, after all."

With a regretful sigh he gathered in the folds of his cloak and looked down to where it met the tops of the soft leather boots he had received as a gift from Lady Alison for his twenty-third birthday. The reminder of Lady Alison did little to lighten his mood. She would undoubtedly call his actions those of an excessively gallant gentleman. After all, he sought the girl only to prove that his eyes had not tricked him.

As he jerked the brim of his hat lower, Revelin wondered why he felt compelled to put forth so much effort. True, the girl had saved his life, but she seemed to want no reward. And there were pressing reasons why he should not dally. It had been no easy matter to persuade his companions to allow him to ride unescorted in the wilds of Ireland, where no English face was welcome.

Revelin smiled. Twelve years in London had ridded him of the lilting brogue that the English found loathsome, but his knowledge of the Gaelic tongue had not vanished. It made it possible for him to search for the girl and for his questions to bring replies . . . of a sort. It was his one advantage over the others in his group.

The countryside swarmed with settlements, but they had not passed a real town since entering Louth. The people were wary of strangers, and as often as not he received only silence in answer to his questions. If not for his good sense in hiding his English dress beneath his long cloak, he probably would have received in addition a pike in the back.

So absorbed was he in reviewing the fruitless day that he

did not hear the riders approaching until they were quite close. The rhythmic thuds of hoofs brought his hand automatically to the hilt of his sword even as he raised his head. Two horsemen came riding toward him, their dark cloaks wound tightly about their bodies. As they spurred their horses forward, he reined in his own and waited.

"Good day, hermit, and well met!" came the cry across the distance, and Revelin's hand relaxed.

"Spying for John, Sir Robin?" Revelin asked dryly when the men had reined in beside him. "Are your days so dull?"

Robin removed his plumed hat with a sweeping gesture and tossed his head, offering the gray day the brilliance of his red-gold curls. "Lud, yes! With John prowling about in his best imitation of a gut-sore wolf, and our parson here...." He made a long face.

Revelin chuckled appreciatively but Sir Richard failed to find humor in the jest. He directed his words to Revelin. "Reade said, were we to find you, we were to bring you back by whatever means necessary."

The idea of John's concern amused Revelin further. "Reade said that? And I thought he cared little for my hide."

"I'd say he fancied you'd found yourself a tidy armful and were loath to leave her," Robin offered with a wink. "But by the looks of you 'twould seem she turned you off without a proper tumble."

Revelin gave a small smile. "My journey had a much simpler goal—the repayment of a kindness. But you are right, I have failed."

"Kindness is its own reward," Sir Richard offered in consolation.

"I must remember that," Revelin murmured and urged his mount forward. He knew he would be questioned relentlessly if they did not start for camp, and he had no desire to share his thoughts or feelings with anyone.

"I marvel at your indifference to your health," Robin commented when he had caught up with Revelin. "With the ceaseless raiding and murdering that abounds in these environs, I would think you'd spare an errant thought for your own security."

Revelin shrugged.

Robin continued irrepressibly. "I can't imagine what sort of kindness demands that you scamper about the countryside to repay it. Perhaps you've simply grown homesick. Or would 'lovesick' be more to the point?"

"Peace and quiet would be more to the point," Revelin answered between his teeth. "Five minutes in your company makes me yearn for the blessings of solitude."

"Perhaps our young friend has sought the guidance of the Divine these past days." Sir Richard's tone was smug. "A man's soul is ever in need of the strengthening offered by denial and prayer. Solitude, like a sojourn in the desert, makes mockery of most men's glory. I've but recently thought myself that young Butler is a man suited to serve the better glory of his God." That said, he spurred his horse forward to enter first beneath the ceiling offered by the forest's trees.

"Greater glory of God!" Robin's guffaw was without any pretense at moderation. "Some parson you'd make. Reverend Revelin, with half the ladies at court begging you for the chance to pray with their knees upward."

Revelin turned a sour face toward his amused friend. "Gently, Robin. Our would-be martyr seems to be laboring under the false impression that I am making myself into pious meat." His painful expression slid into a smile. "If you try to dissuade him of the notion by boasting of my prowess with the ladies, he will only redouble his efforts to save my damnable soul."

"A parson's pox on the man!" Robin replied unrepentantly. In an undertone he added, "'Tis the only kind he's likely ever to catch!"

Ualter heard the sounds first. As he paused, his ears lifted, moving forward and back to pinpoint the source of the noise.

Revelin reined in beside him. "What is it, Ualter? Trouble?"

The dog listened a moment longer, his long powerful body perfectly, tensely still. And then with a yelp he sprang forward at a right angle to the path they had been following and disappeared into the twilight mist.

"Damn dog!" Robin murmured. "Should keep him leashed, Revelin. Revelin? Where are you? Hey!" Before his amazed gaze Revelin had wheeled his horse and taken off after the dog as if both of them knew what they were chasing. "A pox take him! Did you see that?" he questioned as Sir Richard rode back to him.

"What do you propose we do about it?"

Robin's grin broadened to its limit. "Revelin's been up to something this week. Stab me if I let him fob me off this time! Come along, Sir Richard, we're going hunting."

The chance for activity pleased Revelin. Frustrated by the week's fruitless search, this possibility of adventure was too good to miss. Ualter had Satan's own nose for trouble. He would not rest until he found it.

The sight when they came upon it was all a knight errant could have hoped for. In a small clearing beside a burning hut, a horde of ragged men were closing in on two hapless souls. Staffs raised threateningly, the men pelted their quarry with stones. The victims, crouched and bleeding, had raised their arms in a futile attempt to fend off the blows.

Without conscious decision, Revelin reined in and lifted his sword from its scabbard. "Ualter, attack!" he cried.

The dog, who had been trained to respond solely to his master's commands, lunged forward, his vicious teeth bared for combat.

Chapter Four

The shower of sharp-edged stones quickly beat Meghan and Una to their knees. They huddled together, arms locked over their heads to protect their faces. Meghan's back and arms ached in a dozen places where rocks had bruised and bloodied her skin. But even the pain could not convince her that this was happening, that they would be made to die because of the ignorance of strangers.

When a fist-sized stone struck her in the small of the back, rage at the men's brutality overwhelmed her and she leaped to her feet and cried, "Stop!"

Tears blurred her vision as she lifted her hands in a gesture of supplication. "Please stop before ye murder us!" But her cries only fed the bloodlust of the men; they redoubled their efforts, striking her in the right shoulder and hip.

"Aye, kill her!"

"Kill them both!"

It was impossible to duck every missile. A small, slingshot stone struck Meghan in the middle of the forehead and all strength drained from her body as pain radiated through her skull.

Una caught Meghan as she collapsed and pulled her roughly to the ground. "Keep down!" she whispered urgently as she tried to cover Meghan's slender body with her own. "Ye'll only make it worse for us. We can—!" Her warning was cut short by the tip of a staff driven brutally into her side.

"That for the divil's hag!" a man shouted triumphantly, and then: "Take hold of them, lads. There's only one way to kill the divil's spawn and that's burning! Cast 'em into the flames of the hut!"

Una's weight was lifted from Meghan. A moment later she was jerked from the ground by a brutal grip and hauled into a pair of sweaty arms.

"Holy Mother of God! No! *Nooo!*" she screamed, flailing wildly. A rough hand engulfed her mouth, stopping her cries and cutting off her breath as her nose was flattened by the callused palm. She recoiled from the vicious grip, but there was nowhere to go. The hand pressed her tightly against the wall of her captor's chest. The nausea of terror rose to sting her throat as she was spun around to face the heat of the burning inferno that had once been her home. Orange-red flames danced before her, their long hot tongues seeming to reach out for her.

This is how I am going to die! The thought enveloped the chaos of her mind until it blocked every other emotion: the pain, the terror, and even the desire to struggle.

To have it over with—that was Meghan's only desire when through the smoke-laden mist she saw the glint of steel. An errant breeze brushed past her cheek, clearing for an instant the sooty haze, and she saw a horseman galloping toward her. With a resigned sigh she closed her eyes. Dreams, always dreams, from the first moment to this, her last.

Revelin never questioned his ability to rout the men alone. He had fought few battles, yet he knew the power of surprise when used by a sure-handed man on horseback. And then there was Ualter.

Ualter's long strides effortlessly matched those of his master's mount. Instinct directed him. The girl's voice was familiar. Her plaintive cries were what had first drawn his attention. As soon as he saw her, all 140 pounds of him sprang to her defense.

The young herdsman never saw the shaggy-coated lightning bolt that struck him. He felt only the sudden blow that knocked him off his feet and the jarring impact upon the ground that broke his grip upon the girl. A moment later he was crushed by a snarling, snapping weight as he looked up into the gapping jaws off the huge wolfhound.

Revelin rode down the other men, making a broad sweep with his blade to clear a path between them and the women lying in the dust. They scattered like hens before a hound, he observed with grim satisfaction. Clearly, they knew nothing of warfare. This was a mob. No matter what the women had done, they did not deserve death at the hands of rabble.

Reining in his horse so shortly that it reared, he turned and attacked again. Using the flat of his sword, he struck the head of the one man who dared to challenge him with a sickle. With a sound like the whack of an ax the blow felled the man in his tracks.

He reined in a second time and prepared to pass through the throng once more, but the approaching thunder of another horse sent the men running toward the forest, their thirst for blood diminished by the sight of another rider.

Satisfied to see Robin galloping toward him, Revelin turned to his pet. "Ualter, release the man."

The command was instantly obeyed. The dog backed off the herder's chest but bared his teeth and growled as the man sat up, and Revelin enjoyed the sight of the terrified man scampering on hands and knees after the others.

"What sport is this?" Robin cried as he slowed his mount beside Revelin.

"The work of cowards."

"Shall we give chase?" Robin suggested gamely.

Revelin slowly shook his head as he sheathed his sword,

but his gaze did not move from the line of trees until the last man disappeared into the forest. When he finally looked around, the two women had struggled to their feet. Without a moment's hesitation he slipped from the saddle and tossed the reins to Robin. "Bide here a moment," he said quietly. "They've been frightened enough."

His tread was deliberate and slow as he approached the women. He could see bloody patches of skin exposed by their torn garments. At the sound of his approach, the younger of the two looked up, startled, and he paused.

A wild tangle of black hair obscured the details of her features, and what little was visible was bloody and bruised. His gaze flickered over her shapeless tunic, took in her bare feet, and then moved back to her face. This time she raised a hand to her face, as if to ward off a blow.

"Rest easy, girl, there's nothing to fear. The men have run away," he said in deep, soothing tones as he moved closer. "They won't come back. You've my promise on it. Do you understand?"

All at once he realized the foolishness of the question. Of course the women did not understand him. He had spoken in English.

Reluctant to be overheard, he glanced back to where Robin waited. His voice was low as he said in Gaelic, "No further harm will come to you, I swear it." The older woman raised her head and leveled a look at him that made his insides jump.

Una gazed a moment in silence at the handsome young nobleman before her. He had addressed them in English first. There was danger in that. And yet he spoke the Leinster dialect. "Ye best be speaking truly, my lord. By yer battle cry ye're a Leinsterman and I've nae liking for the sort, for all I judge ye a nobleman."

Revelin smiled at the beggarly woman's haughtiness. Her head was high, but the muddy hand gripping the younger woman's shoulder oozed blood from a cut. She swayed slightly, as if about to faint, and he realized that the women leaned against each other to keep their balance. Sympathy for their plight made him move a step closer despite the fierce face challenging him. "Could I be worse than the others?" he asked with a nod toward the forest.

"Ye could be less and still do harm," Una answered unhesitatingly, but she put out a hand to grip his arm tightly. She closed her eyes momentarily against the needle-sharp pain that suddenly shot through her chest. There was no time to give in to the pain, no time to do anything but help Meghan escape before the herdsmen regained their courage and returned. "'Tis the lass. She tried to stop them. I fear she's most hurt."

"Let me have a look at her," Revelin answered. As his hand gently closed over her slim shoulder, he felt a shudder pass through the girl. "There's nothing to fear, lass. I want only to help you."

Meghan's head pounded with blinding fury. The terror of the last minutes was with her still, overriding the realization that she was safe. Only a moment before, hard hands had been about to cast her into flames. This touch was more gentle, yet it prodded her to action. Instead of turning toward him as the pressure of his hand demanded, she jerked free and took a few halting steps before she stumbled and sprawled in the rain-slick grass. The impact left her breathless. Incredibly, the warm, wet edge of a rough tongue reached out and bathed her face before she could even draw a breath.

Ualter sniffed the girl delicately and then licked the wound on the back of her hand. Finally he thrust his muzzle under her palm.

"Ualter!" A few quick strides brought Revelin to the fallen girl's side and he aimed a booted kick at his dog. "Let her be, you mangy cur!"

He knelt and lifted her, turning her over so that her head came to rest against his chest. The fleeting thought of how light she was disappeared as he saw the purple bruise on her right temple where a stone had struck. Had its blow been harder to the fragile spot, he knew, she would have been killed. Restraining a fresh spurt of anger in English curses, he gently touched the trickle of blood at the corner of her lips. Her face was turned from him and for a moment he wondered if the fall had broken her neck. His fingers splayed over the slender column of her throat to the place where her pulse throbbed rapidly.

"Is she dead?" Robin called from his saddle.

"No," he shouted back, not looking up.

Meghan stirred, trying not to moan as she breathed. "Please! Please, don't hurt us any more."

Encouraged by the sound of her voice, Revelin answered, "Hurt you? You've nothing to fear from me, lass." He caught her chin. "Open your eyes and you'll see nothing to harm you," he said gently.

Meghan shook her head, straining against the sensation of comfort in the man's voice. There was no help; why would her dreams taunt her now?

"Look at me, darlin'," Revelin coaxed in yet a softer tone. "I may not be the man of your dreams, lass, but I've never made a lady swoon yet."

No other words could have made Meghan open her eyes, but the mention of her dreams made them fly wide.

His face loomed above her. His bright hair! The rain had darkened it, though, to bronze rings that clung to his brow. They were *his* eyes——the deep green irises ringed by violet now as full of surprise as her own.

The moment she looked up at him Revelin felt a jolt of familiarity. Sea-blue eyes caught and held him a moment in their whirlpool of emotion, then his gaze moved to the hand covering her left cheek. Frowning, he pried loose the fingers she had clamped over her cheek, though her nails curled into her flesh in clawing desperation. The gesture touched him deeply. Was she so afraid of a man's regard? And then he saw it. A perfectly shaped blood-red rose birthmark.

"You!" he whispered, jolted back into English by his surprise. "You are real."

With the lightest of touches his thumb caressed the fine velvety plush of her cheek and then drifted across the distinct floral mark that was no trick of mud or bruise. He had not imagined it. He had not dreamed her.

"So you know her? Trust you to make make the most of your days in the wilds."

Revelin raised his head to find that Robin had dismounted and come to stand over him. His mouth tightened in annoyance. There was little of this he was ready to explain to Robin, least of all why he knew the girl.

"'Twas mean spirited to keep your companions waiting while you exercised your tender charms upon a country wench." Robin bent over Revelin's shoulder with a mischievous grin. "Let's have a look at your Hibernian sweetheart." He cupped the girl's face. "She's a bit muddy, isn't she, but—God's blood!" His full horror echoed in his words as Robin jerked his hand away and took a backward step.

Meghan turned her face into the coat sleeve of the man who held her. She did not need to understand English to know that her mark had once again frightened a stranger.

Revelin's arm tightened protectively as he felt her shrink against him. "What the devil ails you, Neville?"

Robin swallowed hard, his boyish face suddenly pale. "She . . . she bears Satan's mark. Put her down, Rev," he continued as he raised his palm to look at it. "Oh, God, and I've touched her, too!"

"Curse you for a fool," Revelin answered. "What's a mark, more or less?"

"But, Rev—"

"I'll thank you to shut up, Robin," Revelin cut in, amazed by the tide of anger he felt rising within himself and yet sure of its validity. "The girl doesn't need your superstitious prattling; she needs your help."

"My help?" Robin voiced faintly. "Really, Butler. This is above all call of duty, even for a gentleman. Leave her, man. Who's to tell when that rabble may regain their courage and return? We aren't even privy to the reason for the attack. Mayhaps the women are witches and . . ."

Robin faltered, amazed at the look on Revelin's face. Court gossip whispered that the young Irishman had the devil's own temper when aroused, but never before had Robin glimpsed the danger that lay like a treacherous current beneath the surface.

Revelin's voice was taut with anger as he said, "This 'witch,' as you would brand her, pulled me from the bottom of a marshy pond where I was entangled and drowning five mornings past. If she be a witch, then I thank God for it."

"All the same," Robin murmured, glancing anxiously from Revelin to the girl, whose face was hidden in the crook of his arm. She looked so fragile. Though blood streaked, her slim legs were velvety smooth and seductively curved. Long black hair tumbled about her shoulders and pooled in ebony ringlets in the grass behind her. For a moment, envy stirred in his breast that Revelin held such loveliness.

Then reason reasserted itself. Had he not heard from boyhood of the seductive beauty of Satan's consorts? Perhaps she had saved Revelin from drowning. Witches could swim. And there was her mark. The mark always meant evil when found on a female.

Revelin watched Robin's thoughts play across his features. When he saw fear reassert itself he responded quickly. "If the girl frightens you, then see to the old woman," he directed, then looked away to prevent Robin from answering him.

Reluctantly, Robin turned away. And yet he was glad to move from the girl's vicinity. He glanced down at his hand once more. He would almost swear that his fingers tingled where they had touched her. When he looked up again he saw the old woman stagger toward him. Passing his tongue nervously over his lips, he paused as she did. "How do you fare, ma'am?" he asked awkwardly.

Una did not respond though she understood the English tongue. To draw even a breath filled her with pain. She fought it, one fist pressed against her breast, but the pressure increased until she thought her chest would burst. When she opened her mouth to speak, she choked on blood, and the coughing spasm that followed drove the agony through her lungs as she pitched forward.

"Rev!" Robin called out, alarmed by the touch of the old woman, who had fainted into his arms. Yet, he gently laid her on the ground. When his hands came away slick with blood, he shivered. "God strike me, I think she's dead!"

"Una!" Meghan sat up, her eyes dilated with fear. "Una!" she repeated as she struggled to free herself from her comforter's embrace. "Let me go, ye great brute!" she cried when the embrace tightened. "Let go!"

Afraid that fighting her would only hurt her more, Revelin reluctantly released her.

Meghan scrambled to her feet, unaware of her own aches as she hurried across the grass to the place where Una lay. Dropping to her knees, she grasped one of her aunt's hands in both of hers and squeezed the cold, unresponsive fingers. Bending low over the old woman, she whispered, "Una, please, ye cannot die."

Una's eyes opened, and her fingers clenched convulsively over the smaller hand. "Meghan," she whispered, her gaze no longer focused. "Meghan, lass . . . where . . . is he?"

Meghan stared in horror at the trickle of blood that emerged from Una's lips. She dabbed at it with her fingers but succeeded only in smearing it. "Una, ye must nae talk. It makes ye bleed."

"You're right. She should lie quietly."

Meghan looked up, her eyes wild with fright, to find Revelin standing over her. He bent down beside her to offer words of assurance, but the telltale trickle of blood from the woman's mouth stopped him. He had seen enough wounds to know when a body had suffered fatal injury. Each breath the old woman took brought the foam of blood to her lips. She was dying.

"Do something!" Meghan begged, her expression frantic as

she looked from one man to the other. "Do something!" she screamed again when their silence told her what she did not want to believe, and then her eyes filled with tears as she choked back a sob.

"Meghan," Una murmured thickly. Her eyes closed for a moment as the last of the color ebbed from her face, then her gray-blue eyes opened and fastened in urgency on her niece. "Ye must . . . do as I ask. Beneath the turf fire . . . I buried it. Quickly, lass. Bring it."

"What?" Meghan questioned, too numb with shock to comprehend the words.

Revelin had understood the old woman and seized the opportunity to distract the girl. "Robin, take the girl and see what you can do about putting out the fire in the hut. The woman says there's something buried under the hearth. Dig it up and bring it here. Give me your cloak," he added in afterthought. "She's blue with cold."

Robin gave his friend a disbelieving glance. "My cloak? For that wretched creature?" Reluctantly, he swung the costly green velvet from his left shoulder. With a regretful sigh he tossed it onto Revelin's outstretched arm. "I charge you with its replacement if a single drop of blood is spilled upon it."

Revelin placed the cloak in Meghan's hands. "Cover her, lass, and then do as she bids you. 'Tis important to her so you must hurry."

Meghan gazed dumbly at him, her eyes enormous with pain and shock. The face that stared back at her was that of the stranger from the pond. It was not real, not any of this. Beneath her, pebbles dug into the tender flesh of her knees, and the mist-laden sod oozed dampness into the hem of her *leine,* but still she could not believe she was awake. It was a dream. At any moment Una's hard hand would shake her and the gruff but dear voice would admonish her for dreaming away the morning.

"Una won't die. She cannot die." She said it calmly, and

then, when she had lovingly tucked the beautiful velvet cloak carefully about the older woman, a peaceful smile turned up the corners of her lips. "She'll rest easier now." She patted the cloak and then rose to her feet.

Revelin was not pleased by the look of dismay that came to Robin's face as the girl turned to him, but she seemed not to notice Robin's expression as he backed from her as she passed by. "Follow her, damn you!" Revelin hissed in English, and Robin did so, but at a distance.

"Curse you for a coward, Neville," he added under his breath as he watched the girl move toward the now-smoldering rubble that had once been her home. A touch at his knee brought his attention back to the old woman; he looked down to see her regarding him.

Una gazed long and hard at him, eyeing his beardless cheeks with suspicion until she saw the glistening of blond stubble along his jawline. She was dying and she knew it. So much depended upon the next moments. Yet, he was young, so young. Did she dare entrust him with the secret?

She reached out and gripped his thigh. "Hear me . . . Leinsterman. There's nae time. I'm after dying and I know it. Do ye say true when ye say Meghan . . . saved yer life?"

He nodded, pleased at last to know the girl's name.

Una's grip slackened. "Then ye be . . . after owing Meghan, I'm thinking. There's a way . . . to repay her." A cunning light came into her eyes. "Yet, 'tis only fair I warn ye. 'Twill bring ye a deal of trouble."

Revelin answered her readily. "Have you not witnessed with your own eyes how little I fear trouble?"

A ghost of a smile lifted her features. How easily the young rose to the bait of a challenge, she thought. Her estimate of him was not wrong. "Give me . . . yer hand, lad."

Unhesitatingly Revelin placed his hand in her bony grasp. "I give me Meghan into your fosterage. . . ."

"Revelin, Revelin Butler," he supplied.

"Butler?" Una's gaze narrowed suspiciously.

"My mother was an O'Conner," Revelin supplied with a smile of admiration that the dying woman had enough wits about her to balk at his English surname. It was the name Butler that had opened his path to court, that made him acceptable to the peerage at Whitehall, the name whose power he hoped would win him the hand of Lady Alison Burke. How ironic that the old woman should prefer the name that he had not thought of using once in the past eight years.

The tension went out of Una at the mention of the Irish name. After a long moment she said, "Take her . . . take the lass away. She's an O'Neill. Ach, Shane." She sighed and briefly closed her eyes. "There's devils that wish me Meghan dead. Ye must protect her!"

"With my life," Revelin answered.

"With yer life," Una echoed, her eyes closing again as a fresh stream of blood coursed from the corner of her mouth.

"Una! Una! I've found it!" Meghan raced across the clearing and fell to her knees beside her aunt, holding a cloth-wrapped bundle to her chest. "Look, Una," she continued, lightly shaking her aunt's shoulder. "Please, open yer eyes and see for yerself."

Una struggled to break free from the dark recesses of the twilight engulfing her. "Nae time," she whispered. "Leinsterman . . . the knowledge is yers. Use it . . . when the time comes."

Her eyes opened wide as she clawed in the darkness until she again found the solid strength of Revelin's leg. Her nails bit deeply into his flesh as she whispered, "The lass . . . she's not to know. The gift . . . she mustn't touch it! . . . Never betray the secret!

"Meghan," she cried, the name garbling in her throat. "Meghan . . . when the sight comes on ye . . . forgive. . . ."

"Una? Una!" Meghan dropped the bundle to seize her aunt by the shoulders and shake her. "Una! Wait! Una, ye weren't to die! 'Tis my death they wanted, not yers! Una!"

But the eyes that stared up at her saw nothing, and Meghan released her and, with a shuddering wail, flung her body over the older woman's, as though by doing so she could shield Una from the long-fingered grip of death.

"Ye promised ye'd never leave me," Meghan whispered as with gentle fingers she stroked the still face. "Wait for me. I want to go with ye!"

Revelin's mouth tightened as he watched the heaving shoulders of the sobbing girl. There was nothing he could do to ease her pain, and he wisely refrained from cutting short her grief, though her every gasp of misery tore a new rend in his composure. He had heard many people cry, some of them for loved ones, many more for selfish reasons, but never had anyone's misery so touched him. As he looked away toward the forest shadows stretched across the hissing grayness of the rain-darkened clearing, he wondered if there had ever been a more wretched sound than the girl's tears.

One painful moment bled into another until Meghan no longer knew when her sobs turned to dry gasps and then stopped altogether. Una was dead. No tears would return her. There was no reason to live, no place of refuge; no one would ever look upon her again and not be repelled by fear of her ugliness.

And the fault was her own.

Then, overwhelming her conscious thoughts, a vision claimed her. So stealthily did it rise that for once she did not detect its coming. The soft woodsy green and gentle hills gave way to a foreign land where, in a gray sky, sea-swollen clouds dragged their ragged edges over the tumbled-rock mountains. Winds, whipped by the North Sea, careened down through the unfamiliar narrow valley where she huddled, alone with the never-ceasing wail of the wind.

A storm was coming. The fresh tang of salt dried on her lips, and she knew the sea was nearby. The sea's roar came to her now on the breeze and she shivered. It was cold, colder than any winter she had ever known in her life.

From out of nowhere came the thunder of hooves and the whooping battle cries. Two armies of faceless riders surged from the mists before her frightened eyes.

"No! Don't," she cried, rising to her feet and lifting her hands in pleading to those nearest her. "I cannot be responsible for more deaths, do ye hear me? I mean no harm to anyone!"

Her words were lost in the cries of battle. The frenzied roar of bloodlust resounded as the warriors rode forward encircling her. The clash of blade on blade threw sparks above her head as they met. Horses and men whirled about her, forcing her to dodge hoof and boot. Clouds of dust erupted as they fought, obscuring her vision and cutting off any path to safety.

Yet she ran, stumbling between rearing steeds and bellowing soldiers who slashed the air with sword and pike. Past caring for her own safety, she pushed forward with one thought in mind. They fought because of her, because of some evil knowledge she possessed but could not direct. If she did not leave the valley, she would bear the blame for the lives that would be lost. She must get away to make them stop.

"No more deaths! No more!"

Revelin jumped at the sound of her voice. The girl had been still so long that he thought she slept. But she leaped to her feet now with a startled cry. Her eyes were wide and staring vacantly at him as she said, "Always deaths! I must stop it! I must make it end!"

The last thing he expected was the stiff-armed shove in the stomach that sent him tottering back on his heels as she dodged his embrace and raced past him. She should have been easy to catch, for the beating she had taken had left her stiff. When she stumbled and fell, he gasped in sympathy, but she was up in an instant; and when he realized he might, indeed, lose her if she reached the cover of the forest before he overtook her, he rushed to seize her.

The tug on her arm swung Meghan around as easily as if she were a rag doll and brought her face to face with him. His features swam before her eyes, taunting her with their perfection. He was so beautiful, while she was so ugly. "Ye'll nae touch me if ye fear for yer life," she said softly. "Ye must never touch me."

Revelin caught her as she slumped forward and with swift economy he lifted her high in his arms.

All the strength drained out of Meghan as she felt his arms come around her. He was real! Suddenly she knew that this was what she wanted, to be held close. No one had held her since she was very small. She could not even remember the last time Una had embraced her. Una. "Ach, Una, ye're dead now, and because of me," she whispered, turning her face into the supple leather of the man's jerkin.

Revelin's arms tightened as he heard her murmur of anguish, and he pressed his lips against the cool satin of her brow. "It wasn't your fault, lass. She didn't blame you."

The reassuring words were a small but needed comfort. Meghan closed her eyes, accepting the safety of his arms, and her hand stole cautiously across his chest to find an anchor in the curve between his neck and shoulder.

Robin stood by the horses, and as Revelin approached he moved as though to mount up.

"There are several matters that need tending first." Revelin's face was grim as his gaze moved meaningfully from Robin to the body of the old woman.

Robin gasped. "You're joking, are you not?"

Revelin did not reply as he passed the horses and looked about for a place to lay the girl. The broad limbs of a nearby oak offered shelter from the rain.

As he bent to place her on the ground, Meghan suddenly put both arms around his neck and hugged him close. "Don't leave me! Please! They'll come back!" she whispered frantically and buried her face in the sweet warmth of his neck.

Revelin pulled her closer with a reassuring hug. "The herdsmen? They won't come back, I promise you that."

"No! No! The dreams! The dreams will come back if ye leave me," she cried, her voice hoarse with fear. "They always come back, again and again. They never leave me until it happens. Then it's too late!"

She raised her head and gazed deeply into his eyes. "Do ye not understand? 'Tis my fault they're dead. I knew what would happen, the 'sight' always knows, but I couldn't stop it! It isn't my fault, the knowing, I cannot stop it!"

Revelin stiffened in amazement at her incredible talk of strange visions and dreams. Surely the girl was overwrought by the death of her companion. Yet, the eyes holding his were shadowed by very real fear and misery, and he realized that she belived what she had told him. It occurred to him that she had not been surprised by Robin's reaction to her birthmark; she had been frightened. Perhaps Robin's suggested reason for the herdsmen's actions was not far from the truth.

A remembrance of the first moment he had looked into her eyes came back to him. He had been more a stranger to her then than she was to him now. And yet she had rocked him in her arms, held him fiercely tight, spilled her tears upon his cheeks. Even if she were all that some claimed, he would not abandon her.

Poor child, he thought as his fingers moved tenderly to cup the back of her neck and bring her against his chest. The superstitious fools had done their best to kill both women. Of course she would feel the guilt of her kinswoman's death. But her talk of dreams was nonsense.

He raised a hand to stroke her forehead, his voice as soft as his touch as he said, "Do you trust me, Meghan?"

Meghan nodded slowly.

Such vulnerability was rare, and it embarrassed him that she should entrust herself to him so readily. "Then you know I shall not do anything to hurt you. You have my protection for as long as you want it."

His arms tightened as he bent to place a comforting kiss on her forehead. At that moment Meghan lifted her head to speak.

His kiss missed her brow, slipped off the tip of her nose, and found its mark on the soft shape of her mouth.

The instant his lips touched hers, Meghan ceased to think of anything else. The astonishing touch of his lips upon hers lasted but a moment, but it struck like lightning to the core of her being. One kiss was not enough, not nearly enough, and she reached up to bring his head back down to hers.

She had no experience of kissing. The second kiss was a question posed in answer to the first, and she was hardly prepared for the reply. This time, his lips parted on hers. The fiery warmth of his mouth flooded hers and a sensation somewhere between fear and pleasure engulfed her. When his lips lifted suddenly from hers, she was left with a dizzying sensation of disappointment. Not knowing why she felt that way, she stared up at him, her eyes questioning.

Astonishment held Revelin still as his gaze lingered over her mouth, dewy soft and trembling from his kiss. Then he turned away. He had not meant to do that. Merciful heavens! He was not so lost to propriety that he could seduce a girl beside her unburied kin.

He shook his head, refusing even to glance down at her again. 'Twas her fault he so forgot himself. She had pulled him to her the second time, had arched herself against him, had begged the kind of kiss he had given her. No, that was not fair. Had he not only moments before realized how deranged grief had made her? Surely she did not understand what she was doing. She was showing her gratitude, nothing more. The passion in the kiss was his fault, and more was the pity, he thought, for it had set his blood humming.

"Neville!" he called in a tone that brought Robin running. "Come and care for the girl while I dig a grave."

"I won't touch her, Rev," Robin answered, defiance making his complexion ruddy once more. "I'm sorry, but I've done all I can in good conscience." He shrugged apologetically. "'Tis a sorry business but I wash my hands of it."

"You will either obey me or it's two graves I'll be digging

this day," Revelin answered, so angry that his perfect English failed him and the lilting tongue of his youth set the measure of his speech.

"The choice is yours," he continued after a pause. "But consider: death is final. So, you will kneel in the grass and hold the girl with care for the precious thing she is. You will do this or, so help me, you will bury the woman, which is the least she deserves."

Robin drew off his black velvet bag hat before kneeling in the grass. If he gave a thought to the stains he was likely to incur, he kept the misgiving to himself. "Hand her to me, Rev. I've no stomach for the undertaker's part."

Meghan was vividly aware of the gentle strength of the arms from which she was passed. Then the softness of a velvet doublet replaced the feel of smooth leather against her cheek, and the faint, incongruous smells of nutmeg and horse filled her nose. She wanted to protest but she no longer seemed capable of even the simplest speech. She was so very tired. Closing her eyes, she gave up trying to think.

With a spade he found among the ruins of the hut, Revelin dug a grave. The work was painfully slow but he did not think of that. For the first time, the full realization of his promise to the old woman came to him. He had taken on the fosterage of a young girl. That special duty, peculiarly Irish, made him more than her legal guardian; she had become a part of his family. Yet, what did he know of girls and their needs? His interest in the lasses had come about as he reached the age of lust. Well, there was no doubt in his mind, he would have to return to Dublin and then ride to Kilkenny to ask help of his family.

Amusement quivered in his chest despite his somber task. The old woman had warned him that he would be taking a great deal of trouble on himself by accepting the responsibility. She had not lied.

Nearly an hour later, Revelin stood with his arms crossed

before his chest while Meghan, on her knees, murmured prayers over the grave of her aunt. A steady downpour had replaced the earlier mist and he noticed that she shivered in the cold damp. Finally he bent and, taking her by the shoulders, raised her to her feet. "'Tis enough, lass. I have no wish to lose you to a chill. We must go now."

A crystal-clear image of the stranger's face, strained with the effort of his work, filled Meghan's gaze, then she slid gratefully into the cool darkness of unconsciousness.

"Praise be, it's done," Revelin muttered as he scooped her up into his arms. "And the child did not make a scene."

Robin looked at the ghostly pale face lying slack against Revelin's sleeve and said gently, "'Tis hard to be full-tongued in a swoon, Rev."

Revelin blinked back the rain that had gathered at his brow and grinned at his companion. "She's a good lass, Sir Robin, whatever you may believe. She cut me free from the reeds and pulled me to safety, and her only half my weight. She's got more heart than most men of my acquaintance."

Robin gave his friend a curious look. There was an unsteadiness in his voice that had nothing to do with the backbreaking work he had just accomplished. Once more Robin looked down at the young face cradled in his friend's arm. Tiny, bruised, and bloody, she possessed little he could see to interest a man. And yet, he reasoned thoughtfully as Revelin carried her to their horses, there was some connection between the two that would bear watching. So far, his tour of Ireland had been exceedingly tedious. That seemed about to change.

"The journey begins to have great promise," he murmured to himself as he swung into his saddle.

Chapter Five

The fingers of John Reade's right hand beat out a rapid tattoo on his thigh. His lids had drooped, his glare of rage reduced to two slits of silver.

"God's blood!" he roared suddenly, overturning his chair as he came to his feet. "You've the nerve to come before me and say you and Butler have set the countryside to rout for the sake of a slattern and her bastard? Is the tender morsel Revelin's slut? Well? Speak or be damned!"

"So much fury, John," Robin commented amicably, only to have the front of his doublet seized in one of John's broad hands.

"Cease that prattle or I'll have your tongue for supper!"

Robin looked up at John's flushed face and smiled lazily. "Say it again, Reade, I beg you."

The needle-sharp prick of a stiletto just below his seventh rib startled John. A second, more-deliberate jab loosened his hold on the smaller man's clothing.

"God rot you!" he exclaimed, recoiling.

"Better, much better," Robin commented pleasantly and turned the blade away. "As I was saying, the chit may own the most seductive pair of eyes this side of perdition, but as to Revelin's interest, I cannot say."

Robin looked down at the jeweled handle of his weapon, fingering the tourmaline set in the hilt. He had not relished this interview with Reade. Revelin was better at intimidation and therefore less likely to be forced to draw a blade of any sort; but Revelin had asked it of him, and it seemed easier than spending a hour closeted with the girl. A tingle of alarm passed through him. It was still difficult for Robin to believe that he had actually held her in his arms.

John eyed Robin's slight frame and did not attempt to hide his contempt. "Which chieftain and what number of his *kerne* should we expect? God knows we've little enough with which to defend ourselves."

Robin's laugh was just short of a giggle. "I should not count on more than a score of cowherders armed with staffs and rakes, no army certainly. Of course, there were a few with stones. They're quite stout hurlers. I'd as lief not be in the forefront of the confrontation."

"Do you speak the truth? There were no signs of a clan's business in the deed?"

Robin smiled. "They were peasants. No doubt the milk curdled, and they thought the women had cursed their cows."

John's lids flickered. "Do not speak to me of curses. What did the girl have to say for herself?"

"You are free to converse with her yourself, if you know the Irish tongue. My own poor talents are limited to French with a smattering of Greek and Latin. *Bon chance, mon vieux.*" Not wanting John to corner him again, Robin turned and walked away.

John stared menacingly at Robin's back, then abruptly struck off in a direction away from camp. Too often his temper had snatched from him the gains he sought when they were within hand's reach. Six months in the Tower, watching the filth and damp run and puddle in the low spots of his dismal cell, had quite convinced him that patience was a virtue deserving more of his attention.

"Someday, *Master* Robin," he murmured, "your noble parentage will not protect you. Then you will answer for each and every insult."

Nothing during the past weeks had galled him as much as the company of Sir Robin Neville. He was a courtier without a buccaneer's heart, a mincing prancing poet whose only toil was rhyming verse and tallying his tailor's bills. In times gone by a knight or nobleman had retained his place by battle deeds and soldierly service to his lord. Now, stripped of their private armies, England's nobles rested upon their wealth and maneuvered through privilege, innuendo, and flirtation. Men like himself had to scheme and steal every opportunity to better themselves, and it sat like cold mutton in his gut to realize that he must defer to a spoiled coxcomb.

"Reade?"

Drawn from his dark thoughts, John looked around to find Richard Atholl trailing him. He paused and beckoned, hoping that Atholl would prove more forthcoming than Neville had been. "Sir Richard. Tell me what you make of Butler's strange conduct."

A faint blush of pleasure colored Sir Richard's cheeks. Too often his opinion was shunned. "I have stood upon this past hour considering the matter and I believe there's more to it than has come to light."

The corners of John's black mustache lifted at the man's words. "Do you, Parson? Very clever. I wonder that the queen saw need of my small talents as a tactician when you are so perspicacious a leader."

Sir Richard offered the thinnest of smiles. "Indeed. Perhaps our sovereign perceived that the Tower is not the only place suitable for a man of your peculiar skills."

Once, such an insult had caused John to kill a man. Now, while anger coiled like a snake in his belly, a corner of his mind perceived a discontent in Atholl. Shared complaints might prove enlightening.

"Aye, a woman's nature. She smites with one hand and offers a sweetmeat with the other. But, we were discussing Butler. Did he explain his absence?"

Sir Richard's expression soured at the memory of being snubbed by the pair of younger men. "There was some mumbling with Neville to which I was not privy. Yet, Butler did mention the owing of a debt."

John's gaze narrowed. "Debt? What sort of debt? Were there others with Butler when you found him? Did he make secret his whereabouts? Dissemble when pressed?"

The barrage of words surprised Sir Richard. John's bombastic temper rarely revealed his true concerns. So he, too, was worried about Butler's long, unexplained absence. But that was no excuse for rudeness. Disapproval stiffened Sir Richard's thin face. "You have a way of dramatizing situations which smacks of the theatrical."

John clenched his fists. The fact that his bastard birth was the result a liaison between a London actress and a West Country squire was no secret, but no one dared to speak of it to his face. Atholl needed a lesson in kind.

"I know my own tales, Sir Richard. Lest we continue under false flags, allow me to apprise you of my knowledge of your provenance."

Sir Richard's lids flickered, and John loosened his hands and smiled slightly. Yes, this was the way, so much better than the physical release he desired.

"To begin, you were born the third son of a drunkard sot, a laird of little consequence. 'Twas your Presbyterian mother who bound you for the clergy, and there you would have rotted in poverty had not your father and two brothers had the ill luck to drown one squally day, opening the path for you to inherit the title."

The trough of a smile deepened beneath John's generous mustache. "The pulpit lost a shade of its charm when placed beside the gleam of a laird's gold, hey? Oh, how pious you seek to appear when you mewl at others who, unlike yourself, are honest enough to say, 'God may damn me, so long as I have my own here and now!'"

Sir Richard's fair complexion mottled as he said righteously, "'As he spake by the mouth of his holy prophets which have been since the world began: That we should be saved from our enemies, and from the hand of all that hate us.'"

"Hate?" John voiced in amazement. "Not so, Sir Richard. For is it not said, 'nothing is secret, that shall not be made manifest'? Aye, I know the Good Book as well as many and more than some. Your piety does not impress me, but your interest in our mutual companion does." His voice became conciliatory, although his expression of challenge did not alter a whit. "Enough of threats. When made between friends they are so much moldy hay."

John resumed his walk and Atholl followed. After a moment he inserted the first needle of doubt under the Scotsman's skin. "This Irishman Butler is a thorn in my side. I ask myself, is his allegiance to the queen but a ruse? Did Her Majesty send me to spy on the fellow? God's breath! Such assignments little match my ability. I would rather . . ." He caught himself. He had nearly overplayed his part.

Sir Richard gazed at John, his affront diverted by his own ponderings. "I have wondered at this journey myself. A military man, a man of God, a fop, and the earl of Ormond's favorite nephew, a strange assortment, indeed."

John remained silent. For his part, he would scarcely have refused any offer that freed him from his cell. Yet, the command to map the Irish countryside was no job for a man of his worth. The Butler whelp was a fair hand at drawing. Still, his production of maps grew steadily less, and a man had to wonder if there were reasons for the ebbing of work other than the lack of visibility caused by the mists. Butler was an Irishman.

Though the family was Anglo-Irish, his father had married a daughter of a clan chieftain against the dictates of English law. One never knew where one's loyalties would come to roost until swords were drawn.

"Did Butler possess a single sketch when you met him on the road?"

Sir Richard shook his head. "He said nothing of maps. Butler's dog led them to that chance encounter with the women. I refused to follow, of course. While I abhor violence," he shuddered, "I did not see cause to interfere in matters we know nothing of. 'Twas Butler who insisted that the girl be brought into camp. The sooner we're rid of her, the better."

John smirked. Though he had seen a little of the girl as Butler carried her into camp, her slim legs and tangled cloud of black hair had attracted him.

"Perhaps her company will prove a distraction. Who is to say that she will not be eager to show her gratitude to us?" John's gusty laughter underscored the lustful gleam in his eyes.

"Sinful creature!" Atholl intoned righteously. "Even Sir Robin felt the impurity of her presence. He would not ride with Butler, nor would I. You would do well to remove her, Reade, before we are all infected."

John watched Atholl's retreat with open disgust. The skinny-shanked man had the heart of a gelding. No doubt he lacked a man's proclivities even with the most willing of partners. Neither the parson nor the dandy was a man he would choose to trust.

"M'lord?"

John looked up as the throaty whisper called to him from behind a nearby tree. A lusty grin stretched his face. In the controversy of the moment he had nearly forgotten the assignation. "Flora."

Minutes later John gazed up into the woman's passion-heated face as he lay in the damp grass. As she rode him he gripped her naked waist, forcing her down as he thrust up deep and hard into her. Atholl and Butler had been against hiring a servant, fearing betrayal. John smiled. He had hired her not to tend them but to assuage his appetite for female flesh. He knew himself as a man with two weaknesses: temper and lust. Most men took what they could and shrugged off the rest. He burned with constant need, the gnawing ache always just below the surface of his skin like the itch of stinging nettle.

Flora was no beauty. With her teeth bared in a mindless grimace and her fair skin reddened by carnal delight, she repelled him. John shut his eyes, the *slam, slam* of their loins inviting vivid memories of other whores and other places.

Other whores, John mused, his mind drifting back to the glimpse of Butler's girl with her slim legs and blue-black hair. Now, she was a beauty. He would enjoy watching her lick his genitals and ride his shaft. He could not decide which attracted him the most, the thought of riding the girl or outmaneuvering Butler. Either case was a delightful prospect.

He dug his nails into Flora's flesh, heedless of her whimper of pain, and rolled her beneath him. Quickly now, on the avalanche of his body's urging he slammed her against the ground, harder and harder until he seemed to burst . . . falling . . . dying . . . and with it, finding momentary peace.

Revelin scowled as he traversed the short distance from his tent to the place where he had left his horse tethered the night before. He had been made uneasy by the lass's unnatural quiet, and so had spent the night and all of this day at her side. Now the pervading purple shadows wrapped the day in twilight, and he could not tell if she slept or was unconscious. He needed advice, but who was to give it?

He glanced toward the main enclosure, where lantern light threw in sharp relief the silhouettes of the three men who were dining. As if on cue, the aromas of mutton stew and ale wafted past him, and a rumbling of his stomach reminded him that he had missed the contentment of a warm meal during the week of his search. That would be easily amended, he thought, as soon as he was certain the girl would recover.

For the first time in years, he was at a loss. He was not a lady's maid or a nanny. He was more at home with currying and ministering to the needs of a horse. He knew little of medicines and the healing art. What if she became feverish? *Dear God, spare us that!* he prayed hastily. What if she died? The thought appalled him.

He was jarred by a sudden memory of another time, ten years earlier, when he had sat by his mother's bedside and watched her slip away on the fevered breath of disease. He hated sickrooms, always had.

"Hail and well met, foolish knight," he admonished himself. If he had minded his own business he would not now be in such a predicament. The mission that he had undertaken in Ireland had yet to bear fruit. His uncle expected him to have learned the queen's plans for Ireland before he returned to Dublin. Yet, he had seen nothing and heard nothing to give him even a clue.

Revelin groaned. He could well imagine the pointed remarks his kinsman would make regarding the girl if he returned empty-handed with a nursery tale of women in distress. "Black Tom" Butler would accuse him of idling his time away with his new whore.

Revelin grimaced. The lass was passing fair, attractive enough to remind him of his celibate life of the past few months. Yet, there was Alison, and he was not so sorely pressed that he would take advantage of the situation that had presented itself.

He had completely forgotten the old woman's bundle until minutes ago. It was an excuse to leave the girl's bedside for a few moments, and he longed for the exercise.

What had the woman said to him? Ah yes, the lass was not to know about the contents, that he was not to show it to her. Revelin smirked as he loosened the leather tie. What could possibly be concealed in a damp moldy bundle that was worthy of such mystery? When the wrapping was removed, he gazed down in amazement.

It was an Irish skean, a double-edged dagger. The jeweled hilt gathered the last of the twilight into its glittering facets, smoldering with reds and silvers and golds. The raised Celtic lettering under his fingertips could not be read in the dark, and he doubted his skills were up to an interpretation. Even so, he wrapped it up and tucked it back into his gear. It was an expensive piece of work and probably a family heirloom. Perhaps the old woman had intended that he should sell it to provide for the lass. He would know when the moment was right, she had said.

"When the moment is right," Revelin murmured to himself. He had more to think of than the mutterings of a dying woman. When the moment was right he would decide what to do with the skean. First he had to assure himself that the girl would live.

Meghan gazed about her through the thick fringe of her lashes. It was a trick she had developed as a child. Without appearing to, she could watch the world with no one the wiser. The light hanging on a post claimed her attention. She had never seen anything like it. Encased in glass, tiny hisses and spurts accompanying the winking of its tongue of flame, it looked like a captured star.

She nearly smiled. She would have liked to capture a star to keep beside her on winter nights when darkness was so long. Una would think her foolish, but Una...

Meghan closed her eyes against the rush of salty tears. She would never again have Una to share her comfort or her joys. Una was dead. Meghan was completely alone.

At the sound of footsteps, Meghan feigned the stillness of death. After a few seconds, she opened her eyes a slit and saw that the golden-haired stranger had entered the tent.

He came to stand over her, and when he bent low she held

her breath. He was scowling at her as though she had done something wrong. The next instant her eyes popped open as icy cold water splashed her cheeks.

"Thank God!" Revelin said and smiled as she stirred under the droplets of water he had flicked into her face. "You've been a long time awakening."

Meghan gaze up at him in perfect calm, wondering why she found the sound of his voice so pleasant.

"How is your head?" At her wince of pain Revelin instantly removed his hand from the bruise at her temple. "I apologize. Stupid of me to think the pain would go away so quickly."

Meghan watched with delight as he spoke. His upper lip was straight and firm, the bow sensitively and deftly molded; the lower lip was more full, with a slight indentation at the center. It was a fine mouth, a lovely mouth, she decided.

"Are you hurt elsewhere?" Revelin asked with more calm than he felt, for her wide-eyed, wordless mien was beginning to unnerve him. More lightly this time he touched her temple. His hand moved to her shoulder and then down her arm as he spoke. "Is there pain here . . . or here . . . or here?"

No one had ever touched her but Una, and even she had seldom done so since Meghan had been old enough to wash and dress herself. And Una's touch had never affected her as his did. Wherever his fingers strayed her skin tingled beneath the covering of her *leine*.

The last touch, between and just below her breasts, was the lightest of all, but Meghan felt as though a hundred-pound weight had suddenly been dropped in her middle, and she gasped, recoiling instinctively.

Seeing her face flood with color, Revelin realized what he had done. Beneath his fingers was the shape of a breast, full and soft and womanly. He snatched his hand away thinking, *Fool!*

Meghan watched his face but could not deduce from his frown exactly what was on his mind. He had seemed worried, then embarrassed, and now angry. Perhaps he was hurt because she had withdrawn from him. Inexplicably, she longed to comfort him, to press the lines from between his bronze brows and smooth away his frown.

Before she had time to think better of the gesture, she reached up to the clean square line of his chin and her fingers curled against his warm flesh. The rough drag of the golden stubble on his chin pleasantly abraded her palm. As her gaze strayed to his mouth, the memory of his kiss moved through her. That had been his way of comforting her. She sat up, wrapped her arms about his neck to bring his head down within reach of her mouth, and put into her kiss all the tenderness for which she had no words of explanation.

Revelin did not move; he could not. He had seen the change in her eyes only an instant before she reached for him, but he could not say that it was a wanton's invitation he saw there. A hundred thoughts collided in his brain: *She's a child. Mercy's Grace! My vow of fosterage makes me her guardian. She is a stranger, a wretched little creature with no knowledge of what she is doing.* He held himself rigid, applauding his strength of character in not taking advantage of her a second time until—thank the saints—she broke away.

Only a moment passed before Meghan became aware that, unlike the first time, there was no answering warmth from him. The muscles of his neck were rigid, his mouth a firm closed line. *He does not want this.* With disappointment she released him.

For a moment each looked deeply into the other's eyes, wary green meeting enormous pools of shocked blue, and Revelin wondered how any creature could look so vulnerable and miserable. Aware that it was somehow his fault, he moved uneasily away from the bed, his step made awkward by the rise of his desire. So much for strength of character, he noted grimly. He was as randy as a young buck entering a brothel for the first time.

A sigh from her that sounded like a sob registered uneasily within him. Her inexperience at kissing was pitifully apparent.

She would not know what effect she had on him. And he, in his clumsy experience with young girls, had spurned her because he could not keep control of his response.

Revelin lifted the tent flap and stepped out, feeling like seven kinds of a fool.

"Made her cry already?" Robin stood just outside, his arms folded casually across his chest. He shrugged carelessly as Revelin glowered at him. "I had wondered if I should intrude upon the cozy quiet, but now I see that you've handled things admirably."

Revelin swore under his breath. Was it his fault that one moment she kissed him in a gesture fraught with delightful possibilities and the next dissolved into tears? Annoyed to discover that he felt he was to blame, he absolved himself with the observation, "She's simply being stubborn."

"A challenge!" Robin announced. "Reade awaits a glimpse of her. If he can coax a smile from her, will you yield her to his greater persuasion?"

For an instant Revelin remembered the sweet fire of her lips upon his. His memory fed him images of her black-velvet hair, from which the lamplight struck blue sparks. "I yield nothing," he replied. "There's nothing to yield," he added over his shoulder as he walked away.

Robin chuckled. He had answered none of John's questions about the girl. His own unease about the girl was not laid to rest, but he did not relish the idea of her encountering John's wrath. "Mayhaps she's already found herself a true and knightly protector," he murmured.

The sun's golden warmth had begun to penetrate into the mists when Revelin turned over and met the unexpected bulk of his bed partner. Ualter, who slept at his master's side, stretched out his paws, arched his spine, and groaned in shameless abandon.

"Give over, you great clown!" Revelin muttered as he realized that his "bed" was nothing more than a blanket on the ground. "Be off! You've snored like a hearth bellows the night long and your breath has all but suffocated me!"

Ualter obediently rolled over and sat up, his serious expression belying the happy thump of his tail on the grass.

Revelin's every bone ached with cold. He eyed his damp-spotted trunk hose and canions in disgust. The mantle in which he had slept was as soggy as the ground beneath it. Although he had spent other nights in the open, he had never before been in such misery, because he had been better prepared.

After his companions had retired for the night, he had left the girl to sleep alone. His mistakes were so many that he no longer trusted himself near her. As if that were not bad enough, he had had physically to drag Ualter from her side.

He glowered at his pet. "Ten years' loyalty cast away for a pair of innocent blue eyes. I swear, fidelity is dead when a man's own beast is lost to a fair face." He directed the dog toward his tent with a pointing finger. "Well? Go wake her."

Ualter jumped up and disappeared into the tent. Revelin half-expected to hear a cry of fright from the roused girl. Instead, Ualter poked his head back through the opening after a few seconds and lightly sniffed the morning breeze.

Revelin was on his feet in an instant. One look was enough. He dropped the flap with a curse. There was only one conclusion to be drawn, and it was something he had not considered. "The daft lass has run away!"

Ualter's ears pricked forward at his master's muttering, but he did not abandon tracking her scent. He paced back and forth a few times, sneezed to rid his nostrils of mud and grass, and then his whole body went stiff as the girl's scent wafted up from a shallow footprint in the boggy ground. The hair on his back rose, his huge body began to tremble and he whimpered to be set loose.

With relief Revelin recognized the cause of the dog's excitement. "Why do you linger? 'Tis your fault she got away." He motioned with a hand and commanded, "Go!" and the dog galloped off to the forest with a yelp.

Revelin hurried after him, cursing roundly as his boots made squishy noises with every step.

Meghan paid no attention to the distant barking as she sat in the tree that she had climbed. The pattern of leaf and shadow was comforting because it was familiar, the only familiar thing left in her world. She had come to the forest to be alone to think about what she should do next, but she had found no answers. Instead, she saw a world of loneliness stretching out before her, and it frightened her.

Una was gone. Her home was destroyed. There was no one else on earth who cared whether she lived or died.

She closed her eyes. Those were selfish thoughts, thoughts unworthy of the grieving she felt. She wished Una alive again not only because she was lonely; even if Una could not be with her, she would still wish her alive.

"Meg-han! Meg-han!"

The sound of her name was a shock. Never in all their years together had Una shouted her name, for fear that the cries would attract unwelcome visitors. As the sound of barking neared, Meghan looked down through the foliage to see Ualter break from the underbrush into the open ground beneath her tree. Moments later, his master appeared. She drew back behind the tree trunk, afraid that he would look up and see her.

After a moment the barks ceased and the footfalls died. Her curiosity pricked by the silence, she leaned out until she could see. Revelin had paused beneath the huge elm, a hand on each hip, his dog obediently at his side.

"Meghan?" he called more softly this time. "Meghan, lass, where are you?"

The sound of her name was vaguely disturbing, and Meghan clutched the tree trunk as though his voice had the power to lure her down to the ground against her will.

"Meghan?" Revelin questioned again. The rustle of leaves was his only answer. "Ualter, fetch!" he ordered.

Ualter sprang up, circled the base of the elm, then jumped up against the trunk and barked twice.

Revelin looked up with eyes narrowed against the greenness, but he could detect nothing but the sway of leafy branches in the wind.

In hiding once more, Meghan listened to the crunch of twigs beneath his boots as he walked about. When they began to die away, dismay swamped her suddenly, for she knew she did not want to be alone.

Mischief gleamed in her eyes as she pried loose a section of bark from the tree and then hurled it at him. The chip struck a lower branch and dropped to the ground a few feet behind him. She saw him start and whirl about at the sound. Suppressing a giggle, she pulled lose a second strip. Her second throw found its mark in the center of his chest. His yelp of surprise set free the amusement she had been repressing.

Startled, Revelin glanced up as the sound of impish laughter issued from the treetop. "You *are* up there! Come down this instant!"

Meghan quickly crouched down again, her laughter smothered by her hand.

"Meghan? Come down!"

The command made her shiver, and yet she felt compelled to answer, "No!"

Revelin's jaw dropped. "Are you afraid of me?"

"No."

"Then you'll climb down?"

"No!"

Revelin did not stop to think about what he was doing; he was too irritated by her refusal to obey him. She must have only half the wits he credited her with if she felt it necessary to hide in trees. The prospect of retrieving her from a different tree every morning was not encouraging.

Meghan waited in trembling anticipation. The excitement pulsing in her throat was laced about a knot of fear. Why, oh why had she not simply let him leave? What on earth had she hoped to achieve by encouraging him?

The tree trembled and swayed with his climbing and then

it stopped. After several long moments she opened her eyes.

He sat in a fork of the tree, his head even with her bare feet as she crouched above him. His back was pressed against the trunk, his long legs stretched out, his booted feet crossed at the ankles; and when her gaze came back to his face she saw that he was smiling.

From her tense posture, Revelin recognized that she was terrified. She was crouched in a tight ball with her arms wrapped about her legs and her chin resting on her knees. Her hair had fallen forward like a protective curtain and the curled ends drifted in the breeze. He casually lifted a strand caught on the bark and rubbed it between his fingers. "You are feeling better, I see."

Meghan could think of nothing to say; her gaze remained on him, waiting, watching, afraid.

"Why did you come here?" he asked in his kindest voice. He did not look up, thinking that perhaps she would feel safer if she did not have to respond to his stare.

Meghan shook her head. "'Tis only that I—I . . ."

Revelin combed his fingers through more locks of her hair, enjoying the cool silkiness. "Tell me, Meghan."

She shrugged, a frown drawing delicate lines on her brow. How could she explain what Una had called foolish notions?

"Being atop the world makes you feel powerful and special," Revelin supplied.

Meghan looked at him in surprise. "Ye feel it, too?"

Revelin nodded. Strangely, he did. The pleasure of bouncing on a supple branch was a long-forgotten pastime of his childhood.

"How do ye know my name?" she questioned.

"Your mother told me."

"Una was not me mother," Meghan answered.

"Who were your parents?"

Meghan's gaze slipped away from him. Una had called her a changeling, a child of the fairies left in place of a kidnapped human babe.

A by-blow, Revelin decided. Perhaps an O'Neill clansman's bastard, for Una had told him that Meghan belonged to that Ulster Clan. "Why did you run away?"

A moment passed while Meghan searched for words to fit her feelings. She was accustomed to explaining what her actions were, not the reasons behind them. Unconsciously her left hand stole upward. "Because I'm ugly. It frightens folk."

Pity stirred in Revelin as he said in all honesty, "You do not frighten me, Meghan." He reached out and gently caressed her bare foot. She was female, after all, and deserving of a little flattery. As long as he kept his emotions under control, they both were safe.

Meghan gazed thoughtfully at the hand resting on her foot. It was broad and tan, the fingers long and blunt tipped. But it was his warmth that made her uncomfortable. It communicated itself through her skin, making her vividly aware of how cold she was in every other part of her body. Shyly she asked, "Do ye not fear me?" It was spoken with the candor of a child.

Revelin mastered his smile. "I find you beautiful," he replied, and wondered why it made his voice unsteady to say so.

Meghan gazed at him, aware again of the pleasure that gazing upon him gave her. "Nae, 'tis ye who are beautiful."

Revelin looked up from his play.

She was silhouetted against the shifting pattern of green leaves, her hair a black silky halo shot through with rose and gold from the dawn's light. The light breeze molded her *leine* to her body, outlining perfectly the generous fullnesses and slender hollows of her young body. A jolt of pure delight tightened the muscles of his lower belly. She was born to give pleasure, he thought fleetingly. The response took him by surprise, and he quickly lifted his hand and looked away before the betraying passion could light his eyes.

Meghan's smile dissolved. Humiliation shriveled her momentary happiness into a tight knot of shame. He had looked her full in the face and had not been able to stop himself from retreating at the sight. She should have expected nothing more. She had momentarily forgotten that she was bad luck.

With her free hand she clutched the bark of the trunk until it bit deeply into her palm. "I'll be going me own way. 'Tis not for ye to be worrying about me."

In looking away Revelin had missed her reaction. He glanced back now in surprise. "Go your own way? Faith! You can't seriously be considering living"—he waved his arm about—"here?"

Meghan hung her head in silence, and the realization that she meant to do exactly that nonplused him. Conversing with her was like stumbling down a London alley after dark—he never knew what to expect next.

She was only a simple soul, he reminded himself. He should not fault her for balking at the idea of going anywhere with strangers. What could he say to persuade her otherwise? A moment's thought came to his rescue. "I pledged to your aunt that I would see you kept safe. Would you have me break that promise?"

Meghan considered his words as she watched the passage of an ant along a strip of bark. "I cannot ask ye to break an oath," she said slowly, "but I'll have a pledge from ye, meself. I'll not have ye gawking at me ever again."

Revelin's brows shot up, and then he remembered that she believed herself to be ugly. He schooled his features as best he could. "Aye, 'tis a great concern to me, also," he answered, mimicking her thick accent. "I'll be doing meself a favor not to be so easily distracted by a bonny lass the likes of Meghan O'Neill."

Meghan furrowed her brow in confusion. She did not know what to make of his teasing. Una had never spoken to her in cross-purposes that made her want to smile. "Ye're a fey man," she said simply.

Thinking that he would do better to leave well enough alone, Revelin turned and began climbing down.

Meghan followed reluctantly. When he leaped from the lowest branch, she would have followed had he not immediately turned and raised his arms to her.

"Jump and I'll catch you!"

Meghan stood on the branch for a moment, wondering if she should trust him, and then jumped.

Revelin caught her by the hips, but her *leine* slipped over her body like a loose skin and she slid past his grasp, the momentum overbalancing the pair and sending them onto the mossy floor of the forest.

His body cushioned Meghan's fall as she landed atop his chest. With a toss of her head to bring the hair forward over her face, she looked down at the man beneath her with misgiving tugging at her lips. There was a strange light in his eyes, halfway between pain and pleasure.

"Well, lass, get up," he growled in mock indignation.

Revelin grasped her by the waist to heave her off, but his hands stilled as they encountered the bare satiny warmth of her skin. Her tunic had slid up past her waist, and along either side of his waist her long slim legs were bared to his inspection.

As she shifted her weight slightly he realized that the moist heat of her bare loins was pressed against his belly. She moved again, unconsciously increasing the intimate contact, and his hands curled tighter on her waist. It took the full force of his will not to arch under her weight and press himself against her.

Unaware of the cause of his distress but strangely excited by their contact, Meghan reluctantly began to rise. As she did, Revelin was treated to a vision so tantalizing that he groaned aloud.

"Ye're hurt!" Meghan exclaimed anxiously as she knelt beside him.

Not trusting what his next sight of her might be, Revelin waved her away. "No. I'm not hurt. You go back to camp. I'll be along . . . in a minute."

John was noisily sucking the juice from a handful of berries he had found growing at the base of a boulder when he spied Meghan returning from the forest.

"Well now. The day offers all manner of juicy delights," he said with a smug smile. He met Robin's gaze and deliberately licked the last of the rich red juice from his hand before nodding in Meghan's direction. "Methinks Butler's been at a sweeter fruit than I. He's had her to himself for two days. Will he share, do you think?"

Robin glanced back over his shoulder and saw Revelin emerge from the forest a few paces behind Meghan. John needed little excuse to square off against Butler, since it was Revelin's fault that they had tarried a full week.

"With Rev's puppy prancing about, I'd think twice about pressing the matter, were I you."

John's dark eyes registered for the first time Ualter pacing docilely at the girl's side. "There's ways of dealing with that!" he pronounced and rose suddenly to his feet. He reached down and rubbed his groin. "Once she's had a taste, she'll come begging for it."

Robin's mild blue eyes were full of mirth as John strode across the clearing. Despite his lewd talk, Reade did not approach the girl. Doubtless he was afraid of Ualter!

"You've left little, I see," Revelin said when he reached Robin. He had ignored Meghan when she paused just outside the circle of tents, walking past her without comment.

"Appetites vary, Rev. I have mine." Robin gazed speculatively at Meghan. "And you have yours."

Revelin leaned forward, his chin thrust out in challenge. "She's no whore. Any man who tries to change that will answer to me."

"Your piece, understood," Robin replied with a wink.

"No—man's—piece," Revelin answered, punctuating each word with a finger poked at Robin's chest. "Understood?"

Robin considered this bit of information and found his curiosity unsatisfied. "You dragged her off before day to show her a bit of the countryside?"

Revelin straightened. "As it happens, she ran away."

"Faith!"

"I found her in a tree."

"Even better. I've always fancied a dalliance with a wood nymph."

"Keep your hands off her," Revelin said, and reached for a cold pheasant leg and bit into it.

"John says we ride north this day," Robin offered into the lull of the conversation.

Revelin shook his head. "The girl must be made safe. Four days is all it will take. John will see reason."

Robin studiously ignored this request for backing.

"Watch her," Revelin said curtly as he turned and walked away.

Curious despite his discomfort whenever he was in her presence, Robin reached for a strip of meat, laid it on the last slice of stale bread, and started toward the girl.

With trepidation, Meghan watched the ginger-bearded man approach, her hand covering her cheek. Ualter, who lay at her feet, sat up.

"You must be hungry," Robin said in English and held out the food. "Come, be a good girl and eat," he coaxed, waving his offering under her nose.

The aroma of food filled her nostrils and Meghan's mouth watered with anticipation. She licked her lips, eyes wide and wary on the man before her, but she did not reach for the food.

Robin shrugged. "Then have it your way, darling." Bending down, he placed the food before her.

A shudder passed through Meghan as she saw the dog lightly sniff what was meant for her. Hunger wrenched her stomach and a sigh passed her lips. In an instant she was on her knees, snatching the food from under Ualter's open jaws and stuffing it into her mouth. Ualter growled, baring his teeth, but Meghan merely cuffed him aside with her right hand, and he subsided docilely beside her.

"What madness!" Robin cried in amazement. Ualter raised his head, and Robin took a hasty step backward. "There's a bit more, I'm certain. Let me see what I can find," he continued, taking a backward step with each word.

"Unreasonable, am I? Damn you for a prig!"

Both Meghan and Robin jumped at the sound of John's bellow.

John and Revelin faced each other, their bodies taut and inclined forward, each with a hand on the weapon at his waist.

"God above!" Robin murmured as he ran toward the pair. Whoever drew blood would wish it were his own when the queen learned of their conduct. It was not bravery but sheer fear for all their lives that made him throw himself between them. "John! Rev!" he cried, facing each in turn. "For the love of God, have a care!"

"Out of my way!" John bellowed. "No son of an Irish whore calls me a fool and lives to tell of it!"

"Base-born Englishman that you are, you should be accustomed to insult," Revelin returned, anger glittering in his eyes.

John lifted his sword partway from his scabbard. "Let's see you repeat that, minus your pretty head!"

Revelin reached for his dagger, seeming unconcerned that it was a poor match for John's four-foot double-edged blade. His voice was calm, self-assured, and patient as he said, "You have my permission to try."

Reassured by Revelin's self-command, Robin flung himself on his friend and clasped him in a surprisingly powerful embrace. "Don't be rash, Rev! You stand to lose all for a moment's folly."

"He stands to lose all, regardless!" John jeered and bared his blade.

Forgotten by the three men, Meghan rose from her knees.

She could not understand the shouted insults but she understood a drawn sword. A fierce protective instinct reared up within her as she realized that Revelin was in danger. She ran pell-mell across the grass and leaped upon the black-haired man's shoulders.

The unexpected impact from behind toppled John headfirst into the grass. Badly startled, he cried out, expecting at any second to feel two rows of inch-long teeth ripping into his shoulder or neck. Instead, his neck and head were plummeted with hard little fists as his ears filled with a girl's cries: "No! No! Ye must not harm him!"

Revelin's amazement was no less than John's. In the split second before her attack, he had glimpsed her racing toward them, but his heart had nearly stopped when she leaped upon the man twice her size. Amazement and rage vied for the upper hand as he broke free of Robin's embrace and reached out to snatch Meghan from John's prone body. "God's body! You might have been killed, you little wretch!"

John rolled over and heaved himself to his feet with a gnarl of rage. His narrowed gaze moved from the girl beside him to Revelin and back, and his eyes widened. "You?" Before Revelin could move, John reached out and gripped Meghan's chin. "Let's have a look at the doxy Butler's so willing to spill his blood for! You're a— Bloody Christ! She bears the mark of Satan!"

Meghan recoiled as he pushed her away. A deep tremor began within her. She had seen wolves before. They roamed the twilight underworld of the forest, low-slung skulking figures snatching creatures too young or too weak to defend themselves. As she gazed, locked in the vision, the features of the black-haired man changed. A snout appeared where his broad, broken nose had been. His cheeks grayed, and his beard increased until his face was furred. Only his silver eyes did not change and in them she saw single-minded deadly purpose. He was a predator. Who was his prey?

It was over in an instant and then she heard voices conversing as though nothing had occurred.

". . . John. She's only a child," Robin argued, hanging back even though his desire was to interject himself between John and the girl. "She didn't know what she was doing. She—"

"Shut up, Robin," Revelin inserted flatly into the speech. He reached down and picked up John's sword, wiped it against his canions, and offered it, hilt first, to the soldier. "Another occasion, perhaps."

John hesitated long enough to mutter, "Anytime will serve me," and then took his weapon and sheathed it. He wiped the sweat from his brow and then bared his teeth. "I still command. You will ride to Ulster, Butler, or the queen shall hear of it. I know a little of the Tower's amenities. The rack is worst for a man of good constitution. You're young and strong. You might linger for days."

His gaze darted to Meghan, and she shrank back until she met the wall of Revelin's body and his hands closed over her shoulders. "The bitch is cursed. Keep her out of my path or I'll not answer for the consequences. We ride in a quarter-hour's time."

After a moment Revelin looked down at Meghan. He did not doubt John's threat or the verdict if he knowingly disobeyed the queen's command. And then there was his uncle's request. He could not take her to safety, nor, as matters stood, could he leave her behind. "I must journey to Ulster. Will you come with me?"

He noticed that John swung around in startled interest at the sound of his Gaelic speech, but he did not look up.

Meghan gazed up into Revelin's stern face. Clearly he had not shared her vision, and she dared not speak of it. But he was in danger. The fear she felt was not for herself. She had protected him once. Perhaps she could do so again.

"I will come."

Chapter Six

Revelin stretched out for what he decided, with a lazy smile, would be the best sleep of his life. He had agreed with John's assessment that they must stop using their tents once they crossed the boundary of Louth and entered Ulster; pitching them was time-consuming and they were likely to attract the curious eyes of the Irish. In the relentless war that had never been declared, every Englishman who dared to cross into Ulster was fair game for the clans of the north.

Sleeping on hard ground would have been their fate, had it not been for Meghan's solution.

Fian bed, she called it. Paradise, he and Robin named it. It was simply and quickly assembled by laying green branches together, covering them with rushes, then covering that with a blanket of moss cut from the roots of a tree, and a final covering of rushes. With a wool mantle as a blanket, it was dry and as comfortable as a feather tick.

Revelin rolled over and found Meghan's serious gaze upon him. In fact, he acknowledged with a bit of discomfort, her eyes were always on him. She watched him silently, seriously, unrelentingly. She was lying a few feet away with Ualter wedged between them. She did not answer his smile, and not for the first time in the past few days he wondered about her thoughts.

"Sleep well, lass," he said warmly, hoping she would turn away and give him a little privacy.

Meghan nodded slowly and did look away. She closed her eyes, weary beyond belief. The role of protector was much more strenuous than she had expected, yet she had promised herself to keep him safe through the night. Each night it grew more difficult to lie awake while the others slept. The first night she had been too tense to sleep. The next, she had ached too much from a day on horseback to rest.

She arched her back and sighed. For nights she had listened so zealously and patiently that she now knew the pattern of the breaths that Revelin drew in deep sleep. She knew that the ginger-bearded man named Robin murmured in his dreams. She knew that the tall, beak-nosed man who wore a cross hanging from his neck and made the sign against witchcraft when he saw her tossed and turned in his sleep like a man in torment.

It was deep into the middle of the night when she heard the sound. The one called John had spread his bed well away from the others, eschewing their new-styled bedding for a blanket on the ground. The woman among them had followed suit, placing her bedding near John's.

At first, Meghan thought she must be dreaming. Then she heard it again, the smothered sound of a woman's laughter. Her gaze went first to Revelin; she saw that he slept. Then she turned to find John's place empty. She sat up, lifted back her covers, and silently rose to her feet.

Ualter raised his head. "Stay," she commanded softly, speaking the English word Revelin used when he wanted the dog to remain where he was. The dog did not rise but he did not lower his head.

She heard voices again as she crossed the open ground lit

only by a sliver of a moon. And then she saw them, John and the servant woman, two dark shadows moving against the night. Relieved that they were not clansmen or mercenaries, Meghan nearly turned away, but curiosity kept her gazing at them for a moment longer.

John stopped and leaned his back against a tree, and the woman knelt before him as if to pray. Instead, she tore at his trunk hose with greedy hands, her laughter higher and more excited. Meghan heard the rumble of John's bass voice, and then the woman leaned forward and Meghan heard John's sudden intake of breath.

As Meghan watched in amazement, the woman's head rocked back and forth, faster and faster. She had never before witnessed anything like it. The night was too dark for her to see clearly what was taking place; and yet she found herself gasping softly in time to the woman's rhythm as a strange, fiery sensation swept her.

John groaned suddenly and, reaching down, lifted the woman to her feet. He tore at her skirts, snatched them high above her waist, and then gripped her naked hips in his hands and clasped her to him.

The woman moaned low, her thighs working frantically against his hips, and then she lifted a leg and Meghan saw John thrust against her with a power that elicited a sharp gasp from the woman. Suddenly, Meghan realized what was happening. They were coupling.

She turned and ran, her face blazing with shame and excitement. As a child she had once witnessed the actions of a man and a woman in the high reeds on a riverbank. The woman had lain back and raised her skirts, and the man, his tunic lifted to reveal his erect manhood, had moved between her spread thighs. Later, when she had questioned Una about it, Una had taken a switch to her legs and made her promise never to mention it again. The matter had been forgotten, until now.

Meghan's cheeks stung as though a switch had been taken

to them as she slipped back beneath her covers. Ualter listened for a moment to her rapid breathing and then lowered his head.

Meghan heard nothing but the thudding of her own heart. She felt hot and cold at the same time, afraid that she might have been seen and ashamed of what she had viewed. Over and above it all was the overwhelming awareness of her new knowledge. Men and women coupling together.

She glanced guiltily at Revelin's sleeping face. Did he couple with women? The thought made her heart lurch. Had some woman knelt before him and ... Meghan frowned, trying to piece together the missing parts. She once had seen a man full in his manhood, and since she raised hogs she knew the facts of mating. Yet, John's woman had used her mouth.

A hot blush suffused her skin and she sat up gaping at Revelin, innocent in his dream world. Did he know of such things? Memory stirred. By the pond she had gazed upon his flaccid manhood nestled in a wreath of golden curls. She had nearly touched it, but somehow it had seemed wrong. What was it like when he wanted to couple? Did it grow big and stiff like a mating boar's? Perhaps; for her single memory of another man's organ was of something much larger.

Meghan lay back down with many unanswerable questions occupying her mind. She was staring up at the pale splash of the Milky Way when John and the woman came back into the camp, and when dawn tinted the sky with pale blue light she was still lying wide-eyed.

The next morning, Meghan squatted on a boulder, her arms wrapped about her knees and her hair swung forward to shield her face, and watched Revelin's strange morning ritual. With soap foam swathing the lower half of his face, he stood before a small tin mirror nailed to a tree and scraped the bristly growth from his chin with a blade.

"Does it hurt?" she asked when he suddenly jumped and swore.

"Shaving doesn't hurt," Revelin answered. "Cutting oneself does."

Meghan cocked her head. "Now why would ye want to be cutting yerself?"

Controlling his temper, Revelin passed his tongue over his lips and got a mouthful of soap suds for effort. He swallowed, coughed, and wished she would simply go away. But she would not, and he did not have the heart to hurt her feelings by chasing her off. He glanced at her and saw her head nod forward onto her knees. "Meghan, are you sleeping well?"

Meghan lifted her head slightly, her eyes half-closed. "Aye. 'Tis only me laziness," she answered as her hand moved up to shield a huge yawn.

Unconvinced, Revelin studied her for a moment longer. There were purple shadows beneath her eyes and her skin was pasty. She was not thriving under his care. Some guardian he was. The sooner he found her a home, the better. "Are you too cold at night, or do the night sounds disturb you?"

Meghan lowered her eyes. She would die before she told him of the night sounds that had so disturbed her that she could not sleep. "'Tis nothing."

Revelin sighed and went back to shaving. Obviously she would not confide in him.

"Why do ye do that?" Meghan asked when he was finished.

Revelin rubbed his clean cheeks with a length of linen. "Why do I shave? I admit to a certain vanity which makes me prefer my face to be seen."

"Aye. Ye're lovely to look at," Meghan answered readily. To her surprise, Revelin's cheeks reddened. "Do ye suppose 'tis why Fionn wore his face bare?"

Revelin scowled; he did not like to hear her speak of another man. "Who is this Fionn? A brother?"

Meghan's eyes grew round. "Do ye not know? Ye should, ye being a Leinsterman and Fionn one of yer own. Fionn MacCumail, the leader of the Fian."

Revelin grinned. "The fairy tale, you mean. Yes, I have heard of it."

Meghan straightened up and slid off the rock, her face a study of offense. "'Tis no fairy tale. 'Tis the truth! Ye speak the Irish; aren't ye such?"

Pleased that her pique over his lack of belief in local folklore made her unusually vocal, he crossed his arms and smiled at her. "Tell me more."

"Ye would not be making fun of me?" Meghan regarded him squarely. For the first time in days she had forgotten her discomfort at meeting his eyes. All she felt now was the faint knocking of her heart as she was enveloped by his gaze of tender green. "Fionn was a great warrior of the ancients, which ye'd be knowing if ye were a true Irishman. He dressed in the pelts of wild beasts, with a boar's tusk as his mantle pin."

She gazed at his hair, the thick, amber mane feathered by the wind over his ears and brow. "They say his hair was like spun gold. The same as yers."

Her gaze slipped over his body, stirring her memory of his naked beauty beside the pool, and the wind of desire, though she did not recognize it as such, gusted through her. "He was tall, like ye, and strong, too.

"'Tis said his beauty made women weep and men proud to serve under him. Do ye think 'twas vanity that made Fionn scrape his cheeks?—for they say his face was as smooth as a boy's." When her gaze came back to his face, she nearly reached out to touch him. Always she wanted to touch him. There was a pleasure in touching she had never known until she met him. But she locked her fingers together. He would not want her touch, and she did not want to see rejection in his eyes.

Her voice lowered to a whisper by the ache of wanting she knew not what, she said, "If he were as wondrous fair as ye, I think he had reason to be proud."

She's flirting with me. The thought came as a distinct shock to Revelin and yet he rejected it out of hand. She could know nothing of the idle chatter of men and women. She found him handsome, and he was not above being flattered by that. It did not follow that she saw him as anything other than an oddity, like a new flower or a pretty pebble she had found. Yet, he hoped he was more interesting than a pebble.

"I see my learning is sorely lacking, Meghan. Perhaps you will be kind enough to address the lack while we ride."

Meghan bit her lip and hung her head. "Must we go?"

Sighing, Revelin slipped his razor and mirror back into his saddlebag. "I'm sorry, lass, for dragging you over this desolate ground. I promise to find a horse for you as soon as I can. Then, at least, you won't need ride with me."

Immediately Meghan regretted her words. Riding double with him had been the only pleasure of the journey. She had never been astride a horse before, but riding behind this man and holding on to his waist was worth the soreness that had plagued her from the first. Well, almost. Unconsciously she reached back to rub her aching bottom. "I do not mind so much the riding. I do not—" She paused and shrugged. "The others do not like me."

Distracted by the action of her hands, Revelin did not answer at once. She had arched her spine as she reached back, and in doing so her breasts had lifted, becoming two soft mounds straining against her clothing. Her hands worked a pattern of slow circles over her hips, each outward arc stretching the material of her *leine* over the graceful swell of her bottom.

He tried to look away. What had she said? Lord! He could not remember a single word. "Where in hell is the cloak I gave you?"

Startled, Meghan looked up, her actions halted.

Revelin swallowed. He had not known he spoke aloud until she reacted, but he was committed now. "You should be wrapped against the morning chill. And, saints above, you should be properly dressed!"

Meghan looked down at her shapeless gown and then at her bare legs and feet. "'Tis all I have."

"Well, it's not enough," Revelin grumbled. *Lord love us, not nearly enough!* "You should be dressed like Flora. That's another matter to be mended as soon as possible."

He turned abruptly and walked way. *Stays, the girl needs stays and petticoats and yards of skirts and lace to hide what is too tempting a feminine form by half!*

He forced his breathing to slow and changed the direction of his thoughts by calling to mind each and every part of Lady Allison Burke's face. He began with her brow, its smooth, round, alabaster expanse framed by rows of marigold ringlets. He sketched in her nose, a trifle short for perfection but small and neat. He added her mouth; the short upper lip and the sliver of her lower lip. It was a soft mouth, reminding him of rose petals.

When first she had allowed him to kiss her he had thought it a moment of triumph. What matter that she pursed her lips like a five-year-old and offered her closed rosebud mouth for but a moment? It proved her innocent of the common gossip that circulated about most ladies at court. In time, he would teach her everything she needed to know to please him. She was lovely, irreproachable, a maidenly study in shades of rose and lily with gold filigree.

Desire drifted lazily down through him as he considered the prospect of undressing his bride on their wedding night. By the time he reached his horse, he had forgotten the momentary madness that had slicked his palms with the guilty sweat of lust. Meghan was a trial, albeit a pretty one. When he returned to Alison he would feel doubly pleased to have resisted a considerable temptation. He ignored the corner of his mind that called him a liar and a hypocrite.

Hours later, Revelin rode with Meghan clinging to his jerkin as their horse picked its way through the high grass of a glen. As usual, Reade led the way, followed by Sir Richard and Sir

Robin apace. Flora rode just behind them, prodding and cursing her donkey so that she would not fall in with Meghan and Revelin.

Revelin watched her urge the donkey without much success. Flora, too, was caught up in the fear caused by Meghan's mark. She refused to speak to the girl and would not even fill her plate, fearing what she called the evil eye. If it were not for Reade, he doubted that she would remain with the party.

Reade's taste in women was sadly lacking, Revelin thought. When the slattern had rubbed herself against him the first day, he had turned away in disgust. If only desire were so easily spurned in other quarters, he reflected wryly.

When Meghan had finally fallen quiet, he was pleased. He could not have cared less about the trials of Conn the Hundred-Fighter or of Allen the enchanter, who dwelt in the mountains of Slieve Gullion, but he found himself fascinated by the girl herself. There was nothing calculated about her or the manner in which her words poured out. It was plain to see that she was lonely after a lifetime of suffering from the ignorance and superstition of others. The signs were there, too, that she looked to him as a replacement for her aunt, and that boded ill for them both. If he was not careful she would be badly hurt, and he did not want that.

Meghan hunched her shoulders, trying to adjust the long fur-collared cloak Revelin had draped about her. Its generous folds covered her legs, bared by her leine as she rode astride, and the hem dragged over the grasses. They in turn tugged at it. The cloak slipped farther and Meghan grabbed for it as it slid away.

Unaccustomed to the whipping of cloth about its flanks, the horse shied violently and its two riders nearly lost their seats.

"Have a care!" Revelin called roughly as he brought his mount under control. "You'll tumble us both if you don't sit still."

Meghan jerked the cloak clear of the grass and tucked it

under her thighs. He was angry with her and she did not know why. Since answering her questions about shaving, he had scarcely spoken to her, and what words he had directed to her were terse orders to amend some fault. Perhaps he had not liked being compared to Fionn. No, that did not make sense. Who would not like being compared to a great man?

Her hands flexed on his jerkin as the horse misstepped, and her chest collided with his back. At once Revelin straightened to hold himself away from her and Meghan followed suit. She must not touch him, she told herself, but that was not an easy command to follow. Nothing before in her life had encouraged her to consider the matter between men and women, but the events of the night had stirred old memories and raised a thousand questions. What would it be like to couple with a man? Would it be as fiercely sweet as this man's kiss?

Perhaps he would show her if she asked, Meghan mused sleepily. Yes, she would like that. She would never marry. She was ugly . . . and cursed. She would not expect any man to want her as his bride, but perhaps this man, as a kindness, would show her the way of matters between men and women.

After a few minutes Meghan closed her eyes and leaned her brow against Revelin's back, too weary to realize that she was trespassing once more. The walking gait of the animal lulled her, inviting her to slip silently into the restful arms of sleep.

Revelin felt her grip relaxing on his waist, and his first reaction was one of relief. She was pressed against him and with every step her body rubbed his. For the past hour, in vivid detail his mind had been feeding him images of her breasts pressed nearly flat by the contact and the slow massage of those luscious globes by the muscles of his back. The more he fought, the more unbearable his fantasies became. The small hands clutching his waist seemed to knead his flesh, tormenting him until he wanted to slip to the ground and be free of her.

Now her forehead found the valley between his shoulder blades and her grip fell away. The comfort of freedom was short-lived. The uneven ground made her lurch suddenly and grab him again. Revelin waited for her embrace to drop away. When it did not, he looked down to find her fingers laced together across his stomach. After an interminable minute during which he held himself stiffly, her fingers began to loosen, the inching apart an excruciating process that required him to hold his temper. He had scolded her enough. Soon, he told himself, she would free him, and he would have to manage his discomfort as best he could.

But her fingers did not loosen entirely, and after a battle of conscience he reached down and pried her fingers apart. "You're squeezing me too tight," he said hoarsely, and the words sounded as petty and false as they were.

Meghan drew her hands away, too dulled by exhaustion to realize what she had done. Reluctantly, she gripped his jerkin once more. "Beg yer pardon, m'lord."

Revelin's head lifted. In the five days they had been together he had never told her his name! "I'm not a lord, Meghan. My name's Revelin Butler."

His name wandered through her drowsy thoughts. *Revelin.* An O'Conner name. Butler was not. "'Tis not a name I've heard, this Butler," she murmured.

"'Tis English," he offered.

"English!" Meghan's eyes popped open. *"That,* for the English!" she cried and spat over her shoulder.

Oh Lord! A patriot! Revelin chuckled and shook his head. *What next?*

By mid-afternoon the lush green countryside was silver-laden with mist. The shower had not lasted long. The retreating clouds, streaked with reds and golds from the reappearing sun, sailed rapidly toward the east. Below in the wide valley and up the lower slopes of the hills the myriad shades of green were winged with the brightness of violet blossoms, bitter-yellow tormentil flowers, spikes of blue milkwort, and clumps of rich pink fairy foxglove.

The sensuous beauty was lost on the surveyor of the scene. Sir Richard stood atop a rise shielded by a stand of elms and stared angrily at the three figures in the clearing below. Revelin sat in the grass with his sketch pad balanced on his knee while the girl lay at his feet. She was curled up like a kitten on a cloak, her legs tucked up under her and her hands providing a pillow for her cheek. Just beyond her, Ualter stretched out, a shaggy gray rug on the green sod.

Sir Richard's jaw tightened. When the party paused for their noonday meal, Butler announced his intention of sketching the low rolling hills that surrounded the glen. When Meghan followed, he had thought it wise to watch the pair, fearing a tryst in the making. He silently commended young Butler for not touching the girl, but he would have felt better had he been able to understand the words spoken between them.

"Damn foreign gibberish," he muttered. He had thought Butler unfamiliar with the Gaelic. So had John. Why had the man hidden his skill until the chit appeared? As he watched, Butler suddenly laid his charcoal aside.

Revelin's glance moved from his pad to Meghan's free-flowing river of inky waves, then on to her dirty bare feet and finally back to her face. Her profile was startlingly graceful, the bones sharp yet delicate, spare but pure of form. She presented an undeniable challenge for an artist.

His pad was covered with drawings. He turned his pictures this way and that, squinting critically at them, and then grunted in disgust and tossed the pad aside. Something was missing. A pretty face could be captured on paper but not Meghan's illusive beauty.

Revelin bent and picked up a lock of her hair that the breeze had entangled about his ankle. "You're too young to know what you do to me, lass," he whispered as he carefully disentangled himself. Disentangled, yes; he must free himself from the seeds of desire that she had unconsciously planted and that he, damn him, was nurturing in moments like these.

"I can see you've used your time to advantage."

Revelin did not move. He had not heard Sir Richard's footfalls approach, but Ualter had and raised his head. When the dog made no further move, Revelin knew it was one of his party.

"I've done about all I can here," he said and casually flipped his pad closed. When he looked up, he knew he had acted too late. Sir Richard's expression was bitterly cold. He had seen the sketches.

Annoyed, Revelin picked up his pad. "We should move on. Before the mists gathered I thought I saw smoke beyond that north hill."

Sir Richard's gaze shifted to the distant rise. "I was told the countryside swarms with the Irish. I wonder that we've not seen them ere this." He looked back at Revelin, his light eyes bright. "Would you know why they've left us unmolested?"

Revelin met his stare evenly. "I've warned them off, or haven't you noticed? I ride ahead and tell them we're only spies, and, of course, they open the pathway."

Sir Richard sniffed. "You did not tell us you were conversant in Gaelic."

Revelin smiled slightly. "You did not ask me."

Sir Richard nodded slowly. "Is there something more I should know?"

"Were the clans aware of us, you'd know of it."

Sir Richard stared at Revelin, aware, as he often had been these last weeks, of the energy and vitality of his youth. It was a palpable presence, deserving of obtaining its glory. "You have a brilliant future before you. With the queen's backing you will find your power at court greatly enhanced when you return. To maintain it you will need friends. I believe we are destined to go far together, Butler. You and I, forged in a bond for the greater glory of God, what wonders we may accomplish." He glanced at Meghan and away. "Don't jeopardize what we may yet achieve for a common pleasure."

The ice-water stare scrutinizing him made Revelin uncomfortable. Once before he had heard that urgent plea in this man's voice and wondered at its cause. Now he felt a flush creep up his collar. No, he must be mistaken. He was reacting to his discomfort over the pictures he had drawn when his mind should have been on business.

"Now that you speak of it, we'd do well to seek shelter for the remainder of the day. In Ulster the night is kinder to strangers." He bent and lightly shook Meghan's shoulder. "Come, lass, 'tis time to go." She did not move. "Meghan, lass?"

For reasons he did not understand, she was exhausted, but they could not afford to be stranded in the open while she slept. The smoke of that distant fire was from a large blaze, perhaps a party of reivers. Under Atholl's watchful stare, Revelin scooped her up and carried her back to the horses.

Meghan awoke with a start. She was seated side-saddle before Revelin, her bare legs dangling over his right thigh while his left arm held her securely to his chest. Beyond his shoulders, a dim soggy dusk was settling on the land.

"Top of the day to you, lass. Or rather, what's left of it."

Meghan looked up into Revelin's deep smile only inches above her. His eyes glittered like dark jewels in the twilight as he said, "You're a wee bit damp, but other than that, you've slept as snug as a babe in her mother's arms."

Only half-awake, Meghan sighed and closed her eyes. She felt every bit as safe as his words claimed. His arm supported her back and his hand was on the slim curve of her waist. The heat of his body pervaded hers beneath the cloak that covered them both.

Without thinking about it, she turned her head into the opening of his jerkin where his skin lay bare and nuzzled the heated skin. He was so pleasant in so many unsuspected ways. His body smelled different from her own. The tang of his sweat was undercut by his rich, faintly musky scent, which made her toes curl. He was as warm and fragrant as a loaf of newly baked bread, and she wanted a taste of him.

Her nose was cold, like an icicle, yet Revelin's skin burned at the touch. His felt himself becoming aroused. When her tongue slyly reached out and licked the arch of his throat, he gasped softly. It was not real. He had imagined— Oh Lord! She did it again.

"Meghan?" His voice sounded so strange that it embarrassed him. "Meghan . . . lass . . . you mustn't—"

The sound of horses cut through the thick, sweet torment of his desire, and in an instant he was alert to danger.

Specterlike, out of the mists rose wave after wave of riders on unshod horses. The unholy war cries that issued from their throats rent the stillness with a terror that could chill blood in living veins.

As John's shout of warning echoed back to them through the mist, Revelin reached for his sword, but his way was blocked. Meghan sat across his lap, her hips between him and a free draw.

"Damn!" He kicked his mount, jerked the reins to turn him, and dug his heels unmercifully into the beast's flanks. There was no alternative but to run, yet he doubted they would escape. At best he hoped to find shelter for Meghan before returning to aid his companions.

As they raced across the open valley Revelin bent his head, his lips against Meghan's ear. "I must release you. Hide!" Without checking his horse's stride, he lifted and tossed her from his saddle. He turned and shouted at Ualter, who ran alongside, "Ualter! Stay!" He did not look back as Meghan tumbled with a shriek into the waist-high reeds. The muffled tattoo of hooves close behind signaled that they had been seen.

The rider was closing fast, more certain of his way in the mists than Revelin was. To outrun him was useless. Only in combat was there a chance of survival. Revelin wheeled his horse and freed his sword in time to check the first blow aimed at him.

The rider wore a shirt of mail, an iron cap, and leggings of leather, a specter of a medieval knight in this modern sixteenth century. In his left hand was a burning faggot, and torchlight ran in steely flames along the bared sword in his right.

As Revelin urged his mount forward, lifting his sword to deliver a blow, a second rider appeared out of the fog, and the pair of warriors sandwiched him between their flashing blades. He braced himself for a cut of steel that would sever his head from his shoulders. It did not come. Instead, the flurry of blows and thrusts bent him low in the saddle and then toppled him, bleeding, bruised, and stunned, onto the soft wet grass.

Meghan rose groggily to her feet. The fall had dropped her into the slime of a bog and her feet sank up past her ankles as she struggled to stay upright. The thunder of the hooves and whooping battle cries surrounded her. It was the dream—or was it?—that had come following Una's death. Who would die this day?

"Revelin!" She tried to run but the ooze sucked at her legs, holding her back. Ualter ran in circles about her, his paws kicking up mud and muck as he tried to herd her back into the reeds. "No! No! Leave me be!" she cried, pushing him away. Ualter quieted, eyeing her intently as she looked about.

The glimmer of light, a torch carried by one of their attackers, drew her attention and she waded toward it, her heart thumping wildly in her breast. The cool air stung her lungs, and the mists played cruel tricks before her terrified eyes. She saw Revelin's horse and then it disappeared. She slipped her skean from her wrist and wrapped her small hand about its leather hilt.

"Revelin!" she cried, straining toward the rider bearing light. "God have mercy! Revelin!" She dodged between the stomping, impatient hooves of two battle steeds as one warrior bent over his prize.

"English!" the warrior said, spitting. Lifting the nodding

head by its yellow hair, he dipped the point of his blade toward the exposed throat.

"No! Don't touch him!" Meghan flew at the warrior, her dagger poised to strike, and sank the blade into his left shoulder where his mail gaped away from his neck. He groaned in pain and went down on one knee, but he did not collapse. Recovering more quickly than seemed humanly possible, he grabbed Meghan by the throat with one hand, and with the other reached up to pluck her weapon from the top of his shoulder.

"Are ye bad hurt, Colin?" the torch bearer asked.

"Nae! 'Twill take more than a sting to bring low Colin MacDonald," the other called jovially. "And it earns me a colleen, besides. Let's have a look at her. A bonny piece— The devil's foot!" the injured warrior whispered. "I've caught me a changeling!" Releasing Meghan, he crossed himself and murmured a prayer.

Meghan lifted her face for the torch bearer to see; he expelled a string of profanities, backing his horse a step.

"Have a care if ye would live the rest of yer days in God's grace," she cried fiercely, pointing to Revelin's inert body, which Ualter pawed. "If ye've hurt him, ye're cursed till the day ye die!"

She scarcely knew what she was saying. They might well slit her throat and leave her body to rot beside Revelin's, but her ugliness and their fear of it were the only weapons left her.

The warriors exchanged glances. "I'll fetch Ever," the rider offered, and the second man nodded. The battle had ceased as quickly as it began, leaving an eerie silence.

The injured warrior lifted his sword and pointed it at Meghan's middle. "I'd nae be running away if I were ye. I dinna murder women and bairns, but I could make an exception for a changeling who's drawn me coin."

Meghan recognized his accent: it was Scottish. She squinted at him. Could it be that she had attacked a *galloglaigh?* Her gaze moved to his shoulder where the chain mail was reddening with blood. "A bandage of peat moss will stop the bleeding," she said softly before dropping to her knees beside Revelin.

His skin was cold to her touch where moments before it had seemed heated by embers. Her hand shook as she reached for a pulse, and a tiny whimper of relief escaped her.

"Is he yer lad?" the soldier asked, his voice curiously kind.

"Aye, he's mine," Meghan answered and tenderly lifted Revelin's head into her lap. Ualter whimpered and stretched out beside his master.

Meghan looked up as other warriors neared. The leader was wrapped in a mantle of saffron yellow, which she recognized as the clan color of the O'Neill, her clan. "Let's have a look at ye," he offered. "On yer feet, lass."

Meghan did not rise. Revelin was stirring, his head moving from side to side in her lap, and his nearness gave her courage. "If ye've business with me, ye'd best climb down. 'Tis nae like an O'Neill to forget his manners before a woman."

A murmur passed through the throng of men behind the chieftain, but he did not dismount. Colin, who had held her at sword's point, bent over and lifted her chin high. "Shine the light on her, Farrell."

The wind-whipped flames lit Meghan's face, distorting the angles of cheek and nose and staining her birthmark reddish-black. An involuntary gasp escaped the men closest to her.

"Ye see! She bears the mark," Colin proclaimed.

The leader urged his horse forward and leaned from his saddle as he strained for a better look at Meghan's features. "Aye, she bears the mark." He sat back and sheathed his sword. "As to whether or not she's the one, we'd best ask the one man who'll know."

"She's to come with us, then?" Colin questioned.

The leader was silent for a moment while Meghan felt dozens of eyes watching her beyond the meager light of the torch. "Are ye an O'Neill, lass?"

Meghan stared at him. "Who's asking?"

The leader chuckled. "Ye're an O'Neill, right enough. So

I'll be asking ye this: Why are ye in the company of the English?''

Revelin groaned and Meghan glanced down. His eyes were open, gleaming dully in the night. She touched his cheek. What could she say that would save Revelin? "This man saved me life. I know naught of the others."

The leader stroked his beard. "Ye say ye know naught. Mayhaps we can learn more. Whether they die today or another, I doubt it will matter in the end." He turned and called over his shoulder, "Bring the others. We've questions to put to them."

When Colin reached down and dragged Revelin to his feet, Revelin groaned in pain. Alarmed, Meghan struck the warrior with her fists. "Leave him be!"

Ualter, concerned by Meghan's cry, sprang to her aid. He jumped upon the warrior's shoulders as he bared his teeth in a full-throated growl of rage. The man staggered under the huge animal's weight and reached for his sword.

"Ualter! Heel!" Meghan cried as she had heard Revelin do. Instantly Ualter obeyed, moving to her side, but the hair on his back remained raised in anger.

The Scotsman shot the girl a look of pure enmity. "Ye'll carry the lad on yer back for that," he said, and released Revelin so that he collapsed back to his knees like a sack of meal. "See to him, if ye can, lass," he jeered. Turning, he strode away.

Meghan knelt beside Revelin and caught his face between her hands. "Are ye hurt bad?"

Revelin lifted his head, though it felt as if a hundred-pound weight were tied to his brow, and his tongue felt like a thick sausage in his mouth. It faintly amused him that, for the second time, Meghan's intervention had saved his life. "Don't worry, you won't need . . . to carry me, darling."

The endearment caused blood to rush into Meghan's cheeks, but her voice was solemn as she said, "Ye'll nae die this night, I think. Only, I beg ye, hold yer tongue."

Laughter rumbled in Revelin's chest. She had told him to

hold his tongue, his thick-as-a-sausage tongue! He looked at her pale face with its enormous blue eyes. She was so serious, poor wee lass, and he so much trouble for her. "Don't frown so, lass. A man likes a smile on the face of the lass he loves."

The words were slurred; surely she had heard him amiss. And yet . . . Meghan felt her heart pounding furiously as she ran her fingers briefly over his hair, caressing the brilliant waves. His eyes were dark like the onyx-green surface of a lough in the moonlight. No, he could not know what he said. "We must go, Revelin. They'll come back for us, else."

Revelin had never thought his name especially musical until he heard her say it, the syllables rolling from her lips in a soft brogue. He was about to say so, for suddenly he could not control any of the thoughts that came to his mind, when the sound of hooves neared.

"Here's yer mount, lass," the leader said. "Get the lad in the saddle and keep him there. We've tarried too long. 'Tis nae a night to be abroad, or so ye've seen. No tricks or ye'll suffer the same," he added with a jerk of his head.

Meghan looked past the leader to the three horses he led. Revelin's companions had been gagged and bound, hand and foot, and tossed like so many sacks of barley across their saddles. Flora was nowhere to be seen. Suppressing a shiver, Meghan caught the reins tossed at her.

Revelin slowly rose to his feet.

"Can ye ride?" Meghan questioned anxiously.

"Like the wind, lass, with your arms about me." He smiled, a lopsided grin that bared his teeth. His head ached abominably and he was certain he was bleeding in several places, but that did not matter. He threw an arm about her shoulders and swayed against her. His voice sounded drunk and foolish in his ears but he did not care as he whispered, "I'll not fail you, lass."

He smiled as he lifted his boot into the stirrup, grateful that he had adopted the English style of saddle. Without the help of the stirrup he knew he would never have gotten astride. He was light-headed, dizzy as a leaf in the breeze. He clutched the pommel in one hand and offered his free hand to Meghan. She put her bare foot on top of his boot and swung up beside him.

"Put your arms about me, lass, I have need of the anchor," he whispered.

Meghan grasped him firmly about the waist as he asked and Revelin smiled again. Why he had ever objected to the pleasure of her embrace he would never know.

The O'Neill clansmen fell into step with them, two before and behind and one on either side. When the one on her right reached for her reins, she handed them over gratefully, for it was all she could do to support Revelin's weight.

The morning was dawning in clear soft shades of green and blue as Meghan sipped the last of the dark ale from her wooden cup and watched the moon slide down behind the low-rolling hills. Not content with the capture of five strangers, two separate O'Neill reiving parties had added over a thousand head of cattle to their band. For two days and nights they had ridden, stopping only for meals at dawn and dusk. She had learned to sleep in the saddle and contain her normal bodily functions until she thought she would burst, but she had little to complain about compared with the others.

She glanced at the other captives and then away. They were tethered to a nearby tree, as were their horses, and though they ate in silence, she felt their eyes constantly on her in damning accusation that it was her fault that they were so mistreated. Only during meals were their hands and mouths freed, otherwise they rode trussed and slung across their saddles. It was better than other methods their captors might have devised, but that fact gave little comfort. A woman's laughter echoed through the camp, and Meghan knew that Flora had made her own peace with the O'Neills.

Meghan soothingly stroked Revelin's damp brow as his head lay in her lap. The sweat was a good sign. He had become feverish within hours of attack, and she had not been able to give him water or tend his wounds until the next morning. She lifted a corner of the peat-moss bandage she had made for his sword arm and saw with satisfaction that the wound had begun to heal.

"Mount up!"

As the order rang through the camp Meghan groaned. Her arms and spine ached from holding Revelin in the saddle. Yet she knew they must rise or be subjected to the same humiliation as the Englishmen. She ran her fingers across Revelin's brow one last time and bent to lay her cheek on his. "We must ride. Please wake up."

Revelin stirred, weary beyond measure. "Not yet. Another hour."

Meghan prodded him. "No, no! Now, Revelin. Now!" She dumped him from her lap without regard for his head and stood up, aware that the Scotsman named Colin MacDonald was striding toward them. He had not approached her since the night of their capture. Meghan eyed him cautiously. *He must want something.*

It had been too dark to notice much about him the first time they met, and now she studied him curiously. He wore a long shaggy mantle that brushed the ground, and his fair hair, bare of the steel helmet, flowed about his shoulders. Her gaze lowered to the telltale red leggings he wore and she knew her guess had been right. Colin MacDonald was a *galloglaigh,* a man raised to be a soldier by one of the many warrior clans of the Scottish Isles.

His face was burnt red by the sun, and the irregular features left much to be desired in the way of handsomeness. A long scar cut across the bridge of his nose where a sword stroke had broken it. His skin was seamed by old battle wounds, but his eyes were very alive. His smile deepened as her gaze lingered on his face, and she suddenly realized that he was appraising her in a way that made her very conscious of being female. Disconcerted, she looked away.

"What ails the lad?" he demanded.

Meghan shook Revelin's arm with her foot but he merely rolled onto his side away from her. "He's had a fever. He needs rest."

"He'll ride."

Meghan caught Ualter by the scruff of his neck as the brawny warrior bent down and lifted Revelin easily into his arms. Revelin moved restlessly, muttering, "Meghan?" Colin grinned at Meghan through the wiry tangle of his blond beard. "He's a great babe, yer lad."

Refusing to join him in a jest at Revelin's expense, Meghan regarded him solemnly. "How's yer wound?"

Colin chuckled. "I'd forgotten it." His expression grew serious. "I came to give ye this back, lass, but I warn ye not to use it again. I might have killed ye."

When he lifted her skean from his belt and held it out to her, she took it and slipped it into place under her sleeve.

"Aye, that's the way of it," he said in approval. He turned and heaved Revelin into his saddle. When he looked back at Meghan, there was warm interest once more in his eyes. "Ye'll do well at Lough Neagh."

"Lough Neagh?" Meghan echoed in surprise.

"Ye know the place?"

"Aye," she answered softly. Was it only a fortnight ago that she had longed so fiercely to return home? Now she had no wish for it at all.

By day's end the shimmering surface of Lough Neagh shone in the distance. The lake was huge and irregular, its fingers embracing a dozen small isles. On one of the larger was built the O'Neill island fortress. But the O'Neill warriors turned off the path that would have led to the lake's edge, and, picking up the pace, they rode through the wet woods until a glow in the distance made the men around her give the ear-splitting whoop of the O'Neill war cry.

"What is it? Another battle?" Revelin questioned, jarred awake by the racket.

Meghan tightened her arms about him, her voice dry with trepidation as they halted at the edge of a clearing filled with tents. "Nae. 'Tis only that we've arrived."

She looked beyond the tents to the huge column in the center of the camp. She had never actually seen one before but she knew what it was. Taller and broader than a man, its flame rising more than a foot into the crisp night air, was the great King-Candle, symbol of the O'Neill of Ulster.

Chapter Seven

Meghan gazed about in fear mingled with amazement. The sounds of so many so close frightened her. On every side, people rushed the dismounting warriors, their boisterous voices filled with congratulation. On the journey the clansmen had taken care to keep their distance from Meghan. Now, forgetful of her presence in their joy to be home, they rudely jostled her mount.

Meghan gulped down a cry of fright, squeezing her eyes shut and trying to stop her trembling. Raised in near solitude, she was unaccustomed to the noise and stench of a crowd. The odors of unwashed bodies and stale breath of horses, cattle, and men clogged her nose until she felt she would suffocate. Not even Revelin's presence could still the terror rising within her. The urge to flee, always poised at the edge of her mind when in the company of strangers, overwhelmed her. As a clansman grabbed the reins from Revelin to lead their horse to the center of the crowd, she slipped backward from the saddle.

She was unprepared for the shock of her legs folding bone-lessly beneath her weight. She had believed herself inured to sore muscles. Now, as she dropped into the muck kicked up by the passage of hundreds of hooves, she realized she had not toughened up, only become numb from the waist down.

Revelin turned as he felt her slip away, but the milling crowd prevented him from seeing what had happened to her. "Meghan?" he called out as he turned sharply and started to lift a leg over his saddle. "Meghan, answer me!"

"Now hush, laddie," he heard Colin MacDonald say behind him. An instant later the heavy weight of the warrior's sword hilt connected with the back of his skull and Revelin slumped forward in his saddle, unconscious.

"Ah, my God! Ye killled him!"

Meghan's outraged cry drew Colin's attention. "Ach, lassie, don't look at me like that. 'Twas only a precaution. The laddie has a voice which carries, and him a prisoner and all, how would it look?" He sheathed his sword and then reached down to lift her from the ground with a hand on either side of her waist.

Alarmed and embarrassed that he handled her so familiarly, Meghan struggled in the big man's grasp. "Let me be! I can stand!"

The Scotsman's grip tightened. "Easy, lass. Ye're no' a fool."

His gruff voice, unusually quiet, held a warning, and Meghan looked up to find a half-dozen clansmen watching her. A prickling of alarm went through her as their predatory gazes held her. They were probing, looking for weakness. If she appeared helpless, they would no longer regard her as a threat. Their wariness was all that kept her safe.

Meghan straightened up, grinding her teeth as blood swept in a stinging rush through her legs and feet. When the stinging subsided, she said, "Let me go." When Colin released her, she backed away and into the path of a pair of clansmen.

"Watch yer step, lass!" one of them cried. When Meghan lifted her head, he shrank away. "Name o' God! The *suil trom*. And 'twas me sword arm she touched!"

"Aye, that's an ill omen!" the second man remarked.

The conversations about them died abruptly as other warriors overheard their conversation. Frightened, Meghan raised her hand to her face.

"Ach, none of that!" The man she had bumped grabbed her wrist and wrenched her hand away from her face. "Look me in the eye, lass," he demanded, and shook her hard when she did not respond. "I'll nae go into battle with yer ill luck on me. Pray for me or be damned!"

"She'll no' be wanting to please ye, if ye frighten the wits out of her," Colin offered with a smile. He paused in the process of lifting Revelin from his saddle, his gaze lighting significantly upon the hand squeezing Meghan's wrist, and her captor reluctantly released her.

When Colin spoke again, he raised his voice for the benefit of the circle of men. "Ye're no' so superstitious as to harm the lassie? Let her be. She's no account to curse ye ... yet."

Meghan did not object as he reached out, gripped her chin, and, jerking it upward, turned the right side of her face toward the men. "There now. Where would ye be finding a bonnier cheek? Smooth and pale as cream!" He playfully tapped her cheek. "Smile for the laddies."

Meghan swallowed the knot of fear that constricted her throat but she could not unlock the fear-tensed muscles of her face.

"Ah well, 'twould seem ye've given her a fright, laddies. I'd best be keeping me distance till she's no' so afraid."

He turned away from the group as easily as he had joined it and the clansmen melted away after a moment, their wary looks and mutterings disappearing with them.

Meghan stepped to the Scotsman's side. "Thank ye," she whispered nervously.

Colin looked down as he lifted Revelin's limp body from the saddle. "'Twas no' so great a thing. Ye're a braw lassie or ye would no' of slipped yer skean under me mail when I held a sword more than half yer length. Ye've a trick there, with that mark. Use it to yer gain."

Meghan looked at him in astonishment as he winked at her. There was no fear in him when he gazed at her. The knowledge warmed her, and unconsciously she smiled at him before turning her attention to Revelin. She reached out and gently brushed a lock of hair from his forehead after Colin had heaved him over his shoulder.

Colin frowned at the gesture, his thick reddish brows drawing together. "Stay where ye stand, lass. I'll come back for ye."

The order aroused fresh fears, and Meghan grabbed his sleeve. "Where do ye take him?"

Colin's eyes widened innocently. "Him?"

She pointed at Revelin. "His name is Butler."

"Butler, it is?" the Scotsman murmured. "'Tis a name no' unknown to us. Now I'd thank ye to stand a bit, lass, else I'll show ye the way of it that ye won't like." He turned on his heel and disappeared into the milling throng.

Ualter, who had stood patiently beside Revelin's mount, started after the man carrying his master. Then he halted and looked back at Meghan. His tail drooped and his head dipped in apology before he turned and trotted away.

Meghan slumped against her mount, but the horse objected and side-stepped, exposing her to the bustle of men and women. As before, they paused, some startled, some anxious, all curious.

Meghan looked down, concentrating her gaze on her toes. But, after a few minutes, curiosity got the better of her and she shyly raised her head to look about.

The woodland near the lough teemed with people, more than she had ever seen in one place at one time. They were camped in the open. In the light cast by dozens of fires she saw that peasant men, women, and children, as well as warriors and their families, filled the camp. Of course, she remembered suddenly, it was nearing time for coshering. As was traditional in the spring and summer, whole communities were preparing to move from their homes in the valleys to take advantage of the new grasses growing in higher elevations. Meghan glanced at them and then quickly away, aware that staring would draw their attention.

In spite of her fear, hunger lured her toward the center of the encampment, from which the aromas of beef and pork arose. As soon as she passed the first set of tents, she spotted one of the communal cooking fires. Tied by three corners to stakes driven into the ground, a cured cowhide suspended over a fire served as a vessel for boiling meat.

They will eat well, she thought in fleeting envy. Butter and barley bread had been the staples of her life before this, and she had had little of that in recent days.

When two soldiers passed several feet away she paused. Their voices were low and serious, and when they turned to gaze at her, her heart skipped a beat and she hurried anxiously away. What had become of Revelin and Colin? There were no familiar faces among the press of people, only the droning of voices, the ripple of occasional laughter, and the distant swirling of a lone bagpipe.

"Lass!"

Meghan spun about to face Colin MacDonald. "I've known nary a lass that could keep her word."

"I was hungry," she answered softly.

Instead of answering, the Scotsman motioned her to follow him and she did. When he turned away from the camp and the night quickly closed around them, Meghan fingered the hilt of her dagger, grateful that he had returned it to her. If he meant her harm, he would again feel its sting.

When they were beyond the reach of the campfires he stopped

and turned to her. In the dim light she saw that his expression was thoughtful, even frowning, but the darkness cloaked the look in his eyes. He gestured toward a fork in the roots of a huge tree. "Ye'll sleep here." He unwrapped the woolen mantle from his shoulders and offered it to her. "'Tis better than nothing, and there's nae fire for ye."

Meghan took the heavy mantle from him. She had no fear of the night or the dark woods, but Revelin's disappearance worried her. "Where is Butler?"

"And are ye a whore for the Englishman?" he asked testily.

The word was unfamiliar to Meghan and she shrugged. "He saved me life."

He studied her for a moment before answering. "He's safe enough. Only I've me doubts ye'd care to join him." Before she realized what he meant to do, he reached out, lifted her off the ground, and brought her tight against his chest as his mouth swooped down on hers.

Meghan felt no fear, only a momentary shock. His lips were warm and hard within the scratchy nest of his beard, lingering on hers a long moment before he raised his head and set her back on the ground. "Well now, I ken ye're no' so surprised by that as me. Mayhap ye're a fairy right enough!"

He turned and started away, then paused and shook a finger at her. "I've nae cause to chain ye, have I?"

Meghan shook her head.

When he was gone, she huddled in his mantle, taking what comfort she could from his warmth still trapped in its folds. She knew that before morning she would be more grateful for the mantle than she was now. She did not mind the solitude. She had been too much with people these last days. She was well rid of them . . . all except Revelin.

The intruder who came crashing through the underbrush gave her no time to flee. She had no more than sat up with a half-cry when he was upon her, all damp paws and tongue.

"Ualter!" she exclaimed in relief as she flung her arms about his neck. "Where's yer master?"

She leaned around the dog's bulk, but there was no one following the animal. For a moment she considered ordering the dog to find Revelin and following him, but she quickly rejected the idea. Colin had left her unbound. Betraying his trust did not bother her; if he was foolish enough to accept her word, that was his weakness. But—and the exception killed her desire for adventure—her power to influence the Scotsman was a tenuous thing. If she was caught escaping, she would be shown no mercy, and no power she possessed would save her . . . or Revelin.

She put a hand to her lips, lightly tracing their outline. The Scotsman's kiss was not as pleasant as Revelin's, but it was not unpleasant. She smiled.

She huddled deeper in the rough wool mantle and pulled the fox-fur hood up over her bedraggled curls. When Ualter settled down, his stomach covering her bare feet, she sighed and closed her eyes.

"Revelin? Rev, man! Wake up!"

Revelin awoke slowly, his senses sluggish. He lay on his side, his face half-buried in the cold mire of a bog. He coughed and lifted his head to clear it of the mud, only to choke as the rope about his neck tightened. He was bound hand and foot, his wrists and ankles chained together behind his back and attached to the rope that collared his throat. "God's Grace!" he whispered, realizing that any violent move would strangle him.

"Feeling better, then, I see." Robin's ever-amused voice rose from the darkness beside him. "John and I were just speculating about what you've done to join us after so pleasant a journey."

Revelin turned his head carefully toward Robin. The dawn sky provided faint illumination. He passed his tongue over his fever-chapped lips. "How long have we been here?"

John, on Revelin's right, snorted. "Long enough to decide that your whore can do nothing more for you. God's teeth! If you weren't here with me now I'd be gnawing my chains for a chance to slit your throat. I'll not soon forget, Butler, that you did naught for your companions!"

"'Tis Hell!" Sir Richard cried, his voice echoing up from the bottom of his lungs. "We're cast into the river Styx to drown in the foulness of our sins!" The cry of despair ended in a sob.

"Don't mind the parson," Robin whispered as Sir Richard began to mutter a prayer. "He's been like that since the attack."

Revelin frowned, piecing together the last hours. "I was struck from behind," he said slowly. "How long ago?"

"Last evening," Robin answered.

Revelin remembered now the saffron tunics wavering like flames in the torchlight. Only the O'Neills would dare to flaunt the outlawed color of their clan. "Why didn't they kill us?"

John's bark of laughter was bitter. "Do you complain? But, of course, 'tis a traitor's part to act the innocent. Did you bargain with them, Butler? Did you promise them ransom for us? Or did you promise them the girl? 'Twas easy enough to see at least one Celtic dog panted after her."

Revelin cursed and tried to rise, but the rope cut short his breath and he fell back gasping.

"Gently, Rev," Robin chided. "In this instance I agree with John. It takes no scholar to realize that she's the reason we live."

John chuckled. "I don't doubt but that she's now in the company of Turlough . . . or that ugly red-haired brute with the scarred nose."

"God rot you, you devil!" Revelin whispered viciously. A sick feeling rose in his throat as a dizzying weakness spiraled through him, but he gritted his teeth, willing himself to remain conscious.

John chuckled again, feeling better than he had since their ordeal began. "You bleed too easily, Butler. The girl's one of them; he'll use her well. If she's a clever bitch, she'll trade her charms for your miserable life. 'Tis my hope she pleases him, since our lives have been spared along with your traitorous carcass . . . for the moment."

Revelin continued to struggle against the chains that bound him until he felt a warm trickle flow over his hands and realized he had torn open the wound on his sword arm. He closed his eyes, trembling in impotent fury. Meghan was an innocent. To think of her, afraid . . . abused . . . raped!

"'Tis useless," Robin offered softly. "You can't free yourself. We've each tried. I only hope they remember us before the wolves smell us."

John guffawed. "Are you afraid of becoming a bellyful for vermin, courtier?"

"I'd as lief not be," Robin answered lightly. "Lord! What was that?"

The four men fell silent as the cry rose again, echoing through the marshland woods. It came a third time, a long sustained cry of terror-edged pain, and then it ceased abruptly.

"They're murdering some poor bastard," John muttered, loosing a string of curses behind the thought.

Sir Richard's strident voice rose once more in prayer. "Lord in Heaven! Be to Thy humble servant in extremity as a drink of water in the parched desert! Hear Thy sinner's plea and let this anguish pass Thy servant by!"

"Shut up, you fool!" John growled.

"Easy, Reade," Robin cautioned. "Your bombastic voice carries, and who knows but it won't cause them to look here for other sport."

Revelin lowered his head onto the slick grass, his throat aching too much for speech. The soul in agony had been a male, of that he was certain. But it did not ease his fears for Meghan; they writhed like snakes in his gut. Men who came home in victory had only two things on their minds: whiskey and women. She was so young. . . .

He swallowed hard, forcing his mind away from the horrible thoughts crowding it.

Sweat ran down his face, cutting clean paths on his mud-caked cheeks. There was nothing he could do until the men came for him. At least he spoke their language and would be able to demand an interview with their chieftain. If the O'Neill had heard of their captivity, they might yet live to tell of their adventures. As Shane's successor as the earl of Tyrone, Turlough O'Neill was known to show favor to the English. If he sent for Meghan, then he might learn that a member of the captured party bore the influential Butler name. If Meghan kept her head, if she realized the importance . . . If, if, if!

Revelin shook his head. Such a small word, and so much hung in the balance against it. Why should Meghan remember his name? If she had been frightened or, worse, raped by an overeager warrior . . .

"Bastard!" he whispered. Somehow, he would find a way to kill any man who dared touch her!

The first light of day brought Meghan awake. It was a terrible awakening, a sudden jolt of awareness that raised her up from her mantle with a pounding heart and her hand on her skean. Someone had screamed. Her eyes moved quickly over the ground she had been unable to see the night before. In the distance she saw tents of myriad sizes and shapes. Closer in, there was nothing, no one, save Ualter, who weighed down her feet in his sleep.

Meghan blinked back the cold sweat that ran into her eyes. Her hands trembled slightly as she reached out to bring the mantle up over her shoulders. Then suddenly darkness swamped her, making her shiver with anticipation. Giving in to the sensation, she stared sightlessly, concentrating on the blackness enveloping her.

The vision did not resolve itself into recognizable images. Vague impressions without shape or form skulked along the edges of her consciousness, like a wolf stalking its prey, something unseen yet feared. The choking sensation at the base of her throat tightened. Never before had she felt so vulnerable.

Never before had a vision remained unknown, left no concrete afterimage of itself, once it overtook her.

The cry rose again, then ended abruptly.

Meghan blinked and the blackness vanished, leaving her staring at Ualter, who rose to his feet with a whimper.

"Revelin!" Meghan sprang to her feet. It was a man's voice that had cried out in agony. She flung off the mantle, unsheathed her skean, and ran toward the settlement.

The camp had been roused by the cries, and Meghan followed the people streaming past the tents toward one end of the clearing. Her feet seemed hardly to touch the ground as she sped past the stragglers. No one even glanced at her, for they were all too eager to join the noisy crowd that had gathered on the grass in the clearing. As she pushed at the wall of men's backs that shielded her view, she wondered what blood sport was taking place. Using her elbows, she fought through the avid throng until a small space opened before her and she spied the hastily erected corral made of branches stripped from the nearby woods.

Inside the enclosure, a herdsman lay face down in the grass; a puddle of blood soaked the sod beneath him. A second man knelt nearby, clutching his torn tunic as blood flowed between his fingers.

"He's bewitched!" Meghan heard the man next to her murmur.

"Aye, 'tis Beltane when like picks like," another muttered and crossed himself. "There's nae a man else will brave it after this!"

Confused by their conversation, Meghan pushed closer and the men parted. Standing in the middle of the corral was a full-grown bull, pure white except for red markings on its ears. Its head was lowered, its strangely light eyes rolled up until the whites showed. The animal trembled as if buffeted by a strong wind and its sides heaved like a bellows.

The wounded man struggled to his feet, his eyes fixed on

the animal as he took a halting step toward the fence. The bull emitted a snort of agitation that sent a shiver along its length, then tossed its head and pawed the ground. Frightened, the man paused.

"Run!" one of the crowd called to him.

"Aye! 'Tis certain we cannot help ye," another added.

Meghan saw the wounded man glance about, his eyes dazed with pain, then he looked back at the bull, which had gored him. "I cannae!" he whispered desperately. "I'm bad hurt!"

A sound like a sigh passed through the crowd but none went to his aid.

Meghan drew back a little and sheathed her blade, relief swamping her. This was not her battle. Revelin was not here.

"Da! Da!"

A boy, no older than three, who had slipped out of his mother's grasp, ducked under the makeshift fence beside Meghan. His mother screamed in alarm and a like cry went up from the crowd, but when she lunged toward the barrier, bystanders grabbed her to keep her from going after the boy.

Before anyone else could react, Meghan leaped the fence. She ran across the space and scooped up the boy toddling toward his wounded father. The bull bellowed its rage at this new invasion of his territory, but Meghan did not pause to look back as she turned toward the fence with the squawling boy in her arms.

The shouts of the crowd were her only warnings that the animal had charged. Her heart lurched as the pounding of hooves neared. The fence was more than an arm's length away. Even if she reached it, she knew, she could not climb the barrier in time. In desperation, she lifted the child and tossed him into the pair of arms stretched across the barrier. As she did, she misstepped, turned her ankle, and went down with a moan of despair. A fraction of a second later, she felt the fetid breath of the deranged bull as he passed over her, his hooves miraculously missing her.

She leaped from the ground as the bull pulled up short and then turned with remarkable agility. From the corner of her eye she saw two men jump the fence at the far side and help the wounded man to safety. Grabbing a sturdy limb that had fallen loose from the corral, she faced the animal. The stench of its sweat filled the air, and she realized it was ill. Perhaps that explained its maddened state. Then all thoughts fled as the animal lowered its head and charged a second time.

For a moment, fear held Meghan immobile. She saw the madness reflected in the small red eyes of the beast bearing down on her and heard the shouts of the people, but her legs would not move. Then, at the last moment, she threw the stick as she flung herself out of the path of the charging bull. The branch landed a glancing blow on the bull's back and the animal veered away, missing her a second time. Crawling on her hands and knees, Meghan reached the fence; then, unexpectedly, she was lifted from the ground by arms that encircled her waist and hauled across the fence like a sack of meal.

"God's foot! Can ye no' mind yer own business?" boomed Colin MacDonald as he set Meghan on her feet.

Her natural shyness forgotten in the extremity of the moment, Meghan clung to him, torn between laughter and tears. "Where were ye, brave Scot, that a mere lass must see to a man's business?"

Colin gaped at her, then his laughter drowned out that of the men about him.

When Meghan realized that she was gripping Colin by his waist, she released him. Immediately she was stunned by a heavy slap on her back.

"There's a braw lassie for ye!" the congratulator exclaimed. "Ye might do worse than learn a thing from her, Colin."

As more laughter ensued, Meghan glanced about and saw that she was surrounded by Colin's red-shanked Scots comrades.

"She were a wee thing, Col, but I'd no' so mind were she

to end me cloistered days," offered a red-haired boy who Meghan guessed could not be more than a year older than she.

She gazed at his grinning face in amazement, and when he reached out and pinched her cheek she gasped softly in astonishment. Automatically her hand moved to her left cheek, where she found the answer to the stranger's friendliness. Her face was smeared with mud from the fall she had taken inside the corral. Her mark must be concealed.

"So much merriment and the feast not yet begun."

At the sound of an Irish brogue, Meghan turned and saw that a giant of a man had joined them. He was dressed in the finest of clothes. A torque of gold encircled his broad neck. His full-sleeved tunic, the color of a buttercup, was belted at the waist to form an elaborate array of pleats that reached to his knees, where supple leather leggings covered his calves and ankles. A short jacket of buttery smooth calfskin topped the tunic, and over all was draped a mantle of the purest yellow, lined in moleskin and with a hood of fox. Meghan knew that only chieftains were allowed to dress in such finery. This must be Turlough Luineach O'Neill, the newly elected O'Neill. Curious, Meghan gazed up into his face.

He was a giant of a man. His head, set on broad shoulders, bore rough features that just missed handsomeness. A great mat of black hair, shot through with the first threads of silver, framed the ruddy complexion of a man fond of *poitin*. There was no need to guess it; the breath he expelled was heavily laden with the aroma of raw whiskey. Beneath black bushy brows, bright blue eyes stared down at her. They were so at odds with the rough bulk of the rest of him that Meghan wondered at their beauty.

"As 'tis the custom on Beltane, my herdsmen were bleeding my animals as an offering to the fairies." There was a twinkle in his fine eyes as he added, "My bull was bent on a wee bloodletting himself. Who are ye, lass, that ye would presume to make him see matters differently?"

His cattle. Meghan swallowed her fear and lowered her eyes. "If 'tis yer beast I struck, then I beg yer pardon, only . . ." She paused, struggling against honesty.

"Come, lass ye've saved a lad and his father as well. Ye're entitled to a say," the huge man encouraged.

Meghan raised her eyes until she spotted a small grease spot on his jerkin about midway up his chest. "I wonder why none came to the wounded man's aid."

The chieftain roared with laughter. "Lass! The herdsmen are but peasants. What matters the loss of a life or two? Why, ere the morrow more than one O'Neill warrior will have breathed his last in the drunken revelry of Beltane. A true O'Neill fears nothing but boredom or disgrace."

A man sidled up to the chieftain, his voice low as his leader bent an ear to his whisperings. After a moment Turlough straightened, his eyes wide with amazement. "They tell that my stud bull is dead, that ye, lass, struck him with an elder twig before he died. The elder twig carries the power of death. Did ye curse him?"

Meghan blanched, the victory of the moment fading behind the specter of accusation. Now someone would remember who she was, and the trouble would begin again. She began to shake, tears of humiliation rising in her eyes. "I—I did nae such a thing!" She turned her head quickly from side to side, looking for escape, then the chieftain's hand came down on her shoulder.

"There's nae need for tears, lass. The great beast was gelded with age and mad with the knowing of it. I concede the loss, for it spared the life of one of my best herders. I've little complaint with the world." He placed a finger under her chin and lifted it. "Besides, a face as pretty as yers was made for smiles."

Meghan steeled herself for his reaction and was amazed when he did not release her. Instead, he grabbed her chin roughly, pinching the tender skin hard between his thumb and forefinger as he turned her left cheek toward him for a better view and wiped away the concealing mud with his free hand.

"Who are ye, lass?" he questioned softly.

"Meghan," she answered in a breathless voice.

"Meghan," he repeated to himself, as if it had a special meaning for him. "Ye're an Ulster lass?"

Meghan cast her eyes down, afraid of the avid blue gaze burrowing into her. He seemed to see too much. "Aye," she answered.

Turlough traced the mark on her skin with a fingertip. His eyes widened briefly when he had wiped away the last of the mud, then his lids shuttered the blaze of recognition. "Who were yer parents?"

Meghan shook her head. Why did the question always arise? "I do not know," she whispered.

Turlough grunted, as if pleased, and released her. "Ye say ye do not know. What would ye be thinking were I to say *I* know?"

Laughter erupted from him as Meghan's mouth fell open. "Well now, I'll not be saying more till Beltane is over. 'Tis nae good to stir winter memories in the springtime of the year." He released her after a pat on her cheek. "I'll be learning first if 'tis true ye're the changeling yer mark claims. Ye killed me bull with an elder branch and yet saved two lives this dawn. The question remains, are ye marked for good or ill?"

Meghan said nothing, for, truly, she did not know.

"Colin MacDonald, find the woman Sila. She'll nae fear the lass. Tell her to scrape the mud from her face and the brambles from her hair," Turlough ordered. His gaze swept down Meghan's tattered shift, pausing on the thrust of her breasts and again on the curves of her hips. "I've a suspicion of what these rags hide and I've a yearning for a lovely lass to dance with about the bonfire." He turned away without another word and Meghan was suddenly alone with Colin.

"Where is Revelin Butler?" Meghan demanded of Colin, for he was never far from her thoughts.

"Ye've a long memory for so wee a lass," Colin answered sourly and reached out to take her by the arm. "Ye'll be seeing the English dogs when Turlough is of a mind. For now, ye're to have the privilege of dressing up proper for our chieftain."

Meghan slanted a look at him. "Are ye nae a Scotsman that ye call an O'Neill yer chief?"

Colin grinned at her, his scarred face more pleasing when set in lines of amusement. "Ye're a saucy lass. Mayhaps at the celebration ye'll learn what rules a Scotsman's head and heart."

Chapter Eight

Meghan could scarcely believe her luck as she squatted naked before the turf fire smoldering in the center of the tiny one-room hut. For the first time in weeks she was clean. Outside, Ualter was tethered to a tree, eating a bowl of porridge for breakfast.

She too had been given a bowl of porridge, and then a large wooden bucket and fern-ash soap with which to wash the mud from her body. The water had been icy cold, but when she had asked to have it heated she had been laughed at.

"Would ye spoil the power of Beltane dew?" the old woman had asked with a chuckle and then disappeared to let Meghan attend to her ablution in peace.

When Colin had taken her away from the camp to a tumbling-down *rath* at the edge of the lough she had begun to suspect that he was not following Turlough O'Neill's order. But, as the chieftain promised, there was an ancient crone named Sila waiting with a smile of welcome.

Meghan wrapped her arms about her knees, hugging them to her chest. Where the heat from the fire did not reach, her damp skin puckered with chill bumps. Her *leine* had been taken away by the old woman, who muttered deprecatingly about its containing lice.

Meghan's mouth tightened. Had she not wanted to please the O'Neill, she would have given the crone a ready answer for the insult. Even the poorest *spailpin,* who might share his home with fleas, abhorred lice.

Meghan rose expectantly to her feet as the old woman re-entered. Sila was bent with age, her spine so curved that her head hung like a lantern from the stem of her neck. The lines of age criss-crossing her face were so numerous that it seemed to Meghan that each must mark a year of the woman's life. At first she had thought the old woman blind. Her eyes had no color but were pearly white like the inside of a clam shell. But Sila could see. Her milky-white gaze was on Meghan now, almost greedily, as she stared openly at Meghan's smooth shoulders, full bosom, and narrow waist.

"Well now, and here I was thinking ye a reedy bit." The woman smiled, revealing dark gums empty but for a single tooth. "Ye've enough flesh on ye to please a lad, and udders to carry plenty of milk for strong sons."

Embarrassed, Meghan crossed her arms before her breasts. "Did ye bring me *leine?*"

The woman's grin deepened. "'Tis no shame to stand as God made ye, lass. 'Tis less a sin that some lad should see ye so on Beltane." Her gaze wandered over the flair of Meghan's hips and then she patted the slight curve of the girl's belly. "A braw lad will plant his seed there this Beltane." She made a sign with her fingers and then nodded. "Sila has the gift. A son before Saint Brigid's Eve."

"I'm not wed," Meghan protested.

Sila grinned at her. "Ye're nae a babe and should know there's ways."

Annoyed by the woman's conversation, Meghan squatted back down on her haunches. Everything in the *rath* was poor, ill kept, and comfortless. Even the fire was too small to heat the hut adequately, but its smoke was accumulating in the ceiling. As her eyes followed her thoughts, Meghan noticed that stuck up in the underthatch were charms fashioned from reeds, straw, and bits of wood. Her gaze followed the slope of the ceiling to the powerful charms of rowan and elder hung over the door. Other charms surrounded a wooden cross hung on one wall. When she had taken it all in, she looked back at Sila with new understanding. "Ye're a *bean feasa,*" she whispered in awe.

"Aren't ye the clever girl?" Sila answered with a chuckle. "Aye, I'm a wise woman and a familiar of the fairies. Ye've nothing to fear in that, lass, for ye've the power, too, I'm thinking."

Meghan shook her head and Sila pursed her lips. "Are ye ashamed to claim yer own? Haven't ye felt it, lass, the power that makes ye tremble?" Sila closed her eyes, lifting her face toward the ceiling. "They're here this day. The fairies come into their own on Beltane. Would ye deny their power saved ye from Turlough's bull?"

The chill that swept Meghan had nothing to do with her damp nakedness. "I—I do not want the gift. I'd rather 'twas done to me than that I should hold power over others."

"Ach!" Sila scoffed, moving a step closer to Meghan. "Would ye now? Ye should know ye've no say in the matter." She shook her finger under the girl's nose. "The fairies choose who is to receive the power of charms. Many have tried and failed. I was nae born to it, but as a girl I heard talk of ways of stealing power from the fairies. One Beltane morn I crawled naked through a fairy briar rooted at both ends and then washed as ye've done with May Day dew." She chuckled as Meghan's startled gaze flew to the bowl of dirty water. "Aye, ye've done that this morn, but 'tis no power in that alone. A body cannot

147

know the charm's took hold till the sign comes upon her."

"Yer eyes," Meghan replied.

"Aye. Near on a trice of years passed ere the sign showed itself." She tapped one eyelid with a long-nailed finger. "The whiter me eyes grew, the stronger me power became. Once a body knows where to look, there's power in water and fire, power in meadow and flower and bog. Folks come to me to trap the thief, to set charms against the wicked, and—"

"See the future?" Meghan supplied eagerly.

"What's that?" Sila reached out suddenly and gripped Meghan's arm. "Can ye tell the future, lass? Ye've the power for *that?*"

Meghan twisted in her grasp, trying to break free, but Sila's nails only dug deeper into her skin.

"Tell me more!" Sila demanded greedily. "What charms do ye use? What are the words?"

With a cry of alarm, Meghan broke free and stumbled back against the wall. "I've no charms! I see things, 'tis all, on account of me mark!"

Sila's gums worked agitatedly behind her sunken lips while her hands flexed and unflexed. Then tears began to spill in thick drops from her eyes and tumble over her seamed cheeks. "Ye've the mark of a changeling. I should have seen yer purpose sooner. Ye're a fairy come to torment a poor mortal on Beltane!"

Before Meghan's apprehensive gaze the old woman prostrated herself on the dirt floor and gripped Meghan by both ankles. "Ach, fairy, would ye hurt one who honors ye? Who took ye into her home when the O'Neill dared not ask it of another? Have I not brought ye May dew to bathe in, and wasn't I just now about to bring ye as fine a gown as ever graced a *Ard Righ's* wife?"

Meghan gazed at the woman in amazement. The bite of Sila's long nails still stung her arms, but Meghan found her lips twitching—unaccountably—in amusement. A moment ago she had trembled as the woman boasted of her magical charms. Now Sila groveled before her in fear greater than her own had been.

"Get up, Sila," she demanded, her voice gusted by laughter. When the woman stirred, an exhilarating feeling swept Meghan. The ability to persuade a person to do her bidding was an altogether novel experience. The O'Neill warriors had been wary but they had not obeyed her. She could not resist the temptation to test this new power over someone. Wrapping her arms tightly about her shivering body, she said firmly, "I want me *leine* back, and the fine mantle ye made away with while I was bathing."

The old woman scrambled to her feet. "Ach! Wasn't I just saying the very same thing to meself. A fine new *leine* for me guest and a new mantle as well. To the O'Neill himself I be going to get it." She waved a placating hand at Meghan. "Just ye sit all warm and toasty by the fire while I fetch them. Don't go away, fairy, I'll be back before ye know I'm gone!"

When Sila had slipped out in hasty retreat, Meghan sighed with gentle laughter and reached for the wooden comb she had been given. She lifted her damp hair forward over her shoulder and dragged the comb through her inky black tresses in long even strokes. When Sila returned she would ask her about Revelin. Perhaps, if she was still eager to please, Sila would take her to him.

An hour later Meghan stood in the center of the tiny *rath* staring down at the garment she wore. It was an ankle-length dress of pure white with gold-thread embroidery at the hem and about the wrists of the long tight sleeves. The garment skimmed her body without blatant display, accentuating the high curves of her breasts and the womanly fullness of her hips.

"A fine sight ye are," Sila exclaimed proudly as though she were responsible for the making. "'Tis a special gown, woven of *ceannabhan mona*."

Meghan touched the bog cotton fabric reverently. Nothing

149

she had ever touched was as smooth and fine. All her life, her clothes had consisted of rough woolens and scratchy linens, serviceable and warm but offering none of the beauty or comfort of this gown. It even had a scent. "It smells of spring," she said in wonder.

"'Twas rolled with wild mint and bog myrtle to keep the moths away. A fine sight ye are, and won't the laddies be bursting their britches for the chance to sire yer babe."

A son before Saint Brigid's Eve. Meghan glanced sideways at the smiling woman. Could Sila really know such things?

"There was a Leinsterman named Butler among the English." Meghan felt her cheeks growing warm under Sila's keen gaze, but she continued. "Will ye be knowing where he's been taken?"

"A Leinsterman," Sila repeated, her speculative glance hard on the girl. "Well now, I'd have had it Colin MacDonald held other ideas, but 'tis a small matter. Even a Leinsterman will hold to the custom of bundling. When ye're showing, 'tis to the priest he should be taking ye. If fairies wed," she added under her breath.

Meghan shook her head. She would never dare hope for a trial marriage to Revelin. He was as handsome as the legendary Fionn, while she was as ugly as a troll. Yet, the thought of coupling with him made her tingle with unknown but insistent urges. The same feelings had crept over her while she spied on John and Flora, sensations so tantalizing that a shudder rippled through her.

"Does the mortal of yer choice elude ye like a salmon does the fisherman's net? There's other ways to catch him." Sila pulled a strip of braided ribbons from beneath her mantle and held it out to Meghan. "'Tis a charm for ye."

Meghan backed away. "I do not like charms. 'Tis magic and wrong."

"Ach!" Sila's cunning gaze widened. "Is that the reason, I'm thinking? Or are ye the fairy I believe ye to be and afraid to touch a holy thing?" She dangled the plait of multicolored ribbons before Meghan as though it were a trophy. "'Twas exposed to the night on Saint Brigid's Eve. What harm could there be in a Christian charm, lass, unless ye will lose yer power by touching a holy thing!"

Meghan hesitated. Her aversion to the charm had nothing to do with fear of its being sacred. She did not want the woman to have a hold over her. Yet, if she refused the gift, Sila would believe that Meghan was other than mortal. Reluctantly, she took the ribbons. "'Tis unlucky to give gifts on Beltane," she murmured.

"Aye. Were it fire or salt or water, ye'd have none of mine. Turlough O'Neill does the giving. Wear it in yer hair, and when the moment comes, tie them about the arm of yer chosen one. 'Twill bind him to ye forever."

"The O'Neill sent this to me?" Meghan asked, surprised that he would think of such a thing. Then she remembered Sila's challenge. This, then, was a test.

Sila nodded. "Ye're a quick one, ye are. He said ye'd know it for the trap it was. But ye've not been frightened away, so I must believe ye're no fairy." Sila's mouth drooped in disappointment. "So wear it in good health, Meghan O'Neill, and God speed to ye."

Meghan regarded the old woman suspiciously. "Why do ye call me O'Neill?"

"Aren't ye such?" Sila answered but her gaze slipped away from Meghan's. "Must be I heard it when Turlough questioned the prisoners."

"Which prisoners?" Meghan asked quickly. "The Englishmen?"

"Aye, that must be it," Sila muttered, but she had turned her back, and Meghan sensed that the old woman was hiding something.

"Was the Leinsterman among them? He's tall, with golden hair and eyes the color of shamrocks."

Sila turned with a smile that showed her tooth. "Aye, the pretty lad. I saw him. Tall and straight as an elm. He'll sire a grand brood of sons out of ye if the O'Neills don't lift that handsome head from his shoulders."

Meghan's mouth went dry. "Would they do such a thing? Why?"

"Yer lad's with the English." Sila spat a long stream of phlegm onto the filthy rushes that carpeted the hut. "In Shane's day they'd not have lived long enough to utter a single prayer once he'd found them. But Turlough's another sort." She shrugged, her head sinking lower between her shoulders.

"Shane was a great man," Meghan ventured as she tied the ribbons in a lock of her hair.

Sila chuckled. "He was not! Shane was a bad, bad man, and not a woman among them would have had it any different! Ask Turlough. He was Shane's tanist and cousin." She added with cunning, "No man knew him better, his deeds and his mysteries."

Sila snorted and grabbed the ribbons from Meghan's unskilled hands. "Give them to me. They'll come up shreds before ye're done with them." She grasped a handful of Meghan's hair near the crown and adeptly wound one end of the plaited ribbons about it, then unbraided the length so that the multi-colored ribbons cascaded down Meghan's back and mingled with her raven locks.

When she was done, Sila stood back with her hands on her hips and squinted at the girl before her. "Aye, ye'll do," she said at last.

"What am I to do?" Meghan indicated her gown. "'Tis clothing fit for royalty. Yet I am a prisoner like the rest."

Sila wiped the end of her nose with a finger before replying. "Turlough will send for ye when he's ready. Till then, ye've my company. There's May flowers, gorse bowers, and buttercups to be gathered before morning. Come."

Meghan followed the stooped woman out onto the bank of

Lough Neagh, carefully lifting her skirt over the rocks and damp places. The swish of the lovely gown and the rustles of ribbons in her hair made her feel almost beautiful. If she dared kneel on the bank and look at her reflection in the lough's surface, would she see a new person? She touched her left cheek and sighed. No, only the clothes had changed. Meghan O'Neill had not.

Revelin sat in the grass beside his three English companions, listening with half an ear to a poet's epic tale. For more than an hour the man's melodic voice had droned on, evoking battle after battle won by the O'Neill clan, while the chieftain and his retinue feasted on trenchers of meat and goblets of wine. Such boastful tales had a long and honored history in Ireland. Even Anglo-Irish lords were not above approving recitations in their honor. But the narrations were often tedious and lengthy . . . and boring.

Near bursting from inactivity and a gnawing anxiety over Meghan's absence from the gathering, Revelin gritted his teeth and waited. The celebration of Beltane had begun. They would not die this day. But where was Meghan? What could they have done with her? His gaze combed the crowd over and over, seeking her, but Meghan was not among the hundreds gathered in the clearing.

Giving up his effort for the moment, he turned his attention to the chieftain's table. Turlough sat at the head, enthroned in an ornate chair of gilded carved wood that would have been more appropriate in the regal dining hall of Whitehall than in this outdoor clearing beside the Lough Neagh. Surrounding him were lesser chieftains and officers of his retinue. They were for the most part warriors, still dressed for battle, and their chain mail winked in the late-afternoon sun.

One man in particular caught Revelin's eye, and he noted that the man, in turn, seemed inordinately interested in him. He was staring openly, contemptuously, and the scar saddling his nose made his face unforgettable. Revelin's eyes narrowed as the Scotsman raised his goblet in mock salute. This was the man who had bludgeoned him into unconsciousness the evening before. He was also the man who John claimed lusted after Meghan. Was he the reason she was absent?

Chafing beneath the burden of his chains, Revelin jerked his arms angrily, then regretted the movement, for the faint jingling of his bonds attracted the chieftain's sharp eye.

Turlough frowned slightly as his gaze met the prisoner's. He had sent for the English captives but was in no great hurry to interrupt the festivities for their sake. Besides, the lass had yet to appear.

"What's the wizard expounding upon?" Robin questioned under his breath as he leaned toward Revelin's ear.

The poet, in his long tunic, flowing white hair, and beard, did indeed look like a pagan wizard of yore, but Revelin knew better. "He introduced himself as one of the brethren of a distant monastery. No doubt he hopes to gain a small stipend for his efforts."

"A facile man with words," Robin murmured thoughtfully. "Perchance his skills are for purchase in other quarters? We could use a barrister's skills in ridding ourselves of these cursed chains. Dammit all, Rev, I've a pressing need for a bush, yet here I sit unable even to open me codpiece!"

Swallowing a laugh, Revelin asked, "Have you seen Meghan?"

"Sorry, Rev. Not a whisker." His voice dropped even lower as he said, "Do you suppose they did away with her? Because of the mark, I mean?"

Revelin shook his head. "The Irish are not as eager as the English to murder witches and sprites." He smiled tolerantly at Robin's astonished look. "They believe there are good people among the fairies. Your head is still securely upon your shoulders. If you've any doubt of the cause, let me enlighten you: Meghan is responsible. Even John reasoned as much. Being discovered in her company is what saved us. I only wish I knew where she was," he added grimly.

Robin looked appalled. "You mean you believe Meghan is a fairy?"

Revelin said levelly, "I do not. But I won't argue with the man who does. I'm beginning to believe Meghan's my talisman." Even as he said her name his eyes began searching for her once more.

The oration ended with cheers and much stomping of feet and hand clapping. The noise grew until the ground seemed to shake beneath them, and then the O'Neill battle cry rose from hundreds of throats.

"God's life!" Robin exclaimed. "I think I hear the voice of Hell."

"'Tis sweet music to an Irishman's ears," Revelin answered absently. Suddenly a new face appeared among the women arrayed behind the chief's table, and the startling beauty of her profile captured Revelin's wandering gaze. She was dressed in a gown of white that offered tantalizing clues to the curves of the young body beneath it. Under the tender teasing of the breeze, her blue-black hair garlanded with bright ribbons flowed softly down her back, the ends switching like a mare's tail in the wind.

Revelin's scalp tingled for a scant second before she turned toward him and he saw the blood-red rose shadowing the high ridge of her soft cheek. "Meghan," he whispered. She was alive, and well, and beautiful! The sight gave him a jolt of pure joy.

He did not realize he had risen from the grass until he found his way suddenly barred by a six-foot ax swung across his path. He tried to shoulder past, but his hands were bound behind his back and he was easily and ignobly brought up short by a jerk on the chain that linked his wrists.

"Where do ye think ye're going?" the warrior said with a chuckle. "Mine yer manners, lad. Ye've not been called for."

Revelin lifted his head to answer the insult in kind, but then his eyes met Meghan's across the short distance. She was staring at him with wide eyes. Faintly embarrassed by his humiliating position, he felt his cheeks grow warm. The feeling vanished as he realized that she was struggling to free herself. The reason for it thinned his lips with anger. The Scotsman held her by the wrist. As Revelin watched, Meghan turned to the burly, red-bearded Scotsman and spoke. The man released her at once, and she quickly rounded the table and ran toward Revelin. Joy made her face radiant as she crossed the open ground. Every man who saw her responded to her beauty and envied the dirty, mire-spattered Anglo-Irishman who had attracted her attention.

Revelin watched her too, wishing that he had better availed himself of the lake water he had been given in which to rinse his face and hands before being brought into the presence of Turlough O'Neill. He smelled of the bog and his own sour sweat, while in her white gown she appeared as pure as newfallen snow.

Undismayed by his mud-caked clothes and fulsome aroma, Meghan saw only that he was alive and sound. "Revelin," she said softly, reaching out to touch his face. Her brows lifted as her palm encountered dark golden stubble. "Why, ye've grown a beard!" she exclaimed, as if it were something miraculous.

A feeling of fierce tenderness unlike any he had ever experienced gripped Revelin as looked down into her artless blue gaze. He had spent a few hellish hours wondering what tortures she might have been put to at the hands of some lusty Celt. Yet, here she was smiling shyly up at him, smelling of heather and wild mint and . . . No! It was too dangerous to display vulnerability between them. Instinctively he took a step back, breaking their contact.

Meghan reached for him again, but the look in his eyes halted her fingers a scant distance from his face. It did not show in the arrangement of his features, but she saw in his eyes a reprimand. She recoiled, her hand falling to her side as she backed away a step.

Revelin raised his eyes abruptly to look at Turlough O'Neill, but he could not tell how much the man had guessed from Meghan's actions. He sat easily in his chair, one heavy leg thrown over the arm rest, a gold goblet brimming with wine in one hand. He reminded Revelin of Bacchus, the Greek god of wine. With a slight bow, Revelin addressed the chieftain by his English title: "My lord, earl of Tyrone. A word?"

Turlough did not respond at once. He had missed nothing. He had enjoyed the touching scene between the girl and his prisoner. Quite like a play it had been, with the lass near weeping with joy upon the sight of her lost love. He smiled benignly as his wine-mellowed gaze moved over Meghan's womanly form. Just as he had suspected, she was bonny, despite her blemish. He liked the lass, that he did. It was fitting that she should show a womanly concern for her man's welfare. It was fitting, too, that the man should spurn her maidenly display in public; he did not seem to be the weakling that MacDonald had claimed.

His heavy-lidded gaze swung to Colin, and he was surprised to see anger and jealousy in the highlander's face. Colin's eyes were fixed on Meghan's back and his hands were clenched in tight fists. Turlough pursed his lips. The lass had made another conquest, it seemed.

Colin was one of his best soldiers, Turlough mused, a captain of his MacDonald *galloglaighs* and a man whose loyalty was to be courted. The girl herself seemed smitten with the Anglo-Irishman, while he . . . ? Turlough's long mouth twitched. The evening's entertainment had just begun. He would do nothing to spoil it. But in the end he would decide the girl's fate.

"Release the Irishman," Turlough ordered.

While Revelin's chains were being struck, Meghan stood a little apart. He had made it clear in a single glance that he did not want her near him. Even when he was freed he averted his eyes as the guards escorted him past her. Meghan blinked to keep from spilling the tears that suddenly welled in her eyes. She had been so proud and felt so beautiful when she had spotted his soft green eyes upon her. She could not have mistaken that look. It had beckoned to her and she had responded. Why, then, had he drawn back?

From the corner of her eye she saw Sila coming toward her. The old woman pointed to her head, then gestured at Meghan and winked. Meghan reached up and touched the ribbon streamer. The charm by which to catch a lover. She snatched her hand away. She would not use a charm to trap Revelin's affections.

Sila took her by the arm, saying, "Dinna fret, lass. There'll be another, better time."

Meghan did not answer but she allowed Sila to lead her back to the chieftain's table. Naturally shy, she lowered her head as she slipped into a vacant seat between two clansmen.

"Lift yer head, Turlough watches," Sila muttered. When Meghan did not respond immediately, she pinched her arm hard. Meghan raised her head, anger rushing color into her cheeks, and Sila nodded approvingly. "Better. Childish ways have nae place here."

Meghan glanced once around the table until her eyes came to rest on Revelin, who stood on Turlough's right.

Turlough thoroughly studied the prisoner before him. Certainly the lad's handsome face would have a softening effect on any woman's heart. Well, he was no cloistered virgin and it would take more than a fair face to turn his head. He smiled beguilingly at his prisoner. "Who are ye, lad?"

"Revelin Butler of Kilkenny," Revelin answered promptly.

"And of London," Turlough added with a pointed look at Revelin's English attire. "Yer Gaelic is not as smooth as a true Leinsterman's. Ye've idled too long at the English court of the bastard queen."

It was a direct, deliberate insult to his sovereign and Revelin knew he was bound by his loyalty to Elizabeth to defend her. Honor demanded it. Pride demanded it. "You've a curious lack of regard for a gentlewoman's reputation, my lord. One might think you an ignorant damned Irishman, were it not for the fact your wit is well known."

Humor flickered in Turlough's gaze though it did not color his voice. "Ye think yerself clever. Are ye clever enough to evade the noose I've strung for ye?" His gaze shifted to a nearby tree and Revelin's followed. No rope had hung there a minute earlier. Now a noose swung in the wind; a grinning Colin MacDonald held the free end.

A small smile bloomed on Revelin's lips. The tactic did not dismay him. The Irish had no claim on intimidation. The question of how far the provocation would go concerned him more. If he was not more than clever, he might find himself challenged to mortal combat as part of the evening's entertainment. "'Tis known far and wide that my uncle, the earl of Ormond, holds you in respect. I would be loath to be the cause of dissension between you."

Turlough sat up straighter in his chair before he could stop himself. In an attempt to cover his move, he reached for the jewel-encrusted skean that lay conspicuously beside his trencher and eased slowly back into his slouch.

So this young whelp was the earl of Ormond's nephew! He had guessed there was some connection when he had heard the name Butler. Of course, he could not have known that the lad was close kin. Thomas Butler's reach was long and powerful. If one of his household had ventured into Ulster, there must be a reason other than the set of skillfully drawn maps they had found among the prisoner's belongings. Turlough would learn it, in time. But first the lad's metal should be tested further. "Tell me true, lad. Are ye not one of Ormond's by-blows?"

Good, Revelin thought; the O'Neill had backed away from

talk of a hanging. "Though it might endear me to you, my lord, I cannot call my mother whore. She was born Katherine O'Conner and became Lady Butler upon her vows."

Turlough popped a chunk of meat into his mouth and chewed thoughtfully. So a Butler had had the temerity to marry a full-blooded Irish lass despite the fact it was forbidden by English law for Anglo-Irish lords to marry the native Irish, no matter what their noble bloodlines. He relaxed a little and smiled. Three hundred years in Ireland had done more than change the Norman name Le Boitiler into the Irish name Butler; it had made them proud of their adopted homeland and perhaps more Irish in their views of the world than they realized.

"What brings ye to Ulster?" Turlough pointed a thick finger at Meghan and added, "And do not say 'tis on account of the lass."

Revelin deliberately kept his eyes from Meghan. He had Turlough's attention and he knew he must keep it. "You're right, of course, my lord. A man does not risk his neck for a spot to piss or to couple. They are but calls of the natural man and are easily accommodated to circumstance. But there are other matters which can make the difference between what has gone before and what may never be again."

Turlough grunted. "Ye speak riddles, Butler. Speak plain or I'll have the short truth choked from ye."

Revelin turned his head to where Reade, Neville, and Atholl sat chained together, then deliberately turned back to the chieftain. "Eventide approaches, my lord, and yet not every man is sympathetic to tradition."

"More riddles!" Turlough grumbled, but he had understood Butler's message. Privacy was needed before they continued their interview. He rose and waved the men's guard away. "Release the English but keep a wary eye on them. I'll have the heads of the lot of ye if even one escapes this night. Ye, there," he continued, pointing at a warrior who sat beside Meghan, "yield yer seat to our Leinster guest."

He looked pointedly at Meghan and then at Butler. "Ye've the hospitality of the O'Neills for a night, Butler. Use it well."

Revelin regarded the table with conflicting feelings of relief and chagrin, relief because he had passed some arbitrary testing and deep embarrassment because of his filth among the finery. His nostrils stung with his own stink. Instead of seating himself, he disregarded every rational reason to the contrary and spoke. "I would ask a favor, my lord."

Mellowed by the greater part of the third bottle of wine, Turlough nodded in paternal indulgence. "Name it."

"I do not reject your hospitality but I would prefer to bathe before joining those at your table." He hesitated. He was no diplomat; he had no patience for it. Diplomacy was for elderly men with slow heartbeats and seasoned minds. Yet his next request must be delicately handled or he would insult the O'Neills. "I carried clothing in my saddlebags. If 'tis possible, I would make use of them."

Turlough grinned at him. "Ye've nae cause to fret, lad. The womenfolk are fair to tripping over their skirts for a glimpse of ye." He leaned forward with a leer. "They care not so much for the garments ye stand in but how well ye stand stripped of them!"

The jibe at his expense and the accompanying laughter pleased Revelin, for the chieftain had not taken his request amiss.

Collaring a servant who was passing by, Turlough said, "Give the man what he needs." To Revelin he said, "Yer English friends had little of value, to my mind." He glanced down at the table and smiled as his eyes lit upon the skean lying there and added cryptically, "Only one will answer for what he possessed."

When Revelin had gone, Meghan glanced anxiously at the faces ringing the table. Most of them were unknown to her. When Colin took the empty place beside her, she smiled gratefully. Here was one who did not shy from her.

"'Tis a lovely sight, ye are, lass." He grinned at her and reached for her hand. "Jealous the lot of them are, for 'tis Colin MacDonald who'll take all yer dances."

Meghan's eyes widened. "Dance?"

"Aye, dancing, lass. There's nothing so fine as a swirl of the pipes to lift a man's spirits, unless it be the smile of a bonny lass." His hand tightened over hers. "Me day would be complete this very minute if ye'd favor me with one of yer smiles."

Somewhere deep within her, the woman who had yet to live stirred. The gown she wore made her feel beautiful for the first time in her life. Yet, Revelin had rejected her, and she was sorely in need of a man's approval.

Why should I not smile at Colin? she thought stubbornly. But the wicked light in his laughing blue eyes made her slip her hand from his and reach for her meal. She felt as if she did not know herself. One moment she choked on tears, the next she longed desperately to be admired. But there was only one man's admiration she sought, and he had spurned her.

Evening passed quickly into nightfall as the revelry grew louder and more raucous. Wine and whiskey flowed freely. It was the beginning of the summer, when milk and butter and cheese would be plentiful. No man, woman, or child must go without this day, or, legend had it, they would starve come winter.

There was little protocol among the O'Neills. No rank or order formalized the festivities. Every man held his head high and met his neighbor's eye squarely, for each was considered as good as the next because he was blood kin of the O'Neills.

How wonderful it must be to be a part of so great a family, Meghan thought enviously as the evening progressed. Perhaps here, at last, she would be accepted.

Often her gaze strayed to the head of the table where Turlough carried on a steady stream of conversation, eating, and drinking. He had hinted that he knew something of her parents. When would he tell her?

Now he looked up and met her gaze and paused. She held her breath, waiting for him to speak. Instead he reached for the jeweled skean on the table before him and turned it over thoughtfully in his hand.

"Do ye know this, lass?" he questioned after a long moment. "The Butler lad had it in his possession."

Meghan looked at the beautiful gold work of the hilt with its crystal stones and shook her head. "I've nae seen it before."

Turlough knitted his brows. If the girl did not recognize it, he might be wrong—or she might have her reasons for lying. He lay the blade down and pushed his wine goblet toward her. "Ye're not drinking, lass. 'Tis Beltane. Ye must put the warmth of spring in yer veins!"

Meghan took the cup and tasted a little of the dark red liquid.

Turlough nodded. "Finish it. The night has just begun and the wine will bind ye against a chill." And perhaps it would loosen her tongue, he thought.

But Meghan had less and less to say as the hours passed. When Revelin appeared among them again, he was quickly spirited away by Turlough for a game of chess near the center of camp, where the King-Candle burned brightly. She noticed the Englishmen's silent but wary interest in Revelin's conversation, but, though they had been freed of their shackles, they were kept apart from the gathering by the O'Neill warriors.

When she had eaten and drunk all she could hold, Meghan left the table and went to find a patch of mossy ground near where people were laying a bonfire. It was quieter there, and the evening air was a welcome change from the noise and heat. Stretching out on her stomach, she propped her elbows on the ground and dropped her chin into her hands. Soon the music began. Above the clamor of the crowd the drone of bagpipes came to life. After that the clear notes of a flute joined in. Last came the fluid melody of a great harp. The tune was old and familiar and she hummed along.

The sensation of wine was new to her. The warmth of it hummed in her veins, as the music hummed on her lips. She glanced up at the night sky liberally sprinkled with stars and felt as giddy and light as the single silver-edged cloud racing across the midnight-blue expanse.

"Will ye dance, lass?"

Colin looked down at her, his hand extended in offer.

Meghan grinned up at him but shook her head. "I dinna know how."

"Is that all?" Before she could move, Colin bent over, clamped a hand on either side of her waist, and lifted her from the ground. "I'll show ye the way. The steps are easy!"

Propelled along by his insistent hand at her back, Meghan was soon in the middle of the dancing. His hand again found her waist and she was swept up in his embrace, her feet barely touching the ground as he swung her around the huge bonfire that had been lit on the summit of a nearby rise.

"That's it, lassie! That's me lass!" he cried as Meghan tried to match her short strides to his long ones. As he smiled down at her, his face was as ruddy as the flames and his breath told her that more than the fire's glow flushed his features. Like all the company, he had drunk a healthy share of whiskey, and the liquor was calling a tune of its own for his body.

The music changed, and became a wild country dance with much squealing of pipes and pounding of drums. Faster and faster, the tempo gained speed until Meghan threw her arms about the Scotsman's neck to keep her balance.

Far from being frightened, she rejoiced in the measure. The music filled her heart, pumping furiously to keep the rhythm of her feet. She tasted the joy of her own movement, the flow of her body to the insistent rhythm of life. When the music ended, the other dancers began leaping across the fire's licking flames, and she was seized with a desire to join them. The desire seemed to answer some wild, wanton streak in her spirit that had too often been suppressed.

"Wait a bit, lass," Colin cautioned, holding her back with a hand on her waist. "There's more to come."

Pausing reluctantly to catch her breath, Meghan soon understood why Colin detained her. A man suddenly appeared from the edge of the campsite bearing a pole. Mounted on the pole was a straw doll dressed in a fantastic gown made of ribbons and mayflowers and straw. Close behind her came a peasant man and a woman similarly dressed in brightly colored garments laced with straw and flowers. The music began again as the crowd made way for the procession, and Colin leaned down and whispered in her ear, "'Tis the May Baby and her family."

Fascinated, Meghan strained forward as the press of people closed in around her. Sensing her frustration, Colin shoved aside those nearest to her so that she had an unobstructed view.

Once the procession entered the circle around the bonfire, the couple began to dance together, but it was unlike anything Meghan had ever seen. They twirled together and then apart, the woman thrusting her hips forward and jiggling them and then the man doing the same until finally they clasped each other and rubbed their loins together in a bawdy parody of coupling. It was a custom originating in pagan antiquity, a ceremony meant to promote fruitfulness of the land and of the community.

Meghan felt her face growing warm as she watched, remembering how a few days earlier she had watched a man and woman couple in earnest. The sensations sweeping her were the same as had gripped her then, and the wondrous and frightening feelings were bound up in one thought: *Revelin*.

She did not so much see him as feel him approach. When she turned her head she was not surprised to find Revelin by her side. Somehow she had known he would be there. The jostling, laughing crowd had separated her from Colin as she pressed forward so as not to miss a moment of the show.

The hand that slipped into hers was Revelin's. The insistent pressure he applied drew her willingly from the front of the crowd. No one seemed to notice them as they faded back to the rear. No heads turned in their direction as they hurried silently toward privacy and the lough.

Chapter Nine

Revelin did not stop to think of what he was doing in dragging Meghan away from the celebration. Once he had bathed and changed into clean hose and doublet, he thought he was rid of the fever that raged in his loins and heart. But he was wrong. The moment he returned to the celebration from his very enlightening conversation with Turlough and found Meghan laughing and dancing in the arms of the Scotsman, the wildfire of jealousy consumed him.

The wanton tune that flushed her face had quickened his pulse as his eyes followed her around and around the circle of her admirers. She was oblivious to the knowing grins and snickers of the clansmen and the looks of disapproval on the faces of some of the older women. She moved to the music as if she directed the measure rather than the other way around. Her skirts flew higher and higher as the Scotsman whirled her about, revealing more and more of her shapely legs until Revelin had thought he must steal her away or go mad.

Completely oblivious of the effect she had had on the man

beside her, Meghan had ceased to think at all. Everything was feeling. As the rhythm of her heart kept pace with the dwindling beat of the drums, she seemed to soar, becoming more a part of the clouds racing past the stars than of the earth below. She belonged to the wild country surrounding her. Her soul was one with the night wind that rushed through the dark hills and stirred the purple waters of the lough. She felt brave and reckless and exultant. If not for the anchor of Revelin's hand upon hers, she thought she would simply float away.

But Revelin's hand was on hers, holding so tightly that her fingers ached as he led her to the forest's center. She did not care. The pulsing inside her seemed to have a life of its own and it urged her to recklessness. Wherever he led her she would go—gladly.

Meghan's laughter fell gently on Revelin's ears. He felt the elation, too. The joy came from within Meghan and he wanted to be a part of it.

He stopped so suddenly that Meghan collided with him, her face muffled a moment in the hollow between his shoulder blades. And then he was turning to her, steadying her with warm firm hands on her shoulders. Under the night sky his face was dark and hard, but his touch was infinitely tender as his hands moved up the slope from her shoulders to ride the curve at either side of her neck. When he spoke, his voice was deep and hushed. The words seem to drift into her mind. "Did I hurt ye, lass?"

The Gaelic inflection rippled through her, and pain was not what Meghan felt. But how to explain the vibrant sweetness spreading through her? She reached up and laid a hand on either side of his face. "Ye've shaved!"

Revelin smiled; she could feel the bowing of his cheeks against her hands. "Aye. Do you mind?"

Meghan shook her head. "Ye're so lovely to look at it makes a body ache," she whispered shyly.

"Ah, Meghan." Revelin sighed and lowered his head until his lips rested lightly upon her forehead.

Her skin was like cool fire. He turned his head, letting his lips roam the flower-petal softness of her brow and cheeks. He had not meant to touch her, only to save her from the lust of the Scotsman. But she was so sweet, so soft, and the rapid thread of her pulse under his lips was not to be resisted. Just a kiss, he told himself. He would be content with a single kiss.

The shock of his mouth on hers lasted only a moment. His breath was hot, his mouth a furnace upon her tender skin, and then her mouth blossomed under his, offering heat for heat, kiss for kiss, pleasure for pleasure.

The darkness wrapped them in its intimacy as he cupped her shoulders and drew her lightly against him. Meghan clasped her arms about his neck and closed her eyes, giving up the world beyond his tall, strong body. Whatever it was he wanted of her, she wanted him to have it.

She was sweet, so sweet, Revelin thought as his kiss deepened and the velvet rough tip of his tongue moved to teach her another pleasure. She was warm and softly delicious, her trembling mouth more enticing than any lips he had ever kissed. He felt he could devour her, inhale her until her every essence became part of him. Just a little more, he told himself, just a little more. Then he would stop.

Meghan sighed, the wine in her veins distilling under the heat of Revelin's kisses into a richer, more potent brew. She was filling with the heady infusion, becoming like a berry that had basked in the sun until its pulp swelled with sugary sweetness. What was happening? What was this ripeness near bursting within her?

Her movements were unconscious, born of instinct and the guilty pleasure she had derived from watching the May Day dancers. She pressed herself along his long muscular length, her hips swaying lightly into his groin. She heard his breath catch, and his hands stilled their gentle roaming of her from neck to waist.

Revelin raised his head, arching his neck until he gazed up

at the star-dusted sky. A deep shivering began within him, riding the muscles of his stomach from ribs to groin and back. This was madness, this touching, this longing that tightened and tautened him, urging him on to the brink of forbidden desire. He must stop. Now. No more. Not even a kiss.

The touch of fingertips against the front of his doublet did not seem real. Even as the fastenings gave way before her shy touch he could not believe it was happening. He was dreaming; he wanted this so badly he had gone mad.

The night air against his bare chest did not surprise him. Of course, he had imagined this . . . and much more. It was a guilty pleasure he had kept locked in his dreams from the first night Meghan had shared his camp. For it could not be.

When her light, spidery fingertips brushed his naked belly, he shut his eyes; when her fingers found the shape of his maleness swollen and engorged within his hose, a groan of pure agony escaped him.

"It does grow!" he heard her whisper in awed tones, and he began to shake with silent laughter. Lord! She was a witch! No wonder peasants feared her! He should fear her himself, for he knew then he would not stop, would not be satisfied with just a little more.

His hands slipped down her back, molding the shapely arch of her spine beneath the fine cotton of her gown until he reached the top of her swelling hips. His fingers fanned out, questing the soft curves of her buttocks as he scooped her up and held her hard against the throbbing in his loins.

For a moment neither of them moved. Suddenly he was afraid for her. He could have her and he knew it, but he did not want to be her seducer.

"Meghan!" he murmured in a thickened brogue. "Meghan, you should run away. I should nae touch you, but, darling, I want this so!"

Meghan could not catch her breath. She was all sensation of touch and sound and smell. "Ye smell of the woods," she answered, brushing her cheek against his smoothly muscled chest. "Ye make me burn like there's coals in me middle, Revelin."

It was the first time she had called him by name, and the peculiar lilt of her womanly voice gave the syllables the power of a lover's caress.

Suddenly there were two bodies sharing a single, insistent need. Her hands plucked awkwardly at the lacing that held his hose closed over his hips, while Revelin impatiently gathered her full skirts with his hands, raising the hem until only the cool forest air caressed her naked thighs. Then his hose opened under her fingers and she caught him, heavy and erect, in her trembling hands.

Revelin clasped her to him, his hands curving under her naked hips to lift her completely off the ground. With a deep sensuous chuckle he said, "Nae more words, lass. We shall nae need them."

He carried her to a mossy place beneath a tree. Using his body as a cushion against the hard ground, he pulled her over him until they lay breast to breast. Once more he raised her skirts, his hands stroking the backs of her thighs; the fine silk teased his fingertips. The motion slowed as he reached the top of her thighs and his fingers curled down between her legs, pulling them slightly apart. As one hand rose over the globe of a buttock, the other gently worked its path inward until he touched the center of her feminine flesh.

He expected her to gasp, and lifted his head to catch the surprised shape of her mouth with his in a heavy, drugging kiss.

Meghan gasped repeatedly against his mouth, half-sobs of unbearable delight. He had found a place of pleasure she had not known existed, and it was too much. Her tender, overripe flesh seemed about to burst. She was oozing like a ripe berry. She felt it against her thighs as his fingers worked in and out.

Through the heavy veiling of sensual pleasure Revelin heard

her wondrous cries. She was so sweet, a sweet and innocent wanton whose honeyed delights were for him alone. After he'd stripped her of her gown, he buried his face in the deep cleft between her breasts and breathed deeply of her scent. In that moment he knew it was a smell he would never forget or ever get enough of.

Meghan cried out when he caught the tip of one breast in his lips. Too many sensations were happening all at once. His touch was everywhere, inside and out, on her breasts, her thighs, her belly. And then she was beneath him, his hot hard flesh blanketing her cool trembling body. She thought she would be crushed as his weight sank into her, but she was not. There was a strength in her she had not guessed. His weight became a comfort, a shield, a bearer of indescribable joy. When his hand brushed her thighs she parted them willingly, offering her body up to any whim of his desire.

The moment when it came held no disappointment. The violence done to her body lasted no longer than it took her to realize it. Then his hands and lips were smoothing, gentling away the pain, begging forgiveness, promising a return of sweet pleasure. The slow, heavy hammering of her heart matched the rhythm of his hips as he moved on her, surely, steadily, powerfully.

The pleasure came back and with it a redoubling of the drumlike tension in her lower belly. He was there, Revelin moved there inside her, stroking and stroking until it became too much and the tension burst into shuddering ripples of pleasure.

Her cry of joy was little more than an expulsion of breath into Revelin's mouth, and he tasted her passion with grateful delight until the surge of his own body overcame him and he, too, burst with the ripened promise of life.

Revelin kept watch while Meghan slept in his lap. She was curled against him, her head on his shoulder and her legs under her gown tucked up against his thigh. In the distance the bonfires continued to burn while music drifted through the night. Yet he was barely aware of the passage of time or even of the cold that chased ripples across his exposed skin. He was recalling the last minutes in rapt amazement.

Ye've a great heart in ye, Revelin, me lad. But ye dinna think on the consequences!

His grandfather's words came clearly to mind and Revelin's mouth twisted wryly. That was true. He had little patience with carefully measured plans. If he had been a little more calculating this night, he would not have succumbed so easily to his desire for conquest. There were a dozen young women in camp he could have eased himself with. Turlough had offered to find him a woman for the night.

How easily he had been led by his own jealousy and lust. Perhaps Turlough's mention of Meghan as a bonny lass who had drawn the eye of more than one clansman had determined his action. He had defended her honor and reminded the chieftain that he was Meghan's guardian and would kill any man who dishonored her. Turlough had smiled tolerantly and offered the opinion that Colin MacDonald was a worthy adversary.

Revelin sighed and tenderly kissed Meghan's brow. How amused Turlough would be if he could see them now. When the conversation had turned to England and the traitorous topic of open rebellion by the Irish, he had not been able to concentrate as well as he would have liked. Later, when he had found Meghan dancing with Colin, he forgot that he had come back to the festivities to tell Robin and the others they were free to leave with the dawn. He had even forgotten the lie that had come to mind to cover the reason for their release. He had forgotten "Black Tom's" urgent need for the information now in his possession. He had even forgotten Alison.

Meghan stretched in his arms with a kittenlike yawn before she settled down again. Revelin stroked her hair. Even now, with his carefully laid plans in a shambles, just touching her stirred him deeply. If not for the fear that they would be discovered, he would have made love to her again. He wanted her again, wanted to feel the fierce sweetness of her ecstasy.

Instead he felt the first pangs of guilt. He had betrayed Alison. Though they had never made love and were not officially engaged, they had an understanding that they would be when he returned to England.

And there was Meghan's virtue. The sane, rational part of his mind flayed him for the seduction. But the sane part had never ruled his tender emotions. She had been as eager as he. Despite himself, a smile rose to his lips. He had pleased her. There was no pretense in Meghan. And she had pleased him, more than pleased him. In giving herself she had left a little of herself behind. He felt it now, warm and sweet in his heart.

"What is your secret, Meghan?" he whispered against her hair, though he knew she slept and would not answer. "Who are you?"

John Reade leaned back against the trunk in a shadowy recess of an alder tree and contemplated the scene before him. When Butler and the girl had sneaked away he had followed, hoping to make his escape with them. He had not expected to be followed himself.

He clasped his thick palms together and squeezed, feeling the power of his hands. It had not been easy to strangle the O'Neill warrior barehanded. God's death! He had thought the man would never ease thrashing about. Even when blood erupted from his nose and mouth, the man had continued to struggle. Reade had sweated every moment in expectation of discovery. But no one had heard them.

Reade grinned as his eye caught the movement of his prey. His dalliance with the soldier had lost him a goodly part of the entertainment taking place on the lake bank . . . but not all. He had thought them escaping, but they had merely run away to take their pleasure of each other.

Reade licked his lips. The girl had been lovely to watch, her body like a white flame against the darkness of the night. She had fed his unquenchable fire without knowing it. Her muffled love cries had built a pulsing tugging in his own loins, which he had finally relieved in envy onto the ground while watching Revelin pump his seed into her unresisting warmth.

"Next time," he whispered to himself. Next time she would pleasure *him*. He could already imagine his own satisfaction echoed in Revelin's moan of fulfillment.

He grinned as he watched Revelin rise now and lift the sleeping girl into his arms. He had underestimated young Butler. The lad had pleasured the girl before reaching his own climax. It was a talent often lacking in a young buck, yet one a smart man used to his advantage. Yet, Butler did not impress him as a man who would indulge the weaknesses of others for his own gain. Only a man subject to sentimentality would sit on the cold ground this past hour while the girl slept instead of leaving her for the warmth of the bonfire. Butler's weakness was the girl. Perhaps he had fallen in love with her. It was something for Reade to remember and use when the moment presented itself.

When the pair disappeared along the lake bank, Reade did not follow. They were not escaping and he had had enough of playing the Peeping Tom. There was work to be done. Someone in this cursed place must speak English, someone who could be bribed to tell him what had been arranged between Butler and that sot Turlough. The corners of Reade's mouth lifted. "Flora!"

"Where the devil have you been?" Robin grabbed Revelin's sleeve as he was about to pass by with Ualter trotting patiently at his heels.

Revelin turned a bemused face to Robin, who was crouching in the brushes near the camp. "Ah, Sir Robin! You are keeping well, I trust?"

"Rev! You're drunk!" Robin said in frank disgust.

"Aye, that I am, friend," Revelin agreed as he squatted down and placed a companionable arm about the smaller man's shoulders. "I've drunk from Eros' fountain," he confided in a slurred whisper and leaned against his friend.

Robin shrugged off Revelin's weight. "Listen to me! There's trouble! I found something. I think—"

"There he is! Grab him!"

A party of four O'Neill warriors had broken from a spur of dense woods and were running toward them, their swords bared. "Holy Mother!" Not needing an understanding of Gaelic to realize what he had seen, Robin leaped to his feet and sprinted away.

More slowly Revelin came to his feet. "Wait! Robin! Give over, man!" He grabbed Ualter by the scruff of the neck to keep him from charging after the nobleman.

As the warriors ran past, it suddenly dawned on Revelin that Robin was being hunted by the O'Neills. Was it some new game invented by the warriors to while away the hours? Revelin closed his eyes slowly and then reopened them, the light seeming brighter, his mind clearer. Whatever was happening, Robin was a fool to run. Flight was dangerous and useless.

Revelin's hand went automatically for the hilt of his sword, but it no longer hung from his belt. Even his scabbard was missing.

Robin shrieked when the first warrior to catch up with him grabbed him by the collar. The cry ended abruptly as he pitched forward onto the ground.

Without considering the foolhardiness of his action, Revelin ran toward them, the Butler battle cry erupting from his lungs as he charged with Ualter at his heels.

Belatedly he realized that the warriors could, and might well have, killed him. Even Ualter was no match for a drawn blade wielded by a seasoned campaigner. Instead, the clansmen looked up in easy surprise. An unarmed man was a novelty they could not resist. They turned to face him, their sword tips resting quietly against the ground. As he neared them, Revelin slowed his pace and called Ualter back with a single command. He paused a few feet from the men.

"Is he dead?" He indicated Robin.

The men snickered, and the one nearest contemptuously poked Robin's middle with his foot. "He's nae dead, he's swooned like a lassie in the arms of her first lover."

Revelin smiled in spite of himself. Poor Robin. "Then you'll let him go? He's hardly worthy of the hunt."

"That we'll not," came the prompt reply. "The English bastard murdered a man while trying to escape. We found him standing over the body back there."

Revelin glanced in the direction the man indicated. It was very near the place where he and Meghan had spent the better part of the night. "Because a man is dead, it doesn't follow that he was murdered."

Two clansmen reached for Robin and lifted him to his feet by a grip on each arm. "'Tis not for us to say what happened. He'll be answering to Turlough O'Neill."

Revelin let the matter drop and fell into step behind the men dragging Robin back to camp, satisfied that Robin had not been killed outright. If they sought Turlough's opinion, it would be some time before the matter was settled.

He had spent the predawn hours in Turlough's tent steadily drinking and gaming. Never before had he met a man with Turlough's stamina. The chieftain had consumed enough *uisce beatha* to kill most men, but it was not until he had finally succumbed to the effect of imbibing that much whiskey, a quarter of an hour ago, that Revelin had felt free to leave his host's presence. Turlough would no doubt be dead to the world for hours to come.

Revelin belched. His head spun dizzily and his stomach seemed unusually close to his throat. He reached out and patted Ualter's massive head. He had missed the beast and feared him dead or lying wounded in the woods, but other, more pressing concerns had kept him from asking about his missing pet. Yet, when he had seen him tethered outside the old crone's hut when he deposited Meghan there, he had laughed like a boy and thrown his arms about the great dog's neck. He did not even mind that Ualter had chosen to guard Meghan over himself.

Meghan. Just the sound of her name made his senses sharpen. He glanced down at the bright band of ribbon tied around his upper arm. Against the dark green velvet of his doublet the colors seemed especially fresh and cheerful. Meghan had snatched them from her hair and placed them about his arm just before he had left her. He had not known what to say, nor had she. They had parted without words. He was grateful for that. He needed time to determine what he should do next. But first this accusation against Robin must be handled.

The morning was cool and misty. Against the encroaching dawn the dying bonfires were reduced to embers of orange and red. The revelers were asleep now, most of them snoring in peaceful slumber where they had dropped on the open ground from exhaustion. Only a few dogs raised their heads curiously as the clansmen and Revelin passed through the center of the camp. The O'Neills slept secure in their own land.

Revelin was not surprised when the clansmen approached Turlough's tent and one of them entered, but he was astonished when Turlough appeared a few moments later. He stood firmly supported on his tree-trunk legs, his black hair and beard in snarls about his grim face. "Where's the English dog?"

Robin, who had been dumped before the tent, raised his head as consciousness reclaimed him. Revelin tensed as Turlough stepped outside. The chieftain's angry, red-rimmed eyes rested a long moment on the smaller man, then moved to Revelin. "Ah, Butler! They tell me yer English friend has killed one of me warriors. Ask him if 'tis true."

Revelin nodded and turned to Robin, who was struggling to his knees.

Robin gripped Revelin's arm with clawing fingers, gasping, "What's wrong? What am I accused of?"

"Gently, Robin," he encouraged, slipping a hand under Robin's arm to help him to his feet. "They think you killed a man. I prefer to think you're too wise to commit such folly."

"As God's my witness I did not!" Robin's eyes rolled wildly as he glanced fearfully from one warrior to the next. His face lost all its color. "I swear to you, I did nothing! I only stumbled over the body! You must save me, Rev! I swear I know nothing of what occurred!"

The grip on his arm was painfully tight, but Revelin calmly addressed the chieftain. "Sir Robin knows nothing of the death of your man."

A nerve began to tic beside Turlough's right eye. Clearly, he was not pleased to have been awakened from his whiskey-laden dreams. "Me men say different. The Englishman is my prisoner...as...are...you," he added with pointed jabs of his finger at Revelin's middle. "He was trying to escape. For that he will die. Hang him!"

Revelin stepped between Robin and the warriors who reached for him. "Would you kill a man whose guilt you have not proved?"

Turlough's black brows twitched. "Me men saw him bending over the body. When they approached, he ran. What more proof do I need?"

"How did the man die?"

Turlough motioned a warrior to his side and they conversed in whispers. "He was strangled," he pronounced when they finished.

"With what?" Revelin pressed.

Turlough's blue eyes narrowed on Robin's trembling frame, and his words came reluctantly: "Strangled by hand."

Revelin looked down at Robin's smooth hands, which still gripped his sleeve, and nearly smiled. Robin was no more capable of pressing the life from another man's body than

Meghan was. When he glanced up at Turlough, he saw a look of understanding dawning on the chieftain's face. "So, you see, my lord, we have yet to discover the murderer."

Displeased to have his judgement found in error, Turlough's gaze moved deliberately to Revelin's hands, which were strongly tendoned and long fingered. "A man's been murdered. Strangulation is an assassin's trick. There's none here would stoop to it but the English. One of ye is a murderer." His gaze was wintry as he met Revelin's. "I charge ye with finding the guilty. Ye have until sunset. If ye fail, ye and all yer party will die."

Revelin waited until Turlough had reentered his tent before throwing a companionable arm about Robin's shoulders and leading him some distance from the camp. Finally they came to an outcropping of rock and both men settled themselves to rest. Revelin smiled at Robin and winked. "'Twas an unsettling way of beginning a morning, hm?"

Robin's smile was a pale reflection of his usual impish grin. "I made a right fool of myself. Christ's wounds! I thought I was lost." He hung his head a little. "Perhaps it would have been better had I been."

Revelin slapped his back heartily. "'Tis early yet for pity. You may yet have a chance to die."

Robin's head snapped up. "What?"

Briefly, Revelin repeated Turlough's demand. "So, we've a murderer to catch before nightfall."

Robin sighed deeply. "I'm not guilty. I was afraid. God! 'Tis plagued me all my life. I cannot bear to be startled. 'Tis my heart. It gallops away, leaving darkness in its wake. I cannot control it!"

"You are no coward," Revelin said. "You came to my aid some days ago with the herdsmen and again when the O'Neills attacked. I stand by what I say."

But now that he had begun, Robin was determined to finish his confession. "I can control it most often now that I am grown, but there was a time when it took very little to ..."

He wet his lips, his boyish face ashen behind his freckles. "My father despises me for the weakness. One winter's meal, when I was about twelve, I scalded him when a friend thought it a merry prank to jump out and surprise me while I held a tureen of gravy. Lord, but I can recall my father's face when I came to. He ordered me to be dressed up as the girl he said I resembled and paraded in public for all in the village to see and ridicule."

He swallowed again, his voice less steady as he continued, "I was put in the stocks in the town square and left. Come morning I was without my maidenly trappings and without my innocence, after a fashion."

Robin looked Revelin in the eye, his smile full of self-mockery. "I had learned a lesson during the night, thanks to a pair of drunken farm hands. Regardless of my father's opinion to the contrary, my affliction was not a manifestation of my sexual proclivities."

Revelin met his gaze evenly, knowing that it cost Robin more to speak than it cost him to accept the confession. "The dead clansman, did you recognize him?"

Robin blinked, disconcerted by the question, for it had nothing to do with his revelation. Then his smile eased into more natural lines. "I knew him. He was one of the ones who kept watch over us during the celebration."

"I do not suppose you saw him leave or who was with him?"

Robin's grin deepened. "Truth to tell, Rev, I was murmuring shameful endearments into the ear of one of Ireland's own sweet lassies."

"I thought you hobbled by language."

"'Tis so, but the scholar in me has discovered an alarming degree of literacy among these wild Irish. There's something to be said for popery I had not counted. The girl knew Latin, Rev! 'Tis a fair enough language for love."

Revelin reflected a moment on his own evening and then thrust aside the thoughts. "How long did you and the girl keep each other occupied?"

"Until first light." Robin wrinkled up his nose. In spite of his mud-crusted clothes he was first and foremost a gentleman. "I did not mind sharing her tent with relatives, but I draw the line at hogs and dogs. I was in desperate need of fresh air. The body was hidden under the brush. I tripped over it before I knew what it was. When I knelt to uncover the thing, the O'Neills suddenly appeared."

Revelin snatched up a blade of grass and began nibbling it thoughtfully. Robin had not killed the clansman, of that he was certain. So, who might have? Any dispute between warriors was settled by challenge. There was no need for stealthy death when Brehan Law sanctioned legal combat. No, the man who had died had been killed for other reasons. "Where are Sir Richard and John?"

Robin shook his head. "I've not seen them since supper." His face brightened. "Do you suppose they killed the man while escaping?"

That hope vanished before Revelin could answer. Coming toward them from the camp were Reade and Atholl, flanked by armed guards. When his surprise wore off, Revelin noticed that they again wore handcuffs and that the clansmen carried two extra pairs. He tensed. He could run and, perhaps, escape. But Robin would be left behind. And Meghan.

Revelin stood as they neared and held out his wrists. They had until nightfall to discover the murderer, and he had a few questions to ask Reade.

"But why must I stay here?" Meghan questioned for the twentieth time that day.

Sila merely dished up a bowl of milk with bread and butter and passed it to the girl. "Eat it. They'll be coming to fetch ye soon enough."

Meghan accepted the bowl with an ungracious grunt. They, whoever "they" were, could not possibly come soon enough to please her. It was nearly dark, the day gone, while she had idled it away inside the close confines of Sila's *rath*. Where could Revelin be, and what would keep him away the day long?

Meghan gazed down into her bowl as she remembered Revelin's face as she had last seen it, warmed by Sila's fire. The wavering flames had danced shadows across his face, licking up like golden tongues in the spring green of his eyes. She could have looked into his eyes forever. They changed color with the watching, the new green becoming the sea green of waves, then the dark unguent waters of a lough at evensong. She had bared herself to that gaze, given her body completely to his charge, and he had taken her on a journey that had changed forever her perception of herself. She had felt beautiful, like the summer sea, rising and flowing, warm and wet in his arms. If not for Sila's presence she would have slipped off her gown and offered herself again to the pleasure of his touch.

"A lass who smiles on her supper thinks of more than her belly," Sila said with a chuckle. "Aye, yer lad's more golden than honey and sweeter too, I've nae doubt. Did he give ye taste of his honey?" She cackled obscenely and patted Meghan's belly. "A son before Saint Brigid's Eve!"

Meghan's face flooded with embarrassment. "I do not take yer meaning."

Sila chuckled. "Ye will, soon enough. Ye'd best eat yer fill, there's work to be done before morning."

Meghan cocked her head to one side. "What work?"

Sila lowered her eyes. "Ach, that's for Turlough O'Neill to be saying. Only, I'll warn ye to play no tricks. He's nae a man for such. If ye've the power, ye'd best use it."

"I've nae power!" Meghan cried, spilling her supper as she jumped to her feet. "Ye've nae right to claim 'tis so!"

Sila sipped her milk, undisturbed by the outburst. It had been her idea that Meghan should be able to name the identity of the strangler. The settlement was too interested by half in the lass. The death of the O'Neill's bull convinced them that she had powers far greater than Sila's.

Sila glanced sideways at Meghan. It was a difficult enough task to work magic when the populous believed in one's power. Now that the girl had come, they would turn to her unless she was discredited and soon.

Sila raised her head, listened intently for a moment, and got to her feet. "They've come at last." She thrust out her chin as she gazed down at Meghan. "Now we'll see who has power!"

The night was warmer than most but Meghan shivered as she approached the O'Neill's tent. The King-Candle burned brightly near the entrance, and Turlough was already seated near it, his broad frame bare to the waist but for a thick furring of black hair.

"Come, lass, sit beside me," Turlough encouraged with a wave of his hand.

Glancing right and left, Meghan moved forward reluctantly. Where was Revelin? Why was he absent?

Turlough watched her, aware of the face she sought among the gathering. He knew he had not been wrong in thinking the girl was attached to Butler when they slipped away early the night before. When Sila came scratching at his tent at midday with the news of the lass's night in the woods, he knew he had young Butler right where he wanted him. But how far would that attachment go in cementing relationships between his clan and that of the English-Irish Butlers? Time would tell soon enough. He had more than one surprise in store for his audience. Before the evening was out, they would learn that Turlough O'Neill was a man of unexpected knowledge and statesmanship.

Turlough held out his hand to Meghan. "Give me your hand. Ach! Ye're as soft and smooth as new-churned butter, lass. Will ye melt before a harsh truth, or are ye hardier than ye seem?"

Meghan watched him in silent puzzlement. What did he

expect of her? She felt an anxiousness in the great hand clamped over hers, but she could not tell what it meant.

Turlough smiled at her, a wolfish gleam in his eye. "Do ye remember, lass, that I told ye I could name yer parents, a thing ye say ye cannot?" Meghan nodded slowly. "Well, I will do that very thing this night, if ye will aid me in a small matter first."

A tightness crept into Meghan's throat. Her parents! Did he really know who they were? Did *she* want to know? She hung her head. Where was Revelin? She needed him desperately.

Satisfied with Meghan's silence, Turlough signaled his men, and the four prisoners were shoved forward.

Meghan could not still a gasp of outrage at Revelin's man-acled hands, and she turned on Turlough such a furious look that he was momentarily surprised into releasing her hand. "What is this?" she demanded in a tone unlike any she had ever used to another human being.

Turlough smiled inwardly. She was an O'Neill, when she chose to be. Still, it would not do for her to be allowed to speak to him in such a manner. He rose, glowering down at her slight height. "I preferred yer silence, lass. Hold it or be gagged!"

Meghan looked from Turlough to Revelin and saw him nod once. She bit her lip, unconsciously raising one hand to smooth back the loose tendrils of hair that the evening breeze had feathered forward onto her cheek. This was the first she had seen of Revelin since their night together, and it was not as she had imagined while whiling away the day.

Turlough reseated himself and beckoned Revelin forward. "Tell me, young Butler. Have ye an answer for me?"

Revelin shrugged, holding out his chained wrists. "You've left me precious little room to maneuver in, my lord."

"When have wits needed hands?" Turlough returned with a smirk.

"Hands are the beasts of wits' burdens," Revelin replied as

quickly. "There were things I might have done, questions I might have asked, things I might have seen, had I been able. As it is, I have had only my instincts and imagination to keep me company."

"And yer answer?" Turlough prompted, leaning forward in his chair.

Revelin's gaze did not falter, but neither did he hurry into speech. Something was amiss; he had caught the spirit but not the substance of the restless whisperings that had begun among his jailors just after mid-morning. The restlessness, like a withheld breath, pressed him now in the midst of the silent onlookers. If he did not tread warily, he might trip himself up. "My lord, you asked me to prove Robin Neville innocent of the crime of strangulation. He is his own best defense. He lacks not only the ability but the reason to commit so base a crime. As for the guilty party . . ." He paused to gaze significantly about the ring of faces. "I would no more point to you than to any present. I do not know the murderer by name or shape."

Turlough did not move so much as an eyelid, but behind his blue stare his cunning mind raced. So Butler could not be frightened into betraying one of his party to save his own skin. That was admirable, as far as it went. It did not follow that Butler did not know who was guilty.

His mouth turned down slightly as he looked at the slight, freckled man with red-gold curls. Once he had seen the Englishman up close he knew him to be innocent. As for the other two . . . Turlough's inscrutable gaze roamed contemptuously over the sober form of Richard Atholl. From what he had heard from his guards, this man mouthed oaths and prayers with nauseating regularity. No heart there for brutal murder. Finally he settled with concentrated intent upon John Reade.

Here was a soldier. Reade's square face with its heavy features bore the stamp of a man capable of any and all crimes. It was a face of virtue in war and vice in peace. Turlough had seen that look too often not to recognize it. Aye, Reade was his man. But how to smoke the fox from the brush?

Turlough chuckled and reached out to take Meghan by the hand. He pulled her about to face him and with his free hand lifted her chin. "Ye've the power. I've seen proof of it in the mark laid so boldly upon ye and in the death of me bull. Do not fear that I would harm ye. I've a healthy respect for the workings of the fairies and the otherworld. But I tell ye now ye're an O'Neill, lass, and yer allegiance is to yer chief. If ye've traffic with the fairies, make them give ye the name of the murderer so that yer lad can go free." He leaned closer until his breath fanned hotly across Meghan's face. "Sila tells me ye've the sight. I've given me promise, the murderer shall be named this night or all the prisoners must die."

The pronouncement struck Meghan dumb. How could he expect her to look into a face and read guilt or innocence? And murder? She had been told nothing of a murder. "I—I know nothing of murder, my lord," she murmured so softly that none but Turlough heard her.

He patted her cheek. "Ach! Then yer answer will truly have come from the fairies." Gripping her by the shoulders, he turned her to face the four prisoners. He held her still with his heavy hands. "Look at each of them, lass. Look good and long. One of them is a murderer. Ye'll be reading it in his face. Tell me which, and the others will go free."

Meghan shook her head wildly. "I—I cannot! Do not make me! There's no magic in me! 'Tis an accident the bull died. I swear it!"

Turlough shook her by the shoulders. "Dinna fret, lass. Ye're troubling young Butler, and we cannot have that, can we?"

Meghan stilled, seeking Revelin through the blur of her tears. He had advanced toward her but his way was blocked by a warrior. She saw in his eyes fear for her and an odd bewilderment. *He's remembering,* she thought.

Revelin was remembering. What had come to his mind were

Meghan's strange babblings the day her aunt died. She had blamed herself, saying that she knew about the death of some poor herdsman and that his companions had blamed her for it. Surely she had not been foolish enough to spread that tale here, not when even a single glance at her face was enough to repel all the most practical of minds?

"My lord, she's but a lass," Revelin began. "You cannot hold her responsible for childish daydreams."

Turlough did not respond. His fingers dug into the soft flesh of Meghan's shoulder as he leaned forward to whisper in her ear, "Ye've the sight, lass. I know! 'Twas not yer nurse's name Una?" She jumped under his hands, and his grip eased. "Aye. Ye're the one. Read their faces, all, and save young Butler's life."

Meghan closed her eyes. She would try, if it would save Revelin's life.

She waited, becoming so still that she could feel the tremor of each heartbeat within her chest. She waited for the trembling, the shadow that always flooded her before the revelation of the dream that was not a dream. Nothing.

"Open yer eyes. Study them," Turlough encouraged, his lips on a level with her shoulder.

Meghan slowly opened her eyes. This time she did not look at Revelin. She knew he was innocent. She saw Robin shiver as her deep blue stare encompassed him. He was afraid but innocent. The conviction came easily to her mind, without a heralding of foreshadowing. She took a deep breath and moved her gaze.

The tall, white-faced man held up the cross that he wore about his neck as she focused on him, and she heard him murmur a prayer. Amusement struggled in her, a senseless amusement caused in part by terror that she might at any moment be plunged into a vision and in part by a certain knowledge that it would not happen. She felt nothing as she looked at him, neither guilt nor innocence. Nothing.

It was hard to move to the final man. She did not like him. She feared him. Looking into his black eyes was like gazing at danger. His smile was a beguiler's smile. His strong face might be thought handsome by some, but to her his black beard and thick head of hair too closely resembled a predator's pelt. His well-fed smile repelled her. She knew that, given the chance, he would eat her alive. Meghan looked away. *Guilty.*

The thought flashed clearly and calmly in her mind. It was not a vision, it was a simple reading of the truth, and she wondered whether Turlough already knew the answer. Of course, he did. She was being tested; he would have to know the answer in order to know whether she had succeeded.

"Well?"

Meghan closed her eyes. "I do not know. I cannot tell."

Turlough's hands left her. That was not the answer he expected. He had felt the tension rise in her when she gazed at the one called Reade. Turlough himself had surmised the black-haired man's guilt, though not the reason for it. She knew it, too. So why did she plead ignorance when Butler's life hung in the balance? He smiled slowly. Perhaps she did not believe he would carry out his threat.

Turlough gripped the gold hilt and freed the skean from his belt. He had carried it with him constantly since Colin had pulled it from Butler's saddlebags. "If ye cannot name the murderer, mayhaps I can aid ye. I'll remove a choice for ye. 'Twill make it easier."

Megan did not understand Turlough's intent. She did not understand even as he moved past her toward the four chained men. It was only when she saw the long thin blade catch the King-Candle's flame with its edge that she knew what he meant to do. Even then she was slow to react. He had stopped before Robin and grabbed the man by the hair, his blade lifted to plunge into the arched throat, when the power of motion came rushing back into her.

"Not him! Not him!" She flew at the O'Neill chief, her

hand outstretched to catch the powerful arm on its downward stroke.

She leaped upon him, grasping his fist in one hand and the bare blade in her other, and wrenched the skean to deflect its blow. She felt no pain as the metal bit smoothly into the flesh of her palm. She was falling, tumbling into a black abyss without pain and without bottom.

Chapter Ten

The pinpoint light of the vision grew steadily brighter until its icy brightness stung like sleet against Meghan's skin.

The light flared and disappeared.

The hissing grayness of a rain-darkened dusk replaced the brilliant light as Meghan found herself standing in the shadowy stillness of a *rath*. The room was not empty.

Clad from shoulders to boots in a grat mantle of saffron wool, a young Irish nobleman filled the doorway. His head was bare, in defiance of the elements that had plastered his wild black mane to his back. Above his raven-black beard his face was a fierce blend of feral savagery and mortal comeliness. Heavy brows formed ominous ridges over blue eyes so brilliant they resembled those of an osprey; sharp, inquisitive, and with the ceaseless roving of a predator.

A low moan tore Meghan's attention away from the man. From the formless shadows a naked young woman appeared lying on a bed of rushes, her knees bent and her back arched in support of her distended belly. Fever had painted a scarlet patch on each cheek and matted her beautiful flame-colored hair to her pale brow.

Transfixed, Meghan watched the man move to the bedside. For the space of three heartbeats there was only the girl's harsh breathing as he knelt by her side. Then she moaned as a new birth pain began.

Meghan began to shake like a wind-wrung leaf. It would happen now, something terrible, something she could not stop or prevent, something that might drive her mad!

The girl's cries rose higher and higher until the very room shivered with the long pealing screams of agony. Meghan pushed her hands against her ears but the cries were inside her, keening like a banshee's wail.

When the cries ceased, it was like the bursting of lungs. Silence rushed in to fill the void in a curious hiss like an expelled breath.

Choked with terror, Meghan saw the man rise, anger turning his eyes dark as he gazed on the now-silent girl. The lightning flash of a dagger appeared in his hand, the same skean Turlough had drawn.

The blade slashed through the air toward the girl's defenseless abdomen. Meghan screamed. The downward stroke cleaved the vision. It ripped apart before her horror-filled eyes, spewing blood and darkness . . . and the mewling cry of a newborn.

"No! No! The blood! There's so much blood!"

"Meghan! Meghan, darling! 'Tis nothing. A mere cut. Open your eyes and see for yourself. 'Twill mend, lass, 'twill mend."

Revelin hardly recognized his own voice as he took Meghan's face in his hands and kissed her again and again. He did not know how else to still her cries. Her lips were so cold that he feared she would die of shock. Yet, there was no reason for it. After he had carried her into Turlough's tent, Sila had wrapped Meghan's wound in clean linen. The cuts on her palm had been long but not deep.

"Meghan, love," he whispered, offering the heat of his breath to her frozen mouth. "Meghan, please open your eyes."

Meghan resisted the seductive call in the voice she remembered as Revelin's. She knew she would go mad if the vision continued. And yet, she knew she could not prevent a single moment of it when it chose to return. She was cold, numb with the horror of its memory. What more could happen? She opened her eyes.

Revelin thought he would be relieved to look down into her eyes, but facing the deep blue bruising that was Meghan's gaze was like an unexpecting blow to the stomach. His arms tightened convulsively about her.

"Meghan, 'tis over. No one's been hurt. Look here." He reached for her hand. The bandage was spotted in places with rosettes of red, but the main bleeding had stopped. "See, love. You are not hurt badly."

Meghan gazed at the white expanse of cloth covering her hand before her eyes drifted back to Revelin's face. "What happened?"

"Don't you remember? Well, 'tis not important." Revelin lifted her from the rush-and-bough mattress that served as the chief's bed and turned to Turlough. His heart had nearly stopped when he'd seen Meghan fly at the earl of Tyrone. Turlough was a soldier, capable of a death-wielding response before he knew his intended victim. Yet, her cry had warned him and he had not hurt her. Meghan had cut herself.

Revelin tried to keep that in mind as he addressed the chieftain. "I think we've provided enough of a spectacle for one evening. With your permission, my lord, I will find shelter for the lass."

Turlough regarded the two young people before him with detachment. They were a picture of contrasts, the golden-haired lad and the girl with her delicate dark wildness. A more sentimental man might have wished them well and left them to their hearts. But he was a chieftain and warlord. They were pawns in his strategy. "Did ye understand the lass's ravings?"

The question took Revelin by surprise. What had Meghan said? There was something about visions of blood. "She said nothing of consequence, my lord. She was frightened. She has spells of imagination, that is all."

"Is it now?" Turlough looked down at the skean he still held. The girl had recognized it. He had seen her staring at it in horrified fascination before she had passed out. "There's more to it than that, lad. Put her down."

Colin had followed his chieftain into the tent. Now he moved from the corner of the room, and the look in his eye betrayed his wish for any excuse to attack Revelin. After a short hesitation, Revelin placed Meghan back on the bed.

"That's a good lad." Turlough moved to the foot of the bed and held up the skean by its blade so that the intricate pattern of the hilt was displayed. "What meaning does this have for ye, lass?"

After one brief look, Meghan turned her head away. "Nothing."

"Ye're a poor liar, lass, and I've little patience with a good one. Ye had a vision, did ye not? Aye, that's better," he said as she turned back to him. "What did ye see, lass? The truth."

Meghan shook her head in denial, but the words came tumbling out without her permission. "A woman, giving birth. And a warrior. He wore the O'Neill mantle but I—I did not know him. He had that. He—" Her eyes fastened on the blade. "He killed her! Plunged it into her belly." Meghan's hands flew up to cover her face as hard sobs racked her.

"That's enough," Revelin said angrily. "You're torturing a simple girl who cannot tell nightmares from reality."

"Can she nae?" Turlough replied, contemplating the weapon in his hand. He licked his lips nervously. It did not seem possible, but . . . the girl herself had described it all, just as he remembered it.

His gaze switched to Meghan. She had the same dramatic

coloring, the wild black hair, pale skin, and blue eyes. And the birthmark was real; he had touched it. And yet, it could be a trick to make his claim to Ulster less secure. There had been persistent rumors over the years. Perhaps the girl had been coached. There was Sila, of course, to school the girl in such tales. Sila was the one who had proposed the test of naming the murderer. But he was not so easily led. Turlough closed his hand on the hilt. He would need more proof of the girl's gift of visions. He would begin again, from the beginning.

"Ye're nae a believer in fairies, are ye, young Butler?" he said after a moment. "Yer English upbringing makes ye deaf and blind to the nature of the blood that runs in yer veins. Yet, every man knows there are things beyond his mortal understanding. The lass is different. 'Tis plainly marked on her for all to see. If ye were a wise man, ye'd claim her for yer own. When I'm done, I may give her to ye that ye will make of her a proper wife."

"No!" Colin shouted. He strode into the center of the tent, his hand moving to the hilt of his sword. "I offered for the girl this very morning. Ye promised ye'd consider it."

Turlough's brows drew together at the tone of the Scotsman's voice. Colin's indignation held no weight but it angered him.

He turned to Colin. "The lass is not for ye, lad. If she proves to be who I suspect, ye'll be knowing it, too." He walked back to the bed where Meghan lay. Her sobs had subsided, but tears dampened her cheeks. "Take this, lass, hold it tight. Ach! Don't turn away. It will not pass ye by, ye must see that now."

He is right, Meghan thought as she stretched out her hand. The skean was a little longer than the one she had carried for years, but it seemed much more dangerous, evil. And it was warm to touch, as if alive. She shivered, and would have released it had Turlough not wrapped his big fingers over hers to hold it in her palm.

"There's a lass," Turlough continued in an unexpectedly gentle voice. "The man ye dreamed, what was his form?"

"Tall," Meghan answered in a whisper. "And black like ye, but more handsome," she added in innocent honesty.

Turlough smiled. It was common knowledge that his cousin had been the more handsome of the two. "What of the lass?"

As Meghan stared at the blade a dark shadow of the vision drifted through her mind. "Red-haired she was, and beautiful." The vision crystallized, not with soul-quaking intensity but with the blunted edge of far-off memory. "He killed the woman. He plunged the skean into her pregnant belly. I heard the babe cry out in protest!"

Maura Fitzgerald and Shane O'Neill. Turlough crossed himself, muttering a seldom-used prayer. "Saints preserve us, ye've witnessed yer own birth!"

"You're mad!" Revelin broke in, reaching past Turlough and snatching the skean from Meghan's hand. "No one dreams his own birth. You're putting thoughts into her mind and she's too frightened to realize it."

Turlough's sharp gaze focused with new understanding on Meghan's troubled face. "'Tis not I who led her, lad. There's fairy business in this. It began seventeen winters ago." Turlough wiped the sweat from his brow. "We should have known something was amiss. Shane and I were but lads together, basking in the heat of our lust, until he set eyes on Maura Fitzgerald. She was betrothed to an O'Donnell, but Shane was so taken with the lass that he stole her from under the O'Donnells' noses. He wanted her child, and paid the priest to pray every day that the babe would be a lad."

"I've heard the story." Colin jeered. "The lass died and the babe with her. They still talk of Shane running mad with the grieving of it. Ye can't expect a man to believe this lass is the dead child."

"Can't I now?" Turlough responded, turning on the younger man. "What would ye be knowing of O'Neill business, Scotsman? Aye, 'twas pain that maddened Shane, but not all for loss of Maura. The priest had promised him a son. When he realized Maura was dead and no child to show for it, he..." Turlough paused. How to tell what so badly shocked him, even now as a memory of sixteen years?

He extended his hand to Revelin for the skean and received it. "This was Shane's. He was wild with grief, ye'll understand. I saw it, too—and the woman Una—the feeble kick within the dead womb. What was a body to do? 'Twas his heir. The babe had a right to life."

A shocked silence followed Turlough's confession.

"The babe was a lass," Revelin said at length.

"Aye, a lass." Turlough's thoughts turned inward to memories he had tucked away. "'Twas his punishment, Shane said. He wanted a son too much, and to mock him the fairies stole his lad and replaced it with a changeling. I took fright on seeing the babe and ran away to fetch the priest, but Una and the babe were gone when we returned, and Shane would never speak of what had happened."

He looked up into Revelin's doubtful gaze. "Nae a man else knew, ye understand? Ach, 'twere rumors, but until this Beltane I had not seen the lass since her birth."

Turlough shook his dark head, as much amazed by the tale as if he were hearing it for the first time. He reached up unconsciously and touched his left cheek. "'Twas easy to recognize her. The mark is the same."

"Born of a dead woman," Colin murmured, making the sign of the cross. He seemed to remember that he had once kissed her, and wiped his lips as though they had tasted poison. "She's not human, she's a *cailleach!*" He backed toward the entrance. "I take back my claim. Let him who dares take the lass!" Throwing back the flap, he disappeared into the night.

Turlough, too, moved toward the entrance with heavy steps. From the moment he saw her mark he had suspected that the lass was Shane's daughter. He was a Christian man, but more than a millennium of pagan Celtic blood ran in his veins. It was commonly admitted that the O'Neill's cunning, skill, and tireless vigor owed to a knowledge older than that of the Norman world of monks and cathedrals. He himself had trafficked with more than one wise woman over the years. Yet, this slip of a girl possessed a power greater than any he had witnessed. She could see into the past. What then of the future?

Turlough swung around. "Ye can see the past, lass, but what of the future? I'm not an ungenerous man. I will give ye whatever ye name if we will look into my future. What I want to know is, will I rule Tyrone in peace?"

Meghan looked at the black-haired man so like and yet different from the vision of the man he claimed was her father. "Ye will not rule in peace, nor would ye want to."

Turlough's old grin returned as he conceded the wisdom of that. "But will I rule long?"

Meghan closed her eyes. She could tell him nothing. Yet he had promised her anything for a prediction. Her eyes opened. "I want to go free. And I want you to release Revelin Butler and his three companions."

Turlough's gaze darted away. If she was truly able to tell the future, she might prove invaluable to him. He knew that he was considered by some of the O'Neill minor chieftains to be lacking the cunning and bravery of his predecessor. Shane had borne the title of earl, yet he had continued to rule Ulster according to Brehan Law and had dispensed with the lives of other English-titled Irish noblemen with a furor bordering on mania.

I do not lack ambition, Turlough thought. *But neither do I undervalue the worth of compromise.*

Shane had been slaughtered by an act of treachery among men he had sometimes counted as friends. Turlough did not long for a similar fate. He saw the possible and the impossible. It was possible he could live long and die a chief. The likelihood would be greatly diminished if he shed the blood of a Butler.

Then, too, the presence of the lass in his camp might cause

more trouble than good. Colin MacDonald, as stout-hearted a warrior as any man in camp, had run away in fear. Others might seek her out, following her advice above his own if she proved to be strong in the power of the otherworld. He could not afford a divided clan.

"I agree. You and the men shall go free. Tell me, lass, will I rule Tyrone a long while?"

Meghan wet her lips. She did not know the answer, but to save Revelin's life she replied, "As long as ye draw breath, ye will rule Tyrone. Long life to ye, Turlough Luineach O'Neill."

Turlough grunted and nodded his head. "I accept that. But I must satisfy the slain man's widow."

"There's *eraic*," Revelin offered quietly.

"How will you pay it?" Turlough demanded.

Revelin smiled. "We came to Ulster not as beggars. There was gold and silver and jewelry among our belongings. The gold and jewels in Sir Neville's rings alone are worth the ransom of ten lives. The widow's *eraic* could be paid from a fraction of their worth."

Turlough reached for the flagon of wine on the table and poured it into the goblets before turning to the younger man. "I'm a reasonable man. And ye're nae a slow-witted lad. Let's drink to the agreement."

"We will ride at dawn, our horses and belongings returned," Revelin added with a genial smile.

"Oh, aye." Turlough nodded. "Ye'll find them unmolested."

Revelin sipped his wine, wondering how best to tell Robin that his prized rings were gone forever.

Meghan watched them in unease. No one had mentioned her from the moment they began haggling over ransom. Did Revelin want her with him? He had not mentioned it. She stared at him but could not catch his eye. Perhaps her vision had frightend him as much as it had Colin MacDonald.

She touched her cheek. Colin had wanted her before she

revealed herself as a changeling. He had turned away—nay, fled, for fear of his life. Maybe Revelin, too, was afraid to be near her now that he knew what she was. Perhaps he regretted lying with her. Maybe he...

Suddenly she longed to be free of the stifling confines of the tent.

The fruity taste of the wine hardly slaked the dry-mouthed wonder of the last moments, and Turlough quickly refilled his glass. "A toast to the sovereignty of Ulster," he proclaimed in a hearty tone.

Revelin drank unhesitatingly. The question of *whose* sovereignty was not mentioned.

Turlough drained his cup and was contemplating the pleasure of a third, but when he looked down over the rim his eyes were suddenly serious. "One of yer companions is a murderer, ye know that?"

Revelin shrugged. If he suspected as much he would not admit it, not when he had yet to be released.

Turlough lowered his cup. "The lass knows the murderer's name. Do ye think he'll rest easy with her having the knowledge?"

"If she knows, she isn't saying," Revelin answered lightly, but his heart was heavy with foreboding. Reade had killed the guard; he knew it though he could not prove it. Nor did Meghan possess the power to do so. But Reade might be superstitious enough to accept this nonsense about Meghan's ability if it came to his ear.

Turlough's thoughts ran a similar course. "Yer Captain Reade is nae a man I would trust at me back. The lass will need yer protection every moment."

Revelin frowned. "You needlessly frighten the lass," he said reprovingly, and turned his head toward the bed to find that it was empty. "What? Where is she?"

Amusement pleated the corners of Turlough's eyes. "The lass had a great craving for clean air. She slipped out a wee while ago. I saw nae reason to deprive her of it."

Revelin's expression hardened. "Then you're a poorer judge of people than I thought! No doubt that Scotsman is spreading the story of her nightmare, and there'll be the devil to pay if the people take fright!"

Turlough stopped Revelin with an iron grip on his arm. "Ye've a fondness for the lass, so I will overlook yer tongue, this once. She will come to nae harm. She's Shane O'Neill's daughter. They will remember that always. But ye'd best make it legal between ye, lad, or Black Tom will hear of the mischief ye've been up to on the banks of Lough Neagh. Aye, I know how you spent Beltane night."

Taken aback, Revelin felt his cheeks burning. No one had taken him to task for misconduct since he was fourteen. He said shortly, "Meghan is my foster child; I will see to her care."

"'Tis yer whore ye've made her," Turlough returned baldly. "Ye were the man to take her virginity. Don't deny it. She may be different from ye and me, but she's nae a wanton, lad. Now go find her and tell her handfast will do till ye have the earl of Ormond's blessing on the match!"

Revelin jerked free of the bigger man's grip and left the tent with Turlough's genial laughter ringing in his ears. Black Tom's blessing indeed! His uncle would have him flayed alive for considering marriage to a native Irish girl and a Catholic to boot!

Revelin halted in his tracks outside the O'Neill's tent. People still milled about the center of camp, curiosity about the recent happenings holding them to the spot, but Meghan was nowhere to be seen.

"Revelin?" Robin rose to his feet beside Reade and Atholl, who were seated between battle-ax—wielding guards. "What is going to happen to us, Rev?"

Revelin stared vacantly at Robin's manacled wrists and then said brusquely, "We are free to leave. See to the horses and belongings. We ride at dawn."

Without looking back, he set off toward the lake. Meghan might not have gone to Sila's hovel but it was as good a place as any to begin looking for her. He paused at the edge of the camp to take one of the many burning faggots lashed to poles to light the clearing.

Why had Meghan run away? She was as contrary as a spring day, all sunshine and warmth one moment, all dampness and black moods the next. If she had the least bit of common sense she would not have been led on by Turlough's blustery combination of superstition and cunning. But it was not all her fault. She had been brought up to think of herself as different by ignorant people who feared what they could not understand. Well, he would to put an end to that. Once she was properly dressed and learned a bit of English, she would learn to think of herself as just another pretty lass. It was unfortunate that Turlough knew the girl's weakness and had exploited it to his own advantage.

Revelin wondered if Meghan was really Shane's daughter. It made sense. Despite the fakery that went into the telling of the tale, Turlough had vowed in public that the lass was the unknown daughter of Shane O'Neill. The skean that Una had given him seemed to bear out the connection. Of course, it could have come into her hands through other means. Yet, he believed what he had been told, at least that Shane had saved his child by cutting her out of her mother's womb. Turlough had said the babe had a birthmark like Meghan's. Perhaps Meghan was that child.

If he had been considering marriage to Meghan, that fact alone would have given him pause. By allying himself with Shane's daughter he would be obligating himself to the Irish clans: a serious breach with the queen.

Revelin shook his head briskly, willing himself to calm, rational thought. Meghan was comely. In his arms she had been uninhibited to a degree that had overridden his good sense. He had not forced her. Dear Lord! She had given him, against his better judgment, the sweetest joy of his life. But what they had shared did not necessarily lead to marriage. Just the thought of her aroused him, but rational judgment told him that she was not a proper bride for him.

Nor is she a whore. The thought halted Revelin outside Sila's door. Meghan was not a light-skirt to be enjoyed and then passed on to another. So what was he to say to her?

The pulse beating insistently in his throat was a reminder that he was not as calm as he would have liked to be. He should simply turn back, leaving Meghan to the O'Neills. But he could not. He had promised to guard her life. And if he could be blamed for his lack of vigilance regarding her virtue, he would accept the consequences of that. He had known the sweetest part of her. It would serve as a just penance that he must take her back to Dublin by his side and yet never touch her again. Satisfied in his own selfless intent, Revelin rapped on the hovel.

Meghan watched from the cover of night a short distance away as Sila invited Revelin into her *rath*. A sudden decision had made her stop short of Sila's home. Part of her had hoped Revelin would follow, yet another part longed desperately to escape him.

Now, before she had time to think of where else she might take refuge, Revelin exited Sila's hut and picked up the torch he had laid outside her door. For an instant his face was lit by the torchlight, and Meghan's heart skipped a beat. She saw anger in his expression, but also a desperation that matched her own. His body tensed as he searched the darkness, and then his shoulders slumped forward in defeat.

"I told ye, ye'll not be finding her this night, lad. A changeling with the gift can turn herself into a hawk, a hare, or even a wolf. Dinna search for her. Come back in the morning and I'll have word for ye then." Sila's voice was positively gleeful, Meghan noted with annoyance.

"She's a frightened child," Meghan heard Revelin answer. "And not even the poorest beggar's brat deserves to lie alone shivering in the dark."

Is that how he sees me, as a child? Meghan wondered.

As Revelin started back the way he had come, Meghan rose, her eyes on his retreating back. He would go back to the O'Neill encampment and in the morning ride south, and she would never see him again. It was better so, she told herself, but ached anew with the thought.

She took a step toward him, spurred by an emotion stronger than her caution. The snap of a twig beneath her foot startled her. She was not so clumsy as a rule. She glanced up and saw that Revelin, too, had heard it and had paused to look back over his shoulder.

She stilled, becoming another shadow among so many. But the breeze was in a whimsical mood. It caught the hem of her white gown and surged beneath to swell the skirt like a bellows. The undulating, pristine whiteness gathered to it all the meager sum of starlight and lake reflections, and she saw Revelin spin about. "Meghan? Is it—? Meghan!" he cried in certainty and came running toward her.

As he approached her, Revelin remembered the morning she had run away and he had found her hiding in a tree. She had told him that she did not want him gazing upon her. What was the matter now? Did she think him as great a fool as Colin MacDonald and afraid of her claims to sorcery? Well, he would soon put an end to that nonsense.

Revelin halted a few feet from her. "Why did you run away?" He saw her tense as if about to flee, but she did not. "I warn you, if you do so again, I'll not follow, I'm tired and hungry and damned short of humor!"

Meghan tilted her head to one side, suddenly shy. She no longer wished to run away. She wanted, instead, to run toward him, to feel his arms close about her. She needed more than ever before the comfort of his embrace.

Revelin waited patiently for her to speak. Her gaze wandered over him, halting pointedly at his codpiece. Her lips parted unconsciously and the tip of her tongue peeked through. With distinct surprise mingled with a surge of answering warmth, he realized to where her thoughts had wandered. He stood irresolutely still. One moment she was a waif startled by a gruff voice or a harsh word. Now she stood before him, her cheeks flushed by desire, a thoroughly seductive woman. Damn her, she was a flirt!

"I'm going back!" he said shortly and turned away before his body betrayed to her inquisitive gaze just how effective her allure was. She had snatched the upper hand from him without a word.

Meghan watched him retreat once more, taking the light with him, and her pulse began to pound in her throat as if she were about to cry. "I—I . . . My lord!"

Revelin paused, the emotional break in her voice more than he had the heart to deny. "Meghan?" he asked softly.

Meghan was grateful that he did not turn to face her. She felt strangely vulnerable, more fragile than a hen's egg. If he turned the full heat of his gaze on her as he had the night before, she knew she would flee. Never with another had she felt the dissolving of herself as when she gazed into his shamrock-green eyes. It was a little like dying, she thought, a breaking away from her own body.

She had only a vague notion of what she wanted from him. She could not even recall why she had run away. As she neared him, she could feel his warmth. She stopped only a hand's breadth away. "Do ye nae fear me?" she asked.

Revelin smiled slowly. "What I fear in you, lass, is nothing more or less than any man feels in the presence of mortal temptation."

He did not expect her to undersand that, but she did. "Ye have nae fear of charms and curses?"

Revelin wet his lips. He stood in an ancient forest whose inhabitants had once believed in rites that were old long before Christianity began. To deny them might be foolhardy. "I do not deny the ways of old, but I am not afraid of a beautiful girl who believes, to her detriment, things which are not so."

Meghan's hand fell lightly on his shoulder, and the firm strength of his body emboldened her. "'Tis said that fairies have the power for good as well as ill."

Her touch sent a quiver of desire through him. The hesitant exploration of her fingers against his nape was brief but powerful in its effect. The knot of desire tightened in his groin, roughening his voice. "Meghan, lass, when you think back to last night will you tell me that anything you've experienced was better than that?"

Now it was Meghan's turn to shiver in delicious response. "In all me life, I . . . nothing—ever!" The moment of remembrance was too beautiful for words.

Her trembling fingers against his skin were cool as silk and Revelin could not resist reaching up to capture and hold them for an instant to his burning cheek. He felt hot, on fire, a raging inferno that she had stoked despite his resolve to the contrary. "It was a mortal woman I held in my arms last night, a mortal whose lips kissed mine. You are as real as I. I feel your pulse beneath my fingers. We are flesh and blood, Meghan, God help us both!"

When he released her hand it slipped from his neck but she did not pull away. Her fingers traced the path of his spine through his velvet doublet. It seemed to Revelin that all life, all nature, came to standstill. He did not believe in the black arts, was skeptical of most pious "miracles," but Meghan's touch had in it the power to persuade him to betray his most cherished beliefs about himself.

He was not a profligate seducer of innocents. All the women he had ever taken were willing, aware of what they offered, and asked for nothing more than carnal satisfaction and an amicable fondness for shared pleasures. They were for the most part married women, delivered of the obligatory heir and ripe for romance. They had taught him much of the art of lovemaking and he had been an eager pupil. But pure love had never stirred him until he met Alison. But if that were true, then what was this glorious, frightening thrall in which Meghan held him?

The slender arms that came around him from behind seemed a miracle of grace and benediction to his harried thoughts. The world ceased to exist outside the circle of her arms. "My love, take pity," he whispered hoarsely.

Meghan rested her brow in the valley between his shoulder blades, her hands splaying over the flat expanse of his abdomen. *My love!* He had called her his love. He loved her. She felt the rapid rise and fall of his breathing under her hands and it comforted her to know that he was as moved as she. One hand moved up over the wide contours of his chest while the other descended, reaching lower until she found him.

"Mercy's Grace!" Revelin shut his eyes and arched his back, involuntarily pressing himself into her hand. Her second hand joined the first and she cradled him.

He felt alive, like a dove, warm and throbbing. "Did ye always feel so?" she questioned in a serious voice.

"Always feel . . . what?"

Meghan considered this as her fingers searched his clothing for the placket that would allow her entrance. "Ye're like a bull. The sheathing does not tell the whole of it."

Revelin felt the rumble of laughter first in his belly, the immoderate kind of guffaw that was part amusement and part guilty shame. When he loosed it, the explosion startled the night, set the stillness crackling with human warmth and reality. It broke the spell and he stepped away and out of her embrace.

"Ah, Meghan, ye've not a bone of modesty in ye!" he said, mimicking her accent. Yet she was not crude or base. She had no experience of holding her tongue or censoring her words. He must not make the mistake of judging her by his standards again. When he turned to her he thought he had command of himself. The command did not last.

She threw herself against him, twining her fingers in his

hair and pulling his mouth down hard on hers. Her lips burned their soft impression onto his. She was like a womanly vine, curling her small body about his. Her belly caressed his abdomen and her graceful thighs melted into his hard-muscled legs as her tongue, with one day's tutelage, cleverly invaded his mouth.

He was drowning, going down into the depths of a sensation so strong that he feared he would not survive. He gripped her waist with his free hand, whether to hold her away or simply to keep from drowning he did not know, but he could not hold her still. Beneath the thin wool her warm fragrant body undulated in fluid softness as she rubbed herself against him. Her pelvis brushed his groin with ever stronger grazings, demanding and achieving his arousal.

Revelin threw back his head, breaking their kiss. He was drugged by her taste, her fragrance, her desire. From where had she learned this? Was it magic? Aye. And the magic was in the sweet places of her body.

Suddenly Meghan released him, bent to catch the hem of her gown, and lifted it over her head.

Revelin caught his breath at the perfection of her young body. Grateful for the torchlight, he could not tear his eyes away. The night before it had been too dark to fill his eyes with what his hands touched. The flame bathed her in its golden halo. It sought the narrow curve of her waist, rode the flare of each hip and the smooth-squared angles of her shoulders. Looking at her, he understood the reasons why women guarded their bodies with gowns and veils and shawls. Few of them could match Meghan's perfection of form, and fewer still had the simple honesty to offer themselves with the joy with which Meghan now offered herself to him. She was not vain. He saw the need for assurance in her eyes. In her beauty there was a vulnerability that brought him to a conclusion nothing else could have. He would not take advantage of her a second time. He bent, picked up her gown, and offered it to her.

Confused, Meghan refused the gown but reached up self-consciously to cover her breasts. "Am I ugly to ye? Did ye prefer the dark?"

Each word embarrassed Revelin more. What could he answer? "You're lovely, Meghan, more beautiful than any woman I've ever—" He bit off his statement too late. It was a blunder unworthy of a man of his experience. But her expression did not alter.

"Have ye known a great many women?" Meghan questioned in simple curiosity.

"Aye, thousands," Revelin lied. Why not? It might make her angry enough to turn away from him.

Her hands fell to her side. "Do they all have great udders like me?"

Revelin's jaw dropped.

"'Tis not many I've seen to compare," she continued in a conversational tone. "Una's were flat like griddle cakes with raisins in the centers." She indicated the glorious globes that his hands itched to touch. "Tell me true, now, will they serve?"

Will they serve? Revelin raised a not-quite-steady hand to his brow and closed his eyes. Passion made him tremble, and the unreal quality of their conversation was not dampening it. If she asked him to count and examine her teeth he would run screaming from the spot.

"Meghan, put . . . on . . . your . . . gown."

Meghan's mouth quivered. "Ye do not like me. I'm ugly."

It came as a distinct shock to find her mouth once more under his; stranger still was the fact that he knew he had initiated the crushing embrace. She was driving him mad. When he had thoroughly explored her mouth he set her away again, his stiff-armed grip on her shoulders a defense to hold her back.

"You're a beautiful lass! You're a seducer, a harlot in Madonna's clothing! A charm, a potion, a danger to my sanity! So put on yer gown and keep it on, no matter what! Even if one day I should beg ye to take it off! Keep it on! Do ye understand me, lass?"

He was shouting, he knew, raving like a lunatic, but he could not help himself. She drove him beyond self-control. She was so bedeviling that had she been a man he would have struck her. Lord! If she were a man he would not feel as he did now.

Meghan regarded him for a long moment. "Ye liked me the night before. Why do ye not want me now?"

"It isn't a matter of wanting, Meghan." He sighed, searching for words. "Ye've had so little experience of the world, of men."

Meghan cocked her head to one side. "If I had more experience with men, would ye want me then?"

Revelin did not trust himself with a reply.

"Ye're a fey man, Revelin Butler," she said at last and pulled her gown over her head. Twisting this way and that, she struggled to work the clinging material over the flushed swells of her body.

Each flash of skin, a hip, a leg, made Revelin more uncomfortable. "Mercy!" he cried finally and turned his back. "When you've done, go back to Sila's hut. I've things to see to before we leave. Stay there until I come for you in the morning!"

He hurled the words over his shoulder like pikes but they fell gently on Meghan's ears. *We* ride tomorrow. He was taking her with him! "Will I like London, do ye think?"

Revelin sighed like an aged man. "We go to Dublin and then to Kilkenny."

Meghan shook out the last wrinkle in her gown before answering. "I will try not to shame ye."

Revelin sucked in a long breath. "Nothing you do shames me, Meghan."

Meghan kept her skepticism to herself. "Do they make the beast with two backs in Dublin Town?"

Revelin groaned.

"'Tis Sila's name for it," Meghan explained. "I think I like honey-making better."

Revelin walked away without a reply, but in the dim recesses of his mind he recalled a husky whisper during their love-making: "What are we doing, Revelin?" "Making honey," he had answered without hesitation.

Chapter Eleven

"I've decided I'm quite attached to my freedom," Robin declared with a sigh of contentment as he rode beside Revelin. "No one will believe the tale we've to tell of Ulster. Captured by the barbaric O'Neills, brought as prisoners to Turlough himself, feted at the pagan feast of Beltane, and then set free by a fairy's trick, 'tis deserving of a sonnet!"

"I would wait until we've crossed back into the pale before committing your doggerel to parchment." Revelin winked at his friend. "You cannot tell when we may meet an O'Neill who might take exception to your verse."

Robin nodded seriously despite Revelin's bantering tone. A day and a half out of the O'Neills' company had not been long enough for his fear of Ulstermen to fade completely.

He glanced down at the angry marks circling his wrists and then at the rolling green countryside where every rocky outcropping or stand of trees might hide a warrior. "I've had enough of blindfolds and manacles to last me a lifetime! Do you suppose they thought we might be tempted to find them again?"

Revelin urged his mount ahead down a steep slope, leaving the question unanswered. Turlough was a seasoned warrior. He would suspect the motives of every Englishman sent to Ireland. If they had been able to state the exact location of the O'Neill camp, Turlough would not have set them free. He had vowed that the O'Neills would remain neutral, siding neither with the Irish nobles nor with the Crown if war came to the southland. But times were uncertain and the queen's memory long. Any information she received would not go to waste if she perceived an advantage in a change of strategy.

Meghan's arms tightened about Revelin's waist as they began the climb down and he automatically reassured her by patting her clasped hands. "Are you comfortable, lass?"

"Aye."

Revelin frowned at the simple, lackluster answer. She had scarcely spoken three words together since they'd begun the morning's journey. Her moods were mercurial, flowing seamlessly from joy to moodiness to sadness. He had hoped that she would be happy to leave Ulster and the superstitious prattling of the O'Neills.

His expression lightened at the thought of the Scots *gallowglass*. There, at least, the problem had solved itself: Colin had disappeared from the settlement the night of Meghan's supposed vision.

Meghan moved again, adjusting her body for a more comfortable ride, and tucked her hands up under Revelin's doublet. Her fingers moved across his middle, splaying out onto his chest as she leaned her head against his back. The cradling warmth of her body reminded him that beneath her mantle she was nearly naked. She had traded her Beltane gown for a new *leine*, and the straight-lined garment was ill suited for riding astride. Yet, she seemed unaware that the inviting softness of her naked thighs was a torment that he could scarcely ignore.

This was no better than the preceding day, when she had ridden up before him, he decided. Constantly assailed by her sweet scent and tempted with delightful glimpses of the upper curves of her breasts when her neckline gaped, to escape the torment he had finally slipped from his saddle on the pretense of checking his horse's hoof for stones. After that, he had relegated her to a position behind him.

What he needed was female companionship, the kind that could be bought without emotional entanglements. Once he had lain in the bed of an accomplished courtesan, no doubt his pathetic tendre for the girl would dissolve. And if it did not, if he would forever regret their brief hours and the fact that there were not more, none but he would ever know.

What Meghan needed was a trustworthy lady, preferably a married lady, to explain to her that she must not in the future concede her charms to every eager man.

As he reached the bottom of the hill he reined in to wait for the others. "Have you a married sister, Robin?"

Robin smiled beatifically as he and John approached. "Thank the saints, I do not! But I have a pair of plaguey girl cousins. Why do you want a sister of mine when you have one of your own?"

"She's not married," Revelin replied cryptically. That Katherine was unmarried was not the real problem. She was a young widow who had broken more than her share of hearts. Her advice to Meghan would be practical and not overly judgmental. Kathy would sympathize, send Meghan to confession, and then set out to find a husband for her.

The trouble lay in the fact that Kathy and Alison were fast friends. Kathy was a dear but had a loose tongue. If he took her into his confidence, Alison would learn of his indiscretion. He could not risk that when he meant to bring Meghan to live in his household after his marriage. Meghan was his responsibility, and Alison would unhesitatingly open her heart to the girl unless she had reason not to.

"I have a sister," John volunteered. "She's married these

six years, with three children to her credit. If you've need of a discreet lady, you'd not do better than Margaret."

"Discreet lady? Do we speak of indiscretion?" Robin questioned. "I thought Rev was in need of a kind-hearted soul to take our Hibernian lovely in hand."

"'Tis exactly my need," Revelin answered. "Meghan must be taught how to deal with English society."

Meghan had been daydreaming until she heard Revelin mention her name. She looked up to find his companions gazing at her.

"She's gotten rather prettier, don't you think?" Robin commented.

"I think your cowardice blinded you before," John answered. "She's the same marked pigeon, only you're not so particular now because the squab saved your worthless life."

"Hm," Robin murmured as his interested gaze remained on Meghan. "Do you suppose you could teach me to say 'thank you' in Gaelic, Rev? I'd like to offer my sincere thanks to her."

Revelin shook his head. "Speak to her in English. She must begin learning the language."

"There's our wayfarer at last," Robin said as he looked up to see Richard Atholl topping the rise down which they had already ridden. "I must say I'm tired of waiting for him. 'Tis no reason for us to lag about because he will not come within fifty paces of the girl."

"He's afraid she'll fry his giblets and send the rest of him to roast in Hell," John added with a snicker. "God's light, he's a queer bird!"

"One of you should remind him that the lass he holds in contempt saved his wretched life!" Revelin spurred his horse and rode away.

Robin chuckled. "Our Rev has a temper."

"Go on, I'll wait for our timid parson," John suggested. "When I've done with him, he'll keep our pace!"

As Robin moved away, John crossed his arms to wait until Atholl had negotiated the narrow slope. The man's face was gray with weariness and he seemed thinner than before. *He would break like a brittle twig in my grasp,* John thought. But he had no intention of breaking Atholl, just bending the parsimonious hypocrite to his will.

"Parson, you slow us."

Sir Richard licked his lips nervously. "I—I feel most unwell. Is London much farther?"

John's black brows lifted. The man's wits were failing. "Aye, we're a far ride from London. You should rest." He did not wait for the man to agree but swung a leg over and slid from his saddle. Choosing a small keg from the generous provisions provided by the O'Neills, he offered it to his companion. "Have a swig, Atholl. You've lost the blood in your cheeks."

Sir Richard lowered himself painfully from his saddle and reached for the spirits, taking a healthy gulp that burned like fire in his dry throat. "Devil's brew!" he exclaimed, refusing a second swallow.

John took the keg and helped himself. "Does not the Bible say that men must sometimes fight fire with fire?"

Sir Richard covered his eyes with his hands, shaking his head mournfully. "There's a curse on me! I'm losing flesh. My garments hang from me as if from the skeleton I shall soon become!"

"I've no remedies for curses, but I've common sense to aid me," John grumbled under his breath. He stared at the man, torn between contempt for his weakness and concern that he was on the verge of collapse just when he was about to prove useful. "Sit down before you fall. The others will not roam too far ahead."

Too weak to argue, Sir Richard found a seat on a nearby boulder.

John took a second swig from the keg, then corked it. "I'm

glad for the chance to speak with you alone. There are things which I would rather Butler and Neville not hear." He leaned near Atholl. "We've much to gain from our experience. And we owe our luck to the O'Neill lass."

Sir Richard shuddered. "Plague me not with that witch's name!"

"Evil may turn a good deed if wielded by an honest hand." When Sir Richard's wintry eyes lifted to his face, John knew he had the man's attention at last. "Do you know who she is? I will tell you. The girl is the daughter of Shane O'Neill. Shake the cobwebs of fear from your mind and think of the implications!"

Sir Richard's expression was disbelieving. "How could . . . Nay, you've been lied to."

John thundered an oath and thrust his ruddy face closer. "Would I consider a tale that had no bottom to it? Turlough himself claimed the girl as his cousin's child. It was the talk of camp. I heard it from one who spoke a little of the queen's English. 'Tis said Shane put the girl aside as a changeling when she was born—"

"The devil's spawn!" Sir Richard interjected.

"Damn the devil!" John roared. "The blood tie is what counts. Shane got her on a gentlewoman. The queen recognizes handfast. It will serve as well as marriage for our purpose."

"Which is . . . ?"

"If the girl is brought under the queen's protection, the Crown will gain a stake in its claim to Ulster. Think back, man. Did not King Henry the Eighth resort to kidnapping in order to raise sons of Irish noblemen as faithful servants of the English Crown?"

"The charge was never proved," Sir Richard answered reprovingly. "You'd best guard your tongue."

John nodded. "I concede the need for discretion, yet it happened. And does not Turlough's own nephew Hugh O'Neill, the rightful heir to Shane's earldrom, reside even now under

English protection at Penhurst Castle? 'Tis common knowledge that the lad is no more than a forced guest of Sir Henry Sidney. The lord deputy of Ireland must nurture hopes of using the boy, when he is grown, to contest Turlough's claim to Tyrone. We may succeed with a claim in Ulster much sooner. The girl is old enough to wed. Turlough himself vows for the purity of her bloodline. If she were married to an Englishman, he would thus be entitled to claim her rights to O'Neill lands. That is a prize worth considering."

Sir Richard stroked his scraggly beard; the dullness had left his eyes. "Do you believe young Butler nourishes such hopes?"

John recoiled. If he did, then Butler was in danger of losing his life, but Atholl must not suspect it. "Upon his return to England, Butler is to be betrothed, with the queen's consent. Some other man must marry the girl."

Sir Richard gazed up at John. "One such as you?"

"Why not?" John stood up and began pacing. "I've the military experience to raise and maintain an Irish army in the queen's name. She gives that right to men like Peter Carew who are too old and stupid to accomplish the task. Yet, he was given lands any portion of which would set a man up as finely as a duke. Once assured my claim, I would pacify Ulster within a score of months."

"Ambitious plans," Sir Richard murmured.

"Aye, ambitious. Is there a man abroad who does not look covetously upon this green land? There," he said, pointing to the surrounding country. "Those forests could be cleared to raise corn and wheat. Over there, that rise is a perfect site for a fortress. A small standing army could protect the eye's distance."

"All of this for want of a witch." Sir Richard slowly shook his head. "'Tis a temptation she has visited upon you. This thirst for riches 'tis her thrall upon you."

John caught the wistful note in the man's voice and replied, "Is it less dangerous than the lust she inspires in Butler? You have seen it, the naked longing that looks out from the lad's eyes whenever he gazes upon her. Her flesh is ripe for mischief."

John moved closer, his voice coloring with the dark timbre of desire. "Have you not glimpsed a naked thigh when she dismounts? Her skin is like fresh cream. It shimmers lewdly. Does she not at every opportunity press herself, wanton that she is, to Butler? In the saddle, I've seen her hands reach—"

"Enough!" Sir Richard rose abruptly, his long face stained by two brilliant spots of color. "Enough of such wicked talk. You tempt yourself and me with the false beauty of that Hellbound she-serpent."

John drew a deep breath. It was true. A sheen of sweat had broken out on his brow. He must have her. He must! "There's a way of drawing her venom, Atholl. Marriage with a true Christian Englishman is the antidote. Butler is too weak a vessel. He is infected by Irish blood. He will succumb to her and she will drag him into everlasting damnation. A true Englishman can defeat her, beat her into submission if necessary. I would strip her of every false pretense, bare her sins and rout them by force."

"Yes, yes!" Images stirred behind Sir Richard's closed lids, images that he could not give voice to for fear of his soul. "Smite the devil within her! Flog the evil out of her. Purify her soul with mortification!"

John wiped the sweat from his face, amused by the trembling man before him. So, he had found another of the parson's weaknesses. The image of Meghan stripped and helpless had its attraction, but he doubted Atholl's methods would be his own.

"We must be clever, Sir Richard. The girl has so enticed Butler that he's loath to leave her side. We must lure her away, and you must help me. Distract Butler at the noon meal and I will begin my campaign to win her trust. Perhaps she can be persuaded to ride with me awhile. I know all the whore's tricks and will play them against her. 'Tis she who will be snared by her own lust."

"And that will save young Butler's soul," Sir Richard said. "I came to save a lost soul. 'Twas my only desire for this journey."

"You will accomplish that in aiding me," John replied.

Though it was still spring, the warmth of the sun was felt beneath the rare, blue-vaulted sky. Having shed her mantle while walking, Meghan pause to gaze up at a stately oak. It was a temptation she knew she must resist. Revelin had lectured her at the noonday meal about the differences between being a child and being a lady. One of them had stuck in her mind: *A lady was genteel*.

The very word made it sound like a difficult thing to accomplish. Ladies did not climb trees, he had told her as an example.

Meghan lowered her gaze. So many things were changing so quickly that she could not keep them straight in her mind. One thought had preoccupied her more than all the others. She was no longer a nameless bastard, a changeling without parents. She was the daughter of Shane O'Neill. She had had a mother and father and was even a member of the Irish nobility. She was someone important.

Meghan hugged herself. Perhaps now she had a chance of winning Revelin's love. Revelin liked ladies; he had said so. So, she must try to become one to please him. He had not told her that, but she was not stupid. She must learn to speak English and act as English ladies did.

She must forget the past. That meant never mentioning the vision that had occurred at Lough Neagh. Revelin had said she had dreamed it. That was not true, but if he wanted her to pretend that it had been a dream, she would. She would do anything to please him.

A friendly, wet muzzle nudged her behind the knees, and Meghan squealed in surprise.

Ualter barked and circled around to jump up on her.

"Ach! Get down, ye great beast!" Meghan cried as she staggered under his weight. The dog obeyed instantly, and Meghan shook a finger at him. "Bad dog!"

"He's rightly named, that brute. Ualter means 'wolf.'"

Meghan looked up and saw John standing there, his thumbs hooked into his belt.

"Aren't you afraid he'll gobble up a tender morsel like yourself?" His dark eyes moved slowly over her until they came to her bare legs. "I'm certainly tempted."

She did not understand his words, but she did not like the look in his eyes. He was a murderer, though she had not confided that to Revelin because he would not have believed her. As he grinned at her, she shook the wrinkles from her *leine* so that the shapeless garment better covered her.

"Ah, why did you do that? We're just getting acquainted. Butler's not the only man who knows how to please a girl." He reached into his jerkin, then held out a few dried prunes and took a step toward her. "I'd be more than happy to please you."

Meghan shrank back a step at his advance.

Ualter's ears flattened and his tail dropped in response to Megan's reaction. He did not growl, but the hair on his spine stiffened and his upper lip lifted.

John saw the dog's actions and hesitated. He hated the filthy animal, but he could not expect to win the girl's confidence if he ran the cur off. She had a fondness for the miserable flea bag.

"A fine dog," he said, wishing that he had a smattering of Gaelic beyond the vulgarities he had aped after Flora. Perhaps they would serve him later with the girl, but now her ignorance was a stumbling block. "Dog," he repeated, pointing at Ualter. "Ualter. Dog."

Meghan nodded once, wondering what the man wanted. "Ualter. Dog," she said.

"Good." John pointed at himself. "John. Man. John."

Meghan cocked her head. She did not mind Revelin's lessons but she resented this man's tutelage. After all, she was an O'Neill; she needed no murdering Englishman's help. "Man," she repeated slowly and smiled. "Revelin."

John's eyes narrowed at her smirking expression. The little wretch was having a private joke at his expense!

Lord, but she tempted him! Her face was flushed and her body trembled with delicious fear. The raw ache, the raging inferno of lust that threatened to consume him each time he was in the presence of a beautiful woman, flamed within him. He took another step toward her. If not for the dog he would have grabbed her and kissed the smirk from her face.

"Meghan, pretty," he said in a coaxing manner. "Have a sweetmeat, sweeting, My desire . . . is you," he added in an undertone.

Meghan watched his strange expression and remembered the day he had nearly fought Revelin. A shudder passed through her and she reached out for the reassurance of Ualter's broad back.

Alive to every nuance of the girl beside him, Ualter smelled her fear and moved to block John's path.

John's lids flickered and his hand went automatically to the dagger at his waist.

In response, Meghan drew the skean Turlough had given her, the one that had belonged to her father, Shane.

"Well, now," John said, the smile on his mouth not reaching his eyes as he stared at her naked blade. "How would you fair, my lovely, were you not so well guarded?"

"Has idleness reduced you to bullying children?" Robin questioned pleasantly as he strolled into the clearing. "For myself, I wouldn't stroll half a yard with you had I not whetted my sword's edge. Now you have a child blinking back tears."

Though it was too late, John moved his hand from his hilt. "The girl is slow-witted, Neville. I merely offered her a sweetmeat and she took it into her head that her life was in danger."

"How odd," Robin remarked. "I wonder what they breed into young girls these days that they start at every rutting boor who happens along." He moved closer to Meghan, inclined his head in a regal manner, then put out his hand to Ualter. "If Revelin's dog snaps at me, I'll be bound to call you out for provoking him. Ah, there, he licks me. We're all safe, I believe."

"Some more than others," John grumbled. He had lost his opportunity, but to leave the girl with another man seemed a defeat. "I would leave, Neville, but I've my doubts about your trustworthiness with the girl."

Robin looked at John with a smile of incredulous delight. "Why, Reade, 'tis the most flattering thing you've ever said to me!"

John turned and stalked away spewing curses.

Robin turned back to Meghan, who had sheathed her weapon. "Don't mind Reade. He cannot help the fact that all his brains are in his breeches."

Meghan responded to his bantering tone with a half-smile. Perhaps it was because he was small, only a few inches taller than she, that she liked him. Looking at his freckled face, which was pink with health, she was reminded of the night Turlough had nearly killed him and his sick-hearted look of fear. She had understood that. It was a shared experience between them.

Encouraged by her smile, Robin held out a hand to her. "I owe you an apology, little one. I behaved as a knave would toward you, and yet you risked your life for mine." When she placed her hand shyly in his, he brought it to his lips for a light kiss. Struck by whimsy, he quoted from Cicero, *"Amici probantur rebus adversis."*

The words were scarcely out of his mouth before Meghan

replied softly in Gaelic-inflected Latin, "'Friends in adversity' should remain friends always."

Robin's mouth worked up and down but no sound would come out, and his comic expression drew Meghan's laughter.

"But of course!" Robin managed finally. He had thought the woman in Turlough's camp was an exception. Of course, Meghan knew Latin, too. She was a follower of the Roman faith. Thrilled by his discovery, he threw his arms about her waist and lifted her off the ground with a sweep.

The discovery Revelin made as he came upon the pair was a distinct shock. Meghan was laughing, her head thrown back and her blue-black hair streaming out like banners in the wind as Robin swung her around and around.

"What the devil do you think you're doing?"

Meghan and Robin stumbled to a halt, looked at Revelin's stern features and then at each other, and dissolved into giggles like a pair of conspirators.

"A happy discovery, Rev," Robin volunteered when he recovered. "'Twould seem we've underestimated the Irish. Our little fairy speaks Latin!"

Revelin frowned, more interested in Robin's hand on Meghan's waist than in her ability to speak Latin. "I thought you feared fairies, Sir Robin."

"That!" Robin scoffed. "I'm no less a fool than most men."

"No doubt," Revelin murmured.

Robin squeezed Meghan affectionately, and to Revelin's further irritation she looped an arm about the young nobleman's waist. "Think of the splash she'll make in London. Many at court have never laid eyes on a native Irish lass. With her wild beauty, she'll make a most persuasive ambassadress."

"An oddity, you mean," Revelin corrected as he strode toward them. "She's not a wild beast to be paraded about on a golden leash, nor is she some New World aborigine to be displayed for the amusement of your dissolute friends."

He knocked Robin's hand from Meghan's waist. "And while

we speak of such things, keep your hands off the lass. I'll not see her seduced and ruined by some libertine."

Robin looked at his friend in surprise. "Is it something I've done? Twice this day I've been accused of having designs on the girl's virtue. I hope the aura lasts until we arrive in Dublin." He lowered his eyes for a moment, and when he looked up again his gaze was bright with mischief. "If there's danger, 'tis not from me. You'd do well to search closer to home."

Revelin's face flushed, despite the cold fury in his voice as he said, "Do you seek to teach me manners?"

"Rev, John's tactics are rubbing off on you," Robin chided.

Meghan stepped close to Revelin, troubled by his look of anger, and laid her hand on his arm. "Have I angered ye?"

Revelin looked down into eyes the color of forest violets and a little of his jealousy receded. "Nay. 'Tis only my temper strained by bad company." He looked at Robin. "I apologize. Sir Richard spoiled my meal with talk of London politics."

Robin's gaze sharpened. "What could Atholl possibly have to say on the subject?"

Hearing the interest in Robin's voice, Revelin contrarily changed his mind about confiding in him, though he had just been seeking him out for that reason. "Nothing that matters. He's in need of a long rest."

Robin did not pursue the matter directly. "Will you be sailing for London with the rest of us?"

Revelin shook his head. "After presenting myself in Dublin, I must take Meghan to Kilkenny. I have relatives there who will understand her needs better than the English."

"Do you believe the queen will indulge the delay?"

"I don't see that it's any of your business." Revelin could not stop the irritated rise in his voice. When Meghan's hand tightened on his arm, he turned to her, his face stormy. "Take Ualter and go back to the horse! And, for god's sake, don't run off again because I've barked at you."

Meghan looked not at all abashed by his temper. "Ye've a nasty mood on ye and I forgive ye it. Only, ye should not blame the little man for what he did." She smiled at Robin. "He's a nice lad." She beckoned Ualter with a snap of her fingers and walked off.

Revelin followed her with his eyes, unable to dampen his appreciation of the way her hips swayed gracefully as she walked. Belatedly he recalled Robin's comment about his own conduct. He looked back. "I will say this once only. Leave the lass alone. She doesn't know better than to think every man's interest is innocent."

Unoffended, Robin said, "Allow me to ask how she is to learn if you guard her as jealously as a she-wolf with a new cub? She must learn of the world, Rev, if she is to survive. She could use a few friends."

Revelin looked skeptical. "You would be her friend?"

"Would you prefer Reade or Parson Atholl?"

Revelin smiled.

"You are new to mothering," Robin said sympathetically.

Revelin swore. "I'm no mother or father, come to that. She's too near a woman for my own peace of mind."

Robin curbed his tongue this time. "You could do worse, you know."

"Worse than what?"

"Meghan has good bloodlines, and she's beautiful despite the devil's trick that mars her cheek. Yet, even that seems to fade from one's mind after a few days. But if court gossip of an impending engagement between you and Lady Alison be true, then you had best let the girl be drawn from your side while you practice a better liar's face. You give yourself away every time you gaze on her, Rev."

Revelin turned away. "I don't think I asked for your advice."

"And I don't often offer it," Robin answered smoothly. "Perhaps 'tis only my sudden fondness for the lass that makes me speak out of turn." He added more seriously, "You're familiar with love's sting and will not be fatally wounded. Not so with Meghan. When she looks on you there's worship in her eyes."

Revelin turned on him. "She doesn't love me!"

"Does she not?" Robin raised his hands in a gesture of futility. "Tell me you've done no more than kiss her, and I'll be silent."

Revelin looked away.

Robin patted Revelin's shoulder. "You did me a good turn in the O'Neill camp. I told you things I'm already regretting, but that's another matter. Let me help you with Meghan. I can be a friend to both of you."

Revelin resisted the urge to shrug off Robin's touch, for he knew his irritation was with himself. The grand plans he had been fashioning on the morning ride had been toppled by a few words of insight. Meghan felt something for him. How could she not? He was her link with the world. If it was not love, it was dangerously close.

What he felt he no longer knew. Alison's features refused any longer to resolve themselves in his mind. He had been so certain that he could not forget her. Now he needed to gaze on her gold-and-rose beauty and be reminded of the feelings that he had carried with him across the Irish Sea, feelings of a promising future and useful service to his sovereign.

When he looked up, there was new resolve in his expression. "If you do not object to bearing Meghan in your saddle this afternoon, I could do a bit of sketching. Turlough kept the maps I made, and I need to commit my poor memory to paper before it fades altogether."

After an hour of Robin's company, Meghan had forgotten her pique at being set aside by Revelin. "Tell me again about how the ladies of London go riding," she encouraged.

Robin smiled down at her, quite pleased that he had been able to coax her into riding side-saddle before him. It gave him an excuse to keep an arm about her waist, and it proved that he was by far the better diplomat, for Revelin had sworn she would only ride astride.

"London ladies ride in coaches; they're like wagons with tops," he answered.

"Golden wagons," she filled in, "with red wheel rims and blue spokes and a driver who wears finery the like of which I have never seen."

Robin's laughter drew a dark look from Revelin, who rode a little ahead. "You sound like a parrot, sweeting."

"What's a parrot?"

"A brightly feathered bird who can talk."

"Birds cannot talk," Meghan answered. "At least, I know no bird that talks. That is not the same thing, is it?"

Robin gave her a pleased look. "Any number of courtiers at Whitehall could benefit from your astuteness. Most educated men show themselves to be fools when confronted with that which they have never before experienced." On impulse, he bent and touched his lips to her cheek.

Meghan's eyes widened. "Revelin would not like that."

Robin's lips twitched. "Whyever not?"

Meghan glanced at Revelin's back. "He did not like Colin MacDonald to kiss me. He will not like it any better if it is you."

Thoroughly intrigued by this bit of news, Robin could not resist drawing her out. "And what of you? Did you like Colin MacDonald's kisses?"

Meghan considered this. "Aye, they were lovely. But Revelin's are nicer."

"And mine?" he encouraged.

She shrugged, aware that he was teasing her. "I cannot say. You did not do it properly."

Robin's whoop of laughter nearly unseated them. "God's light! You saucy wench! We'll see about kisses later!"

Revelin was preoccupied and his Latin rusty. He heard clearly only the last sentence of their exchange, but it was enough. He reined in his horse and turned to wait for them.

"She's a natural flirt!" Robin volunteered cheerfully.

The thought was not a particularly comforting one. Ignoring Robin, Revelin gave Meghan a stern look. "Would you care to ride with me now?"

Meghan did not hesitate. She raised her arms to him and was immediately lifted across his saddle. Revelin turned his mount again, deliberately avoiding Robin.

Meghan encircled Revelin's neck and forked her fingers through the thick golden hair at the back of his head. "Ye're better," she said, reverting to Gaelic. She pressed her cheek contentedly to his. "Ye smell better, ye're better to gaze upon, and ye kiss better!"

"Better than who?" Revelin questioned, with an odd catch in his voice.

Meghan placed a feather-light kiss on his chin. "Better than anyone." After a moment she added, "It's come to me that I'll nae wed any man but ye, Revelin Butler."

So there it was at last, the thing he most dreaded. "Meghan, lass," he began, praying that the right words would come to his aid. "There's mort of difference between what you—what we—may feel and what leads to marriage. A man may meet and like many ladies but he can marry only one."

Meghan leaned her head back to see his expression. "How does a man know which is the right one?"

"The problem exactly!" he agreed heartily, staring over her head with concentrated effort. "That is where the opinions of others help him. He seeks the advice of his family, sometimes even the queen herself. And, of course, the lady must do the same. There are matters of lands and moneys, family tradition, and alliances to be considered."

A pucker appeared between Meghan's winged brows. "'Tis difficult."

"Aye, 'tis that." As much as he disliked the idea, he knew he must be honest with her. "That is why we have a custom called—"

"'Tis called bundling," Meghan finished for him. "If the

230

woman doesn't breed within a year, there's no wedding. But ye've nae cause to worry. Sila said there'll be a babe before Saint Brigid's Eve."

Revelin choked. "Church law, of which you are not ignorant, Meghan, does not approve of—er—bundling before the wedding day."

"Aye. Una said 'tis so. But ye did not wish to wait, Revelin, and I would deny ye nothing."

She smiled up at him so sweetly that Revelin felt the blood rise into his cheeks. "I led you astray, lass, that I did. You're not to blame. 'Tis my fault."

Meghan shrugged, rubbing the fine silk of his hair between her fingers. "I charmed ye. 'Twas Sila put me to it, but I'll nae say a word against her for it." She snuggled closer to him. "'Tis a wondrous thing, this honey-making."

Revelin sighed. "I was telling you about an English custom called an engagement," he said hoarsely. "When a man is engaged he pledges to be faithful to the woman he loves. But sometimes he forgets when he is far away and the temptation is strong."

Meghan leaned back again to look at him. The beauty that had drawn him from the first was still there but drained of its animation. He was telling her something that she did not understand, nor did she wish to, for suddenly she knew it would not be to her liking. "I do not like this 'gagement. We will nae have one."

"You may not have one, Meghan," he said in his gentlest tone. "'Tis I who am engaged."

She heard the words, but as she gazed at him she could not believe it. "If—if ye wish it, we'll have one."

Revelin closed his eyes briefly. "Listen to me, Meghan. I am engaged to another, a lady who lives in London. We are to be married when I return to England."

"Then do not go!" Meghan responded, flushing with dislike for the woman she had never met.

"'Tis not so simple as that. I've given her my pledge."

"Ye do not love her," Meghan maintained stubbornly, but tears had begun to blur her vision. "Ye cannot say ye love her when 'tis me ye chose on Beltane."

Revelin felt her stiffen at his silence and then her arms fell from his neck. He had hurt her, but there was no other way to do this. "I—I want your promise, lass, that you'll not run away again. 'Tis no safe place and I do care what happens to you."

Meghan hunched her shoulders and pulled away until the brisk spring breeze cooled the space between them. "Ye're nae wed. 'Tis no sin to love someone else."

"Perhaps that's so," he answered slowly. "But I've given my word, as I gave your aunt my word that I would look after you. I cannot break my word."

The logic escaped Meghan. A pain had begun to settle in her chest like a great stone pressing down on her, and tears swam in her eyes. "Ye do not like me anymore. 'Tis because I did nae act the lady for ye." She raised her eyes to his, a plea in her voice. "But I can act the lady, I will do anything for ye, ye must know that."

Revelin watched the path of a tear as it ran the high curve of her cheek, crossed the blood-red rose birthmark, and trickled down the slope of her jaw, where he caught it with his fingertip. He had made her cry. That knowledge hurt him more than the broken oath to Alison or the guilt of having taken Meghan's virtue. She knew so little of joy. Now he had added to her burden of sorrow.

"Hush, lass, no tears," he crooned as he brushed away a second droplet and slipped a hand behind her head to bring her cheek against his chest. To his surprise she went willingly, sliding her arms about his waist and pressing her cheek over his heart.

"I love ye, Revelin, that I do!" she said in a hushed, halting voice.

"I know, lass, I know."

There was nothing more he could say. If ordered on pain of his death to tell the truth, he could not say whether the great swelling of emotion that squeezed his chest was love or pity or guilt. And what of Alison? She was as innocent as Meghan.

"God have pity on us all," he murmured.

Chapter Twelve

Dublin: June 1569

Meghan gazed down from an upper window of an oak-beamed cagework house that had been built within the shadow of Dublin Castle. A faint odor of turpentine rose from the surface of the wooden casement on which she balanced her elbows as she stared out in fascination. When they had arrived at the city gate of the walled town, the dark of night had hidden the sprawling expanse of Dublin. Now, in the daylight, the city lay stretched out before her. It was unlike anyplace she had ever seen. Turlough's settlement of tents and wickerwork huts had not prepared her for the grandness of an Elizabethan city. Everywhere rose buildings of wood and stone, some of them reaching to the incredible height of three stories and topped by roofs of slate or shingle. The castle itself was a huge stone structure of Norman design. Smaller examples of Norman stonework dotted the countryside they had ridden through, but none of them compared with the curtain-walled fortress that occupied the opposite side of the street beyond a ditch too broad for an enemy to broach easily.

She leaned out a little farther, eager to see everything at once. The street below teemed with soldiers. Their unfamiliar uniforms of red and blue identified them as foreigners in Meghan's mind. In vain she sought a glimpse of the saffron tunics of the O'Neills. In fact, none of the men below were dressed like the Irish she knew. They wore hose and doublets like Revelin. There was not a man in tunic and trousers among them.

In the distance to the south she saw the spires of a church. Stretching out until she balanced precariously on her hips, she spied the silver-gold flash of a river running beyond the castle walls. Turning her head in the opposite direction, she saw another, wider ribbon of green-brown water flowing past the end of the street. It seemed as if they were surrounded by rivers.

When the door opened behind her, she drew back with a cry of delight. "Ach, Revelin, come and see what—"

Standing in the doorway was a tidily dressed woman of middle years. She wore a white swatch of cloth tied over her long dark gown and a funny-shaped cap upon her head. Except for a pink mouth and wide blue eyes, her broad face was as pale and smooth as cream. She looked vaguely familiar, and then Meghan remembered that she was the one who had guided her upstairs to this room the night before.

The woman's speech pattern was different from her own, but Meghan knew she understood her. "Where's Revelin?"

The woman pursed her lips. "I'll be thanking ye not to refer to the earl of Ormond's foster son by his first name. 'Tis 'Sir Revelin' ye should be calling him. What learning have ye if ye don't know that?"

Meghan lifted her chin indignantly. "And who are ye?"

"Me name's Mrs. Cambra, and I'll have none of yer airs, me wild heathen." She looked about the room, frowning as she took in the unused bed, then turned her inquiring gaze on Meghan. She looked the girl up and down and sniffed. "Ye've soiled yer gown already. I told them belowstairs ye should have been looked to first thing, but Sir Revelin, being a soft-hearted man and seeing as how ye were sore in need of sleep, had me put ye to bed."

Meghan looked down at the brown streak marring the sheer white dressing gown she had been given and knew it was stain that had rubbed off the casement. She looked up with the kind of smile that had always worked on Una. "Would ye look at that, and me that proud of me new English clothes. 'Twill wear off by week's end, never ye fear."

"I should hope not!" Mrs. Cambra responded. She held out her hand. "Ye'll give me that while ye wash proper. Then I'm to have a seamstress up here to make a decent showing of ye."

Meghan took a backward step, clutching the front of her gown. "Where's me *leine?*"

"Burnt it!" the woman said without a hint of regret.

"Burnt? Me clothes?" Anger shook Meghan as she thought of the bog-cotton gown she had lovingly rolled up and carried with her from Ulster. It was the most beautiful thing she had ever owned. Surely Revelin would not have allowed it to be destroyed. "What of me other gown? If ye've burnt it, I'll—!"

"Ye'll learn a few new things here, me girl," Mrs. Cambra said, unperturbed by the girl's outburst. Imitating the English maids she had occasionally shared quarters with when her masters, the Butlers, had guests, she folded her arms resolutely across her ample bosom. "Ye cannot go about in filthy rags; what a shame that'd bring on Sir Revelin. A sound scrubbing with lye soap should best the fleas and lice, and then we'll tame that black devil's nest on yer head."

Meghan gasped in rage, no less angered than when Sila had suggested she crawled with vermin. But Mrs. Cambra stepped back into the hall and snapped her fingers.

A moment later the door opened wider and a young boy carried in a large, steaming copper kettle. His face turned bright red as he cast sidelong glances at Meghan standing boldly before him in dishabille.

"What do ye gape at, ye lazy cur!" Mrs. Cambra scolded. "Skelp ye, I will, and have yer thanks behind it! Out! Out!"

The boy ducked the expected blow and in the process tipped the kettle, which spilled a stream of steaming water onto the polished floor.

"Aarrah, ye're spilling it!" Mrs. Cambra grabbed a poker from the fireplace and swung it half-heartedly at the boy.

He yelped in mock fear and scrambled out the door after depositing his burden on the washstand.

"Good riddance!" the housekeeper exclaimed when the door slammed behind him. With great precision she replaced the poker and righted the frilly cap on her head before turning back to Meghan. "Off with it, me lass, and bathe."

Meghan looked at the shallow porcelain basin doubtfully. "In there?"

"Aye, that's it."

"But, 'tis so very small."

Mrs. Cambra's eyes widened in understanding. "Ye're not to stand in it! Saints preserve us! No woman or man with sense would wet the whole body, else they'd be taken by a chill in a fortnight." She shook her head, mumbling, "Wild Irish!"

Reluctantly Meghan began to fumble with the tiny pearls that had been sewn as buttons down the front of her gown, but she could not loosen them.

"Give over!" Mrs. Cambra said in disgust and came forward to slap Meghan hands away. "I've heard tales of Ulstermen. 'Tis said fair backwards folk they be." The buttons flew open under her hands and then she pulled the gown from Meghan's shoulders and let it fall to the floor.

Mrs. Cambra's slight gasp made Meghan lift a hand to her left cheek. She had forgotten, forgotten so quickly, how it affected strangers. Expecting a rebuff, she looked up into the woman's face.

"Mercy!" But the housekeeper was not staring at her face; she stared at Meghan's breasts and then her narrow waist and slim thighs. "'Tis more to Sir Revelin's generosity than tenderheartedness, I'm thinking," she murmured.

Pursing her lips, she drew herself up to her full height. "If ye think to be bringing whorish ways into this house, ye'll be finding no help from me. I've laid eyes on Lady Burke and 'tis my loyalty she'll be getting. A fine wife she'll make for Sir Revelin."

"'Tis glad I am to know I've your approval in my choice of bride."

Neither of them had heard the knock at the door or its opening. The sound of Revelin's voice came as a distinct shock. Mrs. Cambra spun about as her hand flew up to still her betraying tongue. Meghan, glad of an ally at last, fled past the woman and into Revelin's arms.

"Ach! Revelin, 'tis glad I am to see ye!" Throwing her arms about his waist, she smiled her brightest smile. "'Tis fair hard, she is, burning me clothes and telling lies about me crawling with creatures!"

The thought that she was naked had not fully registered in Revelin's mind when Meghan flung herself at him and he automatically embraced her. The shock of encountering the velvety texture of her skin as he wrapped his arms about her stilled whatever thoughts he had been about to put into words. In her agitation she was dancing about, rubbing her lovely body against him.

"Revelin, please! Ye must do something!" Meghan begged, unaware of the effect her actions were having on the two people in the room. She squeezed him against her, reveling in the strength of his bigger, harder body. "Do not let her burn me Beltane gown. Please! Ye must do something!"

"Do something," Revelin repeated a little stupidly. Of course!

He must do something. But what? His mind was fully occupied with sensation. It recorded with bewildering detail the exact fullness of the naked buttock he had unconsciously cupped, the delicious pressure of wantonly soft breasts, and the exact shade of brilliant blue in her welcoming gaze.

"Harrumph!"

It was an inelegant sound, worthy of a reprimand from her master, but Revelin heard it like a trumpet's blast in the midst of his failing defenses. He blinked. Only an instant had passed. Meghan was staring up expectedly at him. Mrs. Cambra . . .

Mrs. Cambra! "What the devil's going on?" Pleased with the strong, authoritative sound of his voice, Revelin repeated the question: "What the devil's happening here?"

Mrs. Cambra recrossed her arms in the best English-servant fashion and inclined her head once toward the naked girl in her master's arms. "That mad she is, Sir Revelin, standing there in nothing but what the good Lord give her! Begging your pardon, but 'tis not in me power to do a proper job with such as her."

Revelin, who could think of no reasonable answer to that, remained silent. It suddenly dawned on the housekeeper that perhaps Sir Revelin was waiting for her to do something about the girl. She ran and grabbed a sheet from the bed.

"Let the poor man be!" she scolded as she wrapped Meghan in the linen and then pulled her out of Revelin's arms. "Ach! None of that or 'tis a good slap ye'll be getting," she continued when Meghan began to struggle. "Just look at what ye've done. Mortally offended the gentleman what's housing ye, ye have!"

Meghan glanced back at Revelin to see a blank look on his face that might have been offense or bewilderment or even simple surprise.

In fact, it was the latter two, combined with a sudden realization that the wealth of emotion swirling through him was not composed solely of lust. He should have been shocked, embarrassed, furious with Meghan for her hysterical behavior in front of a servant. But he did not feel anything like that. Her artless actions inspired a rush of protective tenderness within him underscored by an irrational spurt of anger that Mrs. Cambra's presence prevented him from sweeping Meghan up and carrying her to the bed that stood so invitingly nearby. But this was his household and it was badly in need of authority.

In his best master-to-servant voice he said, "Dress and groom the girl decently. I shall require her presence below within the hour."

Revelin discovered with relief that his feet still functioned to his command. They carried him out through the door without mishap. But in the hall, with the door closed safely behind him, he suddenly slumped against the wall, his breath coming in quick gasps.

He was in love—with Meghan!

"You grand fool!" he sputtered before laughter overcame him. How simple. How natural. How terrible.

Meghan, unaware of his conclusions, had squared off against Mrs. Cambra for the second time. "Ye'll not be using them great shears on me. I'm nae a sheep!"

Mrs. Cambra opened and closed the long sewing shears she had pulled from her pocket. "Aye, a sheep ye look with that tangled head of filthy black wool. 'Tis the only way, lass. The beasties must come out!"

In one quick, economical gesture, Meghan picked up her skean from the mantel and held it menacingly. "We'll see who carves which sheep!" she cried and lunged at the woman.

Horrified, Mrs. Cambra dropped her scissors with a scream that shook the rafters and ran for the door. The door opened under the assault of her considerable bulk and she was propelled into the hall's opposite wall with a resounding crash.

Revelin pulled himself upright as Meghan reached the doorway. Holding her cover in one hand, she waved her weapon at the breathless older woman. "That for yer shearing! And do not come back till ye've learned something of manners!"

Revelin and Mrs. Cambra exchanged looks as the door was slammed shut on them.

"'Twas mild as a lamb she was 'ere this, I swear it!" Revelin offered before hilarity claimed him a second time. "Lord love us!" he sputtered between gales of laughter. "What have I brought upon myself?"

Sweating and puffing, Mrs. Cambra righted her cap once more. "There's no proper feeling in them barbarous northmen! Ye'll rue the day, I'm thinking, Sir Revelin!"

"Aye," Revelin said as he sobered. "Mayhaps 'tis my just reward."

Sir Henry Sidney sat behind the massive trestle table and studied his guest through narrowed lids. Ordinarily he would have kept a man of John Reade's meager lineage and reputation cooling his heels for a fortnight before agreeing to see him. But the contents of the badly written missive he had been handed with his breakfast impelled him to grant the man an immediate interview.

Even so, Sir Henry was not above making the man stand while he completed his meal. As lord deputy of Ireland he was not merely the queen's representative, he was fully empowered to administer to royal interests in matters both national and civil. He might be eaten with curiosity over Reade's innuendoes concerning Shane O'Neill and Ulster, but Reade, as a commoner, could not be allowed to suspect it.

Sir Henry carefully dabbed his lips with a linen napkin, purposefully refolded it, and laid it aside before gesturing Reade forth with a languid hand.

"John Reade, late captain under the earl of Leicester?" he inquired in a bored drawl.

John stepped forth briskly. "That I am, my lord!"

Sir Henry slowed his approach with a lift of a hand and reached for the piece of parchment that lay beside his breakfast plate. He looked at it briefly and then back at the man. "I do not usually accept interviews on my morning off." He paused to allow the full import of his statement to sink in. "What is so urgent that it could not wait until Parliament is next in session?"

John hated himself for the wince of anxiety that struck him. Sir Henry stood to gain much by the information he had come to impart, but the man made him feel his lack of courtly manners and relegated him to the position of petitioner. Yet he was a soldier, a campaigner, and not about to be quelled.

"Sorry I am to disturb your breakfasting, my lord Deputy. I might full well have waited with the matter, but as I know your opinion of the O'Neills, and seeing as how Shane O'Neill led you such a merry chase those last years . . ."

John noted with pleasure a flash of warning in the elder man's pale eyes. He had skewered the man squarely with the mention of Shane's numerous victories over the lord deputy and his troops. "It came to me that my information might be of benefit to you."

Sir Henry stared mutely at his guest, then laid the parchment aside and drained his tea cup. "You have been a good and loyal soldier, I'm told, John Reade. If not for your uncertain temper you might well be fighting on the Continent with your compatriots rather than leading an expedition of surveyors beyond the Pale. I tend to overlook the matter of temper in most cases, being a soldier myself. But we've a queen on the throne who knows her own mind, and, as loyal subjects, we bow to her wishes—or suffer the consequences."

"As for Shane O'Neill—" he could not quell the distaste in his voice, the anger was too fresh, "as for the rebel and outlaw Shane O'Neill, I have nothing to say. Men loyal to the Crown brought his head in for bounty a year past. The matter is at an end."

John was blinking rapidly by the end of Sir Henry's speech, for he had been censured, pitied, threatened, and dismissed all in the space of a few sentences.

"But—but, my lord," he began as Sir Henry rose from his chair. "My lord, hear me, for matters pertinent to the claimancy of Ulster are at stake."

Sir Henry's expression changed from indifference to distaste. "The matter of Ulster is being decided this very week by the Irish Parliament. The decision they will reach will coincide with the queen's feeling on the matter. Shane O'Neill shall be attainted, his name and title as earl of Tyrone extinguished from the roll of Her Majesty's nobility, and the lands of Ulster forfeited to the Crown to be redistributed as she sees fit."

The first two had no bearing on John's interests, but the third galvanized him. "Ulster is to be opened to private speculation?"

Sir Henry looked down his aristocratic nose at the burly soldier. "Something of the like. As to your interest in the outcome, I was not aware that you have claim to Irish ancestry or title."

The slap at his antecedents did not sting John. He would have a claim once he married Meghan. "I may soon have a most reasonable and urgent claim to lands in Tyrone."

Sir Henry hesitated. Common sense told him it was impossible for Reade to possess what he claimed. Yet, Ireland, as he had learned in his six years as lord deputy, was a land where the impossible occurred on a regular basis. He reseated himself. "Tell me more."

At the end of Reade's fantastic tale of kidnapping, pagan revelry, and the act of superstitious shamming that had saved the lives of his company, Sir Henry was torn between incredulity and an avid curiosity to lay eyes on the daughter of the man he had contested both on the battlefield and in the courts for nearly ten years.

In the end Shane had outfoxed himself and lost. Yet, Sir Henry had never forgotten the personal humiliation of the queen's actions in 1562 during Shane's visit to London. He had expected Shane to be clapped in irons and dumped in the

Tower dungeon. Instead, the queen conceded to Shane official sanction within the realm of Tyrone.

Sir Henry reminded himself philosophically, as he had often in the years following that blow, that the queen was a woman, which had been Shane's advantage. 'Twas the man's brawny form and manly face ringed with black curls that had won Shane the victory.

But all that was past. The present needed and had his full attention.

Sir Henry's penetrating gaze swept Reade. "You say you have brought Shane O'Neill's daughter to Dublin. Why is she not here with you?"

John wet his lips. This was not the moment to be caught in a lie. "As I have said, Revelin Butler saved the girl's life and extracted a pledge of some sort from her dying aunt that he be made her guardian. I do not know to what extent the pledge was forced or even if the pledge was in reality given. You may ask Sir Robin Neville, but he will tell you what he told me: his lack of understanding of the Irish tongue prevented him from knowing exactly what took place."

Sir Henry nodded. He would certainly check Reade's story. "The girl resides with Butler at present?"

John nodded. "However, as young Butler is not married and lives with no female relatives, I would like to see the girl removed to more—ah . . ."

"Appropriate surroundings," Sir Henry offered.

"Exactly, my lord. I call no disrespect upon Butler, but as a man who harbors some feelings in the matter, I—well . . ." John lowered his gaze as he thought appropriate for a man about to divulge his great love for a girl.

Sir Henry did not think much of the performance. Reade was not the sort of man to resort to mannered expressions and long-winded verse. That he was attempting to do so meant that he wanted something. "Tell me, Reade, does the girl feel the same?"

John blushed though not with romantic ardor. Meghan would

not allow him to come within a yard of her, and yet he must make Sir Henry see her reluctance as natural. "She is shy, my lord, raised a country girl with little to recommend her but her beauty."

"And her name," Sir Henry mumbled too low for his guest to hear. "Do go on."

"I cannot tell her feelings. As to the reason, I doubt she is quick enough to know what she should feel."

"The girl's a simpleton?"

"Oh no, merely untutored," John hurriedly corrected. "She is unacquainted with the ways of the world. You, my lord, have dealt with the native Irish and know that many of them do not understand the simplest English customs. So it is with the girl. She clings to Butler as though he were blood kin. And her dress and manner, well, all but those of the weakest of moral fiber would construe her conduct as akin to a whore's."

Sir Henry blanched. "And Revelin Butler, does he possess the moral fiber of which you speak?"

John looked the man in the eye. "Can a man of Butler's age and constitution be blamed for taking what was so baldly offered?"

Sir Henry was surprised to read the truth of Reade's statement in the soldier's eyes. Butler had made the girl his whore. Of course, it was to be expected. Faith knew, the moral degeneracy of the Irish was a constant plague upon the moral fiber of his countrymen. He reached for the bell that stood behind his plate and rang it sharply. "The girl will be removed from Butler's household at once. As for your interest in her, we shall see."

Reade licked his lips. Blasting Meghan free from Butler's protection was only part of his plan. "My lord, I would ask your permission to call upon the girl."

Sir Henry looked startled. "My permission? I have no intention of cosseting the girl under *my* roof. She will be found a room within the castle walls. As for your attentions, the girl has a tongue. She may ask for you as is her wont."

John paled beneath his sunburn. "And if she prefers Butler's company?"

Sir Henry frowned. He would not have the castle turned into a brothel, yet he could not prevent them from visiting in proper surroundings. "I must find a woman to act as companion to the girl. If she is as backward as you say, I may needs hire a bodyguard as well. Dublin teems with Her Majesty's soldiers, and if the girl gives freely to a handsome face, she should be curbed." He looked up under drawn brows. "If the girl is an O'Neill, she is a noble lady and will be treated as such."

"If the girl were wed to an Englishman, my lord, she would be subject thereafter to his and her Majesty's jurisdiction."

So that was it! At last he had Reade's measure. Sir Henry's voice grew frigid. "Lest you forget the Crown's full extent, the girl is already one of Her Majesty's subjects. It is a lesson her father would not learn. As for marriage, I would put the matter aside for the present. Until the matter of Ulster is settled, she is a prize for no man who hopes to further himself with the Crown."

John knew he had ventured too far and could have kicked himself. "As you say, my lord." He bowed grandly. "But understand, what I feel for the girl is not bound up in the promise of dower lands." No, he thought, what he felt and must be relieved of was a lust for her that was driving him mad, despite a strenuous night in Dublin's most famous brothel. It had nothing to do with physical release, this clamoring, rapacious hunger for the girl. It was a need so great that he grew rigid at the mere thought of her. He would have her, again and again, until there was nothing left in his soul to be slaked by her body. But to do that, he must first get rid of the Butler lad.

Sir Henry thought rapidly. Reade must be removed from Dublin. A man of his stamp was bound to cause trouble, else.

"Sir Peter Carew, now the baron of Idrone, is in need of seasoned campaigners to put down a local uprising. An enterprising man could show himself to advantage there before petitioning the queen for favors."

The light of understanding glowed in Reade's eyes as he swept the lord deputy a bow and departed.

When Reade had departed, Sir Henry penned a brief note to be delivered to the Butler home in Castle Street. He wanted the girl safely away from there. He did not care about the girl's virtue—were she any other Gael, Revelin could plow her as long and well as he pleased—but Sir Henry could not afford for a Butler to form an alliance with an O'Neill, not while the Butlers threatened to defend their land with swords. If matters continued to deteriorate in Leinster, he could not be certain that the Butlers would not call for aid from the north. If Shane's daughter was in Butler hands, the O'Neills might feel obligated to join them in rebellion.

Sir Henry sat back and pinched his eyes between thumb and forefinger. He had known Revelin since boyhood. The young man might be shocked when he learned the extent to which his uncles had been drawn into rebellion against the Crown's colonist Peter Carew. Then again, Butler was hotheaded enough to ride off to join them. If that happened, the O'Neill girl must be safely confined in Dublin.

"Confound this Celtic blood!" Sir Henry exclaimed aloud. Ruthless they could be, cruel and hotheaded, but to the last man they were loyal to their own.

"Damn Reade for his presumption!" Revelin crumpled the parchment and threw it into the huge fire that blazed from the hearth in the salon. He had planned to attend Sir Henry Sidney in the morning, had in fact made the appointment. Now he was ordered to appear at Dublin Castle at nine o'clock in the morning with Meghan in tow.

"Reade is concerned for Meghan's protection, is he?" Revelin's laughter was bitter. Reade had shown no interest in Meghan's welfare on the ride to Dublin. Reade must be planning to use Meghan to . . . to do what?

Revelin ran a hand through his newly shorn locks. While waiting to discover what miracles Mrs. Cambra would perform on Meghan's appearance, he had turned himself over to the barber and tailor. When they had left him he felt like a new man. The suit of clothing he wore was a welcome change from the mud-splattered leather jerkin and hose of the last weeks, and he had been eager to see Meghan's reaction. But all that was forgotten now.

He moved from the hearth to the long table that had been set with two places, but he did not really see the silver and gold place settings. Reade was up to something; in some way he thought he stood to gain by luring Meghan away from Revelin.

"Well, I'll not step into the trap until I've learned a little more."

"Sir?"

Revelin signaled to the footman who had been waiting patiently at the door. "Who gave you the letter?"

"A member of the castle guard," the man replied.

"Did he expect a reply?"

The footman smiled. "I told him you had given orders you were not to be disturbed. He didn't like it, but there was naught he could do."

"Good man." At least his staff remained loyal. In these days of bribery and stealth, a loyal household was more valuable than lined pockets. "I don't suppose you told him I would be out for the remainder of the day?"

"Had you told me to say so, I would have, sir."

Revelin saw the man's face fall. "You've nothing to charge yourself with, Owens. 'Tis my fault the missive came into my hands. If I had thought beforehand, I would not have opened it. If I disobey now, I stand in contempt of the lord deputy.

On the other hand, I could not have disobeyed that which I had not seen."

The footman looked at the fire. "I do not see anything, sir. The letter is fair to disappeared. Might have been a draft. 'Tis a fine windy day. A piece of parchment, left on a tabletop, 'tis not a certainty but what it was swept up the chimney and burnt to a crisp!"

A look of revelation came over Revelin's features. "The very thing! An innocent man could stroll into Dublin Castle alone on the morrow with a free conscience."

"That he could, sir."

"Suddenly I'm famished. Inform Mrs. Cambra that dinner will be served immediately upon Mistress O'Neill's arrival."

The footman bowed smartly and left.

Revelin poured himself a glass of port, feeling again the excitement of the afternoon. *He loved Meghan.* Each time the thought struck him anew. But how to proceed. His only serious experience with courting had been with Alison. Meghan was hardly the type to be wooed with sonnets, a minstral's tune, and scented gloves. What could he do or say to her that was proper for their short acquaintance?

He smiled wryly as he realized the absurdity of his concern. He had tumbled her on the banks of Lough Neagh without benefit of pledge or words of love. Why should he now wonder how to treat her?

Yet, he did. All his actions before had been fostered by impulsive emotions. He had not meant to make love to her. He had not meant even to kiss her that first time. Or perhaps he had. From the moment he had awakened to find himself safe, not drowned, with his head pillowed in her lap, he had sensed that she was his destiny. That was why he had scoured the countryside like a madman looking for her. He could not believe that he would not see her again. The circumstances that had brought them back together were incredible, yet he had taken them for granted. Now he shivered in reaction to what might have been. She might have been killed had he been a mile farther away or too tired to chase Ualter.

"Saints forbid!" he murmured feelingly. She was so lovely, so utterly unaffected of manner. He had never known a simplicty of personality like hers. She was clever but more than a little fey with her belief in fairies and myths. And, of course, there was her belief in visions.

He frowned. He would have to caution her against mentioning them to the people she met in Dublin. They would not understand, and she had suffered enough from the ignorance of others. Oh, they would gossip about her birthmark and her heritage, but he would be there to guide and protect her until she was strong enough to face them all without fear or shame. After all, she was not a coward.

Revelin shook his head in wonder as memories assailed him. She had risked her life more times than most men who were not at war. She had saved all their lives. Yet, now Reade saw her as a pawn in some new scheme of his own making.

"Not while I live!" Revelin muttered, and then turned toward the sound of a knock at the door.

Mrs. Cambra stepped inside in response to Revelin's hail, her plump hands clutching the front of her long apron. "'Tis the best I can do on such short notice, Sir Revelin. The lass needs a month of training. Rude she is, begging your pardon, and wanting in modesty." Her face blazed fiery red as she remembered Meghan's scandalous behavior of the morning. "Sorry I am, Sir Revelin, that I could not do more."

"Well, let's have a look at her," Revelin responded, the housekeeper's profuse apology having steeled him for a fiasco.

Mrs. Cambra reached back to open the door. "Come in, lass."

Meghan negotiated the doorway with not a little trouble. The wide skirt of her gown would scarcely pass through the opening, and the heeled shoes she wore wobbled dangerously as she crossed the polished wooden floor.

"Stand straight!" Mrs. Cambra barked, and Meghan stiffened her spine with a grimace. She was nearly choking from the weight and tightness of the garments she had been forced into, and was about to say so when she saw the second person in the room.

"Revelin!" she cried in delight; then, mindful of Mrs. Cambra beside her, she checked her impulse to approach him. Instead she bent her knees in an awkward curtsy. When she rose, her face was contorted with the exertion and the difficulty in breathing.

Revelin could not quite believe that Meghan stood before him. She looked every inch a lady of the English court. Strangely, that did not please him. He walked toward her with a frown on his face. The woman who stood before him did not seem to be the same wild young girl who had ridden astride for half the length of Ireland. The figure did not even appear to be Meghan's. The dark red velvet gown she wore accentuated a waist more narrow than Meghan's naturally slender one, and Mrs. Cambra had filled in the low square neckline with a muslin partlet to hide the thrust of her bosom. His eyes moved lower, noting that beneath the turned-back, bell-shaped outer sleeves and ruffled puffed under sleeves her small hands were curled into tight fists.

His gaze rose to her face. Her hair had been parted in the middle and drawn back behind a black velvet hood of the French design. A black velvet veil fell down her back hiding her tresses. He stared at her face. Even that looked different. She was so pale that she did not seem real. Then it struck him. Mrs. Cambra had covered her with rice powder in hopes of disguising her birthmark. His heart turned over. Poor sweet Meghan, what had he subjected her to?

"You are free to go, Mrs. Cambra. Mistress O'Neill and I are perfectly content to deal together alone. My lady?" he said, offering Meghan his arm as the housekeeper closed the door behind herself.

Meghan did not move. She had been holding her breath, not in fear or anxiety, but because she was afraid something would burst if she took a deep breath. "Revelin," she whispered under her breath. "Please, ye must help me!"

Concern furrowed his brow and he dropped his arm. "What is wrong, Meghan? Are you ill?"

Meghan nodded, spacing her words carefully for fear of running out of breath. "I . . . cannot . . . breathe . . . properly. She said . . . were . . . whalebones . . . and steel . . . in me corset!"

The plea for help and the look of consternation on her face drew a sympathetic chuckle from Revelin. So that was the trouble! "Sweet child, I forgot you're not accustomed to corsets and farthingales. Please, sit down."

Meghan gripped his arm and inched her way across the treacherously slick floor. "Me back's about to break," she whispered breathlessly, "and me feet are pinched something horrid!" She dropped into the chair, only to leap straight up out of it again with a gasp. "It bit me!" she declared, beginning to pull at the stays at her waistline.

Oh Lord! He must not laugh at her, Revelin thought, not when she had submitted to this "beautification" on his orders. But he could see that he must do something when she raised her eyes, dark with confusion and a touching need to please him, to his.

"Sit down, slowly this time," he counseled, and bent on one knee before her. The first thing he did was lift her skirt, petticoats, and farthingale. Any other woman would have cried out in protest at this liberty, he thought in amusement. Meghan only bit her lip, muttering, "Whatever it is ye're about, be quick, Rev!"

Her use of his nickname sounded sweet in his ears as he lifted her foot and slipped the leather-heeled shoe from it. "Poor toes," he murmured solicitously as he rubbed the silk-stockinged foot between his hands.

Meghan began to giggle, then stopped as a stricken look came over her face once again.

Sensing the problem, Revelin dispatched the second shoe and rose, holding out a hand to her. When she stood before him, he put a finger to his lips and then tiptoed to the doors of the salon and slipped the bolt. Moving quickly, he also locked the servants' entrance.

"Now," he said, smiling beguilingly at her. "Will you allow me to loosen your corset, mistress?"

Meghan's expression melted in relief. "Would ye?" She glanced at the door and doubt crept into her eyes. "Mrs. Cambra will nae like it."

"Mrs. Cambra may mind her own business! Turn about, lass, and I'll soon have ye free." When Meghan spun about, he tossed the train of her hood forward over her shoulder and then more carefully lifted the heavy black-silk fall of her hair over one shoulder in order to reach the hooks at the back of her gown.

"Ye've had practice with this," Meghan observed as he quickly opened the fastenings.

Revelin smiled indulgently. He was not about to own up to the circumstances that had developed his skill. When he finished, he pushed the dress from her shoulders, revealing the lovely bare contours of her neck and back. Unable to resist, he traced the fascinating course of her spine with a finger, from the nape of her neck to the top of the leather-and-silk corset that encased her from just below her bosom to her hips.

Meghan gave no thought to being undressed before him. He had seen her nude before. Eagerly she pulled the bodice away from her to free an arm, exposing one perfect breast with its mauve tip. Yet she sensed a difference in Revelin, a hum in his stillness that made her look up at him.

He was staring at her, his mouth slightly parted as though he could not get enough air through his nostrils. He had that odd, quirky look in his eyes, the same she had seen once before when she had fallen out of the tree into his arms.

"What pains ye, Revelin?"

"What?" Revelin shook his head slightly. "Nothing pains me, 'tis only . . . ah, Meghan, how's a man to resist ye?"

Meghan did not know what to make of his complaint, for his arms were suddenly on her waist, turning her to face him. One hand reached for the bodice she held and tugged it from her hands and let it fall.

He did not even glance down when the bodice fell. His gaze remained tenderly upon her wide, serious eyes.

"The first time I saw you I thought we must be lovers," he said softly. He touched her left cheek, brushing away the dusting of powder with the side of his thumb. "I wanted it to be so, though I could not remember holding you or kissing that berry-ripe mouth. I wanted to know that I'd been a part of you."

His gaze lowered at last to her lovely breasts. A delicate rosy tint fanned up and out over the creamy globes as his eyes lingered, but Meghan did not try to hide her nakedness. She straightened her shoulders in defiance of her self-conscious blush.

Revelin felt her need for reassurance. "You're more beautiful than you know," he said softly, and his hand left her cheek to rest an instant on the curve of her neck before lowering to the beginning rise of her breast. "So lovely, so soft, so beautifully made. You were like a dream to me, a dying man's dream of a love he had not known."

He felt a tremor of desire quake through her body and saw the tightening of her pale mauve nipples into dark buds. Desire expanded within him. He would not take her here. He must not do that to either of them. But she must know once and for all how he felt. He owed her that.

His voice drew deeper, huskier, as his touch firmed, skimming the lustrous skin at the side of one breast. "You ran away, my woodland fairy, and I thought I'd go mad with searching for you. Will you promise me, lass, never to leave me again?"

"Aye, Revelin," Meghan whispered, afraid the sound of her voice might destroy the moment.

His hand moved again, circled under and then rose to cover

the lush fullness of one warm breast. Circling her waist with his free arm, he urged her closer.

Meghan lifted her hands, framing his face as his head bent to hers. His kiss was cool, his lips firm and dry and closed against her expectant mouth. Disappointed, she drew her breath to protest, but her corset would not allow the sudden rush of air into her lungs, and she choked.

"Oh, love!" Revelin murmured between regret and amusement as he gently patted her back. "The hell with proper dress!" With quick efficiency his fingers pulled loose the corset strings and opened the hinged metal and whalebone cage, freeing her.

"'Tis a devil's torture, that thing. I'll nae wear another." Meghan looked down at her rib cage and moaned. "Just look what it's done to me!"

Revelin swore as he saw the marked flesh. "Poor lass," he sympathized, and began rubbing the pink pinched skin of her abused diaphragm. Ruefully he wondered how to handle her dress in the future. The thought was quickly replaced by the more demanding exercise before him as his fingers massaged the cruel impressions of the binding corset from her warm, soft skin. "Better?"

Meghan nodded, inhaling deeply under the caress of his soothing fingers. "Aye, 'tis better than anything. Ye've found every place."

"Have I? Let me see." He bent over to make certain he had not missed a mistreated place. The action brought his eyes on a level with her breasts, and the temptation was too great. He caught her about the waist and opened his mouth to the inviting bud.

She gasped as his mouth closed over her flesh. "'Tis a wicked man ye are, Revelin," she murmured unsteadily.

"I know, love, I know," he answered, rising reluctantly and curling a hand behind her neck to bring her head once more against his shoulder. "We mustn't do this, 'tis sinful," he murmured absently as his hands continued to slide slowly up and down her naked back. He held her still for a long moment, willing her not to move and himself not to contemplate the possibilities held within his embrace.

The knock at the servants' entrance could not have been more welcome to Revelin's mind. "'Twould seem our supper's ready."

He released her slowly and turned her about. He was quite pleased, almost proud in a proprietary way, to find that her gown refastened without the aid of a corset.

Chapter Thirteen

Meghan lay in the dark staring at the dancing shadows thrown upon the ceiling by the fire. She was not the tiniest bit sleepy, though she had been abed for more than an hour. She was confused, hurt, and frustrated. Revelin's single kiss had not been followed by others. Once he had fastened her gown, he had unlatched the door so that their supper could be served.

Meghan licked her lips, remembering the creamy leek soup and fresh-baked bread that had been served with it. She had declined the slices of smoked ham after a single bite. Revelin had not seemed to mind. He had moved the remainder of the loaf and the crock of butter to her side of the table and smiled indulgently while she finished it.

"Aye, he smiles, but he keeps his kisses," she muttered as she sat up. Revelin had entertained her with talk of Dublin and what she could expect to see there, but he had not touched her again, not even when she had raised her face to his when he bade her good night.

Meghan swung her legs over the side of the bed and struggled into the new dressing gown Mrs. Cambra had given her.

When she had asked what had happened to the first one, Mrs. Cambra declared she had burnt it.

Meghan gazed at the small bedchamber fire and wondered what things Mrs. Cambra would burn next. Perhaps she should tell Revelin. After all, 'twas his coin that brought those things, he had said so when she asked him. She did not know much about money but she did know the value of good linen. Even though she did not much like the red velvet gown Revelin had given her, she would wear it; for it had been his gift to her.

When she reached the hallway she realized that she did not know where to find Revelin. Like a woodland animal she stood perfectly still a long while in the drafty hall listening for movement below, but there was none. Finally the floor beneath her feet moved slightly as someone moved about the room at the end of the hall. Hoping that it was Revelin so close by, she started toward the room. The door was ajar and the light showing through the crack beckoned her chilled flesh.

Revelin, too, was indulging in a rare sleepless night. He had stripped off his finery to enjoy the feel of the cool night air on his hungry, tensely alive body. It helped only a little and he began pacing before the fire.

He had waited more than three-quarters of an hour before deciding he must follow Meghan up to bed. Three glasses of port had done nothing to blunt his restlessness as he waited for her to fall asleep, so he had turned to *usquebaugh*.

The raw Irish whiskey had not helped, either. Rather, he had become maudlin, deliberately calling to mind every vivid detail of Meghan's undress. With her bodice about her hips she had risen, like Aphrodite, from the folds of the wine-red velvet. Her body was gloriously hued. Beneath a veiling of ebony silk curls, shades of cream and rose had vied for her coloring as a blush had spread delicately across her breasts.

If not for the rap on the salon door, he knew, he would have taken her there, on the table—on the carpet!—and disgraced them both.

"Fool! Knave! Rutting boar!" he cursed first in English and then in Gaelic as his door creaked on its hinges.

"'Tis nae reason to—" Meghan paused on the threshold, her attention snared by the sight before her.

Her voice startled him and Revelin paused in mid-stride before the fireplace. She knew she should not stare, but she could not help herself. His body was sheathed in the fire's golden glow, turning his skin to amber and burnishing his waves with coppery highlights. With aching desire she drank in all of him. Then her gaze slipped down past the fine line of golden hair that began below his navel and fanned out into a ruff of curls from which his manhood jutted.

Her gaze flew back to his face, her body tingling with the hunger she now associated with him alone. "I—I come to tell ye something ye should know. Rev—Sir Revelin."

Revelin inclined his head slightly, realizing that it was too late to order her out or grab his trunk hose, which he doubted he could have donned without making a complete fool of himself. He crossed his arms more casually than he felt. "What is it, Meghan?"

Meghan glanced back into the hallway and then at him. "Could I close the door, it being so cold and all?"

The sense of unreality that often accompanied his conversations with her rose like ether in his mind, leaving him lightheaded as he nodded.

Meghan's eyes were drawn irretrievably back to his erection. "I—well, 'tis Mrs. Cambra. She's been burning things again."

"Again," Revelin repeated, wondering when embarrassment would get the better of his body's arrogance.

Meghan moved from the door. "She burnt me first dressing gown." She caught a fistful of her gown. "'Twas like this, only 'twas a spot on it, here."

As she pointed to the imaginary stain, the movement of her breasts snared Revelin's gaze and his hands clenched on his folded arms.

Meghan's eyes darted downward and then up to Revelin's face. Nothing moved in his expression; it was as if his lovely face were frozen in stone. It was too dark to see the color of his eyes, but they reflected the vivid emotion he struggled to keep under control.

"Are ye in sickening?" she questioned, keenly aware of his agitation, and reached up to touch his face.

Revelin stepped back as if she had slapped him. "I—No. I just—Damnation! Don't ye see? 'Tis wrong, your being here!"

The volume of his voice had not risen but the wealth of emotion had broken his perfect diction. He reached out to prevent her from touching him again. "I'm only flesh and blood, Meghan. You're tormenting me more than 'tis right. Go back to bed, quickly, before I do something we'll both regret."

Meghan smiled with the insight gained from his words. To his utter dismay, she reached out and tenderly clasped his manhood in her cool hands. "Ye're paining here, are ye not? It must hurt something terrible, ye being so swollen."

Revelin didn't trust his voice or any of the emotions of pleasure, torment, anger, humiliation, and tenderness he felt before the girl who behaved as a whore from the most innocent of motives.

Meghan watched him close his eyes and sigh as if the life were draining out of him. And yet she knew it was not, he was warm and tremblingly alive in her hands. "'Tis because ye're engaged that ye won't lie with me?"

"Aye." The one syllable was all he could manage, yet it did not begin to explain the complex reasons for his reluctance.

Meghan felt honey begin to gather inside her where the gnawing hunger had been. She licked her lips. Memory stirred. There were other pleasures for men. She had witnessed one of them in the wilds of Ulster. If she could not lay with Revelin then, perhaps, she could please him in another way.

When Meghan dropped her hands, Revelin thought for one

grateful instant that she would go away. The next, a strangled gasp of astonishment was wrenched from him as the tip of her tongue grazed the most sensitive portion of his body. Blood rushed to his head and erupted through his thoughts in a volcano of scalding desire.

The caress of her lips seared his skin, and then the tip of him was slipped delicately and a little awkwardly between the damp circle of her lips. Just when he thought he would faint from sensation, her tongue moved once, then twice against his flesh, and panic replaced the weakness as he felt his body's push toward eruption.

"Meghan!" he cried between outrage and wickedly delicious enjoyment, and bent to drag her from her knees. "Meghan, lass! Ye can't! Ye mustn't! Ye don't know what—"

Meghan's cheeks were scarlet with her new knowledge. Feelings ran like rapids through her, making her shy and proud and as trembly as a leaf in the wind. "I—I didn't know 'twould be like that! Please!" she begged softly, as the need to be held overcame her and she blindly stepped in to press her body against the long, strong length of his.

Revelin enfolded her tightly against him. "We're mad, ye know!" he murmured as he rested his chin for an instant on the top of her head. The next he lifted her face to his and engulfed her mouth in a kiss.

Meghan wrapped her arms about him as if by pressure alone she could absorb him through her skin. She needed him with her, within her; it was her body's demand drummed out in the tattoo of her pulse. His lips offered the beginning of pleasures she had experienced only once but demanded to know again. "Please, Rev—please!" she whispered frantically against his mouth.

Revelin smoothed a hand down her back, seeking to control the dancing of her hips against his. He needed no more stimulation. "Ah, Meghan, I must have ye after all. And ye'll have me, there's nae doubt of that!" He bent and scooped her up to carry her to his bed. Following her into the depths of the mattress, he covered her body with his as kiss followed kiss.

But it did not help. Finally he dragged his mouth from hers, the pulsing urgency of his body's demand overcoming his pleasure. Yet, he did not want it that way. He wanted, needed, more from her than that, much much more, and he did not know how to obtain it.

He lifted his head and tenderly stroked a long tangle of hair back from her forehead as he gazed down at her. "We were meant for this. I don't know why or what shall become of us, but we are meant to share this." And by saying what was in his heart, the hunger seemed to subside into a manageable need.

In giving in to the sweet passion of her body for his, Meghan offered him her utter and complete love. Every touch, every gesture, every disconnected gasp and shudder came from the joy of simply loving him with all that she had to offer. When the moment of joining took place, the sweet fulfillment of the act, she was vaguely aware that not all the tears that fled across her cheeks to the bedding beneath were hers.

Meghan stroked him from shoulder to thigh, delighting in the soft springy hair that lightly furred his buttocks as he lay on his stomach beside her. The arm he had thrown about her tightened, drawing her closer, and, kittenlike, she snuggled against him. His body was so different from hers and so dear. "Why did ye deny us before, Revelin?"

Revelin raised his head from her shoulder to look into her eyes. "Perhaps 'twas misplaced pride, or perhaps I fear what may happen to you. I'm not an altogether free man. I cannot explain it well, but I owe a loyalty to my family which I cannot forsake even for love."

"I'd not stand in yer way, ye must know that."

He brushed his finger across the furrow marks on her brow, pressing until they were smoothed out by his touch. "'Tis not a matter of your standing in my way, lass. What concerns me is that you may be endangered by being near me. There's talk of war and of the Butlers' hand in it. If war comes, I must intercede. That is why, as soon as I can arrange it, I'm sending you to England."

He felt her gather breath to protest and cut her off. "You must understand that I cannot leave behind my weakness to be exploited if it comes to battle. And you, lass..." his voice dropped lower as he bent toward her and kissed the words, "...are...my...weakness."

"Take me with ye," she murmured against his mouth.

He chuckled as her breath teased his kiss-bruised lips. "Meghan, you play unfairly. Were you with me I'd think of nothing but this!" He kissed her quick and hard. "And this!" His hand moved to her breast and squeezed. "And particularly this!" His hand slid lower until his knowing fingers surprised a gasp from her.

A stubborn frown returned to Meghan's face, not to be smoothed by appeasing fingers this time. "I do not want to go to England. I do not like the English!"

"But, Meghan," he protested with gentle laughter, "*I* am English."

"Ye're not," she answered indignantly. "Ye're a Leinster-man, and while that's nae the same as an Ulsterman, 'tis Irish ye are, and Irish ye must remain!"

"Must I?" Revelin questioned as though the suggestion were a new one to him. And, in a way, it was. He had been born in Ireland, not far from Kilkenny, but he had come under Thomas Butler's care early in life when his parents died. By his twelfth summer he was in school in England, and he could not remember a time when he had spent more than a few weeks in Ireland until now. He had grown up under the earl of Or-mond's influence, a man of tenacious loyalty to the English queen. The earl would not join a rebellion aimed at routing her influence. Could he?

"I'm not so certain as you, lass, where my loyalties should lie."

Meghan struggled to free her body from under his, and Revelin reluctantly rolled to one side, releasing her. She sat up and turned to him. "Ye cannot think to take an Englishman's side against yer own blood kin?"

He might have paid more attention to her indignant tone if the firelight shadows had not been playing a delicious game of hide-and-seek about her splendid breasts. And it was, with his divided attention, he merely murmured, "Hmmm," while seeking one soft nipple with his mouth.

"Revelin!" Meghan cried and gave him a box on the ear with a hard fist.

It was not the worst blow he had received, but its unexpectedness coupled with what he considered its undeserved vigor made him angry. "Why you little—!"

He saw the glimmer of anger a scant instant before he lunged at her, and she, as agile as a doe, slipped past him off the end of the bed.

Caught off guard, his lunge went wide and his momentum sent him sprawling headfirst to the end of the bed. He caught himself with his hands to prevent banging his head, but he could not stop the forward motion of his body and slid off the bed and landed on the floor with a resounding thump.

The noise reverberated through the house, and Meghan could not suppress her amusement. Musical laughter flowed from her like the sound of wind chimes disturbed by a sudden breeze.

Footsteps sounded at once on the servants' steps. Revelin scrambled to his feet and clamped a hand over Meghan's mouth as the footsteps sounded in the hall. Seconds later, a knock at the door sent the portal—which was off the latch—swinging wide, and his footman Owens was treated to the sight of the naked couple.

The servant's eyes vied with his mouth for the greater circumference of surprise. "Begging yer pardon, Sir Revelin!" he cried and hurried out.

Revelin could hold his laughter no longer. "Lord love us! The entire household will know of this before daybreak, and Mrs. Cambra will have a missive in the mail to the earl before first light!"

Meghan cast a dark look at the hilarious man beside her. "Mrs. Cambra thinks nae good of me. Said I was cow-uddered, she did! And 'twas nae proper for ye to be easing me out of me clothing."

Revelin groaned. He had completely forgotten about the little episode with Meghan's corset. But, of course, Mrs. Cambra would have helped Meghan undress and put two and two together.

"Cow-uddered?" he said suddenly, remembering Meghan's statement. "Lass, were the cows of Erin formed like you, there'd not be a family man in all of Ireland!"

"Shall I go away now?" she asked when his mirth subsided.

Revelin thought about that for a moment while his eyes traveled the length of her beauty. "No, lass, I think not. Tomorrow we shall change your residence." He held a hand out to her in a manner befitting a courtier. "Tonight is all we have and the hours shorten. We were best abed!"

Revelin came fully alert in the time it took him to sit up in bed. "Enter!" he called as he reached for his dagger, which lay on the bedside table.

The door opened slowly and Owens the footman stuck his head into the room. "Begging yer pardon, Sir Revelin. But we've a visitor below and I was told to wake you."

Meghan stirred at the sound of voices and Revelin put a hand on her shoulder to reassure her. "Who is it, Owens?" When he saw the footman's eyes veer to Meghan's sleeping form, he added, "She is trustworthy."

"'Tis Sir Piers."

"Uncle Piers, here?" He slid from bed and began reaching for his clothing. "Did he come alone?"

"Aye," Owens answered. "Said I was to tell ye, Sir Revelin. None of the staff is to know he's come."

Revelin nodded as he pulled on his shirt, leaving the lacing open at the throat, then pulled on his trunk hose. "That will have to do," he muttered to himself when he had donned canions, stockings, and soft leather shoes.

Meghan sat up in bed silently watching him. Only when he reached the door did he remember her and look back with a smile. "Sleep, lass. You've had little enough rest this night."

When he arrived belowstairs, Revelin found his uncle seated at the table with several slices of ham and a tankard of English ale before him.

"Revelin, lad!" he cried, and rose to embrace his nephew as though they were meeting in the open light of day rather than the secret cover of night. "Let me look at what five years has done for you! 'Twould seem Thomas has done right by you, for all you've been raised a ward of the English court." He slapped his nephew heartily on the back. "You've topped me height a bit, lad. That's what damned Irish blood will do for you!"

Revelin did not try to calm his uncle's boisterousness. No doubt the entire staff knew the moment he arrived. Of the four Butler brothers, Piers was most Gaelic in his speech, clothing, and attitude. "Uncle Piers, you've not changed." He patted Piers's broad, muscular frame. "You're eating well, I see, and there's nary a gray whisker among the black."

Piers pulled his chin whiskers and winked. "'Tis the lassies that keep me young. Though Thomas, damn him, has the better of me by three. But there's a lass down on the Nore 'tis claimed will bear me twins before summer's end. Let Thomas top that!"

Revelin smiled. The Butlers were of the old school, feudal lords whose amorous exploits among their tenants' nubile wives and daughters were as much a source of boasting and friendly rivalry as were their military adventures.

"Sit! Sit!" Piers exclaimed, waving Revelin into a chair in his own home. "And what of you, lad?" He glanced up at the ceiling. "What's she like, this black-haired changeling you've been sleeping with?"

Revelin laughed. "Lord! Are there no secrets in a Butler household?"

"I should hope not!" Piers answered and reached for his ale. "So, is she breeding yet, lad? You've a far road to go to catch up with Black Tom's dozen."

Butler children born out of wedlock had little to complain about to their sires, for they were well cared for. But the possibility that Meghan might one day bear a child of his had not really taken root in Revelin's mind. He reached for the pitcher of ale and poured some into the tankard Owens had thoughtfully placed out for him. "What would you think were I to tell you I'm considering marriage?"

Piers winked at him. "'Tis a natural course for a man. But I'd not clamp myself in the marriage shackles too soon. There's many a pretty face and pleasing pair of thighs just awaiting a man's touch."

"Marriage does not appear to have restrained you," Revelin observed dryly.

Piers chuckled. "Aye, but I'm not an overly serious man. You, Revelin lad, were always too much a thoughtful soul. Oh, I'm not claiming there's no fire in your blood." His eyes swept speculatively upward once more. "Will she come down and make her curtsy?" he questioned hopefully.

"Not if I can help it, you old goat!" Revelin muttered.

Piers roared his appreciation, waking perhaps even the mice that dwelt within the walls. "So, 'tis that way. Aye, I remember my first love. 'Twas russet-haired, she was, with skin as pale and rich as fresh cream. A fine high bosom and thighs—well, I got me first son on her. There were two lassies after that. She died four years back; the plague took her." His voice turned wistful. "We had rare times, that lass and I."

Revelin did not prolong the conversation. For all Piers's easy manner, he had not ridden into Dublin under the cover of night to reminisce about lost loves. "What news have you brought?"

"'Tis a rare sad business before us, lad. The Butlers stand to lose all if that English slut accepts the hand in marriage of our mortal enemy Leicester." His vivid dark eyes met Revelin's across the table. "There's talk of it. You better than others can tell me if 'twill come to pass."

Revelin shook his head. "I've been absent from court these last six weeks, Piers. The winds of opportunity there change directions as often as the queen changes her gown."

Piers snorted his opinion of that. "Aye. Yet why else does Thomas remain in London while we must sweat out the actions of the Dublin Parliament?" He struck the table with his fist. "Damme, if I give up one inch of my lands to those *faolchon allmhardha*, Carew and Grenville!"

"'Foreign wolves,' indeed, uncle! Are we not 'foreign wolves' to the Gaels?"

"We are not! We are *ghalliobh* and proud of it." Piers leaned forward, his eyes intent upon his nephew. "There's trouble brewing, lad. Great danger for every Anglo-Irishman among us. We've held our lands as good and loyal subjects to the English Crown these last three hundred years. Now that hag of England is ready to throw us over for want of a good swiving. And 'tis Leicester's prick she wants doing the job!"

Revelin paled. He was no prude, but no one had ever dared speak of the English queen in such terms. "Uncle, you're angry, and perhaps with cause. But I caution you, that message carried back to the English with your name attached to it would mean arrest for treason and perhaps the block."

Piers chuckled and shook his head. "You're Thomas's lad, I see. Well, and so you should be. 'Twould be only right that Thomas should carve a place in your heart for the love of his life. He had hopes at one time himself."

He leaned forward again, beckoning Revelin to do likewise.

Whispering, he said, "You're a man and should know. Have you never wondered why Tom dotes so on his eldest bastard, Piers of Duiske? 'Twas rumored some fifteen summers ago that the virgin queen bore Tom a child. Lad! Don't look so stricken. 'Twas most likely her belly saved her from a long idleness in the Tower after John Wyatt's rebellion. She spent not two months in the Tower before being removed to Woodstock, and nary a hair was seen of her for the rest of the year!"

"Does Thomas confirm the story?"

Piers chuckled. "Had he confirmed it, do you think he'd have lived with such a claim on the queen's honor?"

"But if they loved each other—"

Piers shook his head. "You've a lot to learn about loving. It has little to do with the way most men conduct their lives, and even less to do with politics. I've me whores and me mistresses. But I married for consequence, as you will." He winked. "Enjoy your Irish lass. There'll be none better to comfort you the long days of your life, but I hear you are to marry Lady Alison Burke. Mayhaps you should pursue the matter. The Burkes will be generous with her dowry. You should ask for a portion of their land north of Limerick. The more claim Butlers have to Irish soil, the better our chances of keeping it."

Revelin let the matter of his marriage rest. "You've not yet said why you're in Dublin."

"Aye, to that!" Piers drained his cup, looked wistfully at the empty pitcher, then sat back, throwing a leg over his chair arm. "Edmund is refusing to return to Dublin for the next session of Parliament. Sir Henry Sidney is full of schemes and guiles and all manner of treachery. 'Tis he who stands to gain as much as any. If his brother-in-law, Leicester, should win the queen's hand—God forfend!—then Sidney hopes to gain for himself the Crown of Ireland!"

Revelin stared at his uncle. "Surely that is not possible. There is no Crown of Ireland."

"Aye, and there was no unloyal Anglo-Irishman, either,

until Sir Sidney began parceling out our lands to land-hungry usurpers like that West Country dog Carew!" Piers spat out several more-colorful oaths concerning Carew's Devonshire heritage.

"We will not have our lands stripped from us in the name of progress. Have the Butlers not held themselves as the queen's right arm in Ireland? Have we not served England in any rebellion by the Gaels? Aye! We've maintained armies and collected tithes and filled the coffers at Whitehall! Now we're asked to sit idly by while new men despoil and make free with that which is ours."

"Perhaps you overstate the matter, uncle," Revelin replied mildly. "Sir Sidney fears the queen's preference for the earl of Ormond, and Thomas is not a strong earl for lack of reason. He will allow Sidney only a small victory before taking the matter to the queen."

"Do you believe that? Dupe! Do you know what Sidney has done? He's dared to cede to Carew a goodly portion of your uncle Edmund's plowlands in Carlow."

Something about the twinkle in Piers's eyes signaled Revelin that that was not the end of his speech. "And Uncle Edmund— what has he done about the matter?"

Piers shrugged. "What any man would. We've plagued Carew with a bit of reiving."

"Hm," Revelin answered noncommittally. It was a bit of devilry that only an *Irishman* would have chosen.

"Carew's a fool!" Piers claimed. "Carew sent a letter to Sidney complaining of the Butlers' rebellion against him! Rebellion? Now I ask you, a reasonable man, is the loss of a few cows a rebellion? Did he think we could not have taken Idrone and all within it if we were of a mind? Hah!"

Revelin laughed, imagining Carew's consternation. "I do not see the problem. Carew is a sore loser and must learn the ways of the neighborhood. When he comes to view the trading of cattle as an everyday occurrence, he will steal a few of yours and the trade will even out."

Piers eyed his nephew speculatively. "I've scarcely seen you these years you've grown to manhood. I must ask myself if you're your own man or the earl's foster son."

Revelin met the dark gaze levelly. "Both."

"Aye, that's the spirit. But then are you a Butler first or a fanatic loyalist the likes of Thomas?"

"Thomas is a Butler, first, last, and foremost; you'll not say else and remain under this roof." The speech was said softly and without heat, but Revelin saw Piers's eyes widen in understanding.

Piers stroked his beard and nodded. "Good! By God, that's damned good! Would that my eldest lad had the fire in him that you possess! So, I'll tell you the truth. And you'll use it as best benefits the Butlers. Carew is raising an army, though God knows if he understands what it means to raise an army in this country. He's buying men but the likes of whom you've never seen. They're flocking into County Carlow like so many carrion birds on the scent of a dying cow. English militia we can crush like the rabble they are. But there's others, lad. He's offering bounty and sack to Irish and Scottish *bonaghts!*"

"Mercenaries," Revelin murmured. *Bonaghts* were unlike Turlough's Scots *gallowglass.* They were the outcasts of clans both Scots and Irish, men without loyalties or masters and feared by every reasonable nobleman be he Irish or English.

"I'd not have them on me land," Piers continued. "No good will come of Carew's plans, mark my words. So I've come here to tell you to warn Thomas of what happens. There may be a confrontation before the summer's end, and there's nary a man can tell where it will end."

Revelin shook his head. "You can't seriously be considering fighting Carew. Thomas nearly lost his head for the Battle of Alfane. The queen has forbidden personal battles within her lands."

"She hasn't outlawed protecting a man's own lands! Edmund has it right when he says the Butlers will fight to the death Carew's trumped-up pretense to our lands. We're not advocating the overthrow of the Crown in Ireland. There's a difference, lad."

"And you would have me explain this to Thomas?"

Piers nodded. "We may have little time before an attack comes. We'll not provoke, but we'll run them all the way to Hell once they cross the county line!"

Revelin rubbed his brow in weariness. "I had not planned to return directly to London."

"The lass."

Revelin looked up with a brief smile. "Actually, she had caught Sir Sidney's eye and I'm some disturbed by his intentions." Piers raised his brows, and Revelin launched into a brief review of Meghan's history.

"Shane's natural daughter!" Piers whistled in appreciation. "Of course, you'll not hand her over to Sidney."

Revelin shrugged, irritated with his inability to act. "I don't see that I have any alternative, unless I take her to England with me."

"You have that right, since you're the lass's foster parent."

Revelin's laugh was rueful. "She sleeps in my bed at this very minute." He looked up suddenly, emotion burning in his eyes. "I love her, Piers. I will wed her when and where I can."

"She's Catholic, lad. You cannot—"

"You remember," Revelin said kindly when Piers broke off in mid-sentence, "my mother was Irish and Catholic and your brother married her."

"My bastard brother married her," Piers corrected without heat. Both he and Revelin understood that while the Butlers were Protestant in the main, there had never been any persecution of the Catholics among them. "So, all the more reason to keep her from Sidney's clutches. Send her to Kilkenny Castle. She'll be safe enough. Edmund and I have brought our families there, while Thomas prefers the ease of London."

Revelin sat up. "I had thought of that before Sir Sidney's letter arrived. I could leave for London tomorrow if I knew Meghan was safe."

"Meghan," Piers repeated softly. "I once knew a Meghan, hair the color of cornsilk and eyes as deep a green. . . ."

"Black hair and eyes as deep a blue . . ." Revelin answered dryly.

Piers chuckled. "So keep her for yourself. But marry? Ah, lad, I cannot counsel you to that. What of your betrothal?"

"Another reason I'm needed in London," Revelin replied. "Lady Alison is not one to hold a grudge or to stand in the way of happiness."

"Even yours?"

Revelin shrugged. "She'll see nothing of me after this. I'm returning to Ireland and here I shall remain."

"All the more reason for you to fight for what is ours." Piers stood. "I'm away. The light of morning is never so lovely within the Pale."

Revelin rose with him. "But you've not rested."

Piers lifted his eyes to the ceiling once more. "Do you offer your bed?"

"Your horse awaits," Revelin replied.

Piers's laughter shattered the quiet. "Send her to Edmund, lad. His lady wife will know how to deal with her." He clasped Revelin in a bearlike hug. "Give my best to that damned rascal brother of mine and tell him Butler blood should not be spilt for Devonshire dogs. Ah, and the twins, tell him of the twins!"

When Piers had ridden out, Revelin returned to his room. Meghan was stretched out on his bed, wide awake.

"Did we disturb you, lass?" he asked as he walked toward the bed, stripping off his clothes as he went.

Meghan reached out for him as he cast away the last of his clothing and pulled him down hard against her. "Are ye truly going away from me?"

Revelin stared at the midnight-dark eyes just inches from his. "How do you know? Did you listen?—but you don't speak English."

"Mrs. Cambra told me," Meghan answered. "She came in

to make me leave yer bed, and when I wouldn't, she said I would soon enough because ye're going to London Town."

So, the household knew every word they had spoken. Thank the Lord for loyalty.

Revelin lowered his head onto her breast as his hands found her waist and began a slow, sensual rise toward her breasts. "Aye, lass, I must go away for a little while, but when I return I won't be leaving you again. So..." And he let his hands and lips continue his thoughts.

Chapter Fourteen

"Damnation! A farthing for Leicester's head!"

"Quietly, lad," Thomas Butler, the earl of Ormond, counseled his foster son. Seated before the fire of his London townhouse study, Thomas had been rereading a letter from Dublin. Seeing Revelin's mood, he folded the letter and pocketed it. "You've remembered little of court life if Leicester's witless tongue can prick your ire."

Revelin snatched his velvet hat from his head and tossed it onto a table by the door. "'Twas more than that. As I sat in the antechamber of Whitehall this afternoon, Leicester came over to tell me how delighted he was to learn that Meghan O'Neill is his father-in-law's guest at Dublin Castle."

An old hand at handling agitated statesmen, Thomas said merely, "I know."

Revelin regarded him in surprise. "You know? When did you learn of it? For the last week I've thought Meghan safe in Kilkenny. I had left instructions which needed only Uncle

Edward's letter of consent to put into motion." His green eyes suddenly blazed dark and stormy. "You, you've had a hand in this."

Thomas shook his head. "The news arrived only after you had left this morning."

The anger eased in Revelin's expression. Thomas was not above countermanding Revelin's orders, but if he had he would tell him so. "What am I to do? The lass is behind the walls of a fortress. Guest of the lord deputy, indeed! She must be frightened out of her wits. God knows what questions Sir Henry will put to her. She's not clever in the ordinary sense. She could easily be tricked into saying she's a spy for O'Neill or a rebel or heaven knows what! Leicester let drop in parting that the lord deputy of Ireland is most concerned about what he called the likelihood of a Butler Rebellion."

Thomas stroked his black beard. "A Butler Rebellion! It has a ring to it! *Buitiler a buadh!*" he cried in his deep voice until the room reverberated with the Butler war chant.

Revelin collapsed into a chair beside his uncle, straining to keep a smile from his face. "You can jest when the queen herself lends an ear to these lies?"

Thomas's dark eyes narrowed on Revelin as he considered his next words. "You are young, Revelin, and your blood stirs easily. When you have my nine and thirty years, you will better understand that often the best reply is none at all."

"My years are sufficient to tell me that Leicester goes too far."

"He often does," Thomas remarked evenly. "And, thus, he will one day overreach himself."

"Until then are we Butlers to suffer his attacks on our loyalty?"

"We Butlers!" Thomas smiled. "It warms me to hear my kinsman speak with such fidelity."

Revelin's expression soured further. "You are deliberately turning the conversation."

Thomas chuckled. "And you would rather I blacken Leicester's name with every oath and curse that comes to hand? I am ever mindful of Leicester, but the queen is partial to him at present; and though he does not know it, she will tire of him. When she does, she will look about the court for familiar faces, faces that do not remind her of Leicester. Were I to become his major opponent, she would look on me and, through me, be reminded of him. What a waste of opportunity."

Hearing Thomas speak thus, Revelin was tempted, as he often had been these last weeks, to ask his uncle if the story Piers had told him was true. Yet, something held him back. Respect, perhaps, and the desire not to incur his uncle's wrath. Still, those were not the only reasons. There were things a man kept to himself.

"Were you called into the queen's presence today?" Thomas asked.

Revelin shook his head. "I doubt she remembers I exist."

Thomas lazily glanced over his nephew's elegantly clad body and smiled. "She remembers." His gaze lingered on the well-developed muscles of Revelin's thighs until the younger man blushed. "And, lad, she's partial to a briefer trunk hose in her courtiers."

"The devil, uncle! You make me out to be little more than meat on the hoof."

"A passable young buck, perhaps," Thomas agreed with a chuckle. "As to that, where were you last evening? Lady Alison asked about you at the Danver's musicale. I was forced to invent a lie. I told her you are much enamored of the theater and had gone to sample London's latest fare."

Revelin's expression did not change but his gaze became unfocused and remote. Alison had been much on his mind of late, and still he had not found the words to break off their engagement.

"You owe her a better showing while in London," Thomas remarked. "There's talk that needs only a wicked tongue's telling."

"Who would dare?" Revelin demanded.

"Who would not? The lady in question has waited impatiently for her young swain's return, only for court intrigue and fairy tales to keep him fully occupied. The ladies of the court, jealous creatures that they are, have already begun to worry the notion. Lady Alison was not without admirers while you were away. She kept them at bay with whispers of impending marriage. What say you to that?"

Revelin's green eyes twinkled in answer. "I wish Lady Alison and her husband a happy, healthy life."

Thomas fingered the missive in his pocket. "You have spoken to her?"

"No, I have not." Revelin met his uncle's gaze. "But I will, and soon. I cannot marry her. I had hoped that this business at court would not drag on, so that . . ."

Thomas picked up the dangling thread, "So that you could return to Dublin and your Irish mistress. Lad, you're a fool if you think that soft thighs and misty eyes are the length and breadth of love." He smiled paternally. "We Butlers are a lusty lot, 'tis the boon and bane of our menfolk. We make good husbands for docile wives, and our mistresses are all the better for it."

"We've had this discussion before," Revelin reminded him.

"But you were not listening! The lass is in Ireland; leave her there. Lady Alison will not wish to forsake her place at court for the wilds of Ireland. You, on the other hand, have ties that will make frequent trips to Ireland understandable. Two households, two lives. Who's to care a pig's fart whether that one houses a wife and the other a mistress?"

Revelin rubbed the weariness from his eyes with a hand. "You do not understand. She does not understand who or what I am. She loves *me* and nothing more, not even my name. I feel free when I am in her company."

"'Tis a rare luxury," Thomas agreed. "Keep the lass. Marry Lady Alison."

Revelin smiled slightly. "I thought I was old enough to know my own mind."

Thomas sat back, not defeat but disgust showing on his handsome face. "I am your foster father, and I will not give my blessing to any match that does not further your career and standing. Do you understand what that means?"

"Aye," Revelin answered quietly. So it had come to this.

"That we may be perfectly clear, I will say this once. If you persist in your contrariness and do not marry where your family wishes, you will be disowned, your ties to Butler lands forfeit. As for the queen's wrath, you'll find no help from me there."

Revelin had known what Thomas would say, but the words made him shudder inside just the same. "You would like Meghan; she knows many tales of Fionn and the legendary Fianna."

Nonplused at last, Thomas merely stared at his nephew.

"I love her," Revelin said simply.

"God's death! I begin to believe the changeling has bewitched you!"

Revelin's expression changed. "From where would you have heard that?"

Gratified to have pricked his nephew's composure at last, the earl smiled, touching the letter in his pocket. "So 'tis true, what I've heard of the lass. She's marked, is she not? A disfigurement that any sane man would draw back from. You've been tricked, lad. I don't know by what method, but the lass has captured your mind and will not rest until she has your soul as well!"

"Sir Richard Atholl has been to see you, the bastard!" Revelin exclaimed in anger.

Thomas crushed the letter. Atholl was not the only one to plead his case against the O'Neill wench, but Thomas would not play all his cards at once. "Aye. Atholl fears for your sanity, lad, and I thank him for the concern. He believes, as I do, that your passions have blinded your good sense!"

Revelin rose abruptly. "If you want me gone from your home, I will leave this very night."

Thomas rose more slowly and put a restraining hand on Revelin's arm. "Lad, see reason. I do not share Atholl's opinion that the girl has cast some spell on you. I say, have the lass. But is it reasonable that you should throw away any chance for advancement and success because you've fallen in love? It speaks of a lack of reason for you not at least to consider the possibility.

"I need you. You shall become my right hand at court. My brothers, Edmund, Edward, and Piers, are too much like the Irish in their thinking to understand the complexities of my work here in London. But you, Revelin, you can aid me in my struggles at court."

Thomas slid his arm about Revelin's shoulders. "I was young once. I know the pangs of first love, but I was wise enough and strong enough to put those matters in perspective. If she loves you as much as you say, you will find a way to keep her. Tell me, has she declined the position of your mistress?"

When Revelin shook his head, Thomas's face split with a smile. "She has not? Lad, what madness drives you? Ask her. If you do not, there are others in Dublin who will. If she is as beautiful as you say, she will have no trouble making her way in the world of men." Revelin turned on him an incredulous look that Thomas found he could not destroy. If the girl was being unfaithful with his friend Neville, as the letter opined, then Revelin would learn about it soon enough.

Thomas gazed fondly at his nephew. A first love was the most difficult to lose, but Revelin was young and handsome. He would find others, many of them if the Butler tradition was any indication. "To prove my faith in you, I will write the lord deputy tonight expressing my wish that the lass be sent to my castle in Kilkenny. He'll have no choice but to send her and she'll be there waiting when you return to Ireland. In the meantime, you must go to Lady Alison and rebuild the bonds you've been so eager to rupture." He pushed Revelin firmly toward the door. "Go, lad! Now! And kiss her once for me!"

Revelin moved into the hallway of his uncle's home with his emotions in knots. What Thomas had said was true. From the first he had known he was indulging in boyish fantasies. From the first, Meghan had not seemed quite real. She was the stuff of fancy, of lustful adolescent dreams, of a future that could never be in reality. He had known that. Where had he gone wrong? In his love for her, he had lost his perspective.

Meghan was a wildness in his blood. Like Ireland, she held for him ever-fresh delights. Like spring wine, she was tart and sweet and pungent. In her arms he had felt the stirrings of a kind of freedom that no longer existed for men of his ilk. He had responsibilities, duties to family and his sovereign. For a short time, loving Meghan had seemed to release him from those duties. Now he recognized that he was not free nor would ever be.

Alison was lovely. He had forgotten how lovely she was until he saw her in the corridors of Whitehall. And she still loved him, it was there in the gentle blue depths of her eyes. She was well versed in the arts of womanhood and she would grace his home and raise his children and make life easier at court.

"Ah, Meghan," he murmured regretfully as he reached the door. She would be with him all his life.

Meghan sat with her back to the gallery room at Dublin Castle gazing with bright eyes upon the docks of the river Liffey. Revelin had been away a month now, and yet every morning she awakened with the hope that this was the day he would return. When, the morning after Revelin sailed, Sir Henry Sidney had suddenly appeared on the doorstep with an invitation for her to stay at Dublin Castle, she had not wanted to accept. But Mrs. Cambra, unusually subdued, had packed her belongings and bundled her off without a word of protest.

"Daydreaming, Mistress O'Neill?"

Meghan looked up at the sound of a familiar voice and

smiled. "Sir Robin, come and join me," she pronounced in her new halting English. "Is it not a beautiful day?"

Robin followed her gaze out the window to the docks where the river ran in a swift even stream of brown and green. At dockside two merchant ships were reloading. "He won't be back today, Meghan. It could be weeks before he returns."

"It is weeks!"

Robin chided her with a clucking of his tongue. "Such heat, mistress, and with so few words yet at your command."

Meghan looked at him with a mutinous expression. "When will Revelin return?"

Robin sat beside her. "Smile, mistress. We are watched."

Meghan turned to glance back at the long galley, which was far from empty. Clusters of men were gathered in conversation while others strolled the chamber as they chatted. Yet she knew none of them was as interested in what the other was saying as they all were in catching a glimpse of her.

Robin saw her defiance change to uncertainty; he reached out his hand to her and she took it. "Has it been so terribly awful for you?"

Meghan lowered her gaze but continued to grasp his hand. "The meals is worst."

"Are worst, the meals *are* the worst," Robin corrected automatically, for, at Revelin's request, he had taken charge of teaching her English. "In my humble opinion, Sir Sidney provides a fine table."

Meghan smiled a little. "'Tis not what I mean. They stare at me. All through the meal I feel eyes on me."

"How disconcerting," Robin remarked. "I had not considered it before, but I suppose a beautiful woman must feel completely worn after an evening in the company of ogling men."

Meghan gave him a doubtful glance. "'Twas not beauty they stare at." She raised a hand to her cheek. "'Tis this."

Robin smiled. "'The Irish Rose.' Ah, yes, 'tis what the

gentlemen have named you." He would not tell her of the others, less delicate but more expressive of the lust she unknowingly inspired. "I've warned them that you are well protected by a demon of vast proportions, and should they attempt any liberties they risk their lives."

Meghan gazed at him in horror, her English fleeing. "Ye didn't! Ye wouldn't!"

Robin chuckled. "My Gaelic is slower to mature than your English, mistress, but I would have you know I was referring only to your loyal protector." He glanced down at the huge pile of fur at Meghan's feet, and Ualter thumped his tale in appreciation of the recognition.

Meghan reached out and entwined her fingers in the long, stiff fur of the dog's neck. "Aye, Ualter is my protection." She cast an angry look at one of the gentlemen who paused near them to smile at her. " 'Tis black-hearted he is," she confided to Robin.

"Who?"

Meghan nodded in the man's direction. "That gentleman asked me to join him for wine last evening. Said he wanted to learn Gaelic. He tore me best gown before I could free me skean."

Robin frowned, lost in her Irish speech.

Meghan rolled back the sleeve of her gown, revealing the jeweled O'Neill dagger. "I cut his doublet," she said and made an appropriate move with an imaginary weapon.

"Mercy's Grace!" Robin whispered in dismay. "Mistress Meghan, I beg you, carve no English geese! Revelin would not like it."

Meghan nodded and said deliberately in English, "Revelin will be angry. 'Twas a vastly expensive gown."

Robin nodded absently. He doubted that Revelin's concern would be caused by the loss of the gown. A rare glint of anger gleamed in his eyes. He had spent part of every day in Meghan's company, but it seemed that was not enough to discourage the more persistent gallants in Dublin. The noblemen in town for the parliamentary session were accustomed to the more willing ladies of the court, and certainly Meghan's reputation as Revelin's mistress was not likely to deter them in his absence. So, Robin mused with a smile, he would simply let it be known that Meghan was now under his protection.

Forgive me the lie, Mistress Meghan, he thought. For, as he gazed at her he could only wish that it were so. Her simple gowns were not in the height of fashion, but there were such tempting compensations. Praise be!—he had discovered quite by chance, when she had embraced him upon her arrival at Dublin Castle, that she wore no corset! After that, several men who prided themselves as experts in such matters were quick to point out that, like the most bold of courtesans, Meghan wore *nothing* to restrict her charmingly proportioned figure.

Yet he alone knew that she was totally unaware of her effect on other men. She loved Revelin completely, without reservation or hesitation.

"Poor Meghan," he murmured, remembering the letter in his pocket.

"Now that that is settled, I have a small surprise for you." He produced the letter with the seal still intact. "It came this morning."

Meghan took it, running her finger over the Butler seal pressed into the wax. She recognized it as a copy of the shield that hung over the mantelpiece in Revelin's home. Eagerly she tore it open, then sighed in disappointment. It was written in English. Reluctantly, she handed it back to Robin.

Robin took it and began to read, a grin growing on his face.

"Dearest Meghan,
    I regret my words must come to you through Robin's lips but my Latin is abominable and, dearest, I do not know the extent of your reading skills.

The queen has much business to deter Her and I
must wait upon her pleasure. 'Tis my cherished
hope to be with you by the end of the month. Alas,
I cannot promise. To that end, my uncle has
arranged for you to go to Kilkenny at the first
opportunity, where you will be safe with the
Butlers."

Robin paused, reading the next sentence silently.

"Robin, friend, I trust you will take my lady
there. It is better if Meghan is not in Dublin when I
return."

Trouble there, he thought, before finishing aloud.

"Meghan, lass, I am as always.

Fondly,
Revelin Butler

"Well, that's a stingy love letter!" Robin commented dis-
paragingly, only to have Meghan snatch the letter from him
and hold it to her heart.

"Perhaps, I am overcritical," he amended with a rueful
smile. She loved Rev, the lucky bastard!

"Revelin is coming back!"

Robin gazed at her joy-flushed face, wondering why Revelin
wanted her away from Dublin when he returned. "Of course
he's coming back. Did you ever doubt it?"

Meghan frowned, sorting out the English phrases, and then
smiled. "I do not wish to go to Kilkenny. I will wait here for
Revelin."

"But, mistress, Revelin would prefer that you do his bidding."

Meghan shook her head. "Revelin will come back to Dublin, yes?"

"Aye, he will," Robin answered reluctantly.

"I will wait in Dublin."

Robin did not pursue the matter. Meghan was as stubborn as a mule when it came to sticking by a decision. As for Revelin's desire for Meghan's removal from Dublin...

God's light! I wonder if he's married Lady Alison!

Meghan sat up in bed gasping for breath, her eyes wide with staring long before consciousness focused them. For an instant there was only the blind terror of a remembered dream. No, not a dream, a vision...the first since her arrival in Dublin.

She closed her eyes and opened them again. She was awake. She felt her pulse pounding rapidly in her throat, the bite of her nails into her palms, and the clammy cold sweat that enveloped her.

Gradually the blackness softened into the shape of the tower room she shared with two young ladies of the castle. On one side, the faded red-orange glow of embers warmed the darkness. Faint, milky-white light filtered in on the other side, outlining the shuttered casement window. Nothing had changed during the night. She was still in Dublin Castle.

She pressed her hands to her abdomen as a wave of nausea swept up and over her. As the wave of bile crested in her throat, she swallowed rapidly over and over until it subsided into the uneasy trough of her stomach. With a trembling hand she wiped sweat from her brow. Visions had frightened her before but none of them had left her feeling so weak and sick at heart.

She slipped from the bed, leaving the covers trailing onto the cold stone floor as she raced to the window and opened one of the shutters.

Moonlight spilled silver currents upon the dark waters of

the river below. She rose on tiptoe, tempted beyond the ordinary urge to escape from the stone walls that held her prisoner. The river beckoned, its glassy surface undisturbed by barge or carrick at this hour. She longed to feel the waters gathered and pushed away by her arms as she swam. It had been so long since she had been free to ride or to climb a tree or even to sit and simply watch the world. Dublin was a big dirty city where people and houses and wagons and noise drowned out all sense of the land.

She was a prisoner. No one barred the gates to her, but where had she to go? She knew not a soul outside the castle walls but Revelin, and he had put the distance of the Irish Sea between them.

She fixed her eyes on the water, slipping willingly into the tremulous twilight of the vision. Revelin was nearby; she felt his presence like the radiant warmth of the sun after a rain. Yet, there was another presence, something dark, slope-backed, skulking in the shadows of her joy. She closed her eyes, conscious of the brush of her lashes against her cheeks.

The creature of the vision had black eyes gleaming like wet river stones above its pointed snout and yellowed fangs.

She gasped, her hands flying up to cover her mouth as she forced her eyes wide again. It was only a dream. Revelin had told her her visions were only dreams, fears that fed on her imagination. It was only unhappy coincidence that reality occasionally bore a mocking resemblance to her dreams. She could not cast spells or predict the future.

She dropped her hands and took a deep breath. A tremor passed through her and then another. If Revelin were here, he would hold her, warm her body with his, and make her believe as he did. But Revelin was not here and she was afraid of the vision that had awakened her.

She did not reason out her decision. She snatched a dressing gown from a chair and raced for the door.

When she reached the main stairway, she did not hesitate.

She had spent many afternoons in Robin's room poring over English lessons.

The door was shut but unlatched. It opened soundlessly with a rush of warm air from a fire laid to last the night. Rich tapestries threaded with emerald, sapphire, gold, and scarlet lined the stone walls. A massive bed stood against the far wall and from its depths came deep sonorous sounds.

Meghan crossed to the bed on silent feet. Robin's head was propped up on a red satin bolster. A matching red satin coverlet had been thrown back during the night and his naked limbs gleamed like alabaster against the brilliant cloth in the firelight. Meghan came closer, unabashed by his nudity. He seemed larger without clothes, his body well knit for all its slenderness.

She reached out and shook his shoulder. "Sir Robin!"

Robin stirred, a smile forming on his lips. "No, darling, 'tis too soon." He reached out to pat the bed beside him. "Rest, darling, rest. Later . . . we will frolic again . . . later."

Meghan shook him a second time. "Sir Robin, wake up! I must talk with ye!"

Robin opened his eyes reluctantly, certain that he was dreaming. It was a pleasant dream, no doubt of that. Meghan had come to share his bed!

Meghan bent lower and whispered, "I must talk to ye, Sir Robin. Now!"

"Meghan?" Robin sat up in a single fluid motion, taking in the reality of Meghan standing beside his bed and his own nudity. He grabbed the coverlet to pull it up to his waist. "Mistress Meghan, what brings you here at this hour?" He gaze flew to the closed door. "Are you in trouble?"

Meghan sank down in the bed beside him and threw her arms about her neck. "You must help me! Revelin's not coming back to Dublin!"

The sensation of having a beautiful girl weep upon his bare chest was a new one but Robin found himself quite pleased by the experience. He embraced Meghan tenderly and patted her back. When her sobs subsided, he said, "Of course Revelin's coming back."

Meghan leaned away from him. "You know that he returns? When?"

Robin smiled at her, wondering if she was aware that her gown had fallen open to reveal one shapely breast. "Mistress, do you often visit gentlemen in the middle of night dressed as Mother Nature made you?"

The gentle jest was lost on Meghan. "Only Revelin."

A whimsical smile appeared on Robin's lips. "Do you know what the castlefolk say about us? They think we are lovers, Mistress Meghan. At times, I quite indulge in the fantasy myself."

Meghan stared at him in complete seriousness. "Why?"

"Because, lovely creature, I would like to make you happy. That, *ma chéri,* would make me happy."

She considered his statement as she wiped the last of the tears from her eyes. "You love me, too?"

"Too? Oh, of course Rev." Robin looked away, a new tone in his voice. "If Revelin did not return, what would you do?"

Meghan shook her head and a great emptiness seemed to fill her chest. "I would die."

Robin turned his head away. "Die? Of a broken heart? It hardly ever happens, mistress."

"Is Revelin married?"

Robin's eyes widened as he turned to her. "What makes you think Revelin is to be wed?"

"He told me, before we come—came to Dublin."

"Did he, the bastard!" He sobered immediately when he saw her head move in a quick, restless gesture. "Ah, Meghan . . ." He reached out to brush a lock of hair from her face, and his fingers stayed, resting on her cheek. "Revelin is the most honest man I've ever met. He is honest to a fault. I know you don't understand all I say, dear sweetness. He loves you, I do not doubt it. As to whether he can bring himself to take what he wants, I cannot say. I hope to God he cannot, for then you will need to look elsewhere for a protector. Do you understand any of what I say?"

Meghan held his gaze, his eyes like twin opals in the darkness, and felt a twinge of self-consciousness for the first time. "You want me to love you?"

Robin smiled a lopsided smile. "Some such foolish thing, mistress."

"I do."

Robin's fingers trembled slightly as they moved to the tie that held her gown closed at her neck. "Do you? How do you love me, Meghan? As a woman loves a man?"

Meghan shook her head. "I do not understand."

Robin's other hand came up to join the first and they rose to cup her face gently. "You once teased me about my kisses and I promised to prove myself to you. The time is now. Kiss me, sweeting."

As he bent to her, Meghan leaned toward him, part from genuine curiosity and part from a motive new to her but urgently strong. Revelin would not like it if she kissed Robin. She did not like it that Revelin had been gone so long. Perhaps Robin would tell Revelin that she had kissed him, and maybe, just maybe, that would bring Revelin back to Dublin.

Robin's kiss came as quite a shock. She had not thought about the hair on his face until it brushed her cheeks as their lips met. Shyly, she lifted a hand to quest his springy red-blond beard and moved to touch the curls above his ear. When his hand moved to fumble open the front of her gown, she drew back abruptly. "You said kissing, you did not say honey-making."

Robin grinned at her in bemused bliss. Lord! One kiss and he was standing at attention. "Honey-making? Where did you hear such a quaint term?"

"'Tis how I feel, melting inside, when Revelin kisses me," Meghan answered matter-of-factly.

"Did you melt when I kissed you?"

She shrugged, suddenly shy before him. "A little, only not so much as with Revelin."

"Perhaps we should try it again," Robin suggested with great enthusiasm, only to have Meghan draw back.

He rested his hands on either side of her face and leaned his forehead against hers, chagrined by his thoughts. He was behaving like a lecherous courtier. "Why are you here, mistress, other than to tempt my virtue from me?"

"Do you know when Revelin comes back to Ireland?"

Robin raised his head, his eyes only a hand's breadth from hers. "If I do, and if I know that Revelin does not want you here in Dublin when he returns, what then?"

Meghan ignored the twinge of pain his words wrought. "Tell me true."

Robin sighed. "I would not have told you, and I'm motivated by purely selfish reasoning in doing so now. Revelin is expected in Dublin next week. He returns with Sir Richard Atholl . . . and Lady Alison Burke."

The pang returned with new intensity in Meghan's middle and the tide began to ebb in her stomach. " 'Tis married he is?"

Robin could not lie to her. "He is not married, but, mistress, he is still engaged."

Meghan rose from the bed, reverting to Irish as she attempted to explain herself. "I thank ye for the truth, though 'tis not overly to me—me liking." The tide gathered strength. "I—I do not like this engagement. I do not understand it. Revelin loves me, he said so." The swell of bile continued to build, gathering force as it rose. "If 'tis Revelin's wish for me to go to Kilkenny, I will go now, only . . ." Meghan swallowed convulsively as the wave crested. "Only . . . I nae want to go . . . alone. Could ye, would ye— Oh!"

Robin was proud of himself for reacting so quickly to her distress. The bedside porcelain bowl performed admirably.

"Oh, Lord, not that too!" he groaned as he realized the most logical explanation of her distress. No wonder she'd waited so anxiously for Revelin's return.

"'Tis of no great concern. 'Twill pass shortly," Meghan murmured weakly when she was at last free of spasms.

"Aye, in about nine months' time," Robin muttered sagely, but returned innocent silence to her questioning look. "Into bed with you." What did he care what the castlefolk thought? A man's mistress may be sick in her own lover's bed, he should think!

Meghan cast him a doubtful look as Robin tucked her under his covers, but she was too weak to protest. "You've a fine body," she said before a yawn got the better of her.

Robin executed a courtly bow. "Mistress, I am eternal grateful for the observation. Now shut your lovely mouth and go to sleep!"

Sir Henry Sidney paced the floor of his chambers in the predawn light. The events of the last week had wreaked havoc upon his nights until this one he had passed without any sleep at all. What was he to do under the present situation but to give in gracefully? After all, it was not as if the O'Neill girl had been given specifically into his or the Crown's care. He had been able to pry her loose from Revelin Butler by an invitation that few would have ignored. Besides, a young unmarried woman of noble birth could not reside unchaperoned in a bachelor's household.

But this request from the earl of Ormond was not easily ignored. The earl's brother Sir Edward was a married man with a family in residence in Kilkenny Castle. The O'Neill girl certainly would be properly chaperoned. That was not the problem. The problem was that an O'Neill would be cosseted in a Butler fortress at a time when some Butlers were openly defying English law by engaging in outlawed reiving against Sir Peter Carew. Sir Peter had received permission to raise an army to fend off the attacks. He wished Sir Peter Godspeed in putting an end to the matter, but he doubted the old soldier's ability to accomplish that much-needed task.

Sir Henry shook his head. Irish troubles pressed in on him on all sides. The earl of Desmond was a prisoner of the Crown, but in Munster his clansmen, the Fitzgeralds, were making warlike noises. Rumors said that the Butlers, the Fitzgeralds' old enemies, were watching with interest. Any false move would be enough to touch match to wick, and the powder keg that was Ireland would explode in rebellion. No one knew where it would end if the Butlers threw their lot in with the Fitzgeralds.

He could ill afford to have the girl used as an excuse by the Butlers to send to Ulster for aid in case fortunes went against them. But neither could he afford to encourage sympathy for the Butlers by denying a reasonable request. There was sympathy enough for the Anglo-Irish landowners in Parliament. Why, the Palesman Sir Christopher Barneswall had joined Sir Edmund Butler in leading the opposition in The Commons against reform bills. No, he must allow the girl to go to Kilkenny.

"And I must hope to God that I will not live to regret it!"

Sir Henry turned impatiently as the knock he had been waiting for sounded at his door. He was not without a trick or two of this own, thanks to the queen's latest missive. The Butlers had their allies, but so did he. For more than a month he had had an ear in Carew's camp. Now he would plant one in Kilkenny. Perhaps things were turning in his favor after all.

"Come in, Sir Robin," he said, smiling faintly when the opened door revealed his guest.

Chapter Fifteen

Kilkenny: Late July 1569

Meghan could not keep the smile from her face as she rode through the morning with Robin and the troop of Butler soldiers sent expressly to fetch her to Kilkenny Castle. Sunlight brightened the gentle rolling green of the countryside, while in the distance the remnant of a rain cloud dragged its dark curtain of water toward the horizon. The gusty west wind carried in its trail the faint spice of flowers and a tincture of loam. In the startling blue above, the sketch of birds' wings completed the setting of the most beautiful day she could remember.

"'Tis a lovely sight!" Meghan exclaimed to her partner.

"Aye, 'tis lovely," Robin answered in Gaelic. "Almost as lovely as you."

Meghan flung him a surprised glance, then looked away. "Ye're free with yer words, Sir Robin."

Robin shrugged, unusually quiet. He was riding to Kilkenny when every sensible argument that had come to mind had urged him to the contrary. He could easily have turned down Sir Sidney's request to be the Crown's eyes and ears in the Butler fortress. He had reminded the lord deputy that he was free to turn down any order that did not come directly from the queen's hand, but he had not pursued the refusal because returning to England meant leaving Meghan.

And, like a fool, you cannot bear to be parted from her.

For a sennight he had known himself to be in love with Meghan O'Neill. It was foolish, improbable, and destined to end badly. Still, it was impossible to keep from his mind the hope that she would in time come to love him. The nurtured hope had been strengthened by a letter he had received from Revelin the day before they'd left Dublin.

His gaze lingered on Meghan's profile with a touch of pity. He rode on her right, where her birthmark was not visible. The picture she presented was of an absurdly lovely young woman gowned in green velvet with matching gable headdress and black velvet *cale,* which hid the more vibrant ebony of her hair. Little did she know what the future held for her.

But when Revelin came to Kilkenny to break the news of his impending marriage, Robin would be there to comfort, to support, and to love her.

"And that, my lad, will be nearly as good as smashing Rev's face," he muttered to himself. It angered him to think how Meghan had suffered during Revelin's absence, while Revelin, in London, had proposed to Lady Alison. It seemed only fair that Revelin should lose a mistress as he won a wife.

Concern furrowed Robin's brow as Meghan shifted uncomfortably in her saddle. She spied his worried look and favored him with a brief but plucky smile. He looked away.

Poor ignorant girl. She had realized her situation only the day before when one of their soldier guards had made a pointed remark about her frequent bouts of illness on the trail. The look of incredulity on her face followed by her blissful smile at the realization that she was pregnant had twisted the knot of jealousy that already plagued him. If he had not been so amazed by the depth of his feelings, he might have laughed at himself. Sir Robin Neville had fallen in love. How droll!

Riding for days, he knew, might cause her to miscarry; he thrust aside the thought that said it might be best for all if she did.

The day had warmed despite a midday shower and by late afternoon Meghan had pulled off her hood and released her hair in a cascade down her back. "How much longer?" she called to one of the Butler soldiers who rode with them.

"If ye'll look beyond the trees, mistress, ye'll be seeing a flash of light. 'Tis the river Nore which runs through Kilkenny Town. We'll be home afore nightfall, have nae doubt of it."

Squinting into the setting sun, Meghan saw, at last, a liquid ribbon of amber among the green. Kilkenny was a town whose main road led in from the south, so they had to ride past to come to it. Soon the pale crenellated battlements of the castle were visible above gable-roofed houses and green lawns. When the town gate came into view Meghan felt a tremor of misgiving.

Ever watchful, Robin spied the look of trepidation that came over her face and leaned near, offering her his hand. "Have no fear, dear lady. If the Butlers are half the hosts they're reputed to be, we'll be handsomely received."

Meghan squeezed his hand briefly, then let it go. She had ridden several days to come to this place, the home of Revelin's family. They had invited her, but would they genuinely welcome her when they discovered she carried Revelin's child?

Revelin's child! A smile of pride tugged at her lips. It was amazing, unbelievable, and yet...

The cry from their leader that halted the group startled Meghan. "What is it?" she asked. The soldier nearest her pointed to the south. Looking back over her shoulder, she saw a sight that had gone unnoticed until now. In the south a black snake of smoke uncurled as it climbed toward the sky.

"Reivers," she whispered in dismay.

"Nae reivers, mistress," the soldier answered. "The cursed Englishman Carew and his hellhound *bonaghts!*" He spat a Gaelic curse and unsheathed his sword. Immediately Robin and the others did likewise.

"Ride for the gate!" the leader called, though his company needed no encouragement. The thundering sound of four dozen hooves accompanied their gallop for the city. The cry of *Buitiler a buadh!* opened the gates without hesitation and within moments all were safe inside the city walls.

Flushed and exhilarated by the ride, Meghan had no time to regain the tremulous feelings that had crept upon her when she spied the castle. It was not until the drawbridge was lowered and she rode under the portcullis beside Robin that she again felt the stirrings of uncertainty.

The castle took her breath away. She had been impressed by Dublin's castle but had supposed that its grandeur was owed to the fact that it was owned by a queen. Never in her imaginings had she suspected that Revelin's family would own something equally magnificent. Yet, before her stretched a wedge-shaped fortress wider toward the south, the main entrance. A large tower at each angle joined the battlements into a four-sided fortress.

From the outside, it appeared dark and foreboding. Once inside, the impression vanished. The castle teemed with people, and the early evening sun reflected from the long gallery windows facing inward and cast brilliant rainbow facets upon the courtyard below.

People came running from all directions as the travelers halted in the center of the keepless castle. It was not as boisterous as the rousing welcome that had greeted Turlough's returning warriors; but women with children at their skirts embraced a few of the Butler soldiers, while shy young servant girls in caps and long aprons appeared on the edges of the crowd, their faces animated by admiration of the men and curiosity about the newcomers.

"Chin up, mistress. Here come our hosts," Robin whispered

encouragingly as he helped Meghan from her saddle. With a nod he directed her gaze to two men striding toward them.

Too late Meghan remembered the last of Mrs. Cambra's spate of instructions before she'd left Dublin. She was to have asked the party to pause outside the castle gates in order to allow her to set her appearance in order.

With dismay she looked down at her crushed, rain-dampened skirts. One hand went to the neck of her gown, where a ruff should have been, and the other made a desperate grab for her wind-blown tangle of blue-black hair. Without her headdress she was as good as naked to civilized folk, Mrs. Cambra had warned her. But it had been so warm, and Robin had not seemed to mind that she had completely forgotten about her dress until now.

Robin watched her panicky actions in sympathy coupled with purely masculine interest. She was wind-tossed and rain-dampened, true, but she could not have made more delightful impression on the male company. The raven tangles seemed artfully arranged curls, her flushed face a delight of maidenly blushes. As for her missing ruff, it gave them all a glimpse of the upper curves of her splendid breasts exquisitely outlined by her tight bodice.

As Meghan tried unsuccessfully to brush away the worst of the stains on her gown, a deep voice intoned, "Welcome, mistress, to Kilkenny Castle."

Startled by the volume of the deep voice, she looked up into a pair of wicked, warm brown eyes. The man was not tall but his breadth reminded her of Turlough, as did his sundarkened face above his dark beard. He was dressed in the height of fashion, but that could not hide the raw energy of the man. The gold-embroidered jerkin he wore emphasized the width of his shoulders, and the black velvet doublet sleeves did the same for the enormous muscles of his arms. Without thinking, her gaze fell to where tight canions outlined hardmuscled thighs.

The man's sudden bark of laughter made her gaze fly upward

again to find approval in his grinning face. "God's light, mistress! You've looked me over as thoroughly as a bull at market. Would you buy, mistress, 'tis the question."

The laughter of their audience made her brave. "Aye, were I in the market for a bull."

"Mistress O'Neill!" Robin admonished, turning a brilliant shade of red. "'Tis Sir Piers Butler you address."

"Aye, me name's Piers, as if you give a damn," Piers answered, his eyes never leaving Meghan. He rested his hands on his hips and threw out his chest as he looked her over with a more practiced skill than her own.

When his gaze came back to her face, Meghan's complexion vied with Robin's in its vivid hue, but she was not afraid. Only when his gaze fastened on her left cheek did she feel unease returning. Immediately she covered her mark with her hand and glanced uncertainly at Robin.

Piers's black brows rose. "Are ye afeard of me?" he questioned in Gaelic.

Meghan looked back at him in amazement. "I did not think 'twas lawful for Englishmen to speak Gaelic."

"The Butlers are the Butlers, lass, nae more and nae less," Piers continued in Gaelic. "Did ye think to frighten us with that wee mark? We're nae such cowards as that. Revelin tells me ye think yerself a changeling." His eyes lowered with pointed interest to her figure. "Seeing ye, 'tis nae wonder the lad's beguiled, but I'll own ye did so with earthly charms. Mayhaps I should be persuaded to test these charms meself."

The gentleman who accompanied Piers had paused to speak with the leader of the party from Dublin, but Piers's last statement snared his attention. He came toward them with a frown of disapproval on his face. "Enough, Piers. You'll make the lass gallop back to Dublin in fear for her virtue." He turned to Meghan and she found herself staring up into green eyes quite like Revelin's. "Sir Edmund Butler, at your service, mistress."

Of much the same coloring as his brother Piers, he was taller and slighter of build. Where Piers's apparel was stretched over his frame, Edmund's rich attire clothed a courtier's lithe body. This time Meghan remembered her curtsy, which she executed with more grace than she felt. "My lord," she murmured.

"Not 'my lord,' child; 'Sir Edmund' will serve." He turned to Robin and held out his hand. "Sir Robin, 'tis been some while."

"Two years," Robin supplied.

Edmund inclined his head, then turned to his brother. "Show them in, Piers, before they drop in their tracks. I've a meeting at the town gates. I will be back in time for supper."

Meghan watched him mount a horse brought by a groom, then her gaze moved south to where the plume of smoke had flattened out against the darkening sky. She knew that his business must have something to do with the trouble there.

"'Tis that damn fool West Country squire!" Piers exclaimed in disgust.

"Not Peter Carew?" Robin questioned in disbelief.

"The same. If he thinks a bit of parched earth will frighten the Butlers, then he's campaigned too long in heathen lands." Piers's dark eyes flashed as he looked at Meghan. "We Butlers love nothing so much as a challenge."

"You don't think he'll march on Kilkenny?" Robin pressed, disconcerted by this news. Sir Sidney had said nothing of looting and burning.

"He will not, if he knows what's good for him." Piers shot a glance over his shoulder. "Edmund thinks 'tis wise to take his troops out to meet Carew, but I've a mind the walls of Kilkenny will prove too much for the usurper."

Meghan cast a critical eye at the castle walls and agreed that they were stout protection against any enemy. When Piers offered her his arm, she slipped her hand onto it and followed him.

* * *

"Fie on Edmund for his nervous stomach!" Piers had exchanged his black-and-gold jerkin for one of deep wine red encrusted with jewels at the neckline; but as he prowled back and forth before the huge fire in the great hall, he reminded Meghan of a fancy-dressed boar, dangerous and untamed. Dinner had not improved his spirits, and the after-dinner brandy in his goblet did not seem to be helping matters. "God rot the devil who dares to set foot on Butler land!"

"Piers, please, you'll frighten our guests," Lady Mary Butler chided softly, her small, childlike voice a reflection of herself. She was taller than Meghan but as slender as a young girl, gowned in gold cloth and with an elaborate headdress of gold filigree and pearls. Golden hair framed her heart-shaped face with its sky-blue eyes and a small, thin-lipped mouth of pale rose.

Meghan looked from the husband to the wife and wondered what two people who were opposites in size, coloring, and temperament could have in common. For herself, she was a little afraid of the brusque man.

Piers paused before his wife's chair and patted her pale cheek affectionately. "Forgive me, wife. Edmund and I had words before supper which have left me ill tempered."

Robin, who sat on a settee nearby, crossed his elegantly clad leg over the other and adjusted the silk bow of his ribbon garter. "'Twould seem we have arrived at a bad time, Sir Piers. We were not given warning of the troubles in Kilkenny."

Piers snorted, avoiding his wife's look of disapproval at the crudity. "There's been nothing to tell." He winked at his wife. "I wouldn't be privy to how it began. A few cows reived by some rascally Englishmen, and wouldn't you know our lads would have them back again."

"I see," Robin commented quietly. "And then, of course, a few acres of corn are burned, pure mischief, and then a barn, a church, a small loss of life among the peasants."

"Aye, 'tis so," Piers answered, but his eyes had taken on a new light as he regarded Sir Robin. "What think you of our land, Sir Robin?"

"I find the countryside most diverting," Robin answered agreeably, "and the company exceptionally fine."

"Does Revelin know how exceptionally fine you find Mistress Meghan?"

Caught staring at Meghan, Robin could only laugh and give in graciously. "No doubt he would take exception to my interest; but, alas for poor Revelin, he is not present to learn of my unrequited tendre."

Meghan held still under Piers's dissecting gaze, but she wished that she had not left Ualter in Dublin. He was not her pet, that was true, and Revelin would certainly expect him to be in Dublin when he returned; but she missed his massive shaggy presence at her feet when Piers looked as though he would like to swallow her in one gulp.

Robin saw Meghan's discomfort and wondered that Piers's wife had not called her husband's attention away. Then he saw that she was bent over a knot in the thread she was weaving into her tapestry and knew it was up to him to capture Piers's attention. "Has Sir Edmund gone out to—ah—converse with Carew?"

Piers chuckled, not looking away from Meghan. "He has, in a manner of speaking. Carew understands nothing so much as a blow on the nose with a sharp stick."

"A battle!"

The distress in Robin's voice succeeded in claiming Piers's full attention. "You're not the squeamish sort? The lads go out to trade a few blows, 'tis all. I'm told Carew was once something of a soldier. They say at his castle in Idrone he has tiny soldiers with which to play at games of war. He is without the imagination to use the chessboard to sharpen his skills."

"If it is only a sporting game, why has Edmund taken most of the castle's soldiers with him?"

Piers's black brows bristled like the hairs on a boar's back. "Did he now? And you were counting?"

Robin shrugged elegantly. "My bedroom window faces the south gate. I was fascinated by the parade."

"A sad choice of rooms for you," Piers remarked, "seeing how the racket disturbed ye."

"Not at all." Robin smiled boyishly. "As a courtier only, I was impressed by the armed brigade."

"So you're nae a soldier, Sir Robin? I'm curious that you'd come to Ireland at all. 'Tis believed by some that the English send only spies and soldiers to Irish soil."

"Piers!" his wife cried shrilly.

Piers gave her a loving smile but his dark eyes said *Shut up, sweet wife.* "Will you answer that, Sir Robin?"

"Do I have a choice?" Robin tossed back lightly. He saw the beginnings of a frown crease Meghan's brow, and the notion that she was worried about his welfare made his heart pound pleasantly. "I came to Ireland at the queen's request. You know that Revelin was to sketch the north country for the queen's pleasure. I was sent along to bring a little harmony to the group."

"What of the others who accompanied you?"

Lady Mary rose. "Really, Piers, you press our guests too hard. I will not permit it any longer. Mistress O'Neill, you will kindly follow me. If the gentlemen should prefer to cross blades, you and I need not listen."

Meghan rose reluctantly, a silent plea in her eyes for Robin's guidance.

"You must be tired after our journey," Robin suggested, hoping that Lady Mary's hospitality was not a Butler ploy to divide and conquer them. "I'm certain our hosts will understand if you seek your bed instead of our company."

"We would indeed," Lady Mary concurred. "You do not look especially well to me, Mistress O'Neill. You hardly touched your meal, and you are much too pale after being so flushed when you arrived. A warm quiet bed should do wonders." As she talked she led Meghan to the doorway. With a last admonition to her husband, "Be kind to Sir Robin or I shall have to resort to my own methods," she swept the pair of them out of the long hall.

Robin bowed with a smile as the door closed, then turned abruptly to Piers with a piercing look. "Is the castle left entirely unguarded?"

Piers shrugged. "Your concern for our welfare surprises me."

Robin smiled. "'Tis in part concern for my own welfare, since I now reside within these walls."

Piers chuckled. "Revelin said I would like you, and I do, though you are more English than 'tis to my liking."

"That makes us even."

This time Piers roared his approval. "Come, have another brandy and tell me why you've traveled this great distance for naught."

Robin smiled. "Is it for naught to help a friend in need?"

"Is that what she is?"

"What else?"

Piers grinned. "Revelin told me she bore a mark that had the men of Ulster up in arms and that the wee lass herself believes she has visions that foresee the future."

"Revelin told you a great deal," Robin observed.

"Aye, that he did. We're family, and the lass is in need of a home. Her mark doesn't revolt you, Sir Robin?"

"No," Robin said quietly. "I now find nothing but beauty and sweetness in Mistress O'Neill's appearance."

"So, too, do I!" Piers poured more brandy into Robin's goblet. "But you and I are not too proud to admit that there's a certain streak of fear that runs in all of us when we see the work of God marred by Satan's hand."

"Really, is that not a strong word for an accident of birth?"

"Is it that? Revelin said she frightened Turlough O'Neill half out of his wits with her visions."

Robin frowned. He had been unable to learn exactly what

had happened the night Meghan saved his life, but he doubted that the superstitious prattling of the O'Neill chieftain had rational basis. "Mistress O'Neill saved my life. If it was by witchcraft, fairy magic, or Satan's left hand, I will be forever grateful to her."

"And defend her against all attack. Very commendable," Piers finished for him. "Well, 'tis only a bit of advice I give to you, for if you know Revelin, you know the Butler temper. The lad thinks himself in love with the lass, and she, well, I saw her smile at dinner when his name was mentioned."

Robin understood perfectly. Meghan was now under Butler protection and he was to keep his feelings for her to himself. "I'd give my life to aid her in any cause she chose."

Piers nodded. "Good. Now tell me what threats and warnings Sir Sidney has sent with you. Do not look so amazed, lad. Were I Sidney, I'd be sending more than a beribboned courtier to Kilkenny."

"Will it come to war?" Robin asked, not dismayed by the change of topic.

"It should not! Unless Carew's twice as great a fool as he makes himself appear."

"And if it does, is Kilkenny safe?"

Piers nodded. "As safe as a babe at his mother's tit."

Robin smiled. "Then let's discuss Sir Sidney."

At dawn a gray-white mist off the river Nore threaded its path through the streets of the town. The silence of the early-morning hours courted sleep, but Meghan lay awake in her bed listening with half an ear to the muffled sounds from the courtyard below as the servants of the castle prepared for a new day.

I carry Revelin's child within me!

It was miraculous, incredible, wonderful! Would Revelin be pleased? She had never thought to ask him if he liked children. Would he still want her with him? Would the child be a boy or a girl? Would the child be beautiful like his father or . . .

Meghan shut her eyes. Would the child be cursed with her mark? That fear had awakened her before the sky had lightened, and she was no nearer an answer now, hours later.

If the child bore the same mark as she, would Revelin accept it as his own or send it away as her father had? Or, if he kept the child, would he ever after look at her with wariness in his eyes? Revelin was the only person who had looked upon her from the first without fear or revulsion or dislike. That might change if she bore him a son whom the world would look at askance. If that happened, what would she do?

The clamor in the distance grew, and gradually Meghan came to realize that the noise came not from the castle courtyard but from the town.

She sat up in bed as a cry echoed up from the courtyard. Immediately she heard footsteps on the circular staircase that led to the tower room in which she slept. Dragging a blanket from the bed and winding it about her, she was halfway to the door when it burst open. Robin stood there, his hair on end and his shirt unlaced as if he had dressed in a hurry.

"Dress quickly! Kilkenny's under attack! Carew's men have broached the town gates!" He looked about the room and then nodded to himself. "It will serve. Stay here. Barricade the door and do not come out until you hear my voice on the other side. Promise me!"

"Attack?" Meghan looked him over again, noting the sword in his hand. "Sir Robin, ye will nae fight?"

Robin grinned cockily, his sunburnt freckles standing in high relief on his cheeks. "Do you think I should stand idly by while these Anglo-Irish Butlers have all the fun?"

Meghan shook her head. "Ye're English." A thought struck her and her eyes widened. "Ye would nae fight the Butlers?"

Robin's high, infectious laughter filled the tiny room. "'Tis why I love you, Meghan, you say what you think. I'll not betray my hosts. It occurs to me that you might at least wish me luck."

Meghan put out a hand to him and the next moment she was swept up in his embrace. His breath was warm and quick on her cheek an instant before his lips covered hers in a hotly passionate kiss. Almost at once she was released. "That's to remind you that I intend to come back." He smiled radiantly at her. "I've decided 'tis time I took a wife. When I come back I'll fight even Revelin if I must, for I want you. I love you!"

Then he was gone, with his last words ringing in Meghan's ears. Astonishment held her to the spot for the space of several heartbeats. She could not have heard aright. Robin in love with her? How? Why, when he knew she carried Revelin's child?

An explosion in the distance shook the walls of the castle. She raced to the narrow window to look out. To the south near the main gate the town had begun to burn. A second explosion followed the first. The flash of light that appeared through the dense fog and accompanying blast of noise reminded her of lightning striking a tree. But this was not lightning. This was gunpowder.

Below her, beyond the stretch of the moat, men bearing pitchforks, clubs, and spikes were running toward the sounds. Against them came a tide of women and children streaming toward the castle. Mist shrouded them after only a few yards and they were lost. Had Sir Piers opened the castle bridge to these frightened folk? The question decided her course of action. She would not remain shut up in the tower when she could be useful below.

Within moments she was dressed as best she could without help, abandoning most of her petticoats and fastening her gown only halfway up the back. When she had braided her hair and tied it back with a ribbon, she strapped her skean to her arm and went down.

In the main gallery she found Lady Mary with her children, their servants, and a few soldiers.

Lady Mary rose from her tapestry loom as Meghan appeared. "My dear! Sir Robin said he had left you safely behind your bedroom door."

Meghan dropped a hasty curtsy, aware of her inadequacies in the presence of this regal lady. "I could nae hide away, Lady Mary, when there's trouble." She cast a worried look at the tall Tudor windows as another blast shook the dawn.

"Cannons!" Lady Mary cried and bit her lip. "We were unaware that Sir Peter was so well equipped. Piers will be furious."

Meghan looked about. "Where is Sir Piers?"

"Out there," she answered, casting a hand toward the town. "When Edmund did not return before dawn, Piers took a party of men and went to find him." Her eyes filled with tears but her voice was firm. "I am most unhappy with my gracious husband! He leaves us here to wait when he might have commanded the castle forces."

"My lady!" a servant cried as he came unbidden into the gallery. "My lady, Sir Edward is at the gate requesting entrance."

"Edward? Is Elenore with him? Why do you stand there? Let them in!"

The servant looked uncertain. "Sir Piers gave orders to lower the drawbridge to no one but himself, m'lady."

Lady Mary did something that quite surprised Meghan. She reached out and boxed the servant's ear. "Dolt! He could not have known that his own brother would come to the door. Open it immediately!

The servant held his ear but there was a wide smile on his face as he bowed and hurried out.

She turned to Meghan, all blushes. "What must you think of me? There are times when I believe Piers's rough manners will overwhelm me entirely, though I must admit, they are most effective. You must be hungry. Kate, bring Mistress Meghan breakfast."

Meghan had no time to touch her breakfast before the gallery was once more disturbed, this time by a family of nobles who bore the dust of the road on their clothes. The fourth Butler brother was in his middle thirties, and as he moved he clanked from the armor he wore beneath his mantle.

"Mary!" he greeted warmly, and as he pulled his hat from his head, Meghan saw that, like his brothers, he was dark.

"Edward! Elenore!" Lady Mary cried and went to embrace the arrivals. "Just look at Elizabeth," she continued, hugging the tall slender girl who came behind her mother. "And James and John, how you've grown!" she said, ruffling the hair of the two boys. "Come in, come in, we've food and drink for all!"

Edward shook his head. "I've come only to see my family safely behind Kilkenny's walls. Piers is fighting beyond the city gates and Edmund has disappeared."

"Dead?" Lady Mary questioned fearfully.

"Nae, he's ridden home to Clogrennan, I'll hazard, to raise more troops."

Lady Mary bit her lip nervously. "The city gates are broached, truly?"

Sir Edward smiled. "'Tis one thing to broach a city's gates. 'Tis another thing entirely to storm a castle. Carew is not a madman. He would not dare attack the home of the earl of Ormond, who at this very minute sits in the queen's chambers."

Lady Mary nodded, but Meghan, who watched in silence, saw the look of doubt creep into all their expressions, and a feeling of unease moved deep within her. A castle was not impregnable. If this Englishman Carew did attack, Sir Edmund would need to arrive in time to save them. She could not say why she knew that; but the certainty of it further disturbed her, and she backed away from them.

The morning passed slowly, punctuated by the ever-advancing sound of cannon fire as the battle for the city continued. After the first frantic minutes following the arrival of Edward Butler's family, Meghan had retired to an alcove near a window that faced south to watch silently as house after house went up in flame.

The chattering in the room behind her slowly receded until there was only the push-pull of her own pulse in her ears. The mists over the city darkened as though night were falling, and the orange-red tongues of flame grew steadily until they licked the heavens. Cannon blasts increased until the night was showered with sparks. And wherever they fell, new flames leaped up, greedily consuming the town.

Suddenly, she was on the street outside the castle, being shoved and jostled as the terrified townsmen ran past her, their screams of fear bursting in her ears. "We'll die! We're going to die!"

Meghan bit hard on the knuckle she had wedged between her teeth to keep from crying out. The stinging pain seeped slowly into her consciousness until she was once more inside the castle, looking out on a bright sunlit afternoon.

A vision. She had had another vision, but was it real? Would Kilkenny fall completely? And would she die? "No, please God, no! Spare the child!"

"Oh dear! What have you done?" Lady Mary questioned when Meghan's whimpering drew her to the alcove.

Meghan looked down at her bleeding finger. "I hurt meself."

Lady Mary fell back a step before Meghan's bleak look. "Are you ill, child?"

Meghan shook her head. She would not tell them, could not tell them, what she had seen. If they believed her, they would panic. If they did not, they would think her mad. She rose unsteadily to her feet. "I'm a wee bit weary. I'll go to me room now."

She did not look up as she passed out of the gallery and into the corridor but she heard whispering behind her. Once in the hall, she began to run. She had to get away, to lock herself in the tower to protect Revelin's child. When she rounded a corner she collided with one of the servants.

The young girl's cry of surprise turned to horror when she

saw who had bumped into her. "Saints preserve us! She touched me! I'm cursed! Cursed!"

Lady Mary came hurrying across the hall. "What's wrong? What's the matter?"

The servant girl crossed herself, tears pouring down her cheeks. "She's cursed me. Look!" She held out a hand smeared with blood. "She's put the curse of death on me, she has, with her bloody mark! We'll all be killed for taking in that devil's spawn!"

When Lady Mary slapped the servant, Meghan fell back until the cold stone wall stopped her. "I—I did nae do it!" she wailed. She held up her bloody hand to cover her cheek. "I hurt meself, 'twas all. An accident. I would nae curse ye, I would nae!"

Lady Mary gave the girl a quick shake before releasing her. "Go below, you wretched creature!" Turning, she put a hand on Meghan's shoulder. "Pay no attention. The girl's frightened witless by the battle; we all are. Go along to your room and forget the incident."

Meghan hurried up the circular staircase that led to her room and shut and barred her door. She flung herself on her bed and gave in to the tears she had held back. "Revelin, Revelin, where are ye?"

After a few minutes, she drifted off to a troubled sleep.

The blast at the castle gate shattered the pitcher on the table by Meghan's bedside. The stupor of sleep made her limbs feel twice as heavy as usual as she struggled to sit up. The room was in darkness, the only light a dull wavering glow that filtered through the arrow-slit windows of the tower.

The vision had come again as she slept, and for a moment she thought the sounds of battle so close must be the dregs of that unwanted dream. A woman's scream on the stairwell that led to her room dashed that hope. Meghan sat up, her heart beginning to pump in long heavy strokes as her eyes focused on her door. The battle was going on inside the castle walls!

Booted feet clambered up the narrow winding stairs, and then with a loud *whack!* an ax bit into the planks of her door.

Meghan leaped to the floor as the ax slashed through a second time, making kindling of the once stout oak door. Freeing her skean, she dived under her bed as a huge arm reached through the mangled opening and lifted the crossbar.

Meghan felt her heart leap into her throat as she spied two men through the fringe of the bed hangings. They were not English soldiers, nor were they even clansmen to be recognized by the color of their mantles. They were dressed in bloody chain-mail shirts and wore skullcaps of steel. No insignia placed them. They were *bonaghts*, mercenaries.

The room was small and she knew they would find her. They did so almost at once. After stripping the bedding and overturning the armoire, they lifted the bed, frame and all, exposing her.

"A lass! A bonny fine lass!" one of them declared in Gaelic as he reached down and lifted her from the floor by her arm.

Meghan bit off a cry of pain as he jerked her up, and waited until he had set her on her feet before lunging at him. He had not expected her attack and her blade bit deeply into his throat. As he tumbled backward she wrenched it free and ran toward the open door. Roaring a curse, the second man caught her by the open flap of her gown as she gained the doorway.

Desperate, Meghan grabbed the splintered door and jerked. The cloth gave way, leaving her assailant with a scrap of cloth as she ran down the stairwell. The treacherously winding stairway was wide enough to allow the passage of only one grown man at the time, and the man behind her was hampered by his six-foot ax. Prayers formed on Meghan's lips that there was no one ahead as she flew recklessly down the spiral.

When she rounded the final turn she could not stop and sprawled headlong into the corridor. She tasted blood as her chin hit the floor with a sickening jar, but she was up in an instant. Instinct drove her toward the main gallery, where she had left the others. The ringing sound of steel could be heard over the shouts and cries of men in the courtyard, but as she neared the gallery she could tell that there was no battle here; but the sight that greeted her slowed her step.

More *bonaghts* were looting the gallery, tearing tapestries from the walls and stripping the carpets from the floor. Gathered in a circle in the center of the room were Lady Mary and Lady Elenore and their children. One mercenary had Lady Elenore by the throat, the blade of his skean held just above the grip of his hand. With a whimper of fear, Meghan slipped into a dark shadow near the doorway and watched.

"Where be yer husband, bitch?" the man shouted.

Lady Elenore shook her head. "Not here! Dear God! Spare us! We're women and children!"

"Aye, women! There should be something to be had in that, too." The *bonaght* sheathed his skean, then suddenly reached for the neck of Lady Elenore's gown and ripped it open to the waist. The sound of shredding cloth and Lady Elenore's accompanying cry snared the attention of several other men.

"If ye will nae aid our search, ye may as well entertain us." Still holding her by the throat, he kicked out his booted foot and yanked her legs out from under her. He fell with her, not bothering to break her fall. Lady Elenore's ragged gasp of pain was smothered in his brutal kiss as the soldiers nearby came to urge him on with filthy oaths and suggestions.

Meghan leaned back into the shadow and closed her eyes as fear ran like ants over her skin. Lady Elenore was being raped before her own children's eyes! Meghan knew she should do something. But what? And how could she know that anything she might do would stop them? One man she could kill, but a dozen? They would overpower her and then use her as they did Lady Elenore.

Never before had she felt so weak, so helpless, so vulnerable. She did not fear dying, but she did fear the brutality of the scene before her. Tears streamed down her face as Lady Elenore's cries echoed in the rafters of the long hall. No! She could not allow this! She must try to stop it. Suddenly she knew what method to use.

She propelled herself from the corner before her momentary courage could desert her again. "Stop! Stop!" she cried at the top of her lungs and ran forward into the room.

The men looked up in surprise, then one of them smiled. "Another lass! And younger! She's mine first!"

As he started toward her, Meghan drew her skean and fell to her knees in the center of the gallery. Without a pause she reached up with one hand, tore her hair free of its braid, and raised her hands heavenward as she cried, *"Mallacht!"*

When he was a few feet from her, Meghan lifted her gaze to the hulking soldier's face, shutting out the whimperings of Lady Elenore. "Beware *bonaght!*" she challenged, and flung the wild tangle of hair back from her face as she turned her marked cheek toward him.

"'Tis a *bean feasa!*" he whispered as he fell back a step. The men who had been holding Lady Elenore's arms and legs released her and rose to their feet. With her gown spattered with blood from the dead *bonaght,* her eyes wild, and the blood-red mark upon her livid cheek, the girl appeared to them as an apparition from Hell.

"Mallacht!" Meghan repeated and aimed the point of her skean at the rapist still astride his victim. "A curse on ye, *bonaght!*" Then in a loud steady voice she cried, *"No comlund i mbethi memais foraib ocus bethi for seilib agus for sopaib hi cach airiucht i mbed!"*

The offender scrambled to his feet and reached for his skean.

Meghan leaped to her feet and swung her outstretched hand about to include the roomful of men. *"Mallacht!"* she repeated for the third time. "A curse on all of ye who violate this house."

She locked gazes with the men one by one, and their fear seemed to feed her courage. She heard boot steps in the doorway behind her, but she could not release the hold she had on the company of soldiers in order to protect her back.

She stretched her arms heavenward a second time. "'Defeat in all battles until in every camp ye're spat upon and reviled!' That's me curse on ye if ye touch another woman or child!"

The men's voices rose in protest but one overrode the others. "The madwoman's cursed me. I've nothing to lose!" Enraged beyond reason, the rapist lunged at her, his blade raised.

Meghan held her ground. If she was to die, it would be with the knowledge that they would believe themselves cursed beyond redemption.

There came a shout from behind her, and then a pistol shot roared past her ear an instant before a ball slammed into her attacker's forehead. He staggered back and crumpled to the floor.

"I've warned ye, there'll be nae rape of the nobility!"

Meghan swung around at the sound of that voice. Dressed in a battle-stained tunic, his face shrouded in crusted blood from a head wound, she could not distinguish a single feature. Yet she ran to him, her arms outstretched. "Colin!" she cried, tears blurring her vision of him. "Colin MacDonald!"

Stunned, Colin stepped back from her. "Meghan O'Neill?" he whispered hoarsely, and the strength seemed to go out of him. His pistol arm fell limply to his side.

"Ye know her, Colin?" cried one the soldiers. "Care a care, she's cursed us!"

Colin's gray eyes stared down into Meghan's face and she saw the old fear returning. Suddenly he fell to his knees crying, "Do not curse me, *bean feasa!* I'm yers to command!"

Appalled at the look of sick fear on the huge man's face, Meghan turned and ran to where Lady Mary knelt beside Lady Elenore. The woman's lips were bleeding and five large bruises had begun to redden on her neck where the *bonaght* had choked her, but her eyes were open when Meghan knelt over her. "Are ye bad hurt, Lady?"

"No—" Lady Elenore shook her head slightly. "Edward . . . will be . . . so . . . very . . . angry. No pistol! I forgot . . . it."

"We'll take ye to safety," Meghan promised, and with Lady Mary's help she lifted the woman to her feet.

John Reade pushed through the doorway of the gallery, a pistol in one hand and his sword in the other. His battle-weary eyes took in with disgust the scene of rapine and looting. Carew had charged the men to refrain from despoiling the castle, but these men were not soldiers. These men were vermin, scavengers. In all his years of soldiering he had never before seen the devastation and outright slaughter of which these men were capable. With the smell of blood in their nostrils they had not been content until the sanctity of Saint Canice had been broached and the church silver and gold plate stolen. Thank God, he had been able to keep a small group of English soldiers by his side.

"Cowards! Thieves! Irish curs!" he cried, ranging his pistol back and forth among the few remaining *bonaghts* until reluctantly they withdrew to the far end of the hall. "Wilson!" he called over his shoulder to one of his men. "Secure the gallery!"

When he spied the women withdrawing from the room, he called to them. "Are you mad?" he questioned as they turned to him. "You're safe in this room now with my men to guard you. You cannot leave for any reason."

Meghan glanced up and away. *John Reade.* She swayed slightly. It did not seem possible, and yet it was he.

Lady Mary pinned the soldier with a haughty stare. "Is that the best you English can offer women in distress?"

John smiled evilly. "Would you rather I not interfere, my lady? I am certain your gallant Irishmen would be more than happy to return to their tasks ere I came."

Lady Mary's chin lifted a fraction. "If you can compare your conduct with the manners of swine, I doubt it will make much difference."

Angered by the noblewoman's refusal to thank him, John glanced away, and into Meghan's face. "You!" He grabbed her by the arm as she turned her back and forced her to face him.

"It is, 'tis Meghan O'Neill!" he exclaimed in delight. "Is Revelin Butler among the rebels?"

"There are no rebels here, sir, only Butlers defending their home!" Lady Mary answered him icily. "And if you do not allow me to find a place of rest for the earl of Ormond's sister-in-law, I will see that you lose your head for having allowed the violation!"

John smiled as his gaze stayed on Meghan's pale face. "Do as you see fit, my lady. I have business with this girl." He gazed intently at Meghan. "We do have business, do we not?"

Meghan began to tremble as his grip tightened on her arm. Here was a man who would not fear her power. John was more animal than human, a wolf who stalked in the shadows. Perhaps the vision had played her false, for the predatory look now in his eyes was for her. "What do you want?" she asked.

John's eyes gleamed. "English, and so quickly. If you learn all things so well, we shall enjoy ourselves thoroughly. Come with me, girl! We need privacy."

"No! No!" Meghan twisted in his grasp but he did not release her.

"Are you mad? Release her!" Lady Mary demanded.

Instead, John dragged Meghan close and whispered in her ear, "If you truly care for the lives of these people, you will come quietly. If not, I will free the *bonaghts!*"

"You wouldn't!" With revulsion Meghan saw the answer in his eyes. Looking into the black pit of his fathomless gaze, she knew that she was lost. "I'll come," she whispered so softly that only he heard.

Chapter Sixteen

Meghan bit the inside of her lip to keep back the cries for help that trembled on her tongue as John Reade dragged her out of the long gallery. She knew that if she balked, he would withdraw his promise to protect the Butler women and children from further harm.

When John paused in the corridor, she cast a calculated glance at the main staircase, wondering if she might be able to push him down the stone steps. Two *bonaghts,* dressed in animal skins and hauling a chest down the steps from the floor above, bumped a man standing on the landing. He looked up and cursed, and Meghan saw that it was Colin. This time she turned away from his startled glance. He had run away and left her in the gallery; he would not help her now.

"You, soldier, take those two men and set a guard at the gallery doors," John ordered the Scotsman. "And keep your men away from the east tower. I've business there that will occupy me some little time."

Meghan did not resist, but when John jerked her after him she could no longer keep back a whimper of fear. At the sound, he swung around and slapped her.

"Quiet, bitch! You gave your word; will you keep it?"

Meghan shrank back from him as far as the length of her arm's reach and lifted her hand to her stinging cheek, but she did not try to free herself. Aware that the *bonaghts* who had moved out of John's path were openly staring at her, she lifted her chin and looked at John.

"I will honor the bargain," she said softly in Gaelic. "But whatever pleasure you imagine, you'll be disappointed." There it was, said between them, the unspoken knowledge that John was bent on rape.

John's mouth curved. He did not understand her but he saw acceptance in her eyes. "Come, mistress, it grows late and we've the night before us."

Meghan did not know if he chose her room by design or chance, but as he dragged her up the narrow winding stairs she wondered what his reaction would be to the overturned bed and dead man sprawled across the floor. Perhaps he would give up in disgust, she thought as a bubble of hysteria percolated to the top of her simmering emotions. Yet, she was not without a defense of her own. When her sleeve slipped back to her elbow, exposing the O'Neill skean, she reached out and jerked it back to her wrist.

John paused again at the top of the staircase, his jaw beginning to work agitatedly when he saw the ax-shredded door hanging on a single hinge. He debated whether he should find a more-secluded room, for he wanted no intruders. If he retraced his steps he would risk being diverted by orders.

Undecided, he looked back at Meghan's blanched face, and the hot dark currents of his lust rose to the surface. He felt by turns burned and chilled and, above all, stiff. His lust for her was a canker; he was eaten alive with need. He feared that in another moment he would be on his knees before her, begging her to pleasure him. A beautiful woman: she was his weakness. His hand trembled on her arm, which he held in a viselike grasp. He must have her! Now!

John glanced back at the room beyond the battered door and tugged Meghan after him. "God's death!" he roared as he nearly sprawled over the body of the dead *bonaght*.

Meghan kept her eyes averted for fear that the sight would bleach the conviction from her voice as she said, "'Tis my room. I killed that man. I've cursed your soldiers and I curse you, John Reade!"

John looked at her in faint surprise. "Do I seem a man afraid of curses?"

The eyes staring down into Meghan's were glazed with wildness of purpose that made her stomach flutter. Her head ached and her mouth felt like sand but she could not look away. His grip had all but cut off the circulation and her fingers were numb, but she did not concentrate on the pain. She stared at him. "I saved your life on Lough Neagh."

John's clenched jaw eased into a smile. "Did you?"

"You were guilty of murdering the O'Neill clansman. I saw it in your eyes."

"I remember that night well." His smile deepened in recollection. Her body had been like a white flame in the darkness, her skin luminous and inviting. It had been Revelin who had knelt between her thighs and eased himself. This time, he would know that pleasure. The thought of it made him burn. He had hoped to arouse her as much as he was, but he knew now he would not be able to contain himself. After the first time, he would be more in control; then he would teach her games he doubted Revelin knew.

Still holding her by the wrist, he reached down to unhook the metal points of his codpiece. "I remember the night because you were young Butler's slut. You bared yourself to him on the riverbank and then you spread yourself for him." He licked his lips as his hand began to work on his own flesh. "Bare yourself for me, girl, and I'll show you how it feels to be ridden by a real man."

"You . . . you followed us?" Meghan whispered in horror.

"Aye, I did, and now I'll possess what you gave to Butler." He yanked her nearly off her feet as he roughly pulled her close. With his free hand he grabbed the neck of her gown and tore it open to the waist. His gaze greedily covered her naked breasts. "Ah, I remember them proud breasts, how they shone in the moonlight. Revelin suckled them well, I recall. Then that damned nosy Irishman came creeping through the underbrush and I had to kill him."

His breath was hot and fetid on her face, but Meghan kept her eyes level with his, while revulsion and fear shrank her flesh against her bones. What she and Revelin had shared had been pure. Knowing now that this man had hidden in the bushes and watched made their actions seem an obscenity. The thought made her angry and in her anger she forgot a little of her fear.

"If ye rape me you'll nae have another woman as long as you live." She touched her birthmark and then pointed at his groin without looking away from his face. "I curse your manhood!"

John reached out quickly and slapped her. "Curse me and be damned!"

Meghan's head snapped back at the heavy-handed blow and her knees buckled. John did not try to stop her as she slid toward the floor. He released her and she sank to her knees. Unbuckling his sword, he dropped it to the floor and kicked it aside. Before she could rise to her knees, he bent and grabbed a handful of her hair. "But you're not undressing, girl. I'm an impatient man. If you will lag about on your knees, you may give me ease in this manner." He viciously jerked her face toward his open codpiece.

Meghan cried out and, bracing herself with both hands against his thigh, flung herself away from him. She felt the hairs being pulled out of her scalp as he refused to yield his hold, and pain shot through her head. Blindly she reached for her skean and pulled it free, but John was a soldier first and foremost, and the flash of metal in the room's twilight warned him.

His laugh was triumphant as he bent and caught her slender wrist in his powerful grasp. "I like a wench with fight in her. I like the taming of them. You'll learn from me, sweet little bitch, that you will." He snapped her wrist back so quickly that Meghan thought he had broken it as a stab of pain shot up her arm. Her fingers went numb and the dagger slid from her grasp.

"Service me, whore! Now!"

"No!" Meghan screamed as he fell upon her, his great weight knocking the breath out of her. She thought she would suffocate as his mouth found hers and his tongue invaded hers. She fought and heaved, drumming her heels against the stone floor, but he could not be moved. After a few seconds she felt him groping along her thigh, searching for her skirt, and then he began to lift it. Suddenly she realized that she might lose her child if he accomplished this violence upon her. She could withstand a little pain, but she could not bear the thought of losing Revelin's child.

She bit down hard, catching her own lip as she sank her teeth into his beefy tongue. *"Mallacht!"* she cried when he jerked back from her. "Curse ye so that nae woman will lie with ye again!"

John lifted his head and brought it down like a battering ram with a blow to her forehead. Stars exploded behind Meghan's eyes and she went limp under him.

Satisfied that she would struggle no longer, John heaved himself back up on his knees. He had seen too little of her and, blast the narrow arrow slits, there was precious little light in the room. He swung his head to look for a lantern and once more the glint of metal saved him. He dived across Meghan's prone form an instant before a battleax split the air where he had been kneeling.

In one motion he rolled off her and came to his feet a few feet away, her discarded blade in his hand. "Who the hell do you think you are that you dare to interfere?"

"Ye're nae so much a man that ye can rape a wee lass!"

Meghan's eyes flew open as she recognized Colin Mac-Donald's voice.

John looked over the burly Scotsman and instantly realized that it would be suicide to challenge a man with a six-foot ax when he had only a few inches of steel. He lowered his arm. "Do you burn for the bitch yourself? Ah, but of course, I always thought you two had been quite friendly. Have you missed her?" He smiled and spread his arms. "We'll share. 'Tis a fitting sport for men-at-arms."

Colin glanced down at Meghan but she could not be certain of his expression, for her vision was impaired by pain and the oncoming night. Yet, when he put out his hand to her, she took it instantly and was drawn to her feet.

"Are ye hurt, lass?" he asked gently in Gaelic, his big hand tenderly stroking her face.

"Nay, Colin," Meghan answered, and she caught his hand and squeezed it tight. "I—I thought ye'd forsaken me."

John snorted. "What a tender scene."

Colin touched her lips and met the oily texture of blood. "Ye're bleeding, lass. Wait on the stairs for me. I'll see to ye after a wee bit."

He gave her a gentle push, but Meghan did not go. She reached up and touched his cheek. "Ye answered me prayer, Colin. May God go with ye."

"Aye, and still I'll be damned," he said in his familiar cocky tone. "But ye, lass, ye'll nae come to harm after this day. Colin MacDonald swears it."

During the intervening moments, John had taken the opportunity to steal within an arm's reach of his sword. There was not much room to maneuver an ax. One false step and the Scotsman would be open to a sword's thrust. The room was dark, and the *bonaght's* body, obscured in the shadows, might trip the Scotsman up. John almost smiled when Meghan moved into the doorway. He would have her yet, and he would be fresh from victory with the blood of one of her lovers on his hands.

Meghan moved onto the steps as if in a dream. None of the last hour seemed real. She had thought John in England, and she had thought Colin still in Ulster. As the first *whack* of Colin's ax rang against the stone floor in the room behind her, she began to run. She could not wait, did not want to know what happened. If Colin won, she would be safe for a while. If John won...

Once more she flew down the steps, circling around and around until her stomach heaved and her head spun. When she reached the gallery floor she stumbled into the corridor. Immediately, a strong arm reached out to steady her, and she looked up into the face of one of the Scottish *bonaghts* who had accompanied Colin.

The man glanced up as the battle sounded overhead, then winked at Meghan. "Colin's nae a man to see a lass he likes mistreated. Ye best go in with the others." His certainty vanished as his eyes were snared by her birthmark. "Colin's told us of ye. He says ye'll remove the curse if we swear to protect ye."

Meghan nodded, unable to find words.

The man smiled at her. "We swear to protect ye, *bean feasa*, whatever the outcome above."

Meghan looked up once at the stairwell and then away. *Whatever the outcome.* Colin might die. As the man helped her into the gallery, her mind was numb. Without really feeling the emotion, she recorded with relief that all the Butler family were present and that the women were serving supper, after a fashion.

"Mistress Meghan!" Lady Mary cried when she spied her and came swiftly toward Meghan. "Your gown! Dear Lord! You've been raped!"

"Nae, only a little bruised." Meghan glanced down. She

was naked from shoulder to waist. Yet, neither Colin nor the Scottish *bonaght* had even glanced at her exposed breasts. She was a *bean feasa*, a wise woman of many powers: they were afraid to offend her. When the soldier relinquished her into Lady Mary's arms, Meghan shut her eyes. "Please, Colin, live," she whispered.

The seconds seem weighted by hours before she heard footsteps in the hall. Meghan shot to her feet as a man entered the gallery. It was not Colin; but it was not John Reade.

The short, barrel-chested man was dressed as an English squire, and when he pulled off his hat he bared a sparsely populated head of hair. He swept a low, awkward bow to the company assembled and said, "Ladies and gentlefolk, allow me to present myself to you. I am your captor, the baron of Idrone!"

Lady Mary came to her feet, one hand rising to her throat. "Mercy's Grace, 'tis Peter Carew!" She stepped forward. "I am the wife of Sir Piers Butler. Where is he?"

The stocky man wiped his brow with his sleeve before replying, "Your husband is with the rest of the Butler rebels, under arrest."

"Sir Edmund and Sir Edward?" Lady Mary prompted.

Carew's ruddy face displayed both triumph and annoyance. "Sir Edward I have. Sir Edmund has retreated to Clogrennan Castle."

Meghan rose to her feet. "Sir Robin Neville?"

Carew looked at the girl's torn gown and tangled hair with interest and then shrugged. "I've not met the man."

"He's dead!"

Meghan swayed at the sound of that voice. "Dead?"

"Aye, dead, along with your Scotsman!" replied the man entering the room.

Meghan heard John's voice as if from far away. She was falling into blessed darkness where rest and comfort and peace beckoned.

Dublin, August 1569

Revelin's face had lost its color. "That is not possible! Who wrote this?" He looked around the room for the messenger who had brought the letter he held. When he found the man, he beckoned him with a hand. "Did you see Kilkenny fall with your own eyes?"

"That I did, Sir Revelin. 'Twas not to be believed. That mad Englishman's *bonaghts* broached the city walls at dawn. Before nightfall the castle fell to them as well. There was pillage and slaughter, outright murder of babes and women-folk." He stopped to contain his emotions. "Me own youngest daughter was handed about among the troops until she was broken and bleeding."

Revelin slammed his fist on the table before him. For nearly a week he had been traveling from London to Dublin with one thought on his mind: to ride to Kilkenny and see Meghan once more. He had not been able to think of anything else. Even with Alison by his side, he could not shake the undercurrent of excitement that rose nearer and nearer to the surface of his mind as they drew closer to Ireland. He had thought Meghan would be safe once removed from Sir Sidney's influence. Now it seemed he had sent Meghan into the gaping jaws of Hell.

His fingers tightened on the desk until the skin about his knuckles was white. "What of the Butler household?"

The man shook his head. "I heard many of the servants were put to the sword. And Sir Edward's lady, 'tis said she was violated in public. Saints preserve us!" He snatched his hat from his head to cross himself. "I'm only repeating rumor, Sir Revelin."

"Get out!" Revelin roared. "Get out and stay out until I send for you again—but do not leave my house!"

When the door shut behind the messenger, Revelin sank

into his chair and stared out across his salon with vacant eyes. Carew had attacked Kilkenny, the seat of the earl of Ormond. It was incredible, fantastic ... and true.

Pillage, slaughter, rape...

Revelin put a hand to his brow and moaned softly. In all innocence he had sent Meghan where he had believed she would be safe.

Safe for you and your peace of mind.

The chiding voice in his mind flayed him with the rationale behind his decision. He had thought *he* would be safe with his mistress in Kilkenny and his bride-to-be in Dublin. He had neatly arranged matters in a style of which his uncle and the queen would approve. But what of himself and what of Meghan? She had not wanted to go to Kilkenny. He had ignored her wishes and had the matter arranged by the earl. And so she had gone, straight into the center of battle.

What had happened to her? Had she been killed?

Revelin shut his eyes and listened as if the answer were humming at the center of his being. He heard nothing, felt nothing, and after a moment he realized that this was his answer. He did not feel the grief of her loss. No, she could not be dead, or he would know it.

A twinge of guilt drove him from his chair. If the soldiers did not fear her, she would be much desired. And, as much as it comforted him to hope that they feared her, he knew men too well to hope for that miracle. Perhaps she was being protected by his uncles. Then the messenger's words came back to him. If Lady Elenore had been publicly raped, what hope could he hold that Meghan had not suffered the same fate?

He picked up the letter and read again its hastily scrawled message of disaster. She was not mentioned by name, but Meghan's plight was apparent in every line. She was in trouble. He must go to her.

"Oh, there you are, Rev. I had decided that you were not yet back from the castle."

Revelin raised his eyes slowly to the lady who had entered the room. Dressed in a yellow silk gown that perfectly complemented her buttercup curls and crystal-gray eyes, Lady Alison looked the very image of a clear spring day, but his mind harbored an image of blue-black tresses, a fathomless lough-blue gaze, and the delicate sketch of a blood-red rose.

"I'm going to Kilkenny," he said abruptly and began folding the letter.

"Kilkenny?" Alison frowned. "So soon? Before the wedding?"

"Sit down, Alison. We must talk." Briefly, Revelin recounted the story of the sack of Kilkenny, leaving out his more personal feelings and fears.

"My dear, that's dreadful, but what can you do? If, as you say, this Peter Carew is bent upon the capture of Sir Edmund and Clogrennan, then you must return to London and seek help from the earl of Ormond. After all, 'tis your uncle's estate this Englishman despoils. As much as you must feel for your kin, are they not better served by a pledge of the queen's intercession?"

Revelin shook his head. "Any messenger can apprise the earl of the facts. I am needed in Kilkenny."

Alison rose from her chair and came toward Revelin to place a hand on his cheek. "I have often admired the tenacity and loyalty of the Butlers. We Burkes suffer for our divisions. But, Rev, from what you say, your uncles have much blame to bear for the situation with Carew. I do not say that Carew is justified in sacking the town, but who can say how the queen will view the matter? Would it not be more reasonable to stand apart rather than be one of the Butlers who took up arms? I am certain the earl would urge you to weigh the matter carefully."

Revelin looked up into her lovely face, a touch of amusement in his expression. "Have you been taking lessons at my uncle's knee on the management of Sir Revelin Butler?"

Alison blushed a deep pink. "Certainly not! The earl and I have never discussed marriage. It would not be seemly without the official sanction of an engagement." Her lashes lowered over her eyes, their red-gold tangle having proved to be a great distraction to any number of courtiers. Revelin was aware only that he was about to make to her in Dublin the speech he should have made weeks ago in London.

"What if there were no engagement, formal or otherwise, Alison? What if it suddenly came to a man that his ordering of his future had been without substance, that he was missing an elemental portion, without which his life would be simply milling out?"

Alison's lashes fluttered upward. "Do you mean a life without love?"

Revelin's brows rose. "I do not think I quite understand that word. Once I thought I did. Once I thought it was what I feel when I gaze into your eyes as I do now, that this feeling of contentment and goodwill must be love."

Alison's gray eyes clouded. "But something has made you doubt that?"

"Aye," Revelin said softly, the wistful tone in his voice surprising even to himself.

"Is she really such a beauty?" Alison questioned calmly.

Revelin's gaze focused on her. "Who?"

"Her name is Meghan, is it not?"

"Thomas told you, damn him!" Revelin turned away from her. "He had no right! Did he think me too much a coward to fight my own battles?"

Alison reached out to him but did not touch him. "Nay, Rev, your uncle was gravely concerned for you. When you returned to us from Ireland you were so distant, so ready to go back and leave those of us at court to our own devices. I am not such a ninny that I cannot guess what snares a young man's fancy. If it is not war, then it must be a woman."

She smiled as he turned back to her. "I have been long at

court, Rev, and I have seen the very hour when a man first thinks of straying from his present love. Sometimes, his thoughts are no more revealing than a change in the pattern of his hose from clocks to ivy. It does not matter the change, it is only a signal of the inner turmoil. The signs were there in you long before you left London last spring. Your uncle thought that an adventure in Ireland would cure your restlessness, give you direction. I told him you might only fall in love." Her smile saddened. "I thought I could win you back from any mortal, but they tell me she is a witch."

"How well versed you are, Lady Alison. My uncle has been grooming both of us, it seems, like a matched pair of bays for his stable. Oh no, we are to be part of his dynasty, *Buitiler a baudh!* Yet I cannot wish him well in this present matter. I am a Butler myself, and I am partial to my own victories."

"Lud!" Alison exclaimed lightly and sat back, flicking open her fan. "Am I to be rejected, jilted, in favor of a Gaelic lass? My reputation at court will be in shreds." She looked up at him over the lace-edged fan. "I don't think I should like that."

The practiced skill with which she executed the flirtatious actions could not conceal from Revelin's watchful gaze the hurt behind the clear gray of her gaze. Alison was a product of the court, accustomed to bantering and fencing with rapier-sharp words. For all that, she was also young, a maiden, and new to the intrigues and vagaries of romance. He could not find it in his heart to hurt her more than necessary.

He took one of her small, elegantly manicured hands in his, absently comparing it to Meghan's lightly callused palms. "We have been friends since childhood, Alison, and the affection I have for you will never alter." A spasm crossed Alison's face but she did not look away from him. "We will always love each other but we are capable of feeling more. I was not aware of that until three short months ago, when a shy, untutored lass dived into a stagnant pool and saved my life."

He smiled kindly. "You would think her rude and ignorant,

Alison, for, in truth, she as little resembles you as the sun the moon."

"Yet you've grown fond of the moon while the sun shone so favorably upon you?"

Revelin shook his head. "'Tis not like that. When it happens to you, you will understand."

Alison regarded him steadily but her eyes began to fill. "How can you be so certain that it has not already happened to me, Rev? Do you think yourself the keeper of love's secret delights? Do you not know what I feel when I look at you? Have you not felt me tremble in your arms, watched my adoring eyes follow where—"

"Alison!" Revelin warned. "You must not say these things. You will regret it and hate me for allowing the humiliation."

Alison rose slowly to her feet, her hands gripping his with unsuspected strength. "I am not ashamed of loving you. I will never be ashamed of that. If this black-haired witch has bewitched you, then I will wait until the spell wears through. I know you too well, Revelin Butler. What you feel is gratitude, pity, and a sense of responsibility toward the lass." She looked away at last. "I hear she is tolerably fair of face despite a disfiguring mark."

Revelin smiled. "She is beautiful, mark and all. It is like a rose newly budded."

"And you were like a bee to her nectar," Alison replied bitterly and lifted her eyes to his once more. "Oh, I know you've bedded her or rolled her in the grass of some shady glen. I do not care to see the glory of it reflected in your face, Rev. It makes me hate her . . . and you."

"Hate me, if you must," Revelin answered gently. "I have betrayed your trust. But, if you can, remember that I was guilty of nothing more than ignorance. I did not know I could love with the intensity I now feel. She will never outshine your beauty or usurp your place in my heart. But I must go to her, find her, and bring her safely back. I love her."

Alison bit her lip, her expression becoming peevish. "How do you know she has not fled to safety or even been spared by the intervention of another? Was Sir Robin Neville not with her?"

For the first time since reading the letter a glimmer of hope flickered within Revelin. "You're right, of course! Robin would have protected Meghan. Why did I not think of it? They could at this very moment be on their way to Dublin."

"Or elsewhere," Alison murmured.

"What do you mean?" Revelin questioned in puzzlement.

Alison shrugged one slender shoulder and freed herself from Revelin's clasp. She was losing him, she knew, so why not tell him the truth? "Last evening, after we dined at the castle, I chanced to sit with Sir Sidney for a quarter of an hour. He was most talkative, particularly about your foster daughter." She looked pointedly at Revelin. "That is, after I told him I was aware of the child. He apologized for his misunderstanding of the situation between you and thought me most generous to take in an Irish waif practically on my wedding day. He warned me that the task would not be all to my liking, though he hoped that Sir Robin would do the right thing. After all, the lass is of noble lineage."

Revelin's mouth tightened. "It seems my entire life is the subject of common gossip these days. I am not to blame if Sir Sidney sees evil in innocence. Sir Robin was asked by me to look after Meghan while I was away. If the court gossips wish to misconstrue their relationship, it does not overly concern me."

"Does Sir Robin's behavior concern you?" Casting caution to the winds, Alison continued, "Sir Sidney has it on good authority that Meghan O'Neill is with child."

Revelin's jaw fell, then a great smile spread over his face, which he tried unsuccessfully to tame. "I—I am so sorry, Alison, that you had to hear of it. But you must know that I was unaware. . . ."

Alison turned her back on him, unable to bear the shining pride in his face. "You had best be prepared for another shock. Sir Sidney heard from a reliable source that the child is Sir Robin's."

Revelin laughed. "Sir Sidney would say that to spare you, my dear. He is a gentleman, after all, when he wishes to remember it."

Alison turned on him so quickly that her skirts danced out and knocked over a bric-a-brac table but they ignored it. "Are you so arrogant a fool that you cannot hear me? Sir Sidney was told that Meghan is his mistress by Sir Robin himself!"

Revelin stilled, his face losing all animation. "You lie to me!"

The hushed, brittle words struck Alison like shards of glass and she flinched under the tone. "Rev!" she whispered and came to throw her arms about him. "I did not mean to hurt you. I thought, I hoped, that the knowledge would break the spell this she-devil has woven about you."

Revelin did no return her embrace as she buried her face in his sleeve, but neither did he push her away. He was too full of conflicting emotions. In the beginning he had told himself that Meghan would get over him, that when she was much in the company of other men she would find his attentions not so singular or unusual. She would fall out of love with him and, in time, find a man to marry.

"What rubbish!" he muttered to himself. In truth he had never wanted to be free of her. But this feeling of love for her had come too swiftly, too unexpectedly, and had complicated his well-ordered life. It had happened in a space of moment when he had thought himself dead and opened his eyes to find instead that he had been saved by a black-haired slip of a lass with a rose as her talisman. She had clung to him from the first. If he had been wiser or more brave, he would have bound her to him and let the world be damned. But he had dallied, trying to untangle the skein that was his life, and while doing so had lost her.

"I must go to Kilkenny," he said quietly and stepped back from Alison.

She released him, wiping tears from her eyes with the backs of her hands like a small child. "Why? Do you not believe me?"

Revelin looked down at her and retrieved a handkerchief from his sleeve to offer her. "Meghan is in trouble. Whatever she has done, it is my fault. I cannot abandon her now." His lips turned up in a travesty of a smile. "She is my foster child."

Southern Kilkenny: late August 1569

The cries of a distant battle did not stir Meghan from the makeshift bed where she had collapsed an hour earlier after a night tending wounded soldiers. *Perhaps they will all die this time and leave me with no torn limbs to bind,* she thought wearily.

Behind her closed lids, a stream of blood tripped and ran like a brook through the gentle valleys of Kilkenny. It was worse than any vision she had had. This was real, the dying and wounding; the slaughter and pillage followed them like a plague wherever they went. Carew's forces had marched their hostages to Clogrennan Castle and by deceit entered Sir Edmund's home and killed all servants present, the women and children as well as the garrison soldiers.

Meghan sat up with a shudder as the roar of battle neared. A child had begun to cry somewhere nearby. In the dawn misted by the heavy dew she could just discern the silhouette of Lady Mary bending over her youngest, a girl of three. A moment later Sir Piers joined her, the chains linking his arms and feet clinking as he knelt down and raised his daughter up onto his shoulder, where she quieted immediately.

Meghan slumped back against the tree trunk. Of all the harrowing moments of the last three weeks, there was one shining moment. It had occurred that first day. When she had been revived after learning of Colin's death, she had expected to be John Reade's prisoner. Instead, she was hovered over by Lady Mary and Sir Piers. It was Sir Piers who had told her what had happened, and his eyes were bright with a new respect for her that she had seen once before, in Turlough O'Neill's gaze.

Colin MacDonald's men had barred Reade's way when he demanded her as payment for his part in the battle of Kilkenny. The *bonaghts* had drawn their swords against Carew's orders and threatened to kill their leader before turning Meghan over to him. They told how she had cursed them for their part in the sack of the castle, but had sworn to remove the curse if they protected the Butlers from further harm.

Their readiness to face death had won her a reprieve; and even now, though she could not see him, she knew that somewhere nearby a *bonaght* stood over her. Many had died in subsequent battles as they marched from Kilkenny Town to Clogrennan, but her protectors had not even been badly wounded, and that fact had drawn others to her side until now the Butlers boasted more than two dozen loyal protectors. Meghan knew that if not for fear of the children's being caught in the crossfire, Sir Piers and Sir Edward, along with Sir Edmund, who had finally been captured a few days earlier, would have chanced a revolt within the camp using these *bonaghts*.

Meghan shut her eyes. She was filthy and hungry and thirsty and very afraid for the tiny scrap of life that grew within her. It happened then, the soft faint fluttering like the movement of a butterfly's wings within her lower belly. She held her breath, but the sensation was too slight for her to comprehend fully. It had happened the day before, more quickly. It was life that stirred within her, life that Revelin had put there and that she was determined to protect.

Sir Piers came toward her when at last his child was soothed, and Meghan watched him with sympathy, for his gait was made awkward by the short length of chain linking his ankles.

But when he crouched down before her his grin was as broad as ever. "Did ye hear that, lass?," he questioned in Gaelic as the shrill howling of the Irish warriors reverberated through the early-morning air. "Those are Butlers out there. Carew will rue the day he set foot in County Kilkenny. One of the *bonaghts* told me that he saw O'Conner, Burke, and Kavanaugh standards among the attackers yesterday. Our cause has roused the whole countryside. It would never have come to this if the Kavanaughs had stood up to Carew when County Carlow was taken from them; but they're more English than Irish, and that's against them. They're nae fighters. Now, our Butler lads— Lord—I'd give a few years of me life to be out there with them!"

He grinned and chucked Meghan under the chin. "I'm thinking the Butlers will be proud to add more Gaelic-Irish to our bloodlines. My lady tells me ye're breeding, lass."

Meghan looked at him for any sign of disapproval but saw none. "Ye do not mind?"

Piers laughed. "Who am I to deny the lass who's saved my family from murderers?" He glanced back at his family. "Captivity does not sit well with any soldier. To have them here beside me rubs me raw; but if not for ye, they'd be dead, and I know it."

His expression sobered as he looked at her. "I'm not saying I hold to a belief in charms and such, but I've seen yer power wielded over those who do. Ye're a Catholic, to boot, and I don't encourage that among my people; but I'll say not a word against ye and more than a few for ye should Revelin take his case to Black Tom."

Meghan shook her head. "Sir Robin—" Meghan gulped back a sob. "Sir Robin said Revelin might never come back. He is to be married."

"So I've heard. But Revelin's a good lad, and a stubborn one. I doubt he will do much that is against his nature; and that lad needs more than a court lady to satisfy him. But if he proves too stubborn or too fastidious to leave his place at court, come and see me, lass. I can nae offer ye my hand, but ye'll never want for anything, that's me promise to ye."

He patted her cheek, then rose, cocking his head to one side. "Ye hear that? They're closer than usual. God knows I wish they'd win through. No food, little water . . . Kilkenny will become a graveyard from famine if the peasants keep burning the crops just to keep Carew from filling his belly."

Meghan stood up, unhampered by chains. Where was she to go? "Do ye think we will be freed?"

Piers put a fatherly arm about her. "Of course, lass. Carew meant none of this to happen. Oh, he won't own up to it, but I see the haunted look in his eyes of late. He's holding hostage the brothers of the earl of Ormond. How long does he think he can do that? The earl himself will be coming to Ireland soon, and then we shall see what Carew will do."

The earl's name was mentioned by all his kinfolk, Revelin included, with a kind of awe reserved for legends. "The earl must be a great man," she said mostly to herself.

"He'll be the laughingstock of the realm if he does not answer Carew's impudence with shot, and soon!" Piers replied.

When Piers left her, Meghan felt the pressing call of nature, which she had felt more frequently of late. Dawn filtered through the mist as she made her way toward the rear of the camp. Dully, she noted that there were fewer soldiers than usual in the flanks, and she knew that not all of them were fighting or dead. Many of them had deserted. Others had joined the opposite side, their loyalty bought by food and better odds. Many of them were trading the silver plate stolen from Saint Canice's for a loaf of bread.

She pressed her stomach to stop the sharp gnawing of hunger. They were all hungry and weak from traveling on foot. After she found a private spot to relieve herself, she would look for wild berries and edible roots.

The rustling of nearby bushes startled her as she squatted

in the tall grass above a stream. Lowering her skirts, she remained squatting as she stared at the bushes. Once more they shook, and then the glint of metal winked at her between the dripping leaves. Soldiers! But whose? After a moment she heard the faint creak of a crossbow being drawn and a muffled Gaelic curse. Irish warriors. Her heart began to thump like a rabbit's. These warriors were ambushers, waiting for Carew's men to retreat along this path.

Indecision gnawed at her. Carew always drove the Butlers and their families before his army, hoping to curtail many such plots by exposing his captives to the front of the line. Did these men know that? Or would they launch their assault before they realized their targets?

Meghan stood up. "I know ye're there. I'm a Butler. Show yerselves."

Her voice was low but carrying. Still, nothing moved. "If ye won't talk with me, ye should know Sir Piers and Sir Edward's families are forced to march before Carew's army. Do not murder the women and children." She turned, lifted her skirts, and fled through the tall grass.

She had covered no more than ten yards when a shove between her shoulder blades sent her falling headlong into the grass. The breath knocked out of her, her eyes stinging with tears, Meghan raised her head and was assaulted by a warm sticky tongue.

"Ualter!" she shrieked in disbelief as the great fuzzy muzzle came into view.

A moment later, hands reached under her arms and lifted her to her feet. Weak as a rag doll, she slumped against her captor for an instant before fear spurted through her and her head jerked up as her body tensed for a fight.

"Ye've a fair nose for trouble, lass. We must cure ye of it." The Irish brogue was fake, but the leaf-green eyes laughing down at her could only belong to one man. "Revelin?" she whispered, incredulous.

"Aye, lass," Revelin answered in a rough tone. His hands closed tightly on her shoulders. "God's blood! What are you doing wandering about the countryside when there's a battle going on?"

Meghan shook her head, unable to speak with the intense emotions careening through her. Revelin was here, alive, and his hands were on her. The ghost of her dreams had materialized before her as warm flesh and blood.

"Revelin!" she cried softly and threw her arms about him.

Chapter Seventeen

"Lass!" Revelin whispered in her ear as his arms came around her to hold her breathlessly tight.

"Ye came back!" Meghan murmured brokenly against his leather jerkin. "I prayed ye'd come, but I feared ye would not!"

"Poor lass, has it been so very hard for you?" he crooned softly.

Meghan raised her head suddenly and broke away from him. "Ye must go, quickly, before ye're caught!"

Revelin smiled down at her. "You worry for everyone but yourself, lass. Do you find my arms no longer to your liking?"

Happiness flowed through her like a stream tumbling down a rocky embankment. In the morning light he was as perfect a man as she remembered. The mist had gathered in his hair, encrusting the golden waves with pearls of dew. But it was his eyes that held her attention. They were vividly green with warmth and joy and pleasure in her presence. "I love ye, Revelin!" she whispered quickly before she could stop herself.

"Well then?" he prompted gently, holding his arms out to

her once again. She went into them willingly, and he stroked her dirty, matted hair as calmly as though they were alone in a peaceful, secluded valley instead of a quarter-mile from battle and with armed soldiers at their backs. At that moment, nothing existed for them outside the circle of each other's arms.

"Sir Revelin, what is yer pleasure?"

The sound of a man so close to them startled Meghan, but Revelin did not release her. He tucked her head under his chin and spoke over her head to the soldier, who was one of his own. "You heard the lass. Ambush is a chancy thing at best. If Carew is leading with his hostages, he must be tired of them and ready to negotiate their release. I'm about to give him that chance."

Meghan lifted her head. "No! Ye cannot be thinking of going into camp to talk with Carew! He'll kill ye!"

Revelin smiled and touched his lips briefly to her brow. "I think not, lass, when he learns that I've a message for him from Sir Sidney." He looked back at the soldier. "The rest of you remain here. If I have not returned by midday, attack!" When he looked down at Meghan again, his face softened. "Will ye show me the way? I'm certain my uncles will scald my ears for being so long about this business."

Meghan tried to still her trembling. There was something important she should remember to tell him, now, before it was too late. But her poor beleaguered senses would not school themselves to order. Her heart pounded wildly, and her blood sang through her veins to the lilting shrill of pipes as love surged over her. When he urged her toward camp, she turned and led the way, but she would not release his hand, afraid that he would vanish into the misty morning from which he had come.

Revelin refused to think about the events of the last minutes, lest they overwhelm him. Meghan was so thin, her bones felt birdlike beneath his hands, and the sockets surrounding her eyes were so dark that, he had thought at first she had been beaten. What had she endured and seen in the month of her captivity? No, he could not allow himself to speculate. He must think only of his mission and how best to accomplish it.

He had not been able to leave Dublin the day he had received the letter from Kilkenny. To his amazement his uncle Sir Edmund had arrived at nightfall to protest Carew's attack on his home and family before the Dublin Parliament. When support failed to materialize, Sir Edmund had returned to battle, vowing open rebellion, and charged Revelin with waiting for the earl's arrival in Dublin.

Revelin's hand tightened on Meghan's. He had been in agony; a man on the rack could not have suffered more than he, thinking what each new day might bring Meghan and his family. Finally, with Sir Sidney's acceptance, he had deserted his waiting post, only to learn on the ride south that Sir Edmund himself had been captured.

When they came within sight of the camp, Revelin held Meghan back. "Tell me who is wounded, ailing, or dead among the Butlers."

Meghan blinked up at him; his eyes were like sunlit emeralds shining down on her. "None dead. Lady Elenore still ails, but the rest are hardy but hungry."

Revelin smiled. "I want you to announce me to Peter Carew but no other. Do you think you can slip me into camp?"

She nodded. "Do nae let go of me hand or draw yer sword, no matter what. The power will help us."

Revelin did not ask her what she meant but followed her docilely into the shadow of the forest. The sounds of the battle had died down and shadowy figures of men moved under the trees as they returned from the fray.

Revelin pulled the hood of his mantle up over his head and held fast to Meghan's hand as she picked her way unhurriedly through the throng. He had begun to believe that there was no danger at all, when suddenly he was grabbed from behind and the sharp edge of a skean bit lightly into his throat.

Meghan swung about. "No! He's safe!" she bawled loudly enough to attract the attention of the soldiers nearby. Revelin was released instantly, and she reached up and pulled his hood from his head, revealing his bright golden head. "This man is mine. He is protected, do ye understand?"

Revelin watched in amazement as she lifted a hand to her birthmark and then lightly touched her fingers to his lips. "My protection on ye," she said loudly, and then her fingers curved in a caress on his cheek as she smiled at him. As quickly as he had appeared, Revelin's attacker melted back into the misty shadows of the morning.

As Meghan took him by the hand and led him on, confused and suspicious thoughts whirled through Revelin's mind. What had she meant by her strange actions, and why had the men released him? Was she not their prisoner rather than the reverse?

A moment later all was forgotten as he spied one of his uncles. "Piers!" he whispered sharply.

The man came to his feet slowly and Revelin heard the rattle of his chains. "Who dares call me by my Christian name?" Piers demanded.

"Your rascally nephew, of course!"

Piers peered across the distance and his face lit up. "Rev, you young hellion! Are we saved? You've routed Carew?"

"Hardly that," replied a voice from the opposite side of the clearing. Dripping sweat and smeared with blood from half-a-dozen small wounds, John Reade came across the space with his blade bared. "We've won again, but do not despair, Sir Piers, we've yet to catch the last of the Butlers."

Revelin shoved Meghan from him into Piers's arms and unsheathed his sword. The blade came free with a sharp scraping noise and he smiled when the weight of his weapon lay full in his palm. "John Reade. I might have known you would be where the blood runs thickest."

John chuckled. "Such pleasantries, Revelin lad. Are you strolling about Kilkenny in search of a home?"

"As a matter of fact, I was here to retrieve something I'd left in safekeeping at Kilkenny Castle."

John's smile grew. "I'd choose a safer place next time, lad. What with quarrelsome neighbors on all sides, nothing of value is safe from thieves in these parts."

Revelin inclined his head. "'Tis said you urged Carew on in this matter. I wonder at your reasoning."

"Simple. A man who earns his living by the sword has no living if there is no rebellion or war to keep him employed. Carew needed no encouragement, only eager allies."

"Mercenaries, you mean. You have fallen far, Reade. Once you were among the queen's finest. Now you fight with the scum of the earth at your back. Have you spent a single comfortable night among them?" He saw John glance at Meghan and misinterpreted the look. Stepping forward to shield her from Reade's glare, he said with clenched teeth, "If you've even touched her, I will kill you."

John's laughter rang out. "By God! That's good! That witch, I'd not lay a hand on her for all the treasure in Dublin. She's cursed me and she'll curse you if you take her back. She kills every man she snares with her sluttish charms. Ask Colin MacDonald or Sir Robin Neville."

"That's a lie!" Meghan protested, struggling to be free, but Piers held her firmly.

Revelin ignored her. "Robin is dead?"

John nodded once. "She corrupted him to the point that he took up arms against the queen's own. He deserved a sword in the belly."

"You name yourself a liar to call Carew's rabble the queen's men," Piers roared over Meghan's head.

"You killed Robin," Revelin suggested.

John grinned. "Perhaps I did. That popinjay, that priggish fop, he dared to wield a blade against me!"

Revelin glared at Reade. If Robin had taken up arms, it was to protect Meghan; and that made Robin's death his fault.

He had asked Robin to look after Meghan while she remained in Dublin. Robin had obviously come to Kilkenny to be with her.

Alison's insistence that Robin was in love with Meghan and that she carried his child came back to sting him like a bee. He could well believe that Robin had fallen in love with Meghan and that he would protect her with his life. Robin had thought himself a coward in Ulster, but he had been brave when it counted.

"Ho! Carew!" Piers hailed and set Meghan on her feet. When the West Country man turned toward the call, Piers grinned. "We've company, Carew—company from Dublin with a message for you."

Revelin did not look away from John. His sword was in his hand and he itched to finish what they had begun. "There will be another time," he promised quietly.

John smirked. "At your service, lad."

Revelin nodded slightly and replaced his blade. First things first. He turned to his host with a bland smile.

"Sir Peter Carew, I presume? I am Sir Revelin Butler. You have a number of my relatives as your prisoners. I would like to discuss that with you."

Sir Peter Carew regarded the young man before him with amazement tempered with caution as they shared a meal. With his bright golden head, Revelin Butler was like a canary among his raven-haired uncles who flanked him.

Peter scratched his beard as his eyes moved back and forth between the Butlers. Never in his wildest dreams of glory or his darkest nightmares had he thought to capture the three brothers of the earl of Ormond. He had meant only to teach them a lesson, that he was not a man to be trifled with. The sack of Kilkenny was like a nightmare acted out before his eyes. He could not have stopped it any more than he could now turn tail and run back to Idrone as he longed to do. The promise of riches and titled estates had become ashes in his mouth these last weeks. He had no prosperous barony in Ireland. He had full-scale war on his hands. He needed a way out. Yet, it must be one that would not leave him with less than he had before he began.

He envied the youngest Butler. Here was a young man with looks, breeding, and the self-assurance that came with a long line of noble ancestors. That was what he wanted for the generations of Carews who would come after him. More than riches he wanted his family's name to command the respect and loyalty that the Butlers claimed as their birthright.

"Have you read the letter?" Revelin questioned when he realized that Carew would not make the first move.

"Aye, I read it, and little enough it says," Carew replied irritably.

"I was told it called upon you to act with discretion and reserve as regards your differences with my kinsmen."

Carew gave Revelin a sharp look. "It says nothing about me giving up my claim to Idrone. I'll not stand idly by while degenerate English nobles who dress and speak as common clansmen run riot over my land."

Sir Edmund rose to his feet, his face flushing. "Degenerate? Who are you to call another degenerate, you thieving, conniving, base-born son of a country knight!"

"You call me that, you sorry excuse for an Englishman?"

Carew heaved himself up, but he was encumbered by the weight of his armor breastplate and Sir Edmund easily tipped him backward with a shove. "That for you, you ne'er-do-well! Give me a sword and let's make an end to this!"

Revelin looked from one red-faced man to the other and knew that unless he acted quickly, a duel would take place that might tip the balance of restraint and turn the camp into a bloodbath. He stood up. "If this is your pleasure, then I fail to understand why you did not simply wait for the fair in Enniscorthy on Great Lady Day to face each other as combatants. Two men of your stature deserve an audience worthy of your exertions."

Revelin spoke lightly, but his face was tense until he saw the light of mischief twinkle in his uncle's eye. "The fair," Sir Edmund repeated. He looked at the short, stout West Countryman and smiled. "You fancy yourself a knight, Sir Peter? You should attend one of our degenerate Irish fair days and test your mettle."

Sir Peter spat on the ground. "I've tested the mettle of the Butlers and 'tis like slicing butter with me sword."

Sir Edmund shook his manacled fists at Sir Peter. "If there were no chains binding me, you'd find yourself hard put to utter those words!"

Sir Peter looked about, roaring, "Where's the key? Free and arm the blackguard!"

At the call for arms, Carew's soldiers began to gather in noisy anticipation of a fight.

"Before you resort to hacking each other to death," Revelin inserted calmly into the fracas, "allow me to put a question to each of you. Uncle Edmund, if you should kill Sir Peter, how will you explain your position to the queen's Parliament which acted in favor of Sir Peter against you? Will they not conclude that you resorted to outright murder to achieve your goal of ridding yourself of an enemy?"

"I would not call it murder when a man's armed against me," Sir Edmund maintained.

Laughter erupted at his elbow. "Think again, brother," said Sir Piers. "I say 'tis like murder to fight a man weighted down less by the armor on his back than the stones in his head!"

Piers's joke drew appreciative laughter from the company of men, and Revelin began to relax. Looking about earlier, he had realized that most of Carew's force were Irish. Now he saw a method of using that fact to his advantage. The Irish prized a man's wit above nearly every other virtue, and Carew was a dull, slow-witted foreigner.

"Sir Peter, I now put a question to you. If you should kill

my uncle—it is a possibility, Edmund," he added at his uncle's snort of derision. "If, Sir Peter, you kill the brother of the earl of Ormond, how will you explain to the queen, who counts the earl of Ormond as the most loyal of her Irish subjects and a man well loved in this land? Will the queen think kindly of a man who set the torch to the wick of rebellion in Ireland?"

Sir Peter glared at Revelin. "If what you say it true, 'tis no doing of mine. I'm only protecting what was given me by right of law!"

"Damned English thievery, you mean!" Piers jeered. "You took lands set aside for widows and orphans. You're taking the bread out of the mouths of babes, and pleased to be doing it, you fat sot!"

"Sot, am I? Fool, am I? Thief, am I? Then where does that leave you, my fine Butlers, seeing as you're prisoners of a thieving, sodden fool?"

Revelin swallowed his inclination to smile as new laughter filtered through the crowd. Perhaps he had underestimated Carew. Yet, as he eyed the condition of his relatives he could not help but notice that in spite of the enmity between Sir Peter and Sir Edmund, Sir Peter had not subjected his prisoners to any ill treatment that might later be held against him. One might almost say he was reluctant, nay, regretful that he had gathered this august host of hostages.

Revelin sighed inwardly. If this farce had not resulted in such tragic consequences, it would be laughable. But there were so many deaths, so much destruction; all because one misguided man had more pride than sense. Yet, one might suspect that Sir Peter would give anything—but loss of pride—to rid himself of the Butlers.

Black Tom had once told Revelin that he could have a brilliant future as a diplomat. This seemed the appropriate moment to test that. After all, Meghan was safe.

Revelin glanced at her and away. No, he must not think about her yet, when Robin's death was so fresh in his mind. Later, when he could think rationally, he would think of Meghan.

"I wonder, given a moment's reflection, if the Butlers and the Carews might come to a mutual agreement." Revelin turned to Sir Peter. "What exactly do you hope to gain by marching my kinsmen to and fro through Kilkenny County?"

"I would rid myself of them gladly," Sir Peter pronounced, "would they give their word that they would leave quietly and return to their homes, there to plague me no more."

Revelin turned to his uncles. "Is this true? Have you been offered clemency?"

Edmund turned away but Piers nodded. "Aye, he talks of oaths of surrender and pledges of not taking up arms against him, but I'll nae surrender on me own land to anyone, be he Irish, English, or the Devil himself!"

Revelin began to see the light. "But an agreement to part company is preferable to a lengthy stay in the dungeon of Idrone?"

Accepting his uncles' begrudging nods, Revelin turned his attention once more to Carew. "Sir Peter, it seems to me that you could do no better than to show your largess by freeing your enemies. The queen, I'm certain, would be impressed by that act. Only a man of great of stature can afford so magnanimous a gesture. As for the folk of Kilkenny, what action would better convince them that you mean them no real harm than the release of their masters?"

Sir Peter scratched his chin. "You've a glib tongue for so pretty a face, boy. Yet your words make sense."

Indeed they did, he thought. He was cramped by circumstance and strapped financially by the exorbitant cost of his war. He knew he could expect no help from the Crown treasury. He had promised to subjugate his Irish holdings and turn a profit. So far, he had seen what little he owned go up in smoke as war ravaged his new home.

His eyes narrowed on his hostages. "I would have something back for me trouble. A hundred pounds for the freedom of each hostage!"

Edmund and Piers reared to their feet with vocal protests, but, Revelin noted uneasily, Edward did not. In fact, Edward had contributed nothing to the conversation; but there was a black anger in his gaze that was more forbidding than Edmund's insults and Piers's wicked humor. Trouble there, Revelin decided, but put it aside.

"... I'll have your heads!" Sir Peter roared back in answer to the final insult hurled at him and drew his sword.

"We were speaking of clemency," Revelin reminded him smoothly, moving to stand between his chained uncles and Carew's blade. "You've the gold and silver of Kilkenny. Let that be the price of your hostages. You defiled a church, man!"

Sir Peter fell back before the accusation. "I did not! My troops overran me. I did not touch a single piece of church plate!"

"Then let them go," Revelin demanded.

Sir Peter looked from one Butler to another, nervously gnawing his lip. He was a man of action, not decision making. Bloodletting was one thing. Negotiations of state were beyond him. He wanted nothing more than to return to Idrone. "If I grant you clemency, you'll swear not to attack me?"

"Are you afeard we'll sneak back within an hour and throttle you?" Piers jeered.

"Do you give your word?" Revelin questioned inpatiently.

Piers shrugged. "Certainly. I'll not waylay you, Carew. I've me family to see home."

"Nor I," Edmund seconded.

Edward did not answer, merely nodded a single time.

For the first time Revelin smiled. "Then it's over."

"Aye, for now," Piers said ominously. He leaned closer to whisper in his nephew's ear, "Only I wonder if Sir Peter has heard that parole is an idea little accepted here in Ireland." He chuckled. "On the whole, the man's a great deal to learn before he will be comfortable among us."

Revelin did not answer that, for suddenly he wondered just

who was "one of us." Was he one? He glanced at Meghan, who sat silently regarding him. Did he intend to become one?

When he raised his head again he saw Reade staring at him from the edge of the clearing. He rose and spoke quietly to Piers. "We'll leave as soon as you can gather everyone together. In the meantime, look after the lass. She has a way of getting into trouble if she's not watched."

Piers regarded Revelin in surprise until he saw the direction of his gaze. He reached out and touched his nephew's arm. "Don't let the fire in your blood rule your head, lad. He's a bruiser but he lacks style. He won't last long."

Meghan watched with alarm as Revelin strode toward John. She cried out and Piers clapped a hand over her mouth but it was too late. Immediately, a dozen *bonaghts* armed with axes and crossbows surrounded the two men.

Meghan struggled free of Piers's grasp when a skean slid under his nose, then she ran to Revelin. "Ye mustn't fight! I won't have another death on me conscience."

Revelin turned to her in surprise. "You cannot prevent this, lass. Here and now, or later, Reade and I will settle the matter of Robin."

Meghan bit her lip. "Ye might be killed."

Revelin shook his head. "Not by him." He looked about. "I do not understand it, but if it's in your power to do so, call off these men."

Meghan held his gaze a long time. She had just found him again; she could not lose him. He did not know of her dreams where John, as the wolf, tore out his throat. Yet the feeling of foreboding was lacking as her gaze moved from Revelin to John. John stood before her as a man, no more and no less. When she looked again at Revelin she felt his confidence flowing into her. "Whatever ye say, Revelin," she said softly and waved the *bonaghts* back.

Revelin looked at his uncle. "Take her away from here, Piers."

Grinning, Piers clapped an arm about Meghan's shoulders and turned her away. "Don't be long about it, lad. I've grown quite fond of the lass."

Meghan tried to free herself, but Piers held her in his muscle-bound arms and clapped her so firmly against his broad chest that she thought she would suffocate.

Revelin turned back to Reade. "You slew an untried courtier in Sir Robin, a man more accustomed to scented bowers than the battlefield. You won't find me so easy a conquest."

John's dark eyes gleamed. "I had hoped you would protest. I have waited for this moment for quite some time." He flung his cloak away. "Stay back!" he ordered the men about him. "Under no circumstance are you to interfere until one of us is dead."

When the sharp ring of metal meeting metal broke the silence, a sob escaped Meghan.

"Not to worry, lassie," Piers assured her gruffly as he half-carried, half-dragged her from the clearing. "I saw to Revelin's early training with arms meself. He's nae lacking in skill or strength. He'll come to no mischief."

Meghan closed her eyes tightly. Revelin would come to no mischief. Where were her visions to warn her whether that was the truth? The steady beat of blade on blade became more faint as Piers led her into the thick of Carew's camp. His stride was short but he covered an amazing amount of distance quickly, and Meghan knew at last that chains were not what had kept Piers from escaping.

Meghan trembled. The sound of the swordplay was weaker still, drowned out by the return of the last of the wounded, but her ears seemed attuned to the distant sounds of the duel between Revelin and John. If not for Piers's iron grip on her, she would have run back. She must have been mad to call off her *bonaghts*. Revelin did not know the man he fought. Reade was ruthless, a schemer, he would use any trick that came to mind to best him.

As the minutes ticked by, more slowly than any other moments in her life, she did not notice that the other Butler men had gone to watch or that Lady Mary and Lady Elenore were regarding her with sympathy. She heard only the tinny beat of the blades on and on and on until, finally, they missed a measure.

Meghan held her breath, waiting for the spasm of pain that would tell her that Revelin was dead. An eternity of seconds passed, excruciating in their length, and then there were footsteps nearby.

"Release her. It is done."

Revelin's voice sounded with incredible sweetness in Meghan's ears. Piers's arms fell away and yet she could not move. It took every ounce of her strength to raise her eyes to his face and see the reality of him standing before her.

He was not even wounded, but the look of black fury on his face told her that Reade had not died easily and that there were things between them that she would never know.

Revelin sheathed his sword before approaching her, and he hoped she could not see the blood on his hand as he held out an arm to her. He sighed in gratitude that she did not shy from him but came straight into his embrace. His arms closed hard on her and he knew he must have hurt her but she did not make a sound.

It felt strange to be back in the saddle again after so many days of walking, Meghan decided as she shifted her weight to ease the ache in her lower back. Kilkenny lay beyond the next rise, she had been told, but she no longer held any hope that she would one day call that place home.

She glanced forward to where Revelin rode silently beside his uncles. Two days had passed since Carew released them, but Revelin had been as distant as if they were strangers. The moment in the glade when he held out his arms to her might never have happened for all the attention he now paid to her.

'Tis my fault. Because of me he killed a man.

Meghan lowered her head. She was responsible for so many deaths. From the moment the cowherder died in the forest of Louth, she had feared that she was tainted by evil. Now she believed it fully. The cowherder was the first, then Una. Robin was dead, and Colin, and John. All of them had died as a result of her actions. Only Revelin had escaped unscathed.

I must leave him.

It had come to her during the night, the knowledge that she must protect Revelin by leaving him. He might have died in his fight with John. She had expected it. The vision of the wolf had been as vivid as any of her dreams. She did not understand why Revelin survived but hugged the knowledge to herself. Perhaps she was being given a chance to save him by giving him up. If she did not, he might not survive another battle. She would take no chances; she would leave Revelin as soon as the Butlers were home. She had not asked it of him, but she hoped that Piers would help her. If not, then she would depend on the loyalty of her *bonaghts*.

She turned her head to smile at the Scots mercenary who rode at her side. There were eight of them in all, and they surrounded her when threats along the road to Kilkenny did not require their attention. It still amazed her that the soldiers had left Carew's camp to follow her. They swore that she had protected them from death these last weeks and that as long as they were faithful they would not be defeated. Were they right? She wondered. If so, they were the only ones ever to benefit from her dubious powers. Their leader, Colin Mac-Donald, had died defending her.

The splatter of raindrops came as a welcome relief to the unusual heat of the August day. She lifted her face to the gentle rain and felt the grime cracking on her cheeks as she smiled, enjoying the cool wet upon her skin.

"Ye'll come to mischief, mistress, if ye're wet through," the *bonaght* said gravely as he swung his great mantle from his shoulders and drape it about her. "We're nae so much fond of anything as we are of a wee bairn." He winked at Meghan's shocked face, and then she shot a fearful look at Revelin, but he rode too far ahead to have overheard the man.

Meghan gathered the hot stinking wool more closely about her so as not to give offense to its owner, but she did not like the thought that the company of soldiers knew of her pregnancy. If they had guessed and the Butlers knew, it would not be long before Revelin heard of it, though she had begged his family to keep it from him. What would she do if he would not release her? After all, the child was his, and he was entitled to want it.

Misery settled over her. She had not considered that giving up Revelin might include giving up his child when it was born. The child was to be her consolation. Could she give it up? How could she not, if it meant its safekeeping?

Amethyst mauves and watercress greens tinted the early-evening sky as the spire of Saint Canice's and the Norman towers of Kilkenny Castle came into the view in the valley beyond.

A roar went up from the company, led by Sir Piers's cry of, *"Buitiler a buadh!"* Spurring their horses, the Butlers headed home in full gallop.

"I'd nae do that, mistress," Meghan's bodyguard advised, catching her reins in his hand as she moved to join the others.

Vexed, Meghan dropped her reins. "I'm nae a bit of glasswork. I will nae break!"

"That's so, mistress," he said gravely, but his face was split in a wide smile.

She looked at him, realizing for the first time that a very young face lay behind the bushy tangle of dark blond beard and shoulder-length hair. What was more, he was flirting with her. "What's yer name?" she demanded as he continued to stare back at her openly.

"Conn," he said, making two syllables of the one.

"Well, Conn, ye'd best keep yer eyes in yer head, or I'll shrivel yer most precious treasure!"

So saying, she snatched up her reins and urged her horse toward the town gates. Conn's laughter flowed behind her, and the pleasant sensation of seeing herself reflected with warmth in a young man's eyes raised her spirits. Sometime within the last days her *bonaghts* had lost their horror of her. It had changed into fondness. It was a better feeling than fear. Perhaps their friendship would make up a little for the loss of Revelin.

She did not notice that Revelin had fallen out of the gallop toward Kilkenny until she came abreast of him.

"A good evening to you, mistress," he intoned formally with a nod.

Meghan looked at him in surprise, never quite certain of what she should answer when he treated her like a lady of the court.

"We are nearly home," he continued as he urged his horse into step beside hers. "No doubt you will go straight to bed. But in the morning, I would ask that you grant me an hour of your time. We have been long apart, mistress, and there are matters to be decided between us."

"Aye," Meghan answered solemnly, and, as there seemed nothing else to say, they rode into Kilkenny in silence.

"But you are dead!" Revelin protested.

"Am I? And here I thought I looked the picture of health. Ah, what matters your opinion? I rather think the ladies of Whitehall will favor my pallor."

Revelin swept his friend up in a bear hug. "Robin, you never change!"

"I should hope not!" Robin returned brightly, but he groaned when Revelin released him.

"Did I hurt you?" Revelin asked contritely. "Here, sit down, man, before you collapse."

"I think I will," Robin said breathlessly as he resumed his

seat. "Reade tried to split me in half and he very nearly succeeded." He held a hand to his middle as he gingerly sat back. "The leech they call a doctor says I've more stitches than his aunt's best quilt."

Revelin stared at Robin, his eyes dark with concern. "I killed him; I killed John in a fair fight."

Robin heard the distess in Revelin's voice and knew that it had not been as easy as it sounded. "Well, a fair fight is more than he gave me. We met on the street, and when I told him that I was a guest at the castle he slashed me open without a blink of an eye."

Revelin's green eyes glittered. "I wager you exchanged a few more words than that."

"We did, now that you mention it." Robin shot Revelin a measuring glance. "I believe he ran me through just after I told him I had accompanied Meghan O'Neill."

Revelin nodded. "Did you know of his passion for the lass?"

Robin's eyes glinted with laughter. "Were you surprised to learn of it? Come, Rev, what do you feel when you look at her? Why should you doubt any other man with breath in him feels the same?"

"You're a man with breath in him," Revelin said slowly. "What do you feel when you look at Meghan?"

"If I told you, you'd run me through, too, and I haven't recovered sufficiently to merit your ire."

Revelin's mouth straightened into a hard line. "There was gossip of an ill nature in Dublin. Some say the lass is breeding." His eyes narrowed on Revelin. "What do you know of it?"

"Have you not asked the lady?" Robin's mirth bubbled over. "That's priceless!"

Annoyed, Revelin rose from his chair and went to stand before the fire, bracing himself with a hand on the mantel. "The general gossip in Dublin is that the child is yours." His voice was cool, but Revelin felt as though he had stepped into the flames dancing in the grate as he waited for Robin's answer.

Robin did not reply. He studied the tall, broad-shouldered

man before him. Even in his travel-stained clothing he was a most excellent example of a man. In profile his face was breathtaking, the handsome angles and high cheekbones bronzed by the same summer sun that had bleached his hair an even riper shade.

Revelin Butler was everything Robin was not: tall, handsome, brave. Yet, he had a weakness: he was not certain of himself with Meghan. But then, what man could hold the wind or keep the seasons in his pocket? She eluded definition. Most women would have run to their lovers in expectation of a wedding or with bitter tears of recrimination. Revelin's speech had told him that Meghan had done neither.

So, Robin thought with satisfaction, his lie had worked. All believed that he had fathered Meghan's child. If he told Revelin that the lie was the truth, Revelin would leave without questioning the girl. A Butler was too proud to beg a woman's favor. With one simple sentence he could win Meghan for himself.

And yet, that was not why he had told the lie. He had told it to protect Meghan from unwanted advances and outright ostracism. It was considered outrageous for a single woman suddenly to be pregnant, but there was a certain amount of acceptability when one's mistress came to bed with a child.

"I love her," Revelin said suddenly and raised his head to look at Robin.

I love her, too. The words trembled on Robin's tongue but he could not say them. That would make a travesty of Meghan's love for Revelin . . . and for himself. Revelin had trusted him to look after Meghan in his absence and Meghan had trusted him with her love for Revelin. Yet, Revelin had won that love too easily and stood in need of a lesson.

"If you love her, then why question me?"

Revelin felt his pulse quicken as a red stain suffused his face. "I would not stand in her way if she . . . she loves another."

"God's death! You hypocrite! You're afraid she might care

for another man and you can't stand to hear her say it." Robin rose to his feet, his voice lacerated by the emotions he had sought to keep in check. "You're a coward, Rev. Oh, you're brave with a sword, but you cannot face the possibility that a woman you fancy might have grown lonely with waiting and found someone who was glad to dry her tears."

"Is that what you did?" Revelin's voice turned to ice. "Did she come to you for comfort and you took her to your bed to give it?"

"You'd like to hear that, wouldn't you? Robin Neville played the seducer to your lady's innocence. I'll take it as a compliment that you find me a worthy rival for the lady's attentions."

"A woman needs more than a handsome face and a braw body," Revelin answered quietly.

"Really? You've become an expert on the matter?"

Robin's breath came and went like a bellows in his chest; noting it, Revelin came toward him. "Sit down before you burst your stitches, Robin. I apologize to you for the suggestion. If Meghan gave herself to you, then she did so because she cares for you."

Robin was aware of the cost in pride of that admission to Revelin, and he sank gratefully back into his chair. "Ah, Rev, why did we have to love the same lady? I swear I never knew the feeling until you left us in Dublin. She's not like any lady I've ever known."

Revelin sat down and braced his arms on his knees, his clasped hands hanging between. "Meghan carries a child."

Robin closed his eyes. Anything other than the truth would hurt Meghan, and as much as he loved and wanted her, he could not do that. "She carries your child, Rev."

Revelin thought he was beyond feeling anything, but he was wrong. His heart seemed to soar up out of his chest, and the smile that wreathed his mouth nearly split his face in two. He leaped to his feet. "Truly?"

Robin smiled a bitter-edged smile. "If it were mine, I'd not give her up to you, you damned Irishman, for anything on God's green earth!"

Through his own elation Revelin sensed Robin's defeat. "I have not told Meghan that you're alive. She will want to see you."

Robin raised his brows. "Were you in doubt that I would still be alive once we had talked?"

"She loves you," Revelin said gently. "She cried when she told me of your death."

"Tears," Robin said thoughtfully. "I'm not worth her tears. Send her to me and I will make her smile again."

Meghan closed the door that led to Robin's chamber with a full heart. She had not stayed long. For all his bantering, he had seemed listless; and his eyes, when he did not know she was watching him, were infinitely sad.

Meghan shook out the skirts of her gown. It was her favorite, a deep green velvet with a low-squared neckline. In the sack of the castle, many things had been left behind, most of her clothes among them. It felt good to be clean and have a full stomach. She looked down the long corridor to where Lady Mary directed the rehanging of a tapestry that had been dropped as Carew retreated from the town. In the courtyard below, work had begun on the rebuilding of the south gate. It would take time, but the town would regain its former glory and perhaps improve.

"Mistress Meghan, 'tis time we talked."

Meghan looked back over her shoulder in surprise; Revelin had come so quietly up the hall that she had not heard his footsteps. He looked full of life in his trunk hose and canions of deep blue and a black velvet jerkin over his blue doublet. "Sir Robin is better today," she said softly when she realized that she was staring at him.

Revelin looked beyond her. "I think we will take a turn

about the battlements. We should be out of earshot, and yet you will not be compromised." He took her by the elbow and directed her toward the stairs.

From this vantage, the sight of Kilkenny was more encouraging than it appeared at street level. The trees shielded many of the burned-out houses, and the frameworks of others were filled in or blurred by the kindness of distance. Meghan ran her hand along the stonework as she walked, but she could not entirely forget the hand at her elbow. They strolled the length of the north wall before Revelin pulled her to a stop and turned her to face him.

"There should be so much we have to say to each other, but I can think of nothing . . . other than I love you."

Meghan turned to lean her arms upon a stone embrasure. "I've little liking for cities," she said, using her English. "I've little liking for things English," she continued, switching to Gaelic.

Revelin moved closer to her but did not touch her. "Do you have any liking for Kilkenny?"

Meghan gazed out at the leafy treetops, realizing that here on the battlements of the castle she was higher than she had ever climbed in her life. She liked it, she liked Kilkenny, and the Butlers, but Revelin must not know that.

She turned to look at him, her expression closed. "I dinna like the stink of a town nor its dirty streets."

Revelin looked down into her wide blue eyes and wondered how he had been able to leave her at all. "You favor a country setting, a tree house in the forest, perhaps?"

The mockery in his voice should have angered her. Instead, the faint lilt that crept into his voice when he spoke his native tongue made tiny bells ring in her heart. It would be difficult to loose their music, she thought, but she must keep Revelin safe.

"I've me *bonaghts* to think of." She turned her head away, a difficult task when all she longed to do was gaze at his face until it was seared permanently upon her mind's eye. "Mayhaps we'll journey back to Ulster."

"And begin a new branch of the O'Neill clan?" Revelin questioned lightly. "I wonder that you pin such hopes upon its being a boy."

"Ye know?" Meghan looked up in astonishment to find him smiling a smile that seemed to melt her bones. He was so close she could see her reflection in his eyes. All she had to do was rise on tiptoe and her lips would be against his. As his smile changed to knowing laughter, she realized, too late, that she had given herself away. He was too close; she felt stifled by his nearness. With a sudden movement she stepped away from him.

Revelin frowned as she walked away. The Meghan he had known before would never have dissembled. What had Robin been teaching her this summer? He crossed his arms before his chest and leaned against the parapet. "I am thinking of accepting a bit of land my uncle offered me. 'Tis near Ballygub, south of the Blackstair Mountains and north of the river Nore. I've little liking for court life, and 'tis time I was married."

Meghan closed her eyes. She knew that Lady Alison was in Dublin. "Have ye chosen yer bride?"

"Aye," Revelin answered softly, bemused by the gold and red threads the sun picked out in her black tresses. "She's an Irish lass, willful, difficult to understand, and quite capable of slitting my throat if the desire should arise. By all reasonable accounts, I should throw her over for a more well-mannered lass; but I've grown accustomed to her contrariness, and she tells the best stories this side of Tara."

Meghan turned on him suddenly, her face contorted in a pain whose source he could not guess. "I cannot, I will not marry ye, Revelin Butler!"

She put out a hand to stop him as he straightened away from the parapet. "Dot not touch me! And do not speak to me again! Ever!" Her voice cracked on the final word; and, feeling tears rise to sting her eyes, she snatched up her skirts and ran toward the steps.

Revelin did not try to stop her, nor did he follow her. When her head disappeared down the stairwell he turned to look out at the town. What was wrong? She was not the kind to punish him with a display of temper. Revelin frowned. At least, she had not been when he had left her in Dublin. He had hoped she would learn a bit of sophistication, but he hardly thought her the kind to mimic tantrums. No, there was something wrong, something he had not been quick enough to catch.

She had been afraid. That was what he had seen in her face, pain, yes, but also fear. *I love her. What has she to fear?*

Chapter Eighteen

Revelin shielded his eyes from the sun as he watched the earl of Ormond disembark from the ship at anchor in the harbor at Wexford. After a fortnight of the company at Kilkenny, he had had his fill of idleness. Robin had recuperated well enough to be a constant thorn in his side, while Meghan, damn her impudence, had ordered her *bonaght* soldiers to keep him from coming near her when she was alone.

Since their conversation on the battlement she had exchanged no more than pleasantries with him, until he was driven by temper to the point of unsheathing his sword and taking on the full retinue of her mercenaries. Black Tom's arrival in Ireland was a welcome diversion. If the news had come a week later, Revelin would have been gone to join his uncles in their strategy to reap vengeance on Carew.

The brilliance of the earl's clothing was the first thing that drew Revelin's eye. From the jeweled band winking in his velvet bag hat to his gold-embroidered doublet with the Butler arms hanging round his neck by a heavy gold chain, to his paned trunk hose with wrinkled taffeta canions and silk ribbon cross-garters, the earl of Ormond presented a majestic sight.

"Revelin!" the earl hailed as he reached the shore, and the two men embraced.

"You've come not a moment too soon," Revelin greeted grimly. "Edmund has gathered an army under him at Clogrennan, and Edward is likely to follow."

Tom smiled. "'Tis good to be home, where a man may choose at his leisure from half a dozen quarrels in which to engage." He threw a paternal arm about Revelin's shoulders. "So tell me, lad, have you married the one and bedded the other?"

The sore spot touched with Tom's light hand smarted nonetheless. "I've married none, but congratulate me, uncle: I shall be a father come Saint Brigid's Day."

"Well now," Tom exclaimed with familial pride. "'Tis your first. The first stands out in a man's mind. There's nothing to match it but the birth of his first legitimate heir."

"If she will have me, 'twill be my legitimate heir," Revelin rejoined.

Tom looked at him askance. "Say you've not compromised Lady—" He caught himself in time, for the docks were teeming with travelers.

Amusement tugged at Revelin's stern mouth. "There's only one lass I've any wish to wed, and you know who she is."

Tom frowned. "I thought you had done with schoolboy dreams."

Revelin looked his uncle in the eye. "I have."

Tom's dark eyes met Revelin's green gaze levelly, neither man looking away. "Well, if you must have her, 'tis your folly. I'll not fault a man for doing what he must."

Revelin nearly smiled. "Then I may continue to consider myself a Butler?"

"I would like to see the man who says different!" Tom answered heartily. "But, before you spring the lass on me, won't you first welcome Sir Richard back?"

Revelin looked up to see the tall, soberly clothed figure of Sir Richard Atholl stepping off the second landing boat. "What on earth brings him back to Ireland?"

Tom shot his nephew a speculative look. "You, I rather think. He seems to feel that you will further his desires to found a Protestant settlement in Ulster."

Revelin shook his head. "The man's mad."

Tom shrugged. "My mission is more practical. I've come to learn what my hot-headed brothers are up to so that I may save their necks from the executioner's block."

"You're late in your arrival. We could have used your influence some weeks past, when your family was hostage to Carew's murdering band."

The note of censure in Revelin's voice was a reflection of what he had frequently heard expressed at the dinner table in Kilkenny since his uncles' release. Tom noted this and wondered just how strongly rebellion had taken hold in his absence. As for Revelin... Tom smiled ruefully. He was losing the young man to his Irish homeland.

"Edward and Piers wait for you in Kilkenny. Edmund has been sent word of your arrival and will meet us there. Can you ride?"

Tom grinned as Revelin looked doubtfully at his finery. "Lead me to horse!"

Meghan stared at the regal entourage that crossed the castle drawbridge into the courtyard. Revelin, bare-headed, was the first person she recognized, and she stared her fill. He had been gone a week. If not for Robin's intervention, she would have been halfway to Ulster by now. She did not know what Robin had said to her *bonaghts,* but suddenly they were not eager for her to journey beyond the gates of the castle.

"I must get away!" she whispered to herself. She could not bear to spend another night under the same roof with Revelin and not be near him. More than one night she had stood outside his door, unable to knock or to leave until she trembled with cold. She loved him more now than ever before, and the aching had become a torment that kept her awake at night and near tears during the day.

She moved from her place beside Lady Elenore's eldest daughter, Elizabeth, and would have retreated into the castle had Robin not stepped forward to block her path.

"Coward," he chided softly. "Stay and welcome Revelin home, if you're not afraid," he added as she glared at him.

Meghan swung back to the riders, balling her hands into fists. Once more her eyes were drawn to Revelin's golden head, and this time she saw that he had recognized her and was staring in solemn intensity at her. His gaze did not move away as he drew in rein and slipped from his saddle. He came straight toward her as though she alone waited in the courtyard. His step was not hurried, but everyone present realized that there was purpose in it.

Revelin did not slow until he stood within an arm's length of her. With a formal smile he swept her a courtly bow. "Mistress Meghan."

Meghan dropped automatically into the deep curtsy Lady Mary had drilled her on for meeting the earl. "Sir Revelin," she said in a faint voice. As she rose she was snared by his spring-green gaze, and suddenly she felt the need to say more. "Welcome home."

She had used the words unconsciously and he knew it, but Revelin could not stop the rush of warmth that spread through him at her use of the word *home*. "Aye, I've been away from home too long." He offered her his arm. "Will ye walk with me, mistress? I've a great longing to seek the comfort of my bed." He smiled crookedly. "Or yours, if you prefer."

"Revelin?" Meghan heard Lady Mary call faintly as she followed him toward the steps of the entrance, but neither of them bothered to answer.

Meghan did not so much climb the steps on his arm as rise above them. No one stopped them as they walked the length of the corridor, and when they came to the stairwell that led to her room, she led the way without pause. Neither of them spoke until the door was closed and bolted behind them.

Revelin turned from the door and smiled at her. "I've missed ye, lass. 'Tis a sore point with a man to go long without the company of the woman he loves."

Meghan nodded. "'Tis a burden for the woman also. I know now why people marry." At the questioning lift of Revelin's brow she added, "They cannot do without the honey-making."

Revelin came toward her. "Do you miss me or the pleasure more?"

Meghan lifted her arms to him. "How can I know the answer to that when you bring the pleasure in your coming?"

"Ah, lass," he sighed, enclosing her in his arms. "We've wasted a great deal of time for naught. I should wait a little longer but I cannot. I'll wed you when I can, but I must bed you now."

Meghan shivered at the mention of marriage. She could not, must not marry him, but she could not deny the kiss that he pressed upon her love-thirsty lips, nor would she deny the strong gentle hands that unfastened her gown and slipped it from her shoulders. He was warmth and strength, his body good and heavy and as comforting as a new wool mantle on a winter night. As he lifted her onto the bed, she could think of nothing more compelling than his face tense with passion, his eyes a deeper green than holly, and his mouth pliant with anticipated kisses.

The moment contained all her best hopes and desires. She needed and wanted very little: to be able to gaze upon his face every day for the rest of her life. The place did not matter, nor the conventions of church vows or family alliances or noble ties. He was her love, completely and utterly.

As he sank down into her, Meghan gave a little sigh like a moan of surrender but it was not that. It was a sigh of peace, of completion, of a joining that made whole her world.

* * *

Revelin stroked the hair that spilled in a sooty flood across his chest. "Do you know that I'm as hungry for you now as I was a half-hour past?"

Meghan snuggled against him, pressing her nose into the fragrant warmth of his skin. "I've nae complaint."

He chuckled. "I think that I could spend a week in this bed with you and not begin to sate my hunger, Meghan O'Neill."

"Ye would die for lack of nourishment," she pronounced seriously.

"Oh, I can think of several delicious things I could nibble on," he answered as his hand slid down over a swelling breast to the slightly rounded contour of her belly and below.

Meghan parted her thighs to give him better access to her body. "I like that," she said matter-of-factly.

"I know, love. You like everything, that's a great part of your charm. I wonder that our child will not grow tired of me long before its had a chance to see my face."

Meghan frowned, missing the point of his joke. "I've been thinking."

"Oh no," he murmured, but she seemed not to hear him.

"I will stay with ye if we can be together like this. But I will not marry ye."

Revelin pushed her a little away so that he could turn on his side to face her. "Why not? Do you dislike the institution of matrimony?"

Meghan shook her head, her hair sliding into her eyes. "I'm afeard for ye. Everyone I care about dies. Una, Colin, Robin—"

"Robin did not die," Revelin objected.

"But he nearly did, because of me."

"That was John's doing, not yours."

"John died, too," she said quietly. "Ye killed him because of me."

Revelin lifted the veiling of hair from her face. "I killed

372

John because he deserved it. Had I known what he did to Robin, I would have killed him for that alone. As he fought he told me how he had nearly raped you but was stopped by Colin." John had taunted him with other things, but he would never tell her. John had proclaimed that she was Robin's whore, that he had shared her with Colin before he killed the Scotsman, that she had become the whore of the *bonaghts* who protected her. If she had been, Revelin would not have blamed her if it had meant preserving her life. Later, on the ride to Kilkenny, Piers had apprised him of the nature of Meghan's hold over the mercenaries and the part it had played in saving Butler lives. This morning, on the ride back from Wexford, he had finally put the pieces together and understood her fears. She was afraid she would bring him harm.

"The Butlers tell me you're a *bean feasa*. If that is so, you have the power to protect any you choose."

Meghan shook her head again. "I cannot protect ye, and I could not bear to know I caused yer suffering."

Revelin bent forward and kissed her lightly. "When have you once hurt me? I remember the times you saved my life at the pond and later when the O'Neills attacked. I remember you jumping Turlough when you thought he would kill Robin. Before that, you saved a herdsman and his bairn from a bull. Lady Mary and Lady Elenore, and all the castle, talk of nothing but how you frightened off their attackers. Silly goose, how can you think yourself anything but a beautiful savior?"

Meghan shut her eyes. "But the visions, I hate them and yet they come."

Revelin took her hand in his and held it tight. "Look at me. Do you really believe in visions, or do you only think that perhaps you should believe in them?"

Meghan looked deeply into his eyes and knew she must tell the truth. "I feel things which I cannot explain, and sometimes the visions come true."

"But sometimes not," he added. "What was the last one?"

"There were nae visions this summer," Meghan hedged, unwilling to tell him.

"What was the last one?" he repeated, shaking her lightly.

Meghan wet her lips. "That ye would be killed by a wild beast. I thought John was it, but now he is dead."

Revelin smiled. "So you see, not all your visions of the future are correct. Even if they were, am I not safer where you can share them with me so that I may be forewarned? It would be neglectful of you to leave me unprotected." His hand moved slowly up to the slight curve of her lower belly, and the most tender, unguarded look of love enveloped his face. "And there is our child to consider. I am a strong man. I can protect both of you if you will allow me."

Listening to his confident voice, Meghan felt a great weight rising from her shoulders. "Ye're nae afeard?"

"Am I as superstitious as your *bonaghts?* No, Meghan, I am not. But I do believe in your power over men. I grow rigid at the very thought of you." With a chuckle of triumph he rolled her onto her back and covered her body with his. "Hurry and work your magic before someone comes to fetch us to dinner."

Sir Richard Atholl paced the length of his chamber in the west tower of the Butler castle, back and forth, back and forth, in the hope that the cadence of his steps would lull him into a prayerful trance.

He must concentrate! The extremity of his agitation made him tremble. Sweat, squeezed from every pore, slicked his face and hands. When he reached the end of another prayer he could no longer contain himself and his voice filled the room.

"Lord God, I beseech you! Save this household from the clutches of the unnatural whore who in her unholy power seeks to destroy the souls of the faithful Butlers! Let me be Your instrument. In Your holy name I will smite her! She must be driven out!"

He rolled back his sleeve and began to pick at one of the boils that had erupted on his skin the moment he set foot back in Ireland. She had done that to him. She knew why he had returned and she sought to drive him away.

"But I will not leave that innocent soul to the torments of her foulness!" he whispered.

The torment of the passage across the Irish Sea was nothing compared to the torment he now underwent, knowing that Revelin lay in her bed of foulness. How could Revelin, in his own beauty, look upon her fouled countenance and not see the witch for what she was?

"Ah, but none of them do. She has cast her spell over them all and they believe her a savior."

The Butlers, every one, were filled with praise for this seed of Satan. They saw her wielding of curses to be God's will. Better they had died at the hands of mercenaries than that their souls be bought for the price of their mortal lives! All this he could turn his back on, but not Revelin. Even the earl of Ormond could not withstand her influence. Within an hour of their arrival in Kilkenny, he had pronounced his blessing upon the match.

Sir Richard slowed as he neared a table upon which a decanter of wine and a goblet had been placed. From the first moment he had laid eyes on Revelin, he had known that the young man was his call to God's work. If he could save but one soul, the young Irishman was his calling. He understood now why he had been sent by the queen to Ireland; her schemes were directed by a higher hand. He had been sent as a witness to Revelin's temptation and his guardian if the temptation proved too great.

"And it has, it has!"

He wiped the sweat from his brow. It galled him beyond reason to think how Revelin touched her. Most women were nothing but disease-ridden pockets. The only pure love was that of man for his God and for his fellow man. Revelin must be made to see that. But first he must be rid of the unnatural hag's presence. Once she was gone, Revelin would be released from her trance and able to see the danger in which he stood.

Excitement lighting his pale eyes, Richard withdrew the heavy gold crucifix from his pocket and with an unsteady hand he twisted the latch at the back of the cross to reveal a fine white powder. "'Tis fitting she die in the throes of an agonizing hell."

He tipped the powder into the goblet and then poured wine over it. As he stirred the wine with the cross, prayers tumbled from his lips. When he was done, he lifted the goblet between his hands and held it before him. "Thy will be done, Lord, an end to this wicked business!"

The knock upon Meghan's chamber door roused the pair of sleeping lovers.

"Who is it?" Revelin demanded sleepily.

"A well-wisher," came the muffled reply.

Revelin sat up and shook the sleep from his head. For all the world the voice sounded like that of Parson Atholl, he thought in amusement. "A moment!"

Meghan stirred beside him. "Will ye open the door?"

When she sat up, the covers slipped from her. Revelin's eyes moved slowly over her. Black hair cascaded over her shoulders, hiding all but the rose-brown tips of her breasts and the flushed skin of her throat. He bent and tenderly touched his mouth to hers. "I will see what he wants. Do not stir from the bed, love, unless you would embarrass him."

Meghan watched him slip from the bed and with regret saw the firm curves of his buttocks disappear beneath the trunk hose he pulled on over his nakedness.

Revelin lifted the crossbar and opened the door a crack to find Sir Richard standing there with a decanter and goblet in his hands. The man's gray face seemed stiffer than usual, as if his skin were stretched tightly over a tapestry hoop. Revelin tried for pleasantness in his tone. "May I help you, Sir Richard? Are you lost?"

Sir Richard smiled, increasing the tension in his face. "I am not lost, lad. I've found my path at last. You are to be wed, I hear."

Revelin raised a brow. Black Tom had wasted no time in disclosing the news, it seemed. "Aye, that's so," he answered cautiously.

Sir Richard lifted his decanter. "I would drink a toast to your health, my son."

Revelin glanced back at the bed, where Meghan sat half-naked. "'Tis not a timely idea, Par—Sir Richard." He smiled deprecatingly. "My lady is not prepared to receive guests at present."

"Is she not your bride in the eyes of God, if not yet in the eyes of the Church?"

"That is so," Revelin replied, wondering what wild hand directed the man's actions.

"Then I do not shun to look upon anything that has the sanction of God's will."

"A moment," Revelin murmured and closed the door. "Here, take my mantle," he directed Meghan, scooping up his short Spanish cape to hand to her.

Meghan swung the scented leather garment about her shoulders and tied it under her chin.

Revelin looked at her with warm laughter in his eyes. With her tousled hair and slightly swollen lips, she was the embodiment of every tender dream of love and every eager, lustful urge of which he was capable. He shook his head slowly. Sir Richard would be scandalized to the bone.

"A rare surprise," Revelin said as he opened the door to his guest. "You are the first to congratulate us, Sir Richard."

Sir Richard entered the room slowly, his eyes averted from the bed, which occupied the bulk of the small space. Without seeing her, he could feel the bitch's heat. The faint effusion of love twitched in his nostrils. They had lain here in this room coupling like animals, this beautiful boy and the witch of Ulster.

"Sir Richard, you look unwell," Revelin observed solicitously.

Sir Richard waved him away. "I am tired from the long journey. I must be brief." He shut his eyes for an instant and then turned to the bed. He held out the half-filled goblet. "A toast to you, my dear," he said hoarsely and brought the goblet to his lips.

"Now 'tis your turn," he invited, holding it out to her.

Meghan lifted her eyes to gaze up into the man's face and the room suddenly darkened until there was only a pair of silver-white eyes staring malevolently down into hers. From far away she heard Revelin's words of encouragement, but her muscles were locked in place and she could not even open her mouth to protest.

Revelin saw her pupils expand until the deep blue of her eyes was swallowed by the pupils, and he frowned. She was frightened of Sir Richard. Well, he did not blame her. The man often made his skin crawl. "My lady is not particularly fond of wine, especially in her condition."

Sir Richard's head snapped toward Revelin. "What?"

Revelin squared his shoulders. "I know 'tis wrong to take one's pleasure before the union has been sanctified, but our courtship has been unusual. I intend to rectify the matter shortly. As soon as a priest can be brought to the castle I will wed Meghan O'Neill, and the child will be my lawful heir."

"A child," Sir Richard repeated faintly, and the decanter slipped from his nerveless fingers. Glass splintered and red wine ran like blood over the white stone floor. "She is to bear your child?"

Revelin smiled tolerantly. The parsimonious man had some scruples he could not mask. "Aye, she is, and proud I am to own it to the world."

"No!" Richard shook his head, the fine fringe on the top of his head lifting as air passed through it. "No! 'Tis wicked!"

Fearing another accident, Revelin scooped the wine goblet

from the man's hand. "I am sorry if you do not approve, Sir Richard," he said coolly. "But I cannot see that it matters."

Sir Richard looked at him blankly. Was there nothing he could say to the boy to prevent this disaster? Was there no way to best the harridan who would drag his soul to Hell? He began to tremble. "I apologize, my dear boy. I drank a toast to your bride, did I not? Will you not do likewise?"

Annoyance flickered through Revelin's expression. He did not like the way Meghan sat in the bed like one in a trance. He longed to shove the man out the door. But if drinking a toast would rid them of his presence as quickly, he would finish the wine. "As you suggest, 'tis an excellent idea."

Meghan stared at Sir Richard; she could not pull her eyes away. His face was a mask as Revelin lifted the cup to his lips. It dawned on her that she had once seen that same fixed look in the eyes of a diseased she-wolf. Her fur had been sparse and picked out in places, like the bald patches in Sir Richard's scalp. The female had fastened her purposeful gaze on a young hare in the brush with the same single-mindedness as that with which Sir Richard now watched Revelin. She had waited patiently until the hare turned its back, and then had sprung, tearing the soft fur and strewing the ground with bright red blood.

Revelin tilted back his head and a pearl of red wine appeared at the corner of his mouth and then slid down his chin like blood as he took a swallow.

Blood!

"No! Don't drink!" Released from the nightmare of paralysis, Meghan sprang from the bed and knocked the goblet from Revelin's hand.

"Don't drink! 'Tis, 'tis . . ." She turned quickly on Sir Richard. "'Tis poison ye meant for me!"

Sir Richard pulled his dagger free. "Get back! Stay back from me!"

Revelin looked from Meghan to Sir Richard, the burning

in his middle beginning. He had taken only a swallow, but he knew instantly that Meghan spoke the truth. "Meghan?" he said uncertainly as he reached for his dagger, only to find it missing. The burning in his belly rose into his throat and he moaned.

"Ye would have killed him!" Meghan screamed at the tall man threatening her. "What manner of creature are ye?"

"A holy man!" Sir Richard spat back, the white showing all about his irises. "The Lord sent me to smite you and yours. You'll not bring another creature into this world marked by Satan if I can help it!"

Meghan pulled her skean free, unafraid for her own safety. Tears streamed down her face as she heard Revelin moan again. "If 'tis me ye want, why did ye let Revelin drink?"

Sir Richard wiped the sweat from his brow with an anxious hand. His breath was short. "I had not meant him . . . to die. But he was lost . . . I saw it in his eyes. He would have married you. Married to a witch!" he cried, sending his eyes heavenward. "I'd sooner have him dead than breeding more abominations like you, with the bloody mark of Satan on them."

Meghan lunged at him but he was agile enough to elude her. "I love him," he murmured brokenly. He turned to Revelin, smiling at the man's pain-etched face. "I loved you, truly, but I failed you." Tears streaked down his gray cheeks as he glanced at Meghan. "Now," he said softly as hatred replaced the suffering in his pale gaze, "now I will lose him. 'Tis you who've killed him, you and the demon that grows in your belly!"

Meghan lowered her guard. If Revelin was dying, she had no reason to live. She crossed herself and then, without thinking of what she was doing, she touched her birthmark, then held out her hand toward Sir Richard.

"If Revelin dies, ye'll die likewise. If I'm the demon ye believe, then I curse ye forever. All the pains of Hell will not sear from yer thoughts the murder ye've done this day. Into eternity I curse yer shriveled soul!"

Sir Richard fell back before her words. "No! No! I'll not ... accept ... that!" He turned and ran, stumbling down the narrow stairwell.

Meghan did not try to stop him. She threw her weapon from her and fell to her knees beside Revelin, who had slumped to the floor. "Revelin, me darling, dinna die!" she whispered, as she gathered him in her arms.

Revelin moaned softly and then spasms of nausea bent him double.

"God's blood! Had the young fool drained the cup, he'd not be here to complain of his pains," Piers roared irritably as Revelin's moans issued from the room above. For a day and a half he had lain near death with only Meghan's vigilance keeping him from slipping away.

"I wonder if 'tis true the O'Neill lass has the power of the fairies?" Tom questioned musingly. The miracles he had heard attributed to her in the last days astounded him.

"If she does not, then I do not wish to learn of it," Lady Mary answered forthrightly. "I am not one to encourage superstition, but Mistress Meghan has earned the Butlers' respect and protection; and I'll wrestle with the Devil himself to defend her!"

"Well spoken!" Piers smiled tolerantly at his wife. "I like her, too. If Revelin does not pull through, I will set ye aside and take her meself!"

It was a callous joke, but it was all they had left.

Robin rose to his feet. "If you will excuse me, I will offer once again to spell Mistress Meghan."

"She won't have it," Tom warned.

"I know, my lord, but I will feel better for having made the offer."

The sour smell of the sickroom pricked his nose, but Robin tucked his pomander away lest he offend his friend. When he pushed open the door he saw what he had seen each time he entered. Meghan sat at the bedside, one hand in Revelin's and the other on her cheek.

"Meghan?" he whispered as he came to her side.

Meghan shook her head. "He has not come to his senses." She looked up, her dry eyes red and swollen. "If he dies, 'tis me fault. I killed him."

Robin held her gaze but it tore at his heart to do so. "You saved his life. Sir Richard wanted him dead."

Meghan's face turned hard with rage. "I hope he roasts in Hell!"

The color drained from Robin's face as he looked upon her face, marred not by the birthmark but by the poison of hate.

"No, Meghan, you must not say that. You're a force for good. If you allow bitterness and anguish to warp you, you'll lose the thing Revelin loves most about you."

He reached out to pull her hand away from her cheek. "Atholl has disappeared. He's mad. He's found his own kind of Hell. He needs no help from you. Let it go, Meghan. Let the anger go. Your love is what keeps Revelin alive. You must not allow anything to interfere with that." He smiled as her hand curled tightly on his. "The Butlers look to you for another miracle."

Meghan shook her head. "I have no more miracles. I have no power. I don't know what to believe any more."

She looked down at Revelin's face so ravaged by pain and poison that his skin was yellow and his eyes were ringed by purple bruises. "When first I saw him, I thought him the most beautiful thing I ever saw. Even now he's more lovely than anything I've ever known. I cannot lose him. He's all I have."

"Then you won't," Robin said with conviction. "Lie down beside him and I will keep watch awhile."

Meghan looked up at Robin. "Thank you."

Robin watched her sleep a long while, wondering how a man recovers from the love of a lifetime. Even now, watching her sleep beside the man she loved, he could not suppress a pang of regret, nor the whisper of a secret desire he would not give acknowledgment. Revelin must live, for his sake as well as Meghan's, or guilt would destroy them both.

The taste of bile was the first sensation Revelin was aware of. Then the aching of his ribs and belly. The chill dampness of his skin came shortly after, and the feel of weights upon his eyes. Raising his lids took his full concentration.

The ceiling was not a rousing sight. With great difficulty, he inched his head toward the left and saw that a banner of blue-black silk ribbons lay under his cheek. Raising his eyes, he saw the shape of a tender breast beneath the bodice of a white gown. Looking higher, the sharp contours of her beautiful face came into view. "Meghan."

Meghan jerked awake at the sound of his voice. Looking down, she found herself gazing into startling green eyes. The instant their gazes met she knew that she would never want anything more of life but to be looked at by those wondrously deep green eyes.

"Revelin?" she whispered huskily as she reverently touched his pale cheek.

"Aye, lass."

Tears blurred her vision as she bent to place her lips against his. "I thought ye would leave me!" she whispered against his mouth. "Ye were right, I've nae power at all."

Revelin raised an unsteady hand to touch her cheek. "Nae, lass, ye're wrong. Ye've the power of miracles. 'Tis a miracle ye love me and 'tis a miracle ye've survived, what with me needing so much of ye help.

"Love, love, don't cry," he chided softly. "I'm too near tears myself, and how would it look?"

Meghan sniffed back her tears, wiping away the ones that had spilled onto his cheeks. "I love ye, Revelin! Ye'll never be rid of me. I'll protect ye always!"

He smiled wanly. "I'm afraid we'll need yer *bonaghts* to

keep us both from harm. If I cannot protect one wee lass, how will I ever protect the brood of bairns we're bound to have?"

Meghan's eyes clouded as she remembered Atholl's baleful prediction. "Will ye, could ye love them, if they're born marked like me?"

Revelin reached out to trace the mark on her cheek. "I will love them even more, love, because they will be as beautiful as you. Now kiss me before I fall asleep, my Irish Rose."

Ballygub, Kilkenny: May 1570

Revelin awakened to the splash of rain upon his face. Yet how could that be? The roof of his new home was soundly in place.

"What on earth?" he exclaimed, sitting up in bed.

Meghan's laughter was impish. "'Tis Beltane dew," she informed him, liberally sprinkling him with another handful from the basin she held. "Ye must be quick to catch the power of charms on Beltane morn!"

Revelin wiped the dew from his face, frowning in mock irritation. "Is that all I must do, come soggy to the breakfast table?"

"Oh no," Meghan answered, shaking her head gravely. "Ye must go out and find a fairy bush. When ye do, ye must crawl naked into it."

Revelin's lips twitched. "I'd rather stay here and crawl naked into you!" He grabbed her before she had a chance to guess his intent and tumbled her into bed beside him, uncaring that her basin spilled all over them.

"Ach! Look what ye've done!" she cried. "There's none left for me!"

"You don't need it! Half the county stops by our door each day in hopes that you'll charm away some ailment or another. Your fame has spread so wide that I never have you to myself anymore," he complained as his fingers worked the fastenings of her gown.

Meghan leaned forward, kissing his bare chest. "Ye have me now."

"So I do," he said in perfect pleasure as he lowered her bodice and leaned over to nuzzle her neck. "So I do. Well, fairy, what charm will ye work on me?"

"A love charm," Meghan replied, wiggling to help him pull off her gown.

Revelin's eyes grew warm at the sight of her, soft and flushed with their exertions. "I don't know," he said doubtfully. "Ye keep me weary as it is, with the loving of ye. Another charm may kill me altogether!"

Meghan sat back on her heels, enjoying the open admiration in her husband's face. "Well, I suppose there's nae need for it, seeing as how even now there's a new loaf in the oven."

Revelin looked at her. Her breasts were high and full, the peaks darkened by her first pregnancy, but her belly was as flat as he remembered it before the birth of their daughter, and her waist was incredibly small. Only her hips were a little wider, the flare of her backside a greater distraction than before.

"Well," he said, expelling the word on a long breath. "'Twould only be sensible to make certain, I'm thinking."

"Aye," Meghan agreed, the bright light of passion heating her blue eyes. "Aye, I would make certain, were I ye." And she leaned closer, offering her mouth to his.

An hour later the sound of a rider drew them reluctantly from their bed.

"'Tis Piers!" Revelin announced with delight when he stuck his head out the window. "I haven't seen him in months. There must be news from Black Tom!"

They had meant to dress quickly, but the temptation to stop often to kiss and touch and giggle like the newlyweds they were was too much to resist.

"At last," Piers pronounced when the pair appeared belowstairs. "I was well on my way to reiving the place just to teach you a lesson in the manners of a host. If not for that carrot-topped Scotsman you call a commandant, I'd have died of thirst."

"Don't belittle Meghan's soldiers," Revelin answered as he watched his wife be swept up in his uncle's embrace. "I'll have you know Conn is a wonderful nanny. Sorcha loves him to distraction."

Piers looked about. "Where's the wee lass?"

"I'll get her," Meghan offered and hurried off.

Piers watched her go with a smile. "She grows more beautiful each time I see her. God, but I wish I'd found her first!"

Revelin smiled indulgently. "Did you come only to tell me how much you lust after my wife?"

Piers chuckled. "Nae, I've come to say that the matter with Carew has come to an end."

"He's not dead?"

"Nae, and a sorry thing that is, too. A wee bit of help on Tom's part has settled the matter. The queen has ordered Carew to stay behind the lines of his own property and leave the settling of matters to men with some sense!"

Revelin nodded. The fighting had gone on through the fall before Carew had given up trying to best the Butlers. With spring here, he had feared the trouble might begin all over again. "What will you do now?"

Piers's eyes twinkled. "The queen, rightly so, was a bit peeved with me brothers Edmund and Edward. She's asking them to prove their loyalty by serving in the field against rebels."

Revelin struggled against a smile. "Rebels?" he questioned innocently.

"Aye, there's a few Irish lords who're apt to forget we've a sovereign to obey, a parcel of degenerate Anglo-Irishmen who need a lesson!"

"They would not go by the name of Fitzgerald, would they?"

Piers roared with laughter. "The very name, lad!"

So, the Butlers were going into the field against their Irish enemies, the Fitzgeralds. Nothing had changed.

"Here she is," Meghan cried, swinging her daughter up into her arms. She came forward quickly, pride showing in her eyes. "Is Sorcha not the most beautiful lass ye ever saw?"

Both men looked at the blond, blue-eyed lass with only a pair of dimples marking her rosy cheeks and smiled.

"Aye, she's that," Piers pronounced. He slanted a sly look at Revelin. "But where, lad, are your sons?"

Revelin patted Meghan's stomach, "Here, uncle. Have a little patience."

Piers's face lit up. "Well then, I don't suppose you'll want to go chasing Fitzgeralds?"

Revelin shook his head and smiled. "I like the life of an Irish squire. 'Tis peaceful here with my family, my cattle, and my mercenaries. Two of them are to be wed next month. We'll be a village before you know it."

Piers nodded. "You're a lucky man."

"There's nothing to it, when ye live a charmed life," Revelin replied, hugging his wife and child.

GLOSSARY

1. Anglo-Irish: Ancestors of the Normans who invaded Ireland in the twelfth century. The Butler and Fitzgerald families are two examples.

2. *Arh Righ:* High King, title of king of Ireland.

3. *bean feasa:* A wise woman thought to possess magic powers.

4. Beltane: First day of May, Ancient Celtic holiday.

5. Beltane dew: Dew collected on Beltane. Thought to have magic properties.

6. *bonaghts*: Mercenaries. Not to be confused with *galloglaighs*. Outlaws, men without clan or family loyalty.

7. Brehan Law: Ancient Celtic body of law.

8. *Builtiler a buadh:* "Butler to victory!" battle cry.

9. bundling: A trial marriage of one year during which the woman proves her fertility by becoming pregnant.

10. *cailleach:* Fairy.

11. Carlow: County in Leinster.

12. *ceannabhan mona:* Wild bog cotton.

13. coshering: Seasonal migration of cowherders from valley winter pastures to high summer pastures.

14. *eraic:* Blood money. Fine paid to the family of a dead clansman by the perpetrator.

15. *faolchon allmhardha:* "Foreign wolves," derogatory.

16. Fian, pl. Fianna: A standing army of specially selected and trained warriors who carried out the mandates of the *Arh Righ.*

17. Finn, Fionn: Fionn MacCumail, (Finn MacCool) legendary hero and leader of the Fian.

18. Fostering: The Irish custom of sending noble children to be raised in the households of other noble families. Strengthened loyalties between famillies and clans. Adopted by Anglo-Irish.

19. Gael: Native Irish. The O'Neills are an example.

20. *galloglaigh:* "Young foreigner." A professional soldier of the warrior Scottish clans, they were the mainstay of every Irish Chieftain's kerne (army).

21. *gallowglass:* English corruption of *gallogaigh.*

22. *ghalliobh:* "Foreigner." Term used by the Gaels to distinguish between Anglo-Irish and the "new" English colonists of Elizabeth I. Not derogatory.

23. Idrone: Town in County Carlow.

24. kerne: Irish chieftain's army or retainers.

25. Kilkenny: County in Leinster. Town in County Kilkenny.

26. *leine:* Shapeless tunic worn by Irish women.

27. Leinster: Provence in S.E. Ireland.

28. Mallacht: "Curse" or malediction.

29. Otherworld: The abode of the fairies and other mythological creatures of Ireland.

30. *poitin:* Irish whiskey.

31. reive: Steal, specifically, cattle rustling.

32. Saint Brigid's Day: February 1. Irish holiday.

33. skean: Irish dagger, long blade.

34. *spailpin:* Tramp.

35. *suil trom:* Evil eye.

36. tanist: Second in command to a chieftain and his chosen successor.

37. Ualter: Name meaning wolf.

38. *uisce beatha:* "Water of life." Irish whiskey.

39. *usquebaugh:* Irish whiskey.

40. whiteflesh: Milk and its byproducts: cream, cheese, butter. A summer staple for the Irish for hundreds of years.

The Best Of
Warner Romances

___**BOLD BREATHLESS LOVE** (D30-849, $3.95, U.S.A.)
by Valerie Sherwood (D30-838, $4.95, Canada)

The surging saga of Imogene, a goddess of grace with riotous golden curls—and Verholst Van Rappard, her elegant idolator. They marry and he carries her off to America—not knowing that Imogene pines for a copper-haired Englishman who made her his on a distant isle and promised to return to her on the wings of love.

___**LOVE, CHERISH ME** (D30-039, $3.95, U.S.A.)
by Rebecca Brandewyne (D32-135, $4.95, Canada)

"Set in Texas, it may well have been the only locale big enough to hold this story that one does, not so much read, as revel in. From the first chapter, the reader is enthralled with a story so powerful it defies description and a love so absolute it can never be forgotten. LOVE, CHERISH ME is a blend of character development, sensuous love and historic panorama that makes a work of art a masterpiece." —*Affaire De Coeur*

___**FORGET-ME-NOT** (D30-715, $3.50, U.S.A.)
by Janet Louise Roberts (D30-716, $4.50, Canada)

Unhappy in the civilized cities, Laurel Winfield was born to bloom in the Alaskan wilds of the wide tundras, along the free-flowing rivers. She was as beautiful as the land when she met the Koenig brothers and lost her heart to the strong-willed, green-eyed Thor. But in Alaska violence and greed underlie the awesome beauty, and Laurel would find danger here as well as love.

WARNER BOOKS
P.O. Box 690
New York, N.Y. 10019

Please send me the books I have checked. I enclose a check or money order (not cash), plus 50¢ per order and 50¢ per copy to cover postage and handling.* (Allow 4 weeks for delivery.)

_____ Please send me your free mail order catalog. (If ordering only the catalog, include a large self-addressed, stamped envelope.)

Name _____

Address _____

City _____

State _____ Zip _____

*N.Y. State and California residents add applicable sales tax.   110